DEADLY FALLOUT

Rachel McLean writes thrillers that make your pulse race and your brain tick. Originally a self-publishing sensation, she has sold millions of copies digitally, with massive success in the UK, and a growing reach internationally. She is the author of the Dorset Crime novels and the spin-off McBride & Tanner series and Cumbria Crime series. In 2021, she won the Kindle Storyteller Award with *The Corfe Castle Murders* and her books regularly hit No1 in the Bookstat ebook chart on launch.

ALSO BY RACHEL MCLEAN

Zoe Finch series

Deadly Wishes
Deadly Choices
Deadly Desires
Deadly Terror
Deadly Reprisal
Deadly Fallout
Deadly Christmas

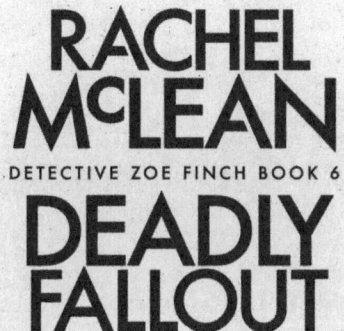

Copyright © 2021, 2024 by Rachel McLean

All rights reserved.

No part of this book may be reproduced in any form or by any electronic or mechanical means, including information storage and retrieval systems, without written permission from the author, except for the use of brief quotations in a book review.

This is a work of fiction. Names, characters, businesses, places, events and incidents are either the products of the author's imagination or used in a fictitious manner. Any resemblance to actual persons, living or dead, or actual events is purely coincidental.

Ackroyd Publishing

ackroydpublishing.com

Printed and bound in the UK by CPI Group (Uk) Ltd, Croydon CR0 4YY

CHAPTER ONE

The house was a burglar's dream.

Nestled at the end of a cul-de-sac, with an alleyway on one side and a high wall on the other, it had no houses overlooking it.

The front garden was shielded by a high hedge, with access to the garden down both sides of the house. Sure, one side had a gate but that was secured with nothing more than a slide bolt.

"Amateurs," he muttered as he strolled along the road towards it, hands in pockets, rucksack shifting as he walked. He'd been keeping an eye on this place for a couple of weeks, working out if and when anyone opened the place up. He'd seen the estate agent come once to collect post and two more times for appointments with potential buyers.

The family had moved to Germany and the house had been on the market for four months. Interest was dwindling, which made it the perfect target. No visitors, no occupants, no neighbours looking in. But the furniture was mostly there, still, making the place attractive to would-be buyers and waiting to be shipped once a sale had been agreed.

He slowed his pace as he reached the bulb of the cul-de-sac. It was twelve minutes past midnight and the residents in this dull suburban corner of the city were tucked up safe and warm. Curtains had been drawn in every window of the neighbouring houses, and most of the lights were out.

He kept moving as he neared the house, and walked onto the front drive without slowing or shifting his gaze. He knew how to look like you were supposed to be somewhere, even if it was gone midnight in a road where no one came home after the witching hour.

He allowed himself a small smile as he placed one hand on the side gate. He knew from Google Streetview that this gate was invisible from the neighbours' windows, even if someone did decide to look out.

There was movement at his feet, the brush of a small body against his leg. He froze, then forced himself to look down.

Don't be such a fucking twat. It was only a cat. The stupid thing looked up at him, streetlights reflecting on its retinas. It had blood on its cheek; it had been killing. *Good for you, pal.* It stared at him a moment longer then swished its tail and moved on, shimmying under the fence separating this garden from next door.

Don't look round, he told himself. *You're supposed to be here.* He hated those scenes in films and TV shows when people looked up and down a street just as they were about to smash a window or break into a car. No one who was supposed to be doing what they were doing would ever check if they were being watched. Sixteen years and four months in this game, and he was the only guy he knew who hadn't been caught. His mates thought he was charmed. He knew he was careful.

He hooked his hand over the top of the gate and slid the bolt back. It squeaked a little; he ignored it. He pushed the door open – swiftly, silently – and slipped through, pushing it closed behind him and sliding the bolt partway back again. Just enough to stop the door from swinging open, but not enough to make it squeak.

He took a deep breath and blew on his hands. It was April, a week after Easter. The day had been warm and the sky was clear, making it chilly tonight. A full moon shone over the garden.

He was wearing his Reeboks. The ones with the thick soles that suppressed all sound. The ones he'd filed down so they had no discernible print. No one was going to finger him via a misplaced step into a patch of mud.

The kitchen was at the back, with a sliding patio door leading to raised decking. He bloody loved Rightmove, all those photos of the insides of people's houses proudly displaying just how shit their security was.

The door looked old in the photos. He'd easily be able to shift its weight and disengage the crappy lock.

At the bottom of the garden, on the side where he was standing, was a shed. He considered checking it out, seeing what tools might be in there. But if the owners had any sense, they'd have taken their tools with them. The photos had shown plenty of stuff inside the house – beds, a monstrous glass-topped dining table, a couple of trinkets on the mantelpiece. But a full shed wasn't necessary to make the house look occupied for those photos.

No matter. He had his rucksack. Nothing in there to

arouse suspicion, but enough to help him get where he needed to be.

He grabbed a screwdriver from the side pocket – flat head, quarter inch blade – and slid it into the bottom of the patio door. He'd been right; these looked like they'd been fitted a generation ago. He jimmied the bottom of the frame and it shifted. He hoisted it up and felt the whole thing pull towards him as the lock disengaged.

Idiots. Leaving their bloody house unsecured but keeping half their stuff in there just to make the place look nice.

His sister-in-law had been shown round a week earlier. She enjoyed being his advance party, loved nosying around other people's houses. She had a way of irritating the estate agents enough that they never called her back. And in return for a substantial fee, she'd pass on to him what she'd found on her little investigations. In this case, there was a box of goodies upstairs.

He shunted the door across and squeezed through. The kitchen was dimly lit by the moon over the garden. The room was as outdated as those patio doors, with tile-topped counters and units that looked as if they'd fall apart as soon as you looked at them. He'd burgled enough houses to know what a half-decent kitchen looked like, and this wasn't it.

The box he was after was upstairs, in the front bedroom. He slid off his Reeboks and shoved them into his rucksack, then crept into the hall, sliding his feet across the bare floorboards so as to not make any noise. Not that it mattered. No one was going to hear.

He hurried up the stairs and rounded a corner into the front bedroom. It had a walk-in cupboard off it, tucked in under the eaves. Tina had found a box in there full of old photos and coins. Knick-knacks, the sort of stuff people never looked at in between house moves. But he had a mate in Digbeth who could get money for those coins. These suckers never knew how much they were hiding in their lofts.

Shining his torch into the cupboard, he found the wooden box precisely where Tina had said it would be. He pulled it out of the cupboard and into the room, hoisting it onto the bare bed. The streetlight shone through the thin curtains. He was careful to keep low, just in case.

He rifled through the box. At the bottom, wrapped in a dingy cloth, was a leather bag full of old jewellery and coins.

His heart rate picked up as he sifted through them. This would sort him out for a few weeks, maybe even months.

He shoved the cloth into his backpack and pushed the box back into the cupboard. He liked to leave places tidy, despised those arseholes who would shit and piss all over their targets. He wrinkled his nose at the thought. *Amateurs*.

He blew out through his mouth and padded down the stairs. Back in the kitchen, he pulled on his Reeboks. As he was about to leave, he spotted the open door.

It led under the staircase in the hall beyond, and a cold breeze wafted out of it. The door eased open and closed, caught in the breeze from the open patio door.

A cellar.

If these people hid old coins in the bedroom cupboard, God knows what they might have down there.

He smiled and pushed the door fully open. He sniffed. He could smell damp, overlaid with something heavier and more cloying.

He grabbed his pepper spray from a jacket pocket and held it up as he shuffled into the tight space. A set of stairs, immediately below the ones he'd just descended, led down.

A light cord brushed his face as he felt his way forward. He wasn't about to pull it, however dark it was.

He put a hand out to the wall beside him and took the stairs slowly in the darkness. After a few steps he pulled out his torch and switched it on. His mobile was back at home, he knew better than to bring it out on a job. He was working old-school.

He directed the torch downwards, his other hand shielding the beam so it didn't shine back into the kitchen. Either side of him, wallpaper flaked off the walls. A patch of damp as long as he was tall adorned the ceiling above him.

He sniffed again. The smell was getting stronger. But he couldn't resist carrying on, finding out what was down here.

The cellar led off to his left, under the house's living room. This house was built on a hill and he guessed this was what filled in the gap between the edge of the building and the sloping earth. He wondered if there was a way out down here.

It didn't matter. He'd tidy up after himself. Go out through the patio doors and leave them as he'd found them. It satisfied his sense of neatness and meant it would be longer before anyone suspected the place had been burgled.

He shone the torch around the low space, ducking to avoid hitting his head on the ceiling. There were more boxes, mostly browning and a few almost disintegrated. He wondered how long they'd been here, if they even belonged to the current owners.

He was disturbed by a sound. Heart thumping against his ribs, he span round to shine his torch into a low nook behind him.

Something moved.

He tightened his grip on the pepper spray and took a step

forward. A small black creature darted out and ran over his foot. It was all he could do not to yelp.

A rat. Now his eyes were accustomed to the darkness, he could see a pile of them, wriggling in the corner. The little fuckers were all over something.

His eyes were watering. He blinked and pulled his scarf up to cover his mouth and nose. Whatever it was, it bloody stunk.

The rats stopped moving as his torch passed over them, then just as suddenly all moved as one, scurrying towards him. He raised his hands, dropping the torch.

He heard them flowing up the stairs, obnoxious little claws scratching on the wood.

He bent down and felt for the torch. It had hit his foot and only rolled a few inches. He raised the beam to the spot the rats had vacated, and gasped.

The rats had been chewing at a face.

Not an animal's face. From what he could tell, it was a man. Thin and yellow, with one eye staring blankly at him and the other an empty socket.

He turned away and retched. Choking, he ran back up the stairs, almost slipping in his haste. He gagged as he slammed the cellar door shut behind him.

He leaned against it, his chest rising and falling. He threw a hand out in front, his latex glove hitting the side of the kitchen worktop. He yelped and pulled it back.

He leaned over the kitchen sink and threw up again, violent and noisy. After he'd emptied himself out, he leaned back. He took a few breaths, slapped himself on the chest, and ran the tap. It worked, luckily.

He washed away the vomit, averting his eyes. When the sink was clean, he washed out his mouth. He hurried through the patio doors and quickly closed them again. He rushed around the side of the house and stumbled into the gate, his fingers fumbling as he pulled the bolt.

Forcing himself to focus, he pushed through the gate and reached back to secure the bolt. He gagged once more, his eyes darting towards the empty street.

Stop it, you fucker. Focus. Slow down.

He pushed his shoulders back and walked out onto the street. He turned left and left again, making his escape via the alleyway next to the house. Twenty minutes later, he was back home, assessing his haul and trying to forget what he'd seen.

CHAPTER TWO

Zoe Finch swung her legs out of bed and let her feet drop to the floor. Carl's flat had parquet flooring throughout, all very nice, but damn cold at this time in the morning. It was 5:30 am. and she'd been lying awake for the last hour, the day ahead circling in her mind.

She felt a hand on her bare back. "Everything OK?"

"Can't sleep. You want a coffee?"

Carl rolled towards her. She looked back at him, her limbs softening.

"That would be great," he murmured. She'd woken twice in the night, and on one of those occasions, he'd found ways to distract her. She still tingled at the thought.

"Great." She hauled on a hoody and pair of joggers she kept at his place and went into the kitchen. There were advantages to living in a flat, she thought. Back at home she'd have to go down the stairs, through the living and dining rooms to get to the kitchen and her morning fix. Here, it was in the next room.

Carl kept his coffee in a tin mounted on a high shelf.

When they'd met he'd been an instant drinker. She'd soon put paid to that. She grabbed the tin – easy enough at five feet eight inches – and spooned some into the filter machine she'd encouraged him to buy. She ran water, then switched the machine on and wrapped her arms around herself.

She went to the window and gazed out while the coffee brewed. The flat was on the second floor, looking out onto communal gardens and then the Bristol Road beyond. The dual carriageway was starting to busy up, a bus rumbling past and a short line of cars in its wake.

She spotted movement reflected in the window and turned to see Carl in the doorway. He wore his work shirt and trousers. She raised an eyebrow.

"It's only half five."

He shrugged. "No point putting one set of clothes on, only to have to change into another one later."

"You not going to have a shower?"

"Who are you, my mum?" He crossed the room and put a hand on her arm. "Besides, we both took a shower just a couple of hours ago."

She smiled. "True." She stepped into his arms and smelled him: clean, musky. She let herself relax.

"You're worried about today," he said.

She stiffened and pulled back. "Of course I'm bloody worried about today."

"Yeah."

She turned away from him and checked the coffee. Today was the first day of the trial of former Detective Sergeant Ian Osman. Ian had briefly been her DS, her second in command. She'd known he was bent, but that didn't make giving evidence against him any easier. She'd met his wife, his kids. She had history with that family.

"They might not call you today, you know."

She grabbed the coffee pot and poured her own mug. "I've still got to be there, just in case."

"Sorry."

She swigged her coffee. Turning to see the disappointed look on his face, she remembered he'd asked for a cup too. She handed him her cup and made a second one.

He closed his eyes as he drank. "The best thing about going out with you, Zoe Finch, is this damn coffee. It's superb."

"The best thing? Really?"

He smiled. "OK. One of the best things."

She nodded and slumped into one of the two kitchen chairs that flanked a minute circular table. She cradled her mug with her hands.

"Penny for them," he said.

"I can't. You know that."

He sat down opposite her, his eyes on her face. "Because I'm a witness too."

"Yup." She drank, not meeting his eye. "I probably shouldn't even be here."

He leaned back. "Maybe you're right. Maybe until the trial's over…"

"Seriously?" she said. "You're doing that to me again?"

"That's not what I meant, Zo."

She raised a hand. "Don't call me that. Only Mo gets to call me that." Mo Uddin was her current DS and her oldest friend.

"Zoe. This is different."

"Last time you thought I was bent."

Carl dragged a hand through his cropped hair. "I thought we'd got over this."

She threw her head back and blew up at the ceiling. There was a stain above the extractor fan. "You're right," she said. "I'm sorry, I'm being a dick. I just want to get this farce over and done with."

"It's not a farce, Zoe. Ian Osman was working for organised crime. He planted evidence at the scene of a terrorist bombing."

"He's not the one you want, and you know it."

"I can't talk about any other..."

She nodded. He was right. Carl's job in the Professional Standards Department, or PSD, made it difficult for them to discuss cases.

"He's been called as a witness too," she said. They both knew who she was talking about.

"How d'you know?"

"I have my sources."

"Lesley." DCI Lesley Clarke, her boss.

She shrugged. "Not saying anything."

"Play it your way then," he said. "But I'm serious. We can't have any suspicion that we're conferring. Not in between you giving your evidence and me giving mine."

She downed the last of the coffee and slammed the mug onto the table. He flinched. "You're right," she muttered. "I'll get my stuff."

"It's only a few days."

She hesitated in the doorway. "We have no idea how long it'll take. There are witnesses neither of us know about. I mean, what if they find Hamm?"

Trevor Hamm had been missing for a couple of months but she knew the Organised Crime team was determined to track him down before this trial. Ian Osman hadn't directly admitted he'd been working for Hamm, but the evidence was there. And if they found Hamm, the repercussions would stretch across the whole region.

Carl said something in response. Zoe didn't hear as she was already in the bedroom pulling on clothes. She had time to go home and change. Her son Nicholas would be there; it would be nice to have breakfast with him. If eighteen-year-olds did breakfast.

"I'll call you when it's all over," she said as she put a hand on the front door handle.

He walked to her and put his arms around her. She let her bag drop to the floor and returned the embrace.

"Sorry," she said.

"I understand. You're anxious. I am too."

"I'll miss you," she muttered into his chest.

"Me too, darling. Me too."

CHAPTER THREE

Anita Randle sat at the kitchen table, watching her husband get ready for work. He wore his blue suit, the new one she'd bought him for his birthday. How many men asked for a tailored suit for their birthday? When she'd met him he'd been the same, but then it was designer jeans and expensive leather or suede jackets. Eighteen years later, and he still knew how to make clothes look good.

He was facing away from her, peering into the mirror in the hallway. He probably didn't even know she could see him from the kitchen; it was dull in here, the low sun still at the front of the house.

He leaned into the mirror, straightening his tie. He frowned at his reflection, licked a finger and pushed a hair into place. She couldn't decide whether she still found this attention to his appearance endearing, or if it had become tiresome.

He straightened, gave himself a final once-over, then strode into the kitchen. Her grip on her mug – porcelain, bought on a trip to Devon – tightened.

CHAPTER THREE

"Darling," he said, smiling with his mouth but not his eyes.

"Darling," she replied, trying to make her own smile more sincere. "Good luck today."

He waved a hand in dismissal. "They won't be calling me. I have to leave the court after they've kicked things off."

"But you'll be in the corridors, monitoring the situation."

His face darkened. "I've got a bloody job to do, Anita. You think being Head of Force CID is easy?"

She felt her chest flutter. "That wasn't what I meant. You know..."

"Hmpf."

She stood up and pulled her dressing gown tighter. It was Italian silk, a present on their fifteenth wedding anniversary. Back before he'd gained that near-permanent harried look he wore right now.

She laid a hand on his shoulder. "I'm worried about you."

He shrugged it off. "You needn't be."

"Still. You haven't been sleeping. I know you've been coming downstairs in the night."

"Sometimes I get a bit of insomnia. Nothing unusual when you reach your fifties, love." He kissed her on the forehead. "Good opportunity to get some work done without interruptions."

She nodded, not ready to pursue this line of conversation further. She'd taken to creeping onto the stairs, sitting halfway down and listening to make sure he was OK. On two occasions she'd heard him on the phone. At three in the morning.

There was only one reason to make a phone call at that time.

She shuddered and pushed the thought to the back of her

mind. If he wasn't going to admit to it, she wasn't going to make any accusations. They had two daughters to think about, each with an expensive education to pay for. She hadn't worked since he'd become a DCI eight years ago. She could never risk letting him leave for another woman.

She lowered herself into the chair, working to control her breathing. *Don't cry.* He had his briefcase open and was rooting through it.

"Have you lost something?" she asked, trying to hide the crack in her voice.

"No," he snapped. "Just being thorough."

"You're going straight to court?"

He looked up. "Yes, I'm going straight to court. Not much point going into the office then having to walk straight out again."

"I'm just interested, darling."

He stared at her for a moment longer than she felt comfortable with. She forced herself to hold his gaze, not to blink. After a moment his face softened. He put a hand on her cheek.

"I'm sorry, sweetheart," he said. "I'm just a bit irritable with this bloody trial. I'll be fine once it's over."

I certainly hope so, she thought. She gave him a smile and swallowed the lump in her throat.

"Right," he said, his voice back to its usual morning brusqueness. "Kiss the girls for me."

"I will." *Like I do every morning.* Maria and Carly hardly saw their father. *She* hardly saw their father.

Anita sighed. She'd known what she was signing up for when she'd married a police officer. Her father had warned her; he'd been a traffic warden and had seen it up close.

David turned and breezed out of the room, leaving a trail

of expensive aftershave in his wake. Anita closed her eyes and breathed it in. His scent still made her heart race.

She heard the door slam. She downed the last of her coffee and threw the toast in the bin – she wasn't hungry. She made for the stairs.

Time to inject some lightness into her voice, to smile through the nagging dread, to pretend to be her girls' bright and happy mother.

CHAPTER FOUR

"Morning all." Zoe pushed open the door to the team room. It was an hour before she had to be at the court. She wanted to spend it grounding herself with a dose of normality.

DC Connie Williams and DC Rhodri Hughes were at their desks, peering into screens. Rhodri turned round, swivelling his chair from side to side. "Morning, boss." He looked her up and down – she was wearing the same clothes as yesterday – but didn't comment. Instead, he gave her a lopsided grin.

She ignored it and walked to Connie's desk. "Morning, Connie."

Connie frowned at her screen then blinked and turned to her boss. "Sorry, boss. I was miles away."

"You working on the Rolands case?"

"Yeah. Got some new forensics in. Implicates Fred Roland even further." Fred Roland had attacked his wife with a hammer after she'd told him she was leaving for another man. "This one's going to be an easy charge, boss."

"Don't count your chickens. I still need to get CPS on board."

"It's a shoe-in, boss," said Rhodri. "You'll walk it."

Zoe laughed. "Thanks for the vote of confidence." She peeled off her jacket and walked to her private office, which was in a corner of the main room, surrounded by glass windows. The main door opened behind her.

"Boss."

Zoe turned to see DS Mo Uddin holding two steaming mugs. She smiled. "One of those for me?"

"I thought you'd need it."

"I already had one at Carl's, then two at home. Nicholas had it brewing when I got in. You're all looking after me." She took the mug off him. "Thanks. And not just for the coffee."

Mo shrugged. "I know how much you've been dreading today."

She glanced at the constables. "I always dread standing up in court. Those lawyers have a way of twisting everything you say, the bastards."

"Bastards," Rhodri muttered in agreement.

"You got a minute?" Mo asked.

Zoe checked the clock over the door. "Better than that, I can give you ten. Come through."

She pushed open the door to her office and sat at the desk. Mo took the seat opposite and slurped his coffee.

"What's up?" she asked.

He twisted his lips, hesitating.

"Spit it out," Zoe said. "You've got me worried."

Mo scratched the side of his nose. "It's Rhodri."

Her gaze flicked out to Rhodri, who was leaning into his

screen more intently than usual. His neck was pink; he knew they were talking about him.

"What's up with Rhodri?" she asked, feeling her chest dip. Not long ago, her DCI had been given a transfer to another region after an injury. Zoe didn't want to lose two trusted colleagues.

Mo leaned back. He cradled his mug.

"Mo, you're getting me worried here. Just tell me, please."

"He's asked to sit the Sergeants' Exam."

Zoe felt her mouth hang open. She forced it shut. She stared at Mo for a moment, trying to read his expression. It told her nothing. He'd practised for this.

She leaned across the desk. "*Rhod* has?"

Mo nodded.

"Seriously?"

"He got that commendation last month. Thinks he's up to more challenge."

She looked out at the constables. Connie was watching Rhodri, who'd turned even pinker.

She looked back at Mo. "Yeah, but... Rhodri."

"He's a good copper, Zo."

"He's a good DC. He hasn't shown any sign of leadership ability."

"Nor do I, not very often."

"That's bullshit and you know it. You're the steady hand that keeps this team on the straight and narrow."

"Oh, great. You make me sound really dull." Mo's eyes sparkled.

"There's more to you than that, Mo, and you know it. You're quick to spot connections in the evidence. You're

CHAPTER FOUR

excellent at engaging witnesses, and much more level-headed than me when interviewing."

"That's not what Dawson said when I—"

"Forget Dawson." Zoe ground her fist into the desk. "He doesn't know you."

Mo sighed. "Anyway, now you've finished embarrassing me with praise, what about Rhodri?"

Zoe shook her head. "He's not ready, Mo. Not yet. You know that."

He looked down. "Yeah. Thought I'd run it past you though, just in case."

"Sorry." Zoe checked her watch. "I really have to go, sorry. I can tell him. We can give him six months, a year. Then review the situation. It isn't a no. Just a not yet. And why is he asking, and not Connie?"

Mo gave her a tight smile. "She's closer than he is, but she's not there either."

"No." Zoe stood up.

"You're busy with this trial," Mo said. "I can tell him."

"It should be me as the team manager."

"It's fine, boss." He stood up. "Go, before you end up in contempt of court."

"It's Zo. And it doesn't work like that."

"No." Mo turned towards the constables. Both of them quickly turned away. "He can read my damn mind, can't he?"

"I think you'll need to have a chat with him immediately, if that's what you're wondering."

"Send him in here on your way out, could you?"

Zoe walked around the desk and patted her friend's shoulder. "Sorry you have to start your Monday morning with this."

"It could be worse," he said, looking up at her. "Say hello to Ian Osman for me, will you?"

CHAPTER FIVE

IAN SAT across the Formica table from his solicitor, his hands clasped between his knees. He was wearing his best suit, the one Alison had bought for him to wear to her brother's wedding last year.

He was grateful that she'd thought to bring it in for him, even if she wasn't living in their house right now. Staying at her ghastly mum's with the kids, having bile dripped into her ear all hours. It was a wonder she didn't hate him by now.

"Ian?"

He screwed up his eyes and forced them open. "Sorry. Yes."

"Did you hear what Mr Syed said?" His solicitor Jane Summer, a ruddy woman wearing an expensive suit that didn't fit properly, cocked her head at him.

Ian turned to the barrister. "I'd be grateful if you could repeat it, please."

Khalid Syed, the barrister Jane had recommended to him, took a deep breath. He was tall and slim, wearing a bright green tie with his dark suit. Ian wondered if barristers were supposed to wear bright green ties. But then, he'd be changing into his fancy dress before the trial began.

"The evidence they have on your connection to Hamm is weak. It's all circumstantial," Syed said, tapping his pen on the table top.

Ian nodded. He'd provided Trevor Hamm with information about police operations. In return, Hamm had arranged for one of his associates, a builder called Stuart Reynolds, to renovate Ian's bathroom. The man was supposed to have fixed his roof too, but work had stopped when Ian had been taken in by PSD.

"Reynolds is connected to Hamm, we can't deny that," said Syed. "They've got evidence of him working on Hamm's old flat in the city centre. But his firm does legitimate work too. You've said your bathroom work was one of those jobs."

"It was." Ian struggled to hold the barrister's eye. "Cash in hand, that's why I've not got a receipt."

"Well, Reynolds could get into trouble with the Inland Revenue for that, but it's not a crime on your part. We can deal with that."

Ian leaned back in his chair, then caught himself as he felt its flimsy back give under his weight. "But..."

Jane shifted in her chair. Ian heard voices outside the door; was he being summoned? He rubbed his fingertips together, trying not to focus on the way they slid against each other.

"But the explosives residue they say you planted on Nadeem Sharif," the barrister continued, his eyes widening. "You were actively involved in an anti-terror operation. Our contention is that you'd been near the plane, and that's how the residue found its way onto you."

CHAPTER FIVE

"And then onto Sharif from your fingers," Jane added.

"When I was checking the bodies," said Ian.

Syed nodded. "When you were checking the bodies. As you were perfectly entitled to do given your place in the investigation."

Ian nodded. Zoe had seen him crouching over Sharif's body. Leave this on one of the victims, he'd been told. Preferably male, preferably Asian. But Zoe hadn't confirmed to PSD which body she'd seen him with; she hadn't known who it was at the time.

He just had to hope she was telling the truth, and would stick to the same story in court.

"One of the prosecution witnesses is the pathologist," said Syed. He checked his notes. "A Doctor Adebayo. I'll plant the idea in the jury's minds that she's just as likely to have planted evidence on the body as you are, that you weren't the only one with access. Which makes the idea of either of you doing it absurd. Two professionals, doing their job. And of course, I'll drive home the fact that you were near the plane."

"Thanks," Ian said. "I owe you one."

"Just doing my job, mate." The barrister stood up. He smelled of soap. His chin was smooth and his hair perfectly neat. "Try not to worry. You won't be called for a while yet. We've got plenty of witnesses to get through before you. And we'll talk beforehand. You'll be fine."

Ian felt his chest tighten. Alison would be in the public gallery, watching him. Her fucking mother might even be there too. The press were here, he'd heard the commotion when he'd arrived in the police van. And his colleagues...

Could he hold up, with all of them watching him? Could he lie?

He caught movement in front of him. The barrister's hand was outstretched, waiting to be shaken. Ian took it, knowing his handshake was damp and weak.

"Thanks," he whispered.

CHAPTER SIX

Zoe sat in her car, tugging at the sleeve of her jacket. She wore a grey blazer and black trousers, not her usual jeans and leather jacket. The blazer was too big and the trousers too tight. She shuffled in the seat, uncomfortable. She had to blank out how uneasy she felt in this get-up. If she fidgeted in the witness stand, it might make the jury distrust her.

It would give Ian's barrister an opportunity to suggest she was shifty, at the very least.

Her first entanglement with a barrister had been twelve years ago, when she was two years into CID. An armed robbery case. She'd been the first officer on the scene, had made the first arrests. The scumbags who'd done the robbery had managed to get a not guilty verdict thanks to their barrister's methodical dismantling of her application of arrest procedure.

She'd been alone when she'd made the arrests, which meant it was her word against the suspects. She'd been an idiot, should have waited a few more moments for Mo to arrive at the scene.

This was worse. There'd been plenty of people at the airport after the bomb that had detonated on Pakistan Airways flight 546, that was certain. But she'd been the only person paying attention to Ian. He shouldn't even have been there; she still didn't know who'd told him to cut short his day off and his family shopping trip and hurry to the airport. She had a good idea though: Detective Superintendent David Randle.

She needed to get moving. She flipped down the visor and checked her face in the mirror. She'd put on a bit of mascara and blusher this morning, it made her face feel heavy. But she was pale, her skin grey through lack of sleep, and she wanted to look alert for the trial.

Zoe pushed the door open and got out of the car in one swift movement. The court was two streets away, and her parking would be up in three hours. She'd have to come back at lunchtime, either move her Mini or feed the meter.

The street was busy, office workers hurrying to their desks to start the week. She wove through the crowds, her gaze straight ahead. When she turned the corner into Newton Street where the Crown Court was, she felt her stomach clench.

The court loomed ahead of her, a slab-like modern building nothing like the rose-brick splendour of the Gothic Magistrate's Court a couple of streets away. People milled around the front steps. Lawyers on the phone, journalists preparing for the day. Witnesses and their families shuffling uneasily, unsure whether to go inside yet.

Get a grip, Zoe told herself. All she had to do is tell them what she'd seen.

But she wasn't entirely sure what she'd seen. And she wasn't entirely sure she'd mentioned all of it when she'd been interviewed by Carl's colleague. She'd been protecting Ian to some extent; the evidence was slim and he was still her DS. And she was worried they thought she was working with him. Keeping to the barest of the facts seemed like the best option.

Randle was at the bottom of the steps, talking on his mobile. He wore a blue suit that made him look taller and slimmer than usual. Her eyes narrowed in recognition of her boss. Should she acknowledge him, say something, or pretend she hadn't seen him?

He shoved his phone into his pocket then turned to take the steps two at a time. The steep steps were like a funnel, wide at the bottom and narrowing into a covered area at the top, pulling people into the building. Zoe watched as Randle slid past a group of people and disappeared inside. She hung back, knowing he would be in condescending mode today. He already treated her like a child half the time, despite having played a part in her promotion. She couldn't face speaking to him, not today, knowing what she did about him. Knowing that he probably knew that she knew.

Go on, she told herself. *You can't wait all day.* She took a long breath and followed him inside.

CHAPTER SEVEN

Zoe needn't have waited. As she passed through the security checks, Randle was right ahead of her. Acting DCI Frank Dawson was with him, the man who had been appointed as her temporary boss after DCI Lesley Clarke had been given ill-health leave.

She sighed and pushed her shoulders back, determined not to let them rattle her.

Dawson turned to her as she grabbed her keys and phone off the conveyor. An insecure smile spread across his face. "Zoe. The woman of the hour."

"Frank."

His face darkened; he didn't like the way she refused to call him *boss*. He was still the same rank as her, so she didn't see why she should. She'd spent years as his DS, tolerating his jibes and casual sexism. She wasn't about to revisit that now.

"All ready?" he asked.

"As I'll ever be."

"They probably won't call you today," Randle said, his

CHAPTER SEVEN

gaze skimming over her. She felt an urge to tug her sleeve. Her skin tingled.

"Still, I have to be here, just in case. Do you think *you'll* be called today?"

"No chance," Randle replied. "I don't even know if they'll need me." He gave her an oily smile. "But I thought I'd show my face, give my officers some support."

She nodded. "Thank you."

"Pleasure. Ian Osman was a blight on our unit, and it's important that the truth about him is told."

Zoe stared at him, her palms damp. She couldn't believe the nerve of the man. Ian Osman had been working for Randle, she was sure of it. And Randle had been photographed with Alina Popescu, the woman who'd detonated the second bomb that day.

She wondered if he'd been made aware of the photo. If her colleague Sheila Griffin in Organised Crime had questioned him yet.

Probably not. You didn't talk to a man like Detective Superintendent David Randle about something like that until you had all the pieces of the jigsaw slotted into place.

"You sticking around, Frank?" she asked, turning to him and wishing Randle would leave them.

"Like the superintendent, I'm here to show support, Zoe." He cleared his throat. "If a member of my team is giving evidence in a case like this, I want to show her she's not alone."

Oh, but I am, thought Zoe. No one else would be standing in that witness box, telling what truth she could remember about the man who'd been her colleague.

"I'll be fine," she said. "Done this plenty of times."

Randle was eying her, his gaze calculating. She wanted to swat him away like a wasp.

"I know you will, Zoe," Dawson said. He lifted a hand, about to put it on her shoulder, then dropped it.

"Thanks, Frank. But I'm sure they need you more back at the office."

Her phone rang. She gave Dawson a look, glanced towards the court rooms, then answered it.

"DI Finch."

"Zo, it's Mo."

"I'm about to go into court. Can it wait?"

"There's a body. Found in a deserted house in Sutton Coldfield. Should be the North Birmingham branch of Force CID attending, but their DI is on leave. Adi needs you at the scene."

Adi Hanson was head of the Forensic Scene Investigation unit, and an old friend of Zoe's.

"Look, can you head over there without me?" she said. "I'll check the roster here, probably find out they won't be calling me till tomorrow, and join you. I'm a bit closer than you are."

"I'm already on my way, but they need you to open the case. I've already spoken to the CPS solicitor, she's told the court."

Zoe glanced at Frank. "What about Dawson?"

"He's acting up, Zo," Mo replied. "Not on operational duty."

Dawson frowned at her. His left eyebrow was raised in a question. She put a hand over her phone.

"There's been a body found in Sutton Coldfield. Erdington can't take it as DI Finks is on leave. They need me there."

CHAPTER SEVEN

He pursed his lips. "Go. You won't be on today and if you are, we can get you put back. I'll speak to the solicitor."

"Mo already has."

"He has, has he? OK, good to see him using some bloody initiative, I suppose. OK, bugger off and do your job."

Zoe moved her hand away from the phone. "Did you hear that?"

"I'll see you there in twenty minutes," Mo replied.

"Yeah." Zoe plunged her phone into her pocket and sped towards the doors, wishing she hadn't worn these damn trousers.

CHAPTER EIGHT

Zoe parked her car at the mouth of the cul de sac. Two squad cars were in front of the address she'd been given, along with three other cars: pathologist and FSIs, most likely.

She grabbed her gloves and overshoes from the boot and walked towards the house, taking in the surroundings. The straight section of the road, leading to the bulb, was flanked by high fences at its entrance, behind which lay the sides of the gardens from the neighbouring street. Only as the road started to widen out did it become populated. The houses faced in random directions, either for privacy or aesthetics. The house with the squad cars outside had a tall hedge in front, and none of the other houses' windows overlooked it.

Invisible, she thought to herself. The perfect place to kill someone. An alleyway ran alongside the house, making it even more convenient. A means to escape the scene, to go undetected.

Either all that was a coincidence, or this crime had been planned.

Zoe approached the front door to the house. A uniformed

constable stood by the bay window at the front, taking names. She gave him her details and passed inside.

The house was clearly unoccupied. Through the open door to the front room, she could see cardboard boxes piled up next to a dusty blue sofa. The low unit in one corner that should have held a TV was bare.

"Hello?" she called. Voices came from the door up ahead, which was glazed with bevelled glass that looked like it had been fitted at least thirty years ago. The whole house felt tired and dated, as if it hadn't been loved for quite some time.

Zoe wondered how long it had been empty.

She opened the door, entering an old-fashioned kitchen that was even more grubby than her own. Heavy wooden cupboards lined the walls and the worktop was tiled. Ugly, but good for preserving prints and any other forensics.

A lighting rig had been set up, pointing into what looked like an under-stairs cupboard. She squeezed past it. The voices came from down a narrow flight of stairs.

She bent down. "Adi? You down there?"

"Zoe! Come on down."

"It's OK to walk on these steps?"

"I've put tape on the spots you can tread on."

She looked down. "I see."

She descended slowly, careful not to touch the walls. The smell of decay grew stronger with each step. Finally she emerged into a low cellar. Adi was crouched in a corner, the pathologist behind him, next to the body.

"Adana," Zoe said. "We must stop meeting like this."

Dr Adebayo turned and smiled at Zoe with her eyes, her mouth covered by a mask. "I'm glad they tracked you down."

"I'm supposed to be in court. You've all done me a massive favour."

Adi stood up, stooping. "I aim to please." A shadow crossed his face. He'd asked her out a few weeks ago, not understanding that her relationship with Carl, however fragile at that time, wasn't over. She hoped he'd return to his normal relaxed self soon.

"I'll only have to go back tomorrow," she said, feeling her skin tighten. She would much rather be here, even with that godawful smell, than cooped up in the Crown Court. "What have we got?"

"Caucasian male, forty to fifty years old I'd say," replied Adana. "Multiple stab wounds to the chest and abdomen. Face has been half chewed off by the local wildlife. He's been here about a week."

"Hence the smell."

"It could be worse," said Adi. "It's dry down here. The heating's turned off and the electricity's erratic to say the least."

Zoe nodded. "Any idea who the owners are?"

"Not yet," said Adi. "Mo's looking into it."

Zoe stood abruptly, hitting her head on the ceiling. Dust clouded in front of her eyes.

"Shit. Sorry," she said.

Adi frowned. "Be careful. He's in the back garden. Go out via the lounge, we're still dusting the kitchen."

"No problem. I'll be back in a minute."

Zoe retreated up the stairs, struggling to turn in the tight space, and felt relief as she entered the kitchen and was able to breathe again. One of Adi's team, a guy called Rav who Connie had worked with on a previous case, was in the doorway. He gave her a nod and went back to his work.

Zoe opened the first door on the left and entered a spacious living room. It had a deep, full-height bay constructed from wood. She could smell the wood along with a tinge of damp. To one side of the bay, a door was open.

She stepped out. The door gave out onto a high deck, which explained the cellar. Mo was below her standing on the lawn, sorely in need of cutting.

"Mo," she called.

Mo turned and waved for her to come down. He was on his phone. She joined him as he hung up.

"What news?" she asked him.

"Thanks for coming. Was Dawson OK?"

"He was fine. Even offered to speak to the CPS."

"Wow. He's trying to be nice."

"Let's make the most of it while it lasts." She gestured at Mo's phone. "So?"

"I've tracked down the estate agent. She's on her way here. Says the house has been on the market for four months, doesn't get that much interest. One of her team found the body, he's gone home."

"Must have been a shock," said Zoe.

"Yeah." Mo grimaced.

She looked up at the house. "No wonder it doesn't get any interest, given the state of it."

"You'd be surprised. Anyway, the owners have moved to Germany. So it's unlikely our victim lived here."

Zoe raised an eyebrow. "He could have come home to check on the house?"

"Estate agent says not. We'll check it out, of course. We'll need to speak to them. But it looks like someone has taken advantage of the fact there's an empty house here."

Zoe glanced back at the house. A small window was below the decking, giving into the cellar. "Someone who knew the layout of the place."

"Yup."

"So this isn't a domestic," she said. "That guy in there was either brought here to die, or someone killed him and then dumped him here."

Mo nodded. "Someone who knew how to pick their spot."

CHAPTER NINE

Zoe climbed the wooden steps up to the deck and went back into the lounge. A few pictures hung on the walls, flanked by bare spots where others had gone with the owners. This room had another sofa, brown leather, with scratches that made her wonder if the owners had a cat. In the far corner was an easy chair that looked like it might disintegrate if she touched it.

She went into the kitchen. Rav was dusting the back door.

"Any prints?" she asked.

He turned, looking surprised. "A few. Not recent, but not four months old."

"Probably the estate agent."

"Yeah." He frowned as he leaned further into his work.

"We'll get prints from everyone who's had access to the place," Zoe said. "For elimination."

He turned to her. "Staff at the agent's would have known there was an empty house."

Even if one of them wasn't the killer, they might have

tipped the killer off, if inadvertently. "You're right. We'll need their prints, either way. And we'll be asking who they talked to about this house."

He shrugged. "It'll be on Rightmove, anyone would have known."

Zoe sighed; he was right. People never considered that the photos they put on listings sites not only told the world their house was possibly empty, but also showcased all the lovely nickable belongings they had inside.

"There's marks on this door," Rav said. "Recent, very recent I'd say."

"Prints?"

He bent over. "Scratches, on the bottom sill. Looks like someone's forced this door open."

"Was it open when you arrived?"

"Nope. Closed and locked. You'd never spot it if you weren't looking."

"You think the killer might have come in that way?"

"It's a possibility."

"But you said they were recent. The body didn't get here recently."

"Victim could have been killed elsewhere, then brought here afterwards," said Adi. Zoe turned to see him standing in the doorway to the cellar.

"Adana will be able to tell us if it looks like he was moved," she replied.

"To be honest, I'd say not. There's evidence of someone going down those steps in the last few days, shoe prints in the dust. But the only disturbance to the dust around the body seems to be the rats' activity."

"Can you get a match for the shoe prints?"

"They're blank. Whatever our killer was wearing, they weren't trainers or work boots."

"Any theories?"

"We've taken an impression of the prints. I'll be able to tell you more when we've analysed them."

"OK. Is Adana close to done?"

Adi shrugged. "You'll have to ask her yourself."

She eyed him. "Everything OK?"

He sniffed. "Bloody stinks down there."

Changing the subject, she thought. *Don't push it*.

"OK." She squeezed past him, noticing that he pulled back so as not to make bodily contact, and went down to the cellar.

Adana was alone, packing up her case. She looked up at Zoe's entrance. "Poor soul."

"Not the best place to end your days."

"Indeed. Getting him out of here without causing any damage is going to be a nightmare."

"Can you do some of the PM here?"

Adana wiped her forehead with the sleeve of her protective suit. "The light's dreadful, we've got barely any space, and the dust'll just contaminate his organs once I open him up. We're going to need to move him out as carefully as we can."

"You want me to summon your team?"

"We'll need more bodies to get this right. Form a kind of conveyor belt, pass him up the stairs instead of having a couple of people heaving him up on their own."

"You want to bag him first?"

"It'll contaminate the area around the body. It's all too tight down here. Charlie and Graham can bag him upstairs."

"Sounds like a plan," Zoe said. "I'll bring some Uniform down."

Adana bent over, her hands on her thighs. "Thanks."

"You want me to get you a bottle of water or anything?"

"That would be lovely, if you've got one."

"Ah. Sorry." She didn't have anything of the sort.

Adana laughed. "Don't worry."

Zoe trudged back up the stairs. Adi and Rav were at the back door, examining the scratches on the sill.

"This was done with a screwdriver, I reckon," Adi said. "Maybe a chisel. Someone jimmied the door from the outside. Lifted it in its frame so the lock would disengage."

"We'll talk to neighbours," said Zoe. "See if anyone's noticed any activity in the garden."

"You've looked at the angle of these houses?"

Zoe shook her head. "From the front, it all looks pretty random, but…"

"No one can see into this garden. Not close to the house, anyway. I reckon if we drew a line from the back of that decking to the fence at the side, it would give us a blind spot."

"Still," she said. "Someone might have seen them come in via the side."

"It's worth a shot. But your killer knew there was an empty house. He knew it was in a secluded spot, with no other houses overlooking it. He did his research, Zoe."

"Don't assume it's a man."

Adi pointed towards the cellar. "The victim's over six feet tall."

"Still," she replied. "We can't assume anything till we've got the evidence."

Adi shrugged.

"Right," Zoe said. "Adana wants to move the body out. Are you ready for her to mess up the staircase?"

"We've dusted the stairs, taken impressions. I know she'll do her best to preserve the area around the body."

"She's setting up a conveyor belt," Zoe told him. "Less disruption that way."

"Good thinking." Adi turned to Rav. "We can help out."

"I'll get some Uniform," Zoe said.

She went out to the front drive and spoke to the constable she'd checked in with. He was one of four uniformed officers on the scene. Within minutes the other three were in the kitchen, filling the space with their bulk.

"Adana!" Zoe called down the stairs. "How many d'you want me to send down?"

"Two please," came Adana's voice. "Two who've got some sense and won't make a mess."

Avoiding the eyes of the constables, Zoe gestured to Adi. "You and Rav."

"Good choice." Adi headed through the doorway and Rav followed him. Zoe heard Adana speaking indistinctly, and then the sound of a heavy weight being moved. She drew in a breath, her eyes on the doorway.

"Right," she said to the uniformed officers, two men and a woman. "What are your names?"

The woman spoke. "I'm PC Gilbert, ma'am. This is PC McDougall and PC Kale."

"Right." Zoe looked at one of the men. "PC Kale, you get close to that door. Be ready to take the body as it approaches and pass it back. Be bloody careful, yes?"

"No problem, ma'am." The constable hurried into position.

"Good. PC Gilbert, you stand two feet behind him, next

to the door to the hallway. Same drill. PC McDougall, you stand in the doorway, make sure that door stays open."

"I'll wedge it, ma'am."

Adana's two assistants were in the hallway. Zoe indicated towards them. "When the body comes through, you pass it on. Slowly and steadily. Be careful not to bring it into contact with the walls and furniture as far as possible. Hand it through to the pathology team. And they'll get it out to their van."

"Ma'am." PC McDougall took up his spot behind his colleagues. The three of them donned protective gloves.

Zoe licked her lips. She went to the window and looked outside. Mo was on the phone again. Trying to get contact details for the owners, she imagined. Connie would be best placed to do that.

She turned at the sound of movement in the cellar doorway. The body was making its way upwards. Adana had secured the limbs in place, but the face was visible. The stench filled the room, making PC Kale gag. Zoe watched him, her breathing shallow.

He took some of the weight off Rav and passed the body through. He did a good job, avoiding contact with the walls despite having to get the body around an angle. Zoe was glad Adana wasn't watching this.

The load moved on, into the waiting arms of PC Gilbert and then PC McDougall. Instead of passing it through to the pathology assistants, he froze.

"Constable, keep the line moving please," Zoe said.

He said nothing, instead staring into the face of the victim, his mouth open.

"Is there a problem?" Zoe approached him.

He looked up at her, the body shifting in his grip. PC

Gilbert to one side and the pathology assistant behind him stepped in to help take the weight.

Zoe was annoyed. She'd given clear instructions. "PC McDougall, what's the matter?"

"I know him, ma'am," he breathed.

She looked down at the body. The clothes were heavily bloodstained and the face was already desiccated, making the victim look twenty years older than Adana had put him at.

"You recognise him?"

PC McDougall swallowed. "He's force, ma'am."

Zoe felt her stomach plummet. "He's a copper?"

A nod. PC McDougall's face was pale. "His name's Detective Sergeant Raif Starling, ma'am. He works out of Erdington CID. Or at least he did, until a couple of months ago."

CHAPTER TEN

The girls had gone to school and Anita was alone in the house. She hated mornings, so empty and quiet with no one here and nothing to do.

She should tidy up. Maria's room was a mess, hair products scattered across surfaces and a pile of clothes next to the desk, among which Anita had no idea which items were clean and which were dirty. Her eldest daughter had a habit of pulling clothes out of her wardrobe when deciding what to wear and then not putting any of it back. The rejects joined the dirty laundry on the floor, meaning Anita did twice as much washing as she needed to.

Maria had gone out last night. It was her boyfriend Joe's birthday, and they'd gone for a pizza with his parents. Carly had shut herself in her room, on WhatsApp with her friends. Anita and David had drifted around the house, him distracted by thought of today's trial and her distracted by her thoughts. More than once she'd been about to question him, to ask him why he'd been behaving strangely lately. But she knew he would be angry at her for raising it when he was under so much stress.

Once this damn trial was over, she'd bring it out into the open. Or she might not. She had no idea what to do. She couldn't risk losing him. But she also couldn't live her life like this, always watching for evidence of another woman. Sniffing his clothes when she pulled them out of the laundry, stopping herself from checking his receipts in the bedroom waste basket.

She heaved herself up the stairs, scratching an insect bite on her arm, and wandered into the bedroom. His trousers from last night lay on the bed, perfectly arranged. If he took the trouble to put them out like that, why didn't he hang them up? Something about airing them, he said. Surely he could air them on a hanger.

She grabbed a hanger from the wardrobe and folded the trousers over it, careful to keep the creases in place. David ironed creases into his trousers after he'd got them back from the dry cleaner's. Thank God he didn't expect her to do it. She had enough on her plate with all the clothes the girls wore.

As she brushed the trousers down, something fell out of the pocket. She frowned. David was fastidious about this. He emptied his pockets every evening when he got in from work. Rubbish went into the waste basket and anything else into the tray on his bedside table. Then he put on his jeans – Levis, he ironed them too – and came downstairs for dinner. Maybe with a detour via his study. Those detours were lasting longer recently.

Anita bent to pick up the object. It was a scrap of paper, folded up. She held it between the tips of her fingers like it might burn her. Was it rubbish? Anything that didn't go into the bin, he filed or photographed immediately. He never left scraps of paper like this in his tray. And he never left *anything* in his pockets.

She pulled in a long breath, her chest shaking. She placed the paper on the bed, trying to pretend it wasn't there.

She turned away from it and placed the hanger with her husband's trousers over the wardrobe door knob. He didn't like that; it made the bedroom untidy. Not as untidy as leaving your trousers lying around on the bed, she thought.

She surveyed the trousers, picking off a couple of white cat hairs – another reason not to leave them lying around, Sheba must have got into the bedroom when the girls were moving around this morning. After what felt like an age, she turned back to the folded-up piece of paper on the bed.

If it was rubbish, she should bin it. It was probably rubbish.

But what if it wasn't?

In that case, she should put it on his bedside table, in the tray. She glanced at the tray; empty. Keys gone, phone gone. Of course. When David wasn't at home, you'd barely know he lived here, so little evidence of himself did he leave behind.

If she put it in the tray, it would be like a beacon announcing she'd touched it. It was probably rubbish.

But what if it wasn't?

She swallowed. Only one thing for it.

She had to know. Then she could decide.

If it was rubbish, she'd take it downstairs, throw it in the kitchen bin. Pretend it had never existed. It was probably rubbish.

She picked it up, thinking of the protective gloves David wore when he handled evidence. There'd been one time they'd suspected Maria had been smoking weed – she hadn't, thank God – and he'd put them on to search her room while she'd been out with friends. As if his daughter would come home and dust for prints.

Anita pursed her lips as she unfolded it. From outside she heard a car door slam. She flinched. *He's not coming home*, she told herself. He never came home in the daytime. David was far too meticulous to leave anything he needed behind.

She opened it further, holding her breath. Inside was a printout of a photo.

She bit her bottom lip as she opened it fully. Her eyes prickled.

It was a photograph of David. He was at some kind of police function, a glass of white wine in his hand and a crowd of people surrounding him. Some of them were in uniform, most not.

Next to him, a blank smile on her face, was a young woman. She had smooth brown hair and dark eyes. She wore coral lipstick. David hated bright lipstick.

He had his arm around the woman. Anita could see his fingers on her waist, his arm encircling her out of sight. He was squeezing her.

Who was this woman, that her husband could embrace her like that?

She stared at the photo.

Now what?

This wasn't rubbish. He'd kept it in his pocket for a reason. Was it a keepsake, a treasured memory?

She lay the photo on the bed, wishing she'd worn gloves now. She took her phone out of her cardigan pocket and snapped an image, jumping as the fake shutter sound kicked in.

She picked it up and refolded it, very carefully. She took the hanger off the wardrobe door and lifted the trousers off it. The photo still in her hand – she needed to let go of it, her palms were sweaty – she lay the trousers on the bed and pushed the photo back into one of the pockets.

She froze. Which pocket had it been in? She felt her chest hollow out. If she put it back in the wrong one, he'd know.

The left pocket. She'd watched him empty his pockets on so many occasions. She knew his habits. Phone and keys in the right, everything else in the left. She patted the pocket, feeling the folded-up image inside, her fingers tingling.

She surveyed the room. The hanger. She put it back in the wardrobe and backed away from the bed. She closed the door.

At the top of the stairs, her grip on the banister tight, she allowed herself to cry.

CHAPTER ELEVEN

Zoe walked into the team room. Connie swivelled in her chair.

"I've got the phone number for the house owners, in Germany."

Zoe nodded. "Ta."

"Shall I give it to the sarge?"

"Did he ask for it?"

A shrug. "He told me they were in Germany. I called the agents."

Zoe smiled. "Yeah," she said. "Give it to Mo. He'll be back here soon."

"Anything you want me to do in the meantime?"

Zoe pulled in a shaky breath. "I need to think."

"Of course, boss." Connie turned away and dipped her head to her work.

Zoe walked into the inner office and threw herself into the chair. DS Raif Starling. That was all she bloody needed, a murder case, and the victim turns out to be a copper.

Not retired, either. PC Kale hadn't known why Starling

had left Erdington. Maybe he'd got a transfer. Maybe he'd resigned.

But her spidey senses were telling her it was neither of those. Had Starling been suspended?

Until she knew whether that was the case, and why, this was a regular murder inquiry. His death might be unrelated to the fact he was a detective. He might just have been unlucky.

Yeah, she thought. *Carry on telling yourself that, and it might turn out to be true.*

Normally she wouldn't even have come straight to the office. She'd have been in front of Lesley, asking for her advice. Trusting her experience.

But Dawson was the one in Lesley's office now. OK, so he was her acting boss, but he wasn't a DCI. And he'd been at court when she last saw him.

No reason to think he wasn't still there.

She opened the door to the inner office. The constables both shuffled in their seats, not looking up. Was she being that obvious?

"Rhod, can I borrow you for a minute?"

Rhodri shared a look with Connie. *Shit*, thought Zoe. *He thinks it's about the Sergeants' Exam.*

She clenched her fists. Might as well address it.

Rhodri stood up, smoothing down his tie, and walked to her office. Connie watched him. Zoe sat behind her desk and waited for him to take one of the other chairs.

"Boss," he said. "How was the crime scene?"

"Bloody smelly," she replied. "Victim had been there at least a week, according to Adana. Mind you, it would have been worse if he hadn't dried out."

Rhodri grimaced. "He killed there, or brought them in?"

CHAPTER ELEVEN

"We're not sure about that yet. There's signs of a break-in, but more recent."

"So he was killed somewhere else, then dumped at the house."

"Not according to the amount of dust around his body." She leaned back. "Adi's still there. If there's anything else to help us work out the sequence of events, he'll get it to us."

"Anything I can do to help?"

"There is, Rhod, but first I wanted to talk to you about something else."

He flushed. "The sarge already..."

"I know. But I'm your DI, and you deserve to hear this from me. I'm impressed by your ambition."

"But."

"You've been a DC for two and a half years, Rhod."

"I was a PC for three years before that."

"I know. And you've got a good record. But if you want to become a sergeant, we need to see more from you."

"That's what the sarge said."

"And he's right. I'm not saying you don't have it in you to make sergeant. Just that you're not ready yet."

He nodded, his eyes lowered. "So how do I get ready?"

"You'll need to take on more responsibility. Cover areas of investigation alone. Maybe with Connie's help. Although I have no idea if she's thinking along these lines too."

Rhodri looked up. "She's not."

"Why not?"

He shrugged. "Dunno, boss. She's only been in CID less than a year."

"Fair point. Connie's more patient than you, that's for sure. But you're both good detectives. You both show potential. I'll talk to Mo, work out how we can help you build on that."

"I appreciate it, boss."

"Good. And sorry to disappoint you."

He grinned. "I kinda guessed it was a long shot."

She smiled back at him. "Doesn't do any harm to ask."

Zoe looked through the glass at Connie, who was on the phone. This was one of the reasons it was so hard for women, especially black women like Connie, to rise up the ranks. Rhodri had role models coming out of his ears. The senior ranks were full of outgoing, confident white men. Men with networks stretching across the region, just like him. He simply assumed he'd work his way up, and fast. Connie, on the other hand, while showing more potential, didn't.

Zoe would need to have a chat with Connie. Plant some ideas in her head.

Was she talking herself into losing half of her team?

"Anyway." She brought herself back to the case. "I need you to do some poking around for me. Use those networks of yours."

"No problem."

"The victim is a copper. DS Raif Starling."

"Whoah." Rhodri's eyes widened.

"Whoah indeed. One of the PCs at the scene, PC Kale, recognised him. They work – worked – out of the same nick."

"Worked?"

"Apparently Starling left a couple of months ago."

"Maybe that's when his killer got to him."

Zoe shook her head. "A DS doesn't go missing for two months without people noticing. No, there's some other reason. It could be ill health, could be that he retired. Or he could have been suspended. There might be a link between that, and his death."

"And you want me to go sniffing around, find out what he was up to."

"Bingo. You know anyone at Erdington?"

"I was on basic training with Sally Gilbert, boss."

"She was at the scene. Good. See what you can get from her. Be subtle, though. I need to go through the official channels, too, inform his DCI of what's happened. Although I imagine he already knows."

"It'll have got back to him in five seconds flat, boss."

Zoe pulled a hand through her hair. "Don't I know it."

She wasn't looking forward to this. DCI Chris Donnelly was a former boss of hers. He'd been her DS when she was a rookie DC. He'd been old-school, 'one of the lads'. And now she was about to tell him he'd lost one of his team, and start asking uncomfortable questions.

She sighed. "OK, Rhod. Let me know how you get on, yeah?"

"Will do." He gave her one of his trademark sheepish smiles and left the room. Zoe picked up her phone, her chest tight.

CHAPTER TWELVE

Mo ended his call from Connie and headed up the stairs to the decking and inside the house. It was starting to drizzle and he was shivering.

He walked into the half-empty living room, his footsteps echoing on the floorboards. He could imagine this place being nice, with a bit of work. Quite a lot of work.

Connie had given him the contact details for the owners, in Dusseldorf. That was his next call. The estate agent had been and gone, kicking up a fuss about the mess they were making of the kitchen. Mo had reminded her this was a crime scene, which gave them the right to examine it as needed. He'd also explained that it would be put back together again. But he doubted this place would sell now. Not when potential viewers knew a body had lain unnoticed in that cellar for a week. And getting the smell out...

He shuddered and stuck his head through the door into the kitchen. He wanted to check for any news on the forensics and update Zoe on that if needed, before he made this call to

Germany. He knew he was procrastinating. The agent would already have told the owners – at least she would have done if she was any good at her job – and so Mo would be the one left to face their confusion and frustration. Anger, too, probably.

"Adi?"

"Down here," came a voice from beyond the cellar door next to Mo. "Come down!"

"On my way." Mo picked his way down the stairs. More lighting had been rigged up which meant the stairway and cellar were now fully illuminated. Two techs filled the cramped space; Adi near where the body had been, and his colleague Rav under the stairs.

"Found anything new?" Mo asked.

Adi turned and stood, stooping to avoid hitting his head on the ceiling. Adi was tall, at least six foot four, and he seemed like a giant in this space.

"We have," he said, giving Mo a quizzical look. Mo thought back to the evening Zoe had asked him to accompany her and Adi to the pub, after Adi had asked her out and she'd said no. Did Adi know how much she'd told him?

"Go on."

Adi turned towards the far wall. "This was hidden by the body."

Mo leaned forward.

"Hang on," said Rav. He shuffled backwards to make space for Mo to approach Adi.

"What am I looking at?" asked Mo. He couldn't see anything.

"It's not the easiest to make out, I'll give you that." Adi grabbed a hand torch and shone it at the wall, holding it at an angle.

As the light swept across the flaking plaster, Mo spotted indentations. He squinted. "Someone scratched that?"

"They did."

Mo stepped forward. He could hear Adi's breath, sense Rav shrinking further into the space behind them. On the wall was what looked like a drawing, scratched into the plasterwork.

"What is it?" he asked.

"It's a symbol, by the looks of it. Almost like a logo. We've photographed it from all angles and I'm going to get a tracing made. UV photography should be the most help."

"What symbol is it?"

The shape consisted of a ring with something else running through it, and the shape of what looked like an animal. Mo bent his head to one side.

"It's a bull," he said.

"Yup. A crude representation, but that's what it looks like to me. The thing sticking out of it, well that's not much more than a line. But I imagine it's meant to be a spear."

"You've seen it before?" Mo asked.

"Nope. We'll put it into the database, find out if it's turned up at any more crime scenes."

"It took time to do that. To stop in the middle of disposing of a body and draw that on the wall. That was deliberate."

"A message," Adi agreed. "But it might not have been the killer."

Mo felt cold sweat run down his back. "You really don't think the victim could have...?"

He tried to imagine the victim scratching this out. He'd have had to be alive, and sufficiently alert to do this. He'd have been alone.

"Dr Adebayo said nothing about that," Adi replied. "But it has been a week. And the full PM hasn't been done yet."

Mo stared at the inscription. "Either way, it's a message."

"A calling card," Adi said.

"Or a clue." Mo looked at him.

"Are there any signs he might have been alive?" Mo asked. "Any evidence of him moving around? Bodily functions?"

"Plenty of blood, not much of anything else. If he was alive after they left him here, he didn't last long. Poor bastard."

Mo whistled out a long breath. "Yeah." Taking your last breaths down here, knowing you were never going to see daylight again. He shuddered.

"I assume Zoe told you who he is," Adi said.

"She did."

Adi nodded. He flicked the light off. "So you've got a DS who's been off work for a couple of months. And this." He gestured towards the wall. "If it *was* him, he was talking to us. He knew we'd see it."

Mo felt cold. "He wanted us to know who killed him."

CHAPTER THIRTEEN

ZOE GRIPPED HER MOBILE, watching the constables through the glass and listening to the ring tone. DCI Donnelly wasn't picking up.

She wondered whether he was unavailable or simply not taking calls. Part of her was relieved; she didn't relish the idea of speaking to him. But a bigger part was frustrated. This was a murder inquiry and she needed to let him know his officer was dead. And to find out what he could tell her about the victim.

If he chose to tell her anything, that was. She hoped this wouldn't end up involving Carl.

She hung up and redialled.

"Erdington police station, can I help you?"

"My name's DI Zoe Finch, I'm with Force CID. I need to speak to DCI Donnelly."

"Oh." Zoe heard muffled movement, followed by voices. She tapped her pen against the desk.

"I'm sorry, he's out. I can give you his mobile number."

CHAPTER THIRTEEN

"Don't worry, I've already tried that. Can you tell me where he is?"

"I'll put you through to his team."

Before Zoe could object, the line went silent. After a few moments, it was picked up.

"Well, well. If it isn't Zoe Finch."

"DI Zoe Finch. Who's this?"

"Don't say you don't remember me. Fin Weeks? We worked together."

She remembered Fin Weeks. He'd been Donnelly's pet, back when she'd worked at Erdington CID.

"Fin. How are you? Still hanging onto Donnelly's coat tails?"

"Nothing wrong with loyalty. I'm a DI now, and I hear you are too."

"Can you tell me where DCI Donnelly is, please? I need to talk with him urgently."

Weeks laughed. "You never did have a sense of humour, did you?" He sighed. "He's at the crime scene you were at earlier, if you must know."

Why was she not surprised? "That's a Force CID operation. He has no—"

"Don't get your knickers in a twist, Zoe. His man has carked it and he wants to know what's going on."

Carked it? If Raif Starling worked for Donnelly, it meant he was Weeks's colleague. *No love lost there*, thought Zoe.

"The victim isn't at the scene anymore. He's been taken away by Pathology."

"Again, nothing I don't already know. You think we don't talk to each other here in Erdington? We're not like you fancy Lloyd House lot."

"I'm not based out of Lloyd House. I'm at—"

"Oh, yeah. Not senior enough. Anyway, I'll tell the boss you called."

"Don't worry. I'm on my way to the scene anyway."

"I'll warn him."

I bet you will, she thought. "Fin, do something for me, will you?"

"Try me."

"Tell him to stay put. It's important that I speak to him. And tell him not to interfere."

A snort. "I'll try, Zoe. Can't say I'll succeed."

CHAPTER FOURTEEN

ANITA SAT at the kitchen table. A mug of tea had long since gone cold in front of her but her fingers were still entwined around it.

That woman. Who was she? Why was David photographed with his arm around her?

She looked young enough to be his daughter. No more than twenty-five. Anita gritted her teeth, resisting an urge to grab her phone and look at it again.

Her phone rang and she jumped, almost falling off the chair. It vibrated on the table, skidding towards her mug. She stared at it, her mind clouded.

At last it stopped. She turned it off, cursing it under her breath. *Leave me alone*.

Was she going to speak to him, this time? She'd suspected him of having an affair for months. The late nights, the evenings when he would come home, eat and then go straight out again. Never telling her where. She'd watched him drive away from the house, trying to imagine what he was thinking.

Whether he felt any guilt for what he was doing to her and the girls.

She loved him, still. Despite the betrayal. Despite the coldness in recent months. He was permanently distracted. She'd asked him more than once if he was OK, but each time he blamed it on work stress. And he had a point; it had definitely got worse since he'd been promoted. Since the murder of Bryn Jackson, the Assistant Chief Constable.

She shivered. She should have made contact with Margaret Jackson, after her husband died. The woman was a grey, mousy thing, scared to speak when she attended work functions. But her husband was dead, for God's sake. Anita should have reached out, shown some sympathy.

It was too late now. Bryn Jackson had been dead for over six months. If she called his widow now, it would look odd. And besides, from what she'd seen of ACC Jackson, the woman would be a damn sight happier without him around.

She was woken from thoughts of the Jacksons by the house phone ringing. She dug her fingernails into the table. No one ever rang that number. Not unless they were selling something. David used his police mobile when he was in his study, and she had hers too. The girls, well the girls barely knew what a phone was supposed to be for. Unless it was posting fifteen-second videos online and taking pouting selfies.

Damn, it wouldn't stop. She shoved the finger she'd been grinding into the table in her mouth and chewed on the nail. She knew she shouldn't: she'd had her nails done last Thursday. If she carried on like this, she'd ruin them.

She didn't care.

Oh for God's sake will you bloody stop? She raised her head to look towards the kitchen door. The landline was in the dining room at the front of the house, best spot for the wifi router. She'd have to answer it, if it was ever going to shut up.

She trudged through to the dining room and grabbed the receiver. She considered putting it straight down without answering but then decided better of it.

"Hello?"

"Mrs Randle?"

"That's me." She wriggled her fingers and surveyed the chewed nail. "What are you selling?"

"Mrs Randle, it's Mrs Healey from the school, Carly's head of year. I tried your mobile but there was no answer."

Anita felt a chill wash over her. She glanced at the clock. "Is everything alright?" It was coming up to 3:00 pm. Her girls walked home from school. It wasn't like she'd forgotten to pick them up.

"There's been an incident. In PE."

"An incident?"

"Another girl alleges that Carly attacked her."

Anita's hand went to her chest. "Sorry?"

"The girl says that Carly bit her. On the wrist."

Bit her? Carly hadn't bitten since she was three. Fourteen-year-olds didn't bite.

"I'm sure it's a misunderstanding."

"Well, we need to gather evidence, as I'm sure you understand. But so far, we have two witnesses who corroborate the allegations against Carly. I can assure you I'll be mounting a thorough investigation, but—"

"Is she alright?"

"Carly's.... Well, she's calm now. But she's angry about something, Mrs Randle. I think it might help if you talked to her."

"Of course."

"And in the meantime, we had to pull her out of PE and I'd be grateful if you could come and collect her."

Anita stared out of the front window. A group of boys in the uniform her girls wore walked past. They looked like sixth formers.

"Yes, right. Of course. I'll be right there." Anita swallowed.

"Thank you. We can set up a more formal appointment for tomorrow afternoon."

"Yes. Right."

"See you shortly."

The line went dead. Anita held the phone out in front of her, her eyes fizzing. She'd spent half an hour already sitting at the top of the stairs, crying. She couldn't start again.

Get a grip, she told herself. She had the snap of that photo she'd taken on her phone. She'd decide what to do with it later, when the immediate crisis had been dealt with. Carly, biting people? It made no sense. She was a good girl, spirited sometimes, but so far she'd kept any rebelliousness to home. At school, she had a flawless record. Or she had done.

Anita sighed and walked into the hall. She grabbed her handbag off the table and checked her keys were inside. She tugged open the front door, her head full of worry.

CHAPTER FIFTEEN

Zoe drummed her fingers on the steering wheel as she sat in the tunnels below Birmingham city centre. This reminded her of the Osman kidnapping case, all those journeys across town, all those hours she and Mo had spent sat in traffic.

This was why they had two branches of Force CID. But DI Jane Finks, her opposite number in the north, was still away. Zoe wondered if she'd be recalled early. If her team would be taken off the case. Jane was OK; a bit territorial, like everybody else, really, but easy enough to work with.

The car ahead of her started moving. Zoe released the brake and inched forward, muttering. By the time she bloody got there, Donnelly would be long gone. She needed to know what Starling had been up to, why he'd stopped work.

Maybe Rhodri would have some intel by now. She hit hands-free and called him.

"Hey, boss."

"Hi, Rhodri, any joy with Starling?"

"A sniff, boss."

"A sniff?"

"Well, nothing official like, but Sally Gilbert reckons he was bent."

Zoe's eyes widened. "On what basis?"

"Just gossip round the station really, but Starling left all of a sudden eight weeks ago. No leaving do, no sign of illness, he wasn't due for retirement. The guy was only forty-six."

Shit. Forty-six. He'd looked twenty years older in that cellar, his skin had been so dry. But Adana had estimated forty to fifty, and she'd been right.

"So he stopped coming into work all of a sudden and PC Gilbert has jumped to the conclusion that he was suspended?"

"Not just her. It's the only logical conclusion."

Maybe not. It was important to consider all the possibilities. That's how a person gets to be a sergeant, Zoe thought. "It's one conclusion, Rhod. And a hell of one. We need to keep our minds open until we get confirmation."

"He'd just bought himself a flash car, boss."

An officer suddenly spending large amounts of money was a red flag for possible corruption. "What kind?"

"A Tesla."

"A Tesla?" She tried to stop herself laughing. She'd never come across anyone who'd spent their corruption money on an electric vehicle.

"Don't knock it, boss. It may be an EV, but it's the best one you can buy. They start at forty-two grand."

She whistled. "Blimey. And that's supposed to save the planet?"

"Don't ask me, boss. So have you tracked down his DCI yet?"

"He's at the scene, apparently."

"OK."

"I'm hoping he doesn't try to take over the case."

"You think he will?"

Zoe wasn't about to give Rhodri the history of her relationship with Chris Donnelly. "Like I say, hopefully not."

"Anything I can do to help?"

"Not right now. You got Connie with you?"

"Course, boss."

"Ask her to talk to Mo, follow up on any more forensics. One of you get onto Dr Adebayo, find out if they've done the post-mortem yet. I'll be with Mo soon, tell him to expect me."

"No problem, boss. You want me to do some more sniffing around Erdington?"

"If you can do it without pissing anyone off."

"That's my speciality." She heard the smile in his voice. Maybe if he did go for the Sergeants' Exam, a unit where this kind of activity was valued would be a good match for him. Like Organised Crime. Or Professional Standards.

"Thanks, Rhodri." Zoe's phone buzzed. She glanced at it; another call was coming in. Her chest sank.

"I've got to take this, Rhod. Speak soon."

She switched to the other call. "Mum. I'm working."

"Zoe love, I'm having a crisis."

Zoe felt her chest grow heavy. Her mum was a recovering alcoholic and had experienced plenty of 'crises' in her time. Some no more serious than running out of vodka.

"What is it? It'll have to be quick." The traffic was moving now and Zoe was on the Aston Expressway. She indicated to change lanes and avoid finding herself on the M6.

"It's my boiler, love. It's packed up."

"I'm not a plumber." Zoe filtered into the lane for the north of the city.

"I was hoping you might know one."

Zoe gritted her teeth. "Look in the Yellow Pages, Mum."

"Even I'm not too old and crap to know there's no such thing as the Yellow Pages anymore."

"You'd be surprised." Zoe knew the Yellow Pages still existed; Connie had used it on a case last year. "Surely you have a number for a plumber, Mum?"

"I'm not the bloody Yellow Pages, am I? Why should I?"

Because most people in their seventies were organised about things like getting their boiler serviced, Zoe thought.

But not Annette Finch.

"OK," Zoe said. "Nicholas is at home studying. Give him a call, ask him for the number of the company we use. It's on the fridge. Don't keep him long, though. He's got to study."

"Don't worry, love. I'll be quick as a lamb's tail. Be nice to talk to him."

Zoe rolled her eyes. "He's studying. Please..."

"It's fine, girl. Stop worrying so much."

The line went dead. Zoe took the fork after Six Ways and headed towards Boldmere and the crime scene, unsure who was more annoying: Chris Donnelly, or her mum.

CHAPTER SIXTEEN

Zoe pulled up at the end of the cul de sac and walked towards the house. A Forensics van was outside along with a squad car, Mo's car and two others she didn't recognise.

She flashed her ID at the constable outside and stepped into the house. Raised voices were coming from the kitchen.

She walked in to find Mo, Adi and Donnelly all shouting across each other. To be fair, Adi and Donnelly were doing most of the shouting; Mo had his arms raised and was trying to get them to calm down.

As she entered, they turned to her as one.

"Guys," she said. "You're making enough noise to wake the dead here."

Donnelly gave her a look of disdain. She approached him, her hand out. "DCI Donnelly. I'm sorry for your loss."

"You don't bloody sound it."

"I know what it's like to lose a colleague."

He grunted. Adi opened his mouth to speak but Zoe raised a hand.

"Surely there's a better place to have this discussion," she said.

"You don't even know what we're discussing," snapped Adi.

Zoe turned to him. Adi had never lost his temper with her. Never.

"Sorry," he said, wiping a gloved hand across his forehead. "I didn't mean to…"

"It's OK. DCI Donnelly, can we talk in the garden, please?"

"One of my team has been murdered, on our patch. I don't see why Force CID are tramping all over this, throwing your weight around. Don't forget you used to—"

"I used to work for you, yes. And so did Mo. But this is a serious crime. As such, it's a Force CID case."

He shook his head. He'd lost almost all his hair since she'd last seen him, and his face had become even greyer than before. Chris Donnelly had always been a nondescript, weaselly man, but now he'd lost even more colour and resembled a ghost.

"How are you?" she asked him.

"I'm fucking fine. Just tell me where the pathologist has taken Raif."

Zoe looked at Mo, shrugging her shoulders. "D'you know?"

"City Hospital," he said.

She turned back to Donnelly. "You'll want to pay your respects. I'm sure Doctor Adebayo will be very accommodating."

"It's not just that, and you know it."

"Sir. I've been made SIO on this case and you have to respect that."

Chris Donnelly had patronised her and belittled her when he'd been her sergeant. She'd tolerated it, focusing on the times he was supportive and even caring. Like when her dad had died. But now he was out of order. He might be her senior officer, but she was in charge.

"Sir, please can we go outside? I have questions I need to ask you."

Donnelly checked his watch. "OK. But I'm straight off to the morgue after."

"Fair enough." Zoe gave Mo a nod and he followed as she led Donnelly into the living room next door. The door to the decking was open.

"We can talk here," said Donnelly. "Unless the FSIs still need it."

"Adi?" Zoe called out. He put his head round the door. "Are we OK to stand and talk in here?"

"Fine. Don't move around too much, yeah?"

"No."

"And I need to talk to you afterwards." He flicked his gaze to Donnelly and back to her. She nodded, understanding that he didn't want to tell her why.

Adi closed the door and Zoe looked at Donnelly.

"I've been told that DS Starling had been off work for a couple of months."

Donnelly's face hardened. "Where did you get that from?"

"It's not exactly a secret."

"No."

Zoe heard footsteps in the hallway outside. Adi raised his voice again. This time a woman was speaking to him. Zoe frowned.

"What the—?" she said through gritted teeth. She needed to get control of this crime scene, and fast.

"D'you mind waiting here for a minute, sir?" she said to Donnelly.

He grunted.

"Thanks." She slid out of the room, not envying Mo left alone with their old boss, and went into the kitchen.

"DS Kaur?"

A short Asian woman with long dark hair tied back in a bun stood with her back to Zoe, speaking to Adi. She turned at the sound of Zoe's voice.

"DI Finch. Good to see you."

Zoe twisted her lips. Seeing Layla Kaur was never good. The woman worked with Carl in Professional Standards; she'd been the one assigned to interview Zoe when she'd been suspected of working with Ian Osman on the airport bomb.

"I'm going to have to halt whatever it is you're doing here," DS Kaur said.

"Sorry?"

The DS took a sheet of paper out of her inside pocket and handed it to Zoe. Zoe looked it over. Unlike Donnelly, Kaur had come prepared.

"PSD are taking over this investigation?" Zoe said.

"We are."

"Why?"

"You know I can't tell you that, ma'am."

Zoe clenched both fists. "I know he was a copper, but there's nothing to indicate this wasn't an ordinary murder. Not yet, anyway."

Adi cleared his throat. Zoe flashed him a look. He knew

something, didn't he? Maybe that was what he'd wanted to talk to her about.

"I guess I have no choice," Zoe said.

"Thanks for your cooperation," DS Kaur replied.

Zoe turned to the door. As she put her hand on it, she spoke to Adi. "I'll see you later, mate, yeah? White Swan, like we said."

Puzzlement crossed Adi's face, followed by a brightening. *Oh hell*, Zoe thought. He thought she was asking him out.

Then he realised. His features dropped and he looked into her eyes. "Of course. Yeah, see you at eight."

"Good." She stepped back into the living room. Mo and Donnelly stood at opposite ends of the room, ignoring each other.

"We've got to leave," she said to Donnelly. "All of us. PSD are taking over this case, and I'm hoping you can tell me why."

CHAPTER SEVENTEEN

Ian allowed the guard to lead him out of the courtroom and into the corridor leading to the cells. He'd been lucky so far; he'd been given bail and hadn't spent more than a few hours in a cell. So he shuddered as they approached the area, the guard's keys swinging on his hip.

Ian had been here plenty of times. He'd given evidence in the courtroom he was being tried in. It was the Crown Court, so only indictable offences were tried here, but he'd seen his fair share of those. Among the more recent ones were an armed robbery in Northfield last June, and a domestic assault in September. He could still see the face of the accused in that last one, silent tears falling throughout the trial. That hadn't stopped the jury finding him guilty, and the judge handing down a sentence approaching the top end of the guidance. His ex-girlfriend's face had been cut to shreds, she'd been lucky to live. Ian shuddered at the memory of it.

He heard footsteps behind and turned to see his solicitor Jane Summer approaching. "I need to talk with my client," she said. "He's entitled to a legal consultation before you lock him up."

The constable grunted. They turned back in the direction they'd come and Jane walked ahead, her footsteps brusque. Her hair was dishevelled and her shirt hung out of the top of her skirt. He hoped the jury wouldn't be affected by the fact that his lawyer looked a mess.

At least he had that Mr Syed, the barrister. He'd conveyed a sense of serenity in court, the air of someone utterly unbothered by what was happening. He probably was. Ian was just a number to him, one in a long line of defendants he had to stand up for, regardless of what he thought of them.

Jane opened the door to a meeting room. The constable stopped outside and unlocked Ian's handcuffs. He rubbed his wrists then entered the room. Syed was already waiting for them.

"Ian. How are you feeling?" he asked. He didn't look like he was interested in the answer.

Ian frowned at him. "Oh, I'm just fine and dandy."

"He asked you a genuine question," Jane said.

Ian held the barrister's eyes. "I've got a splitting headache and my feet ache from all the standing but yeah, other than that I'm doing OK."

"I feel it went well today," Syed said as he sat down.

Ian shrugged. He'd avoided the eyes of the jury while the lawyers were making their opening statements, worried they might think he was shifty if he stared at them. Now he was worried that not looking at them make him seem even shiftier.

"Should I make eye contact with the jury?" he asked.

"Do what feels natural," Jane said. "We can't coach you."

"Yeah, but..."

Syed leaned forward. "If you try to put on an act, they'll see through it. Just hold yourself steady, do what you're told by the clerk and the judge, and react in whatever way is natural for you."

Natural. Standing there listening to them accusing him of involvement in a terrorist attack. He'd had nothing to do with the bomb at the airport, or the one at New Street. He hadn't even known the New Street bomb had happened until he was at the airport.

But the evidence that he'd been accused of planting on Nadeem Sharif... yeah, he knew about that. When they mentioned that in court, that was when he struggled to work out how he should hold his face.

"They were going to call some police witnesses today," Syed said. "At least, that's what we thought. But they were pulled away to a crime."

"What kind of crime?"

"You don't need to worry about that," said Jane.

But he did. He was still a detective inside, even if he'd been stripped of his rank. He wanted to know what was going on.

"Just tell me."

"I don't even know," said Jane. "And I don't think it'll help you to let yourself get distracted."

Ian turned to her, his face hot. "Distraction is good. I need something to think about other than the prospect of going to prison. Do you know what they do to police officers in there?"

She blushed and glanced at the barrister, who sighed. "Very well. We'll bring in a local paper tomorrow. You can

CHAPTER SEVENTEEN

read it, keep in touch with what's happening outside these walls."

"Thanks."

"OK," said Syed. "Sit down and we'll let you know what to expect tomorrow."

He did as he was told.

Syed flicked through a file on the table. "Assuming they bring in the witnesses who were due today, tomorrow your former colleagues will be testifying. DI Zoe Finch and Detective Superintendent David Randle."

"Randle?" Ian hadn't known if his old boss was going to be called.

"Yes. He was on the scene, he'll be appearing for the Crown. I'll be trying to cast doubt on his trustworthiness."

I bet you will, Ian thought. He was still torn between revealing Randle's secrets and protecting the man. Tell all, and he might get a shorter sentence. But then he'd have made some dangerous enemies, and anyway, he stood a better chance in prison if there were people on the outside protecting him. Randle was one of those people, and Trevor Hamm was another.

"Ian, are you sure you don't want to tell us any more about David Randle?" Jane asked. "It could help your case."

Ian shook his head. "There's nothing to say. I hardly had any contact with the man." He avoided her eye.

Syed sighed and closed his file. "Fair enough." He exchanged a glance with Jane. "Maybe tomorrow you might think differently."

Ian gave him a puzzled look. What was he planning to do in his questioning of Randle? The superintendent was cool to the point of glacial, unflappable. If Syed thought he could needle him, he was wrong.

CHAPTER EIGHTEEN

Zoe walked towards the street, her stride brisk. Donnelly stopped at a brown Nissan. It suited him.

"I still need to ask you some questions," she told him. "Can we talk in my car?" She looked back at the house. Two officers she didn't recognise were heading inside: PSD.

"You heard the woman. This isn't your case anymore."

She raised her eyebrows. "You want to find out why DS Starling died even more than I do. If we leave PSD to it, it'll all be hushed up." She paused. "Just one chat."

He cocked his head. "OK. But only because we used to be colleagues, and only cos I can't stand those PSD bastards."

She smiled, trying not to think about the fact her boyfriend was 'one of those PSD bastards'. Did Donnelly know she was going out with Carl?

"Thanks."

"But not in your car. I don't want them seeing us talking. There's a pub on Boldmere Road, a Wetherspoon's. It's big and anonymous. I'll see you there in five minutes."

Zoe nodded and watched him get into his car. She had to

trust that he'd be true to his word, that this wasn't just a way of brushing her off.

"You coming too?" she asked Mo.

He grimaced. "Wetherspoon's."

"Beggars can't be choosers."

He shrugged. "See you in five."

She hurried to her Mini, Donnelly's car passing as she opened the door. Once inside, she looked across at the house, wondering exactly what had brought PSD here. Adi was still inside; had he shared something with them? Did Mo know about it? Everything had happened so fast, she hadn't had a chance to speak to him.

Get this chat with Donnelly out of the way first, she told herself. Then Mo could bring her up to speed.

The lights where Boldmere Road met the Jockey Road were playing up and she waited in a jam for five minutes, tapping her foot repeatedly on the brake.

"Come on," she muttered. The longer Donnelly sat in this, the more likely he was to simply carry on driving and head back to Erdington.

Once through the lights, she sat in slow traffic for a few minutes then spotted the pub on her left. There was a car park just past it. Mo parked next to her and they walked towards the pub. There was no sign of Donnelly's Nissan.

"I hope he hasn't bailed on us," she said as they walked into the pub.

"There he is," said Mo. "At the bar."

Relief washed through Zoe as she approached Donnelly. It was five thirty and the pub was starting to fill up.

"I'll get this," she said.

He smiled at her. "Won't say no to that. Pint of Guinness."

She caught the barman's eye. "Pint of Guinness and two Diet Cokes please."

Mo cleared his throat. "I'll have a cup of tea."

"A cup of tea?" Zoe pulled a face.

"Coke makes me gassy. They do tea here, see?" He indicated a sign above the bar.

"Fair enough."

The barman poured the pint and her Coke and handed Mo a mug with a teabag in it. "Hot water's round there."

Mo wrinkled his nose and went to fill his mug. Zoe walked to the back of the pub and found a table in a quiet corner. Donnelly trailed behind.

When Mo had rejoined them, she took a swig of her drink and placed it down on the table. "So," she said.

"So," replied Donnelly. He wiped beer froth from his top lip. "You want to know about Raif."

"Is it true he's been off work the last two months?"

"I wasn't going to tell you this. It's private."

"But..."

"But now PSD are involved..."

She didn't share his disdain for Carl's colleagues, but she wasn't going to look a gift house in the mouth.

"Why was he off work?"

Donnelly looked around then leaned in. "He was suspended pending an investigation."

This wasn't a surprise. "Why?"

"There was an allegation that he'd been taking bribes."

"Bribes? Who from?"

He raised his pint and took a long drink. She could sense him weighing up how much to tell her.

"You'll just go blabbing to PSD, won't you?"

"Surely you've spoken to them."

CHAPTER EIGHTEEN

"Not yet." He threw his head back to drink more.

"I think PSD know more than you're crediting them for," Zoe told him. "Seeing as they've taken over the case."

"Hmmm."

"Who were the bribes from?"

"I don't know, exactly. Criminals."

Zoe rolled her eyes. "It's hardly likely to be righteous upstanding citizens. What kind of criminals?"

"Drugs. There's an investigation going on. I've been told to appear at Lloyd House for an interview tomorrow. But I'll be square with you here, Zoe. I didn't know what he was up to. I just heard the rumours."

"He was a member of your team, but you knew nothing?"

"He's a DS, I'm DCI. I oversee CID in that nick as well as two others. I don't have my fingers in all the pies."

"Has there been any suggestion other members of the team might have been taking bribes too?"

He held her gaze, unblinking. "None whatsoever."

"None at all? They're not interviewing you because they suspect you?"

He leaned back. "PSD fucking suspect everybody. But no. They've got nothing to worry about from me."

Mo pulled out his phone and held it in front of Donnelly. "Does this mean anything to you?"

Zoe squinted at the phone. She frowned at Mo: *what is this?* He gave her an apologetic shrug.

Donnelly grabbed the phone off Mo and peered at it. "No. Sorry."

"Fine." Mo took back his phone and pocketed it.

Donnelly downed the last of his pint. "I've got a team to get back to, and a bloody unhappy one at that. I've got nothing else to tell you. And you're not supposed to be working this case anyway."

Zoe said nothing. Donnelly knew what she was like. He'd hauled her over the coals for it enough times. But neither of them would say out loud that she was going to keep digging at this.

He stood up. "Nice to see you. Good luck with the Osman trial."

She stiffened. "Thanks."

Zoe and Mo watched Donnelly stride across the pub and leave through the double doors at the front. When he was gone, she held out her hand. Mo handed over his phone.

"What's this?" she asked.

"Adi found it on the wall, next to the body."

"When?"

"While you were at the office."

"What is it?"

"I don't know. Nor does Adi."

"And nor does Donnelly, it seems."

"Hope you didn't mind me showing it to him," Mo said.

"It was useful to get his immediate reaction."

"Seemed legit to me."

"Me too. So who did this? The killer?"

"Could have been the victim."

She almost dropped the phone. "He was alive and functioning for long enough to do something like this?"

"Adi's looking into it. DNA, blood patterns. And the results of the post-mortem will help shine a light."

"Yeah." She stared down at the image. It was a bull, in a circle. A logo, or a callsign. Donnelly hadn't recognised it, so it was nothing to do with the local police.

In which case, what was it? And how had it come to be drawn right next to the dead body of a corrupt officer?

CHAPTER NINETEEN

THE FRONT DOOR SLAMMED. Carly was upstairs in her room, her laptop confiscated. The girl's phone was in Anita's bedside table.

She stiffened as she waited for David to come into the kitchen. She'd made lasagne from a Bolognese she'd found in the freezer. She and the girls had eaten already, an awkward meal conducted largely in silence. David's portion was, as so often, under clingfilm waiting to go into the microwave.

She turned as she heard his footsteps behind her. She pulled on a smile. "Hello, darling. How was your day?"

He shook his head, his face screwed up. "What's for dinner?"

"Lasagne. Yours is in the microwave."

"Heat it up for me, will you, sweetheart?" He gave her a perfunctory kiss on the cheek. "I'm getting changed." He turned and paced out of the room.

Heat it up yourself, she thought as she listened to him thumping up the stairs. She opened the microwave, pierced a hole in the clingfilm, and slammed the door shut. She jabbed at the buttons to turn it on, her vision blurred.

He reappeared at the kitchen door wearing a pair of tan trousers and a blue shirt. He still looked crisp and tailored. "Thanks, love. I'm starving."

"I need to talk to you about something that happened today."

"I haven't got time. I'll be appearing in court tomorrow and I need to prepare."

She approached him and lowered her voice. "It's Carly. She got into trouble at school."

He frowned then looked past her at the microwave, which was bleeping. "I'll eat in here and you can tell me." He turned to the fridge, brought out a bottle of beer and sat at the kitchen table.

Anita stared at him. *You can't even get your own dinner out of the microwave?* She grabbed the plate from the microwave and put it on the table in front of him, her movements jerky.

"Take it easy," he said. "I'm sure it's nothing."

She lowered herself into the seat next to him. She needed to deal with this situation calmly, rationally. Like a concerned mum, not a woman on the edge of losing her mind.

"So." He shovelled a forkful of lasagne into his mouth and spoke through it. "What happened?"

Anita looked towards the kitchen door. She should close it. But she didn't like shutting the girls out. They came downstairs rarely enough as it was.

"She was accused of biting another girl."

He laughed, almost spitting out his food. "Biting! What's this, kindergarten?"

"I'm serious. I got a call from Mrs Healey, the head of year. We met her at parents' evening, remember?"

He shrugged. He'd barely paid attention at parents' evening, he'd been on his phone half the night.

"They told me to take her home. She was kicked out of PE."

"That's no hardship."

"David, this is serious. They think she's angry about something. Suggested we talk to her."

He let his knife and fork clatter onto the plate and eyed her. "Angry about what?"

"I don't know. That's why we need to talk to her. You've always been closer to Carly, maybe you can..."

He shook his head. "Not right now, love." He stood up with his plate and placed a dry kiss on the top of her head. "I'm sure you'll do a much better job."

He took his plate to the sink and left it on the draining board. "I've got to work. Let me know how you get on."

"David. I can't do this on my own."

He turned to her, his fists balled. She shrank back. "And I can't do this at all, Anita. This bloody trial is the biggest thing that's happened to Force CID in years. I've only been head of the unit for six months. This is fucking important."

"More important than your daughter's welfare?"

He grabbed her hand and looked into her eyes. "Right now, yes. This impacts my welfare, Anita, and the welfare of all my team. If I don't get this right, it'll affect yours too."

She frowned, her hand itching in his grip. "How?"

"Don't worry about that. I'm sorry I can't help, but it's just bad timing. I'll be a fully present dad when this thing is over, promise." He gave her a false smile. She stared back at him, her chest hollow.

"Good," he said. The smile dropped. He dropped her hand and hurried to his study, leaving her staring after him.

CHAPTER TWENTY

Zoe's phone rang as she drove across town to Harborne. It was just after 7:00 pm and she wasn't returning to the office. Instead she was making for the White Swan and her meeting with Adi.

"DI Finch," she said, answering it.

"Zoe, I hear you had a run in with PSD today."

"Frank." She wondered if Dawson was still in the office. Maybe she should go in, show willing.

Maybe not.

"So?" he said. "What happened?"

"To be honest I've got no idea. One minute I was talking to the victim's senior officer, the next DS Kaur was throwing her weight around and kicking us all out."

"She give you a reason?"

"You know what it's like. She said this was a Professional Standards investigation and we were to get out. She let Adi stay put, though."

"That's helpful."

CHAPTER TWENTY

Zoe yawned. She'd slept badly the night before, her cat Yoda waking her at 3:00 am yowling for biscuits. "How so?"

"Adi's a mate of yours, isn't he? He can tell us what's going on."

"We've been told to leave the case alone, Frank. I don't think..."

She thought of Adi, waiting for her in the pub. She should have picked somewhere further from the office.

"Come on, Zoe. We both know you better than that. You'll be wanting to know what's going on and why this guy was murdered. Even if it isn't our case."

"I've got a full workload. I'm sure handing this one over to PSD will—"

"Bullshit. You already told me you were talking to the guy's senior officer. What about?"

She indicated to turn off the Five Ways roundabout. "I asked him why DS Starling was no longer working out of Erdington nick."

"How did you know that?"

"Come on, Frank. It's my job to know things like that."

"Fair enough. So what did he say?"

She swallowed. Could she trust Dawson with this? He sounded as eager as her to pursue the case, and if so, it would make things easier.

"He was suspended," she told him. "Suspected of taking bribes."

A whistle came down the line. "That explains it, then."

"Mo and Adi found some sort of symbol etched into the wall where the body had been."

"What kind of symbol?"

"A bull, surrounded by a ring."

"The Birmingham bull?"

"Who knows?"

"Send it over to me, will you? You on your way home?"

She hesitated. "Back to a cosy evening in with my son."

"Sounds nice. I'll see you in the morning."

Zoe hung up, perplexed. When she'd been poking her nose into the Magpie investigation into the New Street bombing, Dawson had come down on her like a ton of bricks. What had changed?

She pulled into the pub car park and found a spot. The pub was busy, even on a Monday night. She turned up the collar of her jacket against the cold and made her way inside.

Adi was at a table at the far end, two pints of Diet Coke in front of him.

"Cheers," Zoe said as she sat down and picked the full one up.

He raised an eyebrow. "Did I say it was for you?"

She put the glass down and looked towards the bar. "Sorry. Is someone else with you?"

He laughed. "Got you, Zoe. Nah, it's yours. Don't worry about sharing your germs with my imaginary friend."

She smiled and took a long swig. "Ta, Adi." It was nice to have him back to normal. "So what did you want to talk to me about at the house?"

"Has Mo told you about this?" He held out his phone with a photo of the etched symbol.

"He has. Means nothing to me or to DCI Donnelly."

"You shared it with him?"

"We did." It wasn't for Adi to question her or Mo's investigative methods.

"OK. Anyway, I did some more analysis of the area around it."

"Go on."

"I'm really not supposed to be sharing this with you. DS Kaur said—"

"I'll worry about DS Kaur. What did you find?"

"There was blood staining consistent with the victim moving around."

"Moving around? Not *being* moved?"

"Yeah. Fingerprints, swipe marks. The angle would be difficult to achieve by accident. And there was urine, he pissed himself."

"Couldn't that be post-mortem?"

"It was on the floor. He'd tried to pull down his fly, we reckon."

She shook her head. "So he was alive down there, on his own."

"Looks like it."

Zoe slumped in her seat, suddenly sombre. "You think he drew that thing."

"It's got blood smears on it. His fingerprints. He could have rubbed against it with his hand, but it's not the kind of staining you'd get if you brushed the wall. It's the kind of distinct prints you'd get if you were using your fingertips to hold something steady against the wall."

"Like a knife. But if he had a knife, why didn't he use it to fight back?"

Adi shrugged. "It isn't a knife. We found an old pen, no ink in it."

"He managed to etch that symbol with a biro?"

"It was cracked, sharper than it might have been. And the plasterwork was soft."

"Prints?"

"The victim's. Nothing else."

"What about the marks on the patio door? You said they were recent."

"They were. We found smears in the dust upstairs, too, a box that had been moved."

"What box?"

"A wooden box full of keepsakes. Old jewellery, photos, that kind of thing."

"That's odd. It was just a convenient empty house to dump a body. Why did they go rummaging around?"

"Someone was rooting through that box, Zoe. I think someone took stuff from it."

"So they killed Starling, dumped him in the cellar, then went upstairs and nicked stuff." Mo would be talking to the owners of the house. Could they be involved in all this, after all?

"Maybe they were there for a burglary and they came upon him," said Adi.

"Taken by surprise? Killed him because of that?" Zoe shook her head. "Not with him being suspected of corruption. It'd be too much of a coincidence for him to find himself mixed up in an unrelated burglary. And besides, why was he at the house?"

Adi shrugged and slurped his Coke.

"Adana says the victim had been dead for a week," Zoe said. "How long do you think he'd been in the cellar?"

"Since no more than a day before death. Probably hours. The condition of the blood stains, the urine."

"So if the killer got in via the patio door, that means he came back after Starling was dead."

"I guess so."

"This makes no sense," Zoe said. "Why come back to check on someone, days after killing them?"

"Maybe the plan was to move him again, and they were disturbed."

"It's a possibility." Zoe drank the last of her pint. "Anything else useful?"

"Not yet. DNA has gone off to the lab, the patio door's going to be removed tomorrow for analysis. The dogs will be coming in, too."

"And the post-mortem will tell us a lot. Not that I'll have access to the report now."

"You don't think Adana would help you out? You two seem pretty tight."

"She's way too professional." Zoe stood up. "Thanks for this. I know you're sticking your neck out."

"Always happy to help my favourite detective." He grinned. Zoe laughed.

"Cheers, Adi. I won't *ask* you to keep me informed, but..."

"I'll see what I can do." He winked at her.

CHAPTER TWENTY-ONE

"Hey, Mum." Nicholas was in the kitchen, stirring a pot of something. Zoe leaned over it and inhaled.

"Smells good."

"Thai curry. Zaf's coming over."

"You want me to get out of your way?"

Zaf was Nicholas's boyfriend. There'd been some tension between the two of them after Zaf had been imprisoned by a killer who targeted gay men, but things seemed to be improving.

Nicholas shrugged. "It's OK, we'll go upstairs."

"I don't mind. I could do with seeing Mo." She hesitated. "And Carl."

Another shrug. "Up to you."

"That's decided then. I'm not going till I've eaten some of this curry, though. Smells bloody lovely."

He gave her a sheepish smile. "Thanks."

She went back through the living room to the hallway and hung up her jacket. She returned to the kitchen, rolling up her sleeves and pulling her long red-brown hair out of the band she'd tied it back in.

"Gran called," Nicholas said as he spooned rice onto a plate.

"Shit. I'm sorry, I forgot all about that." Zoe glanced at the fridge. "Did you manage to find the number for the plumber?"

"It wasn't the boiler, it was her thermostat."

"How d'you know?"

"Because I went round there and took a look."

"You were supposed to be studying."

He ladled a portion of the curry onto the rice and started opening cupboard doors, looking for something. "I'm ahead of my schedule."

"That doesn't mean you can afford to take time off."

He turned to her. "Mum, don't."

She raised her hands in supplication. "I just want you to get the grades you need."

"And I'll do that without you nagging me."

Zoe mimed stabbing herself in the chest. "Ouch. I'm not a nag."

He eyed her. "No."

"The chutney's in the fridge, if you're looking."

"OK." He shuffled to the fridge – it wasn't far, their kitchen was tiny – and grabbed a jar. He held it up. "You want me to put it on, or you?"

"Let me do it." She shoved past him and spooned the condiment onto her curry. Her mouth watered.

"Thanks for this, Nicholas. It's just what I needed."

The doorbell rang. Nicholas's face lit up. "That'll be Zaf. Can you turn the hob off?" He tossed the tea towel he'd been holding onto the worktop and ran towards the front door.

Zoe wandered into the dining room and put her plate on the table. Nicholas and Zaf entered, arms around each other. She smiled at Zaf. He was Connie's brother, a good kid. If *kid* was the right word for an eighteen-year-old.

"Hi, Zaf. How's things?"

"Good, thanks."

"Mum's nagging me about my revision," Nicholas told him.

"I'm not nagging," she said as she forked curry into her mouth. "I'm just concerned."

Zaf laughed. "I bet you're nothing compared to my mum."

"Don't knock mums. We care, that's why we're a pain in the arse."

"Curry looks good." Zaf raised his eyebrows at Nicholas.

"Oh, yeah." Nicholas extricated himself from Zaf's embrace and headed into the kitchen. Zaf sat down opposite Zoe. She waved her hand in front of her mouth; the curry was hot, in both senses.

"You got plans for tonight?" she asked him.

"There's a new film on Netflix Nicholas wants to watch."

"Don't tell me. A documentary about marmosets."

"Nah. It's some kind of arthouse movie."

"Nice." She was glad she'd already committed to going out.

Nicholas came in with two plates and put one in front of Zaf.

"You got any beer?" Zaf asked.

"You don't have to ask," Zoe told him. "I want you to feel you can make yourself at home here."

"He does." Nicholas winked at his boyfriend, who blushed. "Just not when you're around."

She held up her hands. "Alright, alright. I know when I'm not wanted." She grabbed her plate and made for the living room. It was knocked through to the dining room but it gave them a bit of privacy at least.

When she'd finished eating, Zoe went back through the dining room towards the kitchen. "You didn't tell me what happened with your gran," she said to Nicholas as she passed the table.

"The battery had died in her thermostat."

"I didn't know thermostats had batteries."

"This one does. Easy fix."

"She's going to be lost, when you go to university."

He gave her a look. "You can do this stuff. You always have here."

She looked down. "Just not for your gran."

Zoe's relationship with Annette was complicated. Sometimes she wished Nicholas would understand just how hard Annette's drinking had made her life. But at other times, she wanted to protect him from all that.

She put a hand on his arm. "Anyway, thanks for helping her out."

"She was asking when she might see you again. It's been two months, she said."

"It's been a lot less than that." Zoe rolled her eyes. "OK, I'll go round at the weekend. As long as I don't have to work."

"She'd like that."

"Yeah." Zoe went into the kitchen and washed her plate. Since when was Nicholas managing her relationship with Annette? Normal mums nagged their kids to spend more time with granny, not the other way round. But she'd barely seen Annette until recently, seventeen years with no more than a handful of contacts. Pretending to be a normal family wasn't something you just did overnight.

"I'll see you later, boys."

Nicholas grimaced and Zaf threw him a smirk. *Not boys*, she thought. *Not anymore.*

"See you, Mum."

She closed the door and let out a long breath. She needed to talk to Carl, but she knew he wasn't going to appreciate it.

CHAPTER TWENTY-TWO

THERE WERE three men in Zoe's life who she really cared about. Nicholas, Mo, and Carl.

The first was happily ensconced with his boyfriend. The second she hoped was at home, putting his girls to bed or enjoying some peace after they were asleep.

And the third...

She got into her car and sat with her fingers curled around the steering wheel, considering. She wanted to talk to Mo. To tell him what Adi had told her, to find out if there was anything else he knew. But Mo wasn't the sort to go digging around in a case when he'd been told to back off. And he had his family to think of.

She'd speak to Mo in the morning. And the rest of the team.

She started the ignition and drove north, towards Carl's flat. He lived in an Art Deco block set back off the Bristol Road, in the opposite direction from Mo.

The streets were quiet, little traffic heading into the city at 9:00 pm on a Monday night. Zoe was at Carl's flat in under ten minutes. She looked up at the building as she approached. The airport bomb had driven a wedge between them, one they were only just chipping away at. When Ian had been arrested for planting evidence on a victim of the bomb, there'd been suspicions that she'd been working with him. Carl hadn't been able to discount the idea she was bent. And she'd told him she couldn't see him if he didn't trust her.

Two months ago, he'd told her he no longer believed she might be involved, and they'd reconciled.

So why hadn't he warned her about Professional Standards taking over the Starling murder? Why had he sent Layla Kaur instead of coming himself? It was unusual to send a sergeant to take over a case, even for PSD, and he must have made a conscious decision to do it.

There could be an innocuous explanation, of course. He was preoccupied with Ian's trial. He was the lead officer on the case, and he'd have a full workload ensuring that the CPS had everything they needed. Not to mention preparing for his own evidence.

She reached the door to the building and a shiver ran over her. She still hadn't been told if she was expected to give her own evidence tomorrow. In the absence of information to the contrary, she had to assume she was.

She should go easy on him. She clenched her fists and stretched her arms. She knew she had a temper and could bulldoze her way into situations that needed to be treated with tact. Maybe this was one of those times.

Right, she told herself. She still wanted to find out what was going on, and why PSD had taken over this case. But she'd use an indirect way.

She pressed the buzzer for Carl's flat.

"Hello?"

"It's me."

"I thought we agreed not to see each other."

"This is work."

The door buzzed and she pushed inside. The hallway to the building was spacious, decorated with tiling that looked like it had been there for eighty years or more. She climbed the stairs to find him waiting in the doorway to his flat. He wore a crumpled grey t-shirt and a pair of joggers.

"You were getting ready for bed," she said.

He shook his head. "No chance of that for a while. I wanted to relax my mind. Thought getting changed might help."

He stood back and she passed him to enter the flat. She turned to him. "And did it?"

He brushed her arm with his fingertips. "No bloody chance."

She looked into his eyes. They were bloodshot, with grey circles beneath. Occupational hazard. "How did it go today?"

"You know I can't talk to you about it. Not till you've given your evidence."

"Yeah." She went into the living room. Papers were strewn across the dining table and coffee table.

"Hang on a minute, Zoe. I need to clear all this away. You can't stay. We agreed…"

"I've been working a new murder case. The victim was a DS Starling."

"I know the one."

"Why did you send DS Kaur?"

"That wasn't me. Superintendent Ro—"

"You sure you just didn't want to get mixed up with me and my team?"

He took a step towards her. "You know that's not true."

"It would have been nice to have been warned. That she was going to take over."

"Sorry, Zoe. I didn't know myself." He gestured around the room. "Too busy."

She followed his gaze. "You need to work."

"I can't have you here while I do that."

"I'm not here to spy on you, you know."

"No, Zoe." He grabbed her hand. "I know that. But it won't look good, if my boss gets wind that you were here."

She sighed. Bloody Detective Superintendent Rogers. "I'll leave you to it."

"Thanks. I'll call you in a couple of days, maybe I'll be able to spare an hour or so."

She looked into his eyes, aware of the warmth of his hand on her cheek. "This is keeping you busy?"

"It's a big case."

"So you're not involved in the Starling case?"

"You know what it's like, Zoe." He stepped back into the hallway. "We can't tell other departments what we're doing, or why. We never know who knows who, or who might be involved."

She raised her eyebrows.

"For Christ's sake, Zoe. I'm not saying you're involved. But this is protocol. I can't tell you about the Starling case, and I can't tell you what happened at the Osman trial today."

"You shared plenty with me when you wanted me to babysit Ian while he spied on Randle for you."

"That was different."

Zoe dug her fingernails into her palm. She wanted to challenge him, to ask how it was different. But it would change nothing.

She leaned forward and kissed his nose. "I didn't mean to piss you off, Carl. Let's talk later this week."

"Let's." He opened the flat's front door.

She brushed past him, smelling his aftershave mixed with the faint smell of chocolate.

"See you soon, Carl."

"When you've given your evidence."

"Yeah."

"Hey." He smiled.

"What?"

"Come here."

He grabbed her round the waist, pulling her back into the apartment. He kissed her lightly on the mouth.

"Still friends," he said, letting go.

"Still friends," she replied.

CHAPTER TWENTY-THREE

Zoe was the first person in the office next day. She'd struggled to sleep, thoughts of Carl, the trial and the murder investigation running round her head. She'd had a dream about a bull jumping through rings of fire.

She yawned as the door to the outer office opened: Connie. Zoe walked out of her own office.

"Morning, Connie."

"Morning, boss. You look tired."

Zoe rubbed her eyes. "That bad?"

"Sorry. I didn't mean…"

"It's OK. Can I get you a coffee?"

"Herbal tea for me, please. My mum's got me on a health kick."

Zoe took the teabag Connie held out and left the office, wondering if Connie would ever move out of the family home. She was twenty-seven and becoming established in her career. Or maybe having someone to cook and clean up after her made it easier to focus on that. Zoe knew she'd be no

CHAPTER TWENTY-THREE

good if she had to cook for herself instead of Nicholas doing it. And as for cleaning...

By the time she got back Mo had arrived. She handed him the coffee she'd made for herself and headed for the door.

"Might as well make one for Rhodri while you're at it," Mo said. "I saw his car pulling in."

"Right." She went back to the kitchen: black coffee for herself, tea with two sugars for Rhodri.

She returned to the office. The three team members were at their desks. Zoe put the mug of tea in front of Rhodri.

"Ah, thanks, boss. That's fab." He slurped noisily.

Zoe grimaced. "No problem. Before you guys start working, I want to have a conflab."

Mo gave her a warning look which she chose to ignore. She perched on the edge of Connie's desk. The board was behind her, notes and photographs from the murder case still there.

"OK," she said. "How much have you all heard about what happened yesterday?"

"PSD have taken over the case," said Connie.

"And they won't tell us why," added Rhodri.

"So you're up to speed on that."

"Frees us up to work on our other cases," said Rhodri. "Bit of a relief, to be honest."

Zoe tapped her foot against the desk. "No, Rhod. What cases have you got on right now?"

"Well, there's this ongoing spate of robberies in Chelmsley Wood. Connie's been helping me try and identify links between the crimes. And there's the assault allegation in Kingstanding..."

"And the drugs local CID found in that lockup in Perry

Barr," added Connie. "We've been asked to identify links to other cases."

"None of it particularly exciting," Zoe said.

Connie shrugged. "Nature of the job, I s'pose."

Mo was watching all this in silence.

"Come on," said Zoe. "Aren't you just a little bit intrigued? A suspended copper gets himself murdered, and you aren't itching to know more?"

"We've been told to back off," said Mo. "It's PSD's case now."

Zoe looked across at him. "Dawson says otherwise."

"He does?"

She nodded. "He wants to know what's happening. Told me as much on the phone last night."

Mo stood up. "You sure about this? You haven't just interpreted what he said the way you want to, so you can—"

"I don't appreciate being accused of *interpreting* an order from a senior officer."

"I thought he wasn't your—"

Zoe put up a hand. "I'm not saying we go back to the scene. I'm not saying we continue the investigation in anything like the same form. But Adi is still the Forensic Scene Manager. You've got evidence sitting on your phone, Mo. I just want to know what that symbol is. And if it's got any connection to the Ian Osman trial."

"You think it has, boss?" asked Rhodri.

"I've got no reason to. Not directly. But, look. An officer accused of taking bribes turns up dead the day before the biggest corruption trial this force has seen for decades? It might be coincidence. But then again, it might not."

"You think he…" Mo tailed off.

CHAPTER TWENTY-THREE

"I don't know what I think. But the only way to clarify our thinking is to find more evidence."

"With all respect, boss, I think we should leave well alone," said Connie. "If PSD are involved…"

"Have you spoken to Carl?" Mo asked.

Zoe gave him a look. It wasn't like Mo to challenge her like this, not in front of the team. "No. I haven't." *Not about this, anyway*, she thought. *Not successfully*.

The door opened: Dawson. Zoe felt her muscles tense.

"The team's all here, I see." He sniffed as he approached Zoe. "And you haven't wiped the board yet."

"Last night, you said you wanted me to—"

Dawson shook his head. "Things have changed. We've got a suspected murder in Chelmsley Wood. I want you over there right away."

CHAPTER TWENTY-FOUR

Anita hated mornings. Carly wasn't so bad, at least not in terms of organisation. But Maria was a walking nightmare.

"Is my Maths book in my bag, Mum?" she asked.

"How should I know?" Anita checked the clock at the bottom of the stairs: 8:15 am. They should have been gone five minutes ago. "Go and check. And hurry!"

The girl ambled up the stairs, leaving Anita muttering under her breath. Carly shoved past her sister, prompting a yell.

Don't fight, Anita thought. *Not now*.

"I can't do PE," said Carly.

Anita cocked her head. "Why not?"

"I hurt my leg. Can't run."

"Maybe PE will help."

"It won't. Can you write me a note?"

Carly had been sent home from PE yesterday after allegedly biting that girl. And now here she was crying off today's lesson. Perhaps it was for the best.

"Give me a sheet of paper from your bag."

CHAPTER TWENTY-FOUR

Carly ripped a sheet out of a notebook and handed it to Anita just as Maria tumbled back down the stairs.

"Can't find it," she said.

"Bloody hell!" Anita took the stairs two at a time and stood in Maria's doorway, not surprised the Maths book was impossible to find. The room was strewn with books and clothes, magazines scattered on the bed and something Anita would rather not identify spilling off a plate on the floor. She picked her way past it and rummaged through the pile of junk on Maria's desk. At last, she found the Maths book.

"Found it!" She brandished it as she ran down the stairs.

Carly was holding out the sheet of paper. "My note?"

"Sorry." Anita was out of breath. She snatched the paper and placed it on the hall table, writing a scrawled excuse. The teacher would probably be relieved. She hoped.

"Right." She shoved the paper into her eldest daughter's hand. "Out, now." She squeezed past them and opened the front door. The school was a twenty-minute walk away. Maria would go straight there, while Carly walked to a friend's house first. The friend lived in the opposite direction, but the two of them would still arrive at school before Maria with the speed she walked at.

Anita was amazed she'd never had a call asking why her daughters hadn't arrived at school. That they made it there at all seemed like some kind of miracle.

She gave Maria's shoulder a squeeze – hugs were banned since she'd started secondary school – and eyed Carly.

"Keep away from that girl," she said.

"I will," Carly groaned. "She's toxic."

Anita pursed her lips as she wondered what had really happened. She had no doubt she'd be getting a call from the school later today. A summons to discuss how they would deal with her daughter's behaviour.

She hated meetings like that. It always made her feel like she was the teenager, sitting in the headmistress's office being told off for her inadequate parenting skills. David never came along, of course, despite her always giving him the date and time. Too busy with work.

She watched as her daughters turned in opposite directions at the end of the drive. She leaned against the doorframe, exhausted. A van was pulling up. She waited.

The driver, a short fat woman wearing a red cap, smiled as she walked up the path. "Morning."

"Morning." Anita tried to return the smile. David had left at 6:00 am and they hadn't had a chance to talk. Not about Carly, not about the photo. He'd been in his study till gone midnight and she'd been asleep when he'd come to bed.

"Big 'un, this," the woman said. "Heavy."

Anita looked at the parcel the woman carried. It was indeed big. The woman lowered it to the ground at Anita's feet and held out a phone for Anita to sign her name.

"Cheers. Enjoy it, whatever it is." The woman gave her a mock salute.

"I will." Anita stared down at the box, puzzled. She hadn't ordered anything online in the last week. It was nobody's birthday.

She bent down to check the label. Mr and Mrs D Randle. So it was for David, but she'd been added as an afterthought.

But her name was on the label, which meant she was allowed to open it.

She dragged it into the hall and closed the front door. It was too heavy to take into the kitchen so she went to fetch a pair of scissors. She ran the blade against the tape securing the top flaps. There was no logo on the box, no indication of where it had come from.

The flaps opened and she pulled them back to reveal packing material. She shovelled it out. Inside was a basket. It looked like a picnic hamper.

She wrinkled her nose. Who would send them a picnic hamper?

Once all the packing material was on the floor around her, she ripped the box open further to reveal the rest of the basket inside. It had a leather handle, and a logo painted on the side. Fortnum and Mason.

Blimey.

Someone had sent them this hamper, someone with money. Why?

She unfastened the buckle on the leather strap holding the hamper shut. As she lifted the lid, she wondered what she would use the basket for once its contents had been eaten.

It was gorgeous. Cheeses, a bottle of port, red and white wine, chocolates, a loaf of artisan bread. Beneath that, a fruit cake wrapped in muslin.

This must have cost a fortune.

She rummaged amongst the parcels, looking for a note. Eventually she found a small card.

Thank you in advance, it read. No signature. No address. Just one line.

Thank you for what?

She felt her body go cold.

What was David expected to do, that would earn him this expensive gift?

As a serving police officer, this meant only one thing. Unless it was a gift from his colleagues.

No. West Midlands Police didn't send out things like this.

She held the card in her fingers, only the tips touching the creamy paper. He would know she'd opened it. The outer box was ruined. And if he knew she'd opened it, he'd know she'd read the card.

She swallowed. Only one thing for it.

She ripped the card into shreds, not stopping to reconsider, and walked to the kitchen. She tossed the shreds in the bin. After a moment, she opened the bin again and stirred it around with a wooden spoon to make sure the paper was obscured.

She stared through the kitchen door at the parcel and the surrounding packing material, scrunched-up brown paper. Even that looked expensive. She would have to clear it up.

She took the bin bag out of the kitchen bin. She'd put the packing materials in that and dump it in the wheelie bin. That way, David would never see the note.

CHAPTER TWENTY-FIVE

The fastest way to get to Chelmsley Wood was north out of the city and via the M6. The Aston Expressway heading out of town was busy and Zoe had to concentrate on making sure she was in the right lane.

At last they were on the motorway.

"Right," she said. "Let's prepare."

"Not much to prepare for," said Mo. "A dead body, adult male, found in some wasteland in one of the rougher parts of Chelmsley Wood."

"Aren't they all rough parts?"

"Uh-uh. Whole swathes of the area are being rebuilt. Some of it's quite nice."

Zoe rubbed her nose. A lorry braked in front and she pulled out to pass it before getting stuck.

"Dawson said it was called in at four am," she said. "So why weren't we summoned earlier?"

"Maybe they didn't think it was suspicious."

"Which means it's probably an overdose," she replied.

"Or it might look like it could have been a suicide."

"Or a domestic."

"Unlikely," said Mo. "A man dumped in open air."

"Yeah. Could still be drugs though."

Zoe pulled off the motorway and looped back over it to a roundabout.

"This place always confuses me," said Mo. "I feel like we're going round in circles."

"Perfect place to stash a body, then," Zoe replied.

"We're not far from those robberies Rhodri has been looking into. One of them was in that chemists." He pointed to a pharmacy in a squat modern building to their right.

They'd turned off the Chester Road and were taking repeated right turns, rounding a shopping centre and a bright modern Co-op supermarket that clashed with the featureless council blocks behind it. They turned left and stopped behind a squad car that blocked the road.

The 'wasteland' consisted of a patch of grass to their right. Zoe stopped and showed her badge.

"Park over there please, ma'am," the constable said. She pointed towards a row of cars parked further along.

"Dr Adebayo," said Mo. "That's her BMW."

"Which means this is more than a random overdose. She'd have sent one of her team if it was straightforward."

"We don't know that. They might have been busy."

Zoe parked the car and turned to her friend. "Adana's been a pathologist for fifteen years. She's one of the best in this region and a fair few others. She doesn't waste her time on grunt work."

"Well, let's hope she can tell us how this guy died." Mo opened his door.

"Let's." Zoe followed him across the road towards the grass. It was overgrown, littered with discarded cigarette packets and plastic bags.

"I don't think this bit has been gentrified," she said to Mo.

He wrinkled his nose. "No."

Adana stood next to the body, which was partly obscured by a hedge. To the side was a steel fence topped with barbed wire.

"We need to search the industrial estate," Zoe said. "Talk to the people working in those units."

"We've got two officers already knocking on doors."

Zoe turned to see a uniformed constable standing behind her. "Where did you come from?"

"Sorry." He pointed to a squad car parked nearby. "PC Hines."

"We've already met," she said, her stomach dipping. He'd been there when Andreea Pichler had been ploughed down by a car. Zoe had held the woman in her arms as she'd died: one more victim of Trevor Hamm's organisation. "Fill me in."

He nodded, his expression grave. He was remembering it too. Then he took a breath. "999 call came in at 3:48 am. A guy driving along here spotted a shape in the grass. He parked up, got out and threw up."

Zoe followed his outstretched hand towards a patch of vomit on the grass. "Nice."

"Can't blame him, really."

Zoe looked back at the body. The man had been dead a few days, at least. The face had been attacked by animals and the stench was overpowering, even in the open air. The blond hair was matted with dirt and the body was bloated to the point where the seams of his clothes were bursting.

"We need to get a tent over this. Too exposed."

"FSM are getting one out," PC Hines said. He looked back towards where Yala Cook stood by a white van, talking to a uniformed sergeant. "She's with my sergeant."

"Good." Zoe knew Yala; she worked closely with Adi.

She turned to Adana. "What's your initial thinking?"

"He's been dead at least four days, possibly longer given that he's partially buried in the soil. Decomposition is setting in. Not just where animals have got at him, but elsewhere. I've looked at his abdomen and there's greening, meaning his gut bacteria is spreading into his abdomen. There's bloating to his thorax and head and purge fluid."

"I can see." Zoe didn't need to be told about the fluids leaking from the man's nose and mouth. She put a hand in front of her nose. PC Hines seemed unaffected. He looked to be in his late fifties; he'd probably seen worse over the years.

"The top half of his body is much worse than his lower abdomen and legs. It looks like he was more fully buried but something dragged him out," Adana said. "Hence the irregularity in decomposition in different parts of his body."

Zoe could hear Mo behind her, breathing through his mouth. They'd seen worse things than this themselves: in Uniform, the two of them had broken down the door of an elderly woman who'd lain dead in her flat for two weeks. But there was something about the angle of this body, the twisted, bloated neck and the bulging eyes that made the scene disturbing.

"Why's he twisted up like that?"

"He could have fallen, landed like that," Adana replied. "Could have just ended up like that when an animal pulled him out of the soil. If someone tried to bury him, it was a damn shallow grave. I don't think they were too concerned about him being found."

"Or they wanted him to be found, but not immediately." Zoe thought of the body in Boldmere, of Ian's trial. She shook her head: no reason to think this was connected.

She crouched down to get a better angle. The man looked like he was in a yoga position. His legs were bent up to one side, his torso twisted over so his chest faced upwards. His right arm was threaded beneath his shoulder and his face pointed the other way from his feet.

"He's definitely been moved," said Adana. "And not just dragged out of the hedge by a fox."

"Why?"

The pathologist pointed to the legs. The man's trousers were ripped and Zoe could make out dark blotchy flesh on his thighs.

"See the colouration on his legs? That's hypostasis, but it's in the wrong place. Should be on his lower side, as that's where the blood pools after death."

"So he didn't die here?"

"He didn't die in this position, that's for sure. Whether he died *here* isn't certain."

"It's unlikely someone would come back and move him around," said Zoe. "Not without shifting him to another spot. Couldn't a fox turn him over like that? A dog?" There were bite marks on the chin and feet.

Adana shrugged. "Look at the way his arm is threaded under his shoulder. That wouldn't happen by accident. I think someone arranged him like this."

"But after death? After hypostasis?"

Adana nodded. "It would have to have been after rigor

had passed. Which means three days after death. Makes no sense, I know."

"Poor bugger," said Mo. "You definitely don't think foxes could have moved him like this?"

"He's too neat. The way he's twisted, it's kind of symmetrical. Looks deliberate."

"Why would you pose a body like that?" Mo asked.

"No idea." Adana looked at him. "That's your job."

He flashed his eyes at her. "Touché." Adana lowered her mask and smiled.

"OK," said Zoe. She turned to PC Hines. "I need to speak to your sergeant."

"Ma'am." He hurried away. A group of uniformed officers were near the cars. One of them peeled away and walked towards her.

The sergeant was short with long dark hair tied back in a ponytail. She extended her hand. "Ma'am. I'm Sergeant Villada."

"DI Finch." Zoe shook the woman's hand. "PC Hines tells me you have officers knocking on doors."

"We do. There are five units in that estate, we'll have them all covered in no time."

"I'll need CCTV footage. We're unlikely to have witnesses if he was brought here at night." Zoe pointed to the Co-op supermarket. "And we'll talk to the manager of that place."

"There's a church round the corner," said PS Villada. "The vicar has already been round. He almost fainted."

"I'll bet." Zoe looked up as Yala approached. "Thank God. You got the tent?"

"We have." Yala started giving directions to her team of

CHAPTER TWENTY-FIVE

two men. The three of them had the tent erected in a couple of minutes.

"That's better," said Zoe. "How long will you need to keep him here?"

"We'll need to take some more photos," said Yala. "And samples." She turned to Adana, her eyebrows raised.

"I've done all I can here." The pathologist peeled off her gloves. "I'll let the team back at the morgue know they've got a treat in store."

CHAPTER TWENTY-SIX

ANITA SAT in her living room, the hamper open on the coffee table in front of her. She couldn't decide whether to unpack it and put the food in the fridge. If she left it like this, it would spoil. But she'd spent too long living with a policeman; it felt like tampering with evidence.

She pulled out her phone and flicked to the photo of David with the woman. She placed it next to the hamper, her heart racing.

Two things in twenty-four hours. The photo with the woman, and this gift. Could the two be related? Had the woman sent this?

Anita picked up her phone and enlarged the photo. The woman was in her twenties, pretty. She wore a green blouse that looked cheap, and a pair of gold hoop earrings. She didn't look like the kind of woman who'd walk into Fortnum and Mason and order something like this.

Anita didn't even know if there was a Fortnum & Mason in Birmingham. Was there one in Selfridges?

Not wanting to disturb the photo on her phone, she went

into the kitchen and grabbed the iPad she supposedly shared with David. She googled *Fortnum and Mason Birmingham*.

The only one outside London was in Hong Kong. So this had been ordered online, or by someone from London.

Or someone visiting London.

None of this helped her. She searched through the website until she found the hamper that sat in front of her. It cost £150. There was no way the woman in that photo would have spent £150 on a luxury hamper.

Anita sat back on the sofa and rubbed her eyes. She didn't need this. School would call any minute, and she'd be expected to go in and talk to them about Carly. She had no idea if she was going to defend her daughter, or let her get what was coming to her. Maybe that would do her good. David would disapprove, but David wasn't here.

Her phone pinged and she flinched. She fumbled for it, almost dropping it on the floor.

"Hello?"

"Mrs Randle?"

Anita closed her eyes. "Yes."

"Hello, it's Mrs Healey again. How are you?"

"Fine, thanks." *Get on with it.*

"I just wanted to let you know things have calmed down today. Carly was given an opportunity to apologise to the other student and she was very contrite."

"Good." Was that it? No meeting? Thank God! Anita opened her eyes and brushed a stray hair away from her face.

"So I was hoping we could have that chat at the end of the school day, before Carly leaves for home. She can sit in."

Anita stiffened. She hadn't considered that Carly would be a part of this. "OK."

"Is two forty-five alright for you?"

Anita closed her eyes again. "That's fine. Thank you."

"Ask for me, I'll be waiting." The teacher hung up.

Anita let her phone drop onto the hamper. She wished she hadn't ripped up that card now. It was evidence, like the hamper itself.

If the woman hadn't sent it, then who had?

She had to know. But she wasn't about to ask David.

Anita grabbed her phone and stood up. She walked to the window and looked out as she dialled. *Don't hang up*, she told herself. Her hand shook.

"Hello?"

"Hello. It's Anita Randle."

"Anita? Everything OK?"

"Of course." *No*, she thought. *Don't lie.* "How are you? David told me about your injury."

"Well... it wasn't so much an injury. OK, it was. But... oh you don't want to hear my life story." Lesley Clarke sounded confused. Anita had never heard her like that. "What can I do for you?"

"I hope you don't mind me calling you."

"Of course not. It's been a while. And to tell you the truth, I'm bored out of my tiny mind."

Anita had known Lesley quite well, back when both she and David were DCIs. They'd even had Lesley and her husband round for dinner a few times. What was his name? Terry, or Trevor. He wasn't the sort of man you remembered, unlike his wife.

"Was there something specific you wanted to talk about?" Lesley asked.

Anita cleared her throat. "I wanted to ask you about the cases David is working on at the moment."

A pause. "Cases?"

"Is there anything big? Apart from this trial, of course. The corrupt sergeant."

"Ian Osman." Lesley's voice had taken on an edge that gave Anita a chill.

"That's the one."

"Doesn't David tell you about his work?" Lesley asked.

"Oh, you know how it is. I don't want to bother him."

"OK." Lesley didn't believe her, it was clear from her voice.

"So... any big cases?"

"Well, there's Magpie. The New Street bomber investigation. Before that there was ACC Jackson's death, but I assume you knew about that."

"Of course." Anita had been at the Assistant Chief Constable's retirement party. Hours before he'd died.

"Canary, before that. The paedophile ring. To be honest..."

"Yes?"

"I'm sorry, Anita. I really shouldn't be talking to you about this. They're sensitive cases, and I've been off work for a couple of months now. I don't know their status."

Anita knew Lesley too well to believe she wouldn't keep track of what was going on.

"Is there any reason someone might send him a gift?" Anita asked, putting her free hand on the hamper.

"A gift?"

"Chocolates, wine. That kind of thing."

"Anita, I think you need to talk to your husband. Not to me. You know police officers can't receive bribes."

"It's not a bribe," Anita replied, too quickly. Was it?

"Anita, talk to David. Tell him to get rid of it if it's dodgy.

If it isn't, well that's fine. Maybe the new ACC wanted to thank him for something."

Thank you in advance. Anita was pretty sure it wasn't from the ACC.

"Sorry to bother you, Lesley. I'm sure it's nothing."

"That's fine. Are you sure you're OK?"

"Fine. Just got some trouble with our daughter. You know what kids can be like." She laughed.

"It's nice to hear from you, Anita."

"We should get together some time. Meet for a coffee. If you're well enough."

"I'm fine. But I'm moving. Dorset, in the summer."

"Maybe we can meet before then," Anita said. She knew they wouldn't.

"Sounds like a plan. You take care, Anita. Talk to David. I mean it."

"I will. Please don't tell anyone about this conversation, will you?"

Anita caught herself. She shouldn't have said that, it made her look suspicious.

"I can't promise that, Anita. Not if I'm asked. David might ask me, he is still my line manager for now."

"Oh. Alright, then. Thanks."

Anita hung up, her heart racing. She tossed the phone onto the sofa and started to empty the hamper. She would put its contents in the fridge, hide them amongst other things. She would shove the basket under the spare bed.

It would be as if the thing had never existed.

CHAPTER TWENTY-SEVEN

Zoe sat in her car with Mo, waiting for Adana to tell them she was ready for the body to be moved. The space around the tent was limited, so they'd decided to give the FSI and pathology teams some room.

"What d'you think?" Mo asked.

Zoe stared out through the windscreen. A crowd was forming at the cordon, shoppers and passers-by stopping to see what was going on.

"Could be drugs related," she said. "Could be anything, really."

"Yeah."

"Until we know who he is, we've got no idea. We don't even know the cause of death yet."

"He's in a state." Mo wrinkled his nose.

"He certainly is. You think Rhodri will be able to stomach the post-mortem?"

Mo whistled. "That would be cruel."

"He's been bragging about how good he is at them these days. Stomach of iron, he says."

"It would be a challenge."

"If he wants to make sergeant..."

"About that," Mo said. "Did you say something to him?"

"I did. That OK with you?"

"Of course. He's been acting a bit odd, though."

"How?"

"Eager. Bossing Connie around a bit."

"That's not on."

"No. I think she's just as ready as he is, in a different way."

"You're right," Zoe said. "We need to find some way to give them both opportunities."

"Without losing them both."

"Now that would be careless."

Mo laughed. "It would."

"How about we let them lead the planning for this case, when we get back?" Mo asked. "Give them what we have, and ask them how they think we should progress things."

"That could work."

"If you can resist poking your oar in, that is," he said.

Zoe mock-punched him. "Oi."

"Joking. You are the boss, after all. And it's unlikely they'll think of everything. But if we let them kick things off..."

"Both of them?"

"Why not?"

Zoe considered. "It could be carnage, but it might work."

She turned towards the tent. Yala was emerging, beckoning them over.

"You think we should do some thinking of our own, first?" she said to Mo as they got out of the car.

"I didn't say we couldn't do that."

"Good. Cos I can't not process a case once it's in my head."

He smiled. "I know. It's why you're so good at your job."

"DI Finch, we've got a development." Yala was in front of them, looking agitated.

"A problem?" Zoe asked.

"Not a problem as such."

"Go on."

"We've found something in the man's pocket. Come and see."

Zoe exchanged a glance with Mo and followed Yala towards the tent. Next to it, one of the FSI techs was labelling evidence and bagging it up.

"Show them the badge," Yala said.

The tech pulled an evidence bag from the plastic box he was filling. He handed it to Yala, who held it out. "We found it in his inside pocket."

Zoe leaned in. "What is it?"

"A fabric badge. The kind you'd embroider onto clothes. It was loose."

Zoe took the bag from her and turned it over in her hands. She smoothed the plastic down to get a better look at what was inside. "Shit."

She handed it to Mo, her mind racing. "You found this in his pocket?" she said to Yala.

"Inside pocket of his jacket. It was a bit of a mess, we'll have to get it cleaned up before we can analyse it for prints or DNA."

Mo held the bag like it was on fire.

"Get your phone out," Zoe said. He did so, navigating to the photo he'd shown to Donnelly the previous evening.

Mo held the phone out next to the badge. The images

mirrored each other: a bull against a ring. A spear sticking out of it.

"It's the same," Zoe said.

"It is," replied Mo.

"This is not some random drugs crime."

CHAPTER TWENTY-EIGHT

THEY DROVE BACK through the traffic, which was heavier now. It was the middle of the evening rush hour; that coupled with the fact it had started to rain made the M6 more like a car park than a motorway.

"We shouldn't have come this way," Zoe muttered as she turned the windscreen wipers up higher.

"The Stetchford way would have been just as bad," replied Mo. "Worse, probably."

"It's going to be dark soon. Connie and Rhodri will need to get off home."

She and Mo had been at the crime scene for four hours; it had taken three of those to prepare the body to be moved and then they'd waited one more while Yala's team examined the area immediately around the body. A team of uniformed officers were trawling the vicinity, checking other patches of grass and the car parks that were dotted around the area. Officers had been sent in to the industrial estate and the supermarket, as well as the church and a nearby primary school.

So far, no witnesses had come forward. If anyone had seen anything, they hadn't been around today.

"We'll need to do an appeal," Zoe said. "Someone must have seen something. It's built up around there, plenty of people."

"Chances are he was dumped late at night. Could have been deserted. And we've got CCTV from two of the industrial units."

"And the Co-op." Connie and Rhodri were already working through the CCTV footage from the supermarket. Zoe's plan to give them the lead on this case hadn't kicked off yet, but there was still time.

"That badge is the key," she said. "Once we know who the victim is, we can find out why he had it on him."

"Question is, was it already in his pocket, or was it put there?"

The traffic started to move and Zoe muttered at the car in front. "That makes a difference."

"It certainly does."

"We'll show it to the constables," she said. "Give them that, and what we have so far from the body. See what they reckon we should follow up on."

"I'm worried this is going to be taken off us," Mo said as they filtered off the M6 onto the Aston Expressway. The traffic stopped again and Zoe cursed, slamming her palm on the steering wheel.

"Cos of that symbol," she said through gritted teeth.

"If this is connected to DS Starling, PSD might snatch this one off us too."

"Maybe we don't tell them. Not yet."

"Dawson will have to."

CHAPTER TWENTY-EIGHT

"I wouldn't be so sure."

They drove through the tunnels under the city centre. Zoe had the beginnings of a headache. Driving in this weather didn't help. When they arrived back at the office, she was relieved to get out of the car, a rarity for her.

"Right," she said. "Let's see what our two trusty sidekicks have got to say for themselves."

As they walked along the corridors towards the office, a door opened and Dawson appeared ahead of them.

"Just got back?" he asked.

"From Chelmsley Wood," Zoe replied. "We're about to have a briefing."

"I'll join in."

She sighed. "Fair enough." Frank was a brooding presence in briefings. If he wasn't criticising, he was sitting in silence with his arms folded. It made her uneasy.

"Anything interesting?" he asked as they walked.

Zoe glanced at Mo. "Middle-aged man. Plenty of bloating, he's been dead a while. Pathology reckons he was moved. And there's this." She stopped and showed him a photo of the badge on her phone.

"That's like the one in Boldmere."

"It is." She eyed Dawson. "And now you're going to tell me we'll be taken off this case, too."

He cocked his head. "Why would I say that?"

"This was at the Starling murder scene. If the two are connected PSD will want to..."

"It's just a badge, Zoe. Don't get your knickers in a twist. It's your case, and I expect you to lead on it."

"About that," she said as she opened the door to the team room.

Dawson looked puzzled. "Yes?"

"I'm planning a slightly different approach. Humour me on this, OK?"

CHAPTER TWENTY-NINE

Rhodri was getting up from his desk as they entered, shrugging on his coat. His face fell as he saw Zoe, Mo and Dawson coming in.

"Ah."

"Ah indeed," said Zoe. She checked the clock: 6:00 pm. Early, in a murder inquiry. "Sit yourself down. I've got a treat for you."

Dawson snorted and took a seat at the back. Mo went to his desk. Connie was at her screen, tongue poking between her lips. The board had been rearranged: photos and notes for the Starling case in a small area to the top left with photos from this new crime scene occupying a section on the right. Most of the board was blank. Connie had noted the lines they would be taking: CCTV, witnesses, forensics. It looked like much of what Zoe was about to ask her and Rhodri to do was already underway.

"Right," Zoe said. "I won't keep you long, but I want us to get our heads together on this one before going home. We'll have to wait for the forensics tomorrow and I'm not sure when the PM will be taking place—"

"Ten am tomorrow," said Connie. "I checked."

"Good. Do we have a volunteer for that? It's going to be gruesome."

Rhodri paled. Connie raised her hand, very slowly. "I'll go."

"Good. Stick it on the board."

Connie rose from her desk and wrote the time of the post-mortem.

Zoe leaned against the wall at the side of the room, keeping away from the board. It was all she could do not to march up to it and start adding notes. But she needed to let the constables take the reins.

"Mo and I have been talking," she said. "We want to give the two of you the lead in this meeting. We'll work together to identify the lines of inquiry we need to take, but I want to hear suggestions from you first."

Rhodri frowned. "But you were already at the scene."

"Doesn't matter. I've led investigations in the past where another member of the team has gone to the scene before me. It hasn't stopped us getting started before I've seen things for myself. You have to learn to trust the eyes and ears of your colleagues."

"OK." Rhodri exchanged a glance with Connie, who shrugged.

Zoe leaned back. "Go on, then. Who's going to start?"

Connie looked at Rhodri as if she was waiting for his permission. She had to stop doing that if she was ever going to make sergeant. Zoe gave her an almost imperceptible nod. It was her writing up on the board already; she had a head start.

CHAPTER TWENTY-NINE

"OK." Connie licked her lips and walked to the board. "So we've got a middle-aged man, found on wasteland between an industrial estate and a supermarket. Pathology says he's been there...?" She looked at Zoe.

"Dead at least three days," said Zoe. "The bloating indicates rigor mortis has long since ceased. He's barely recognisable."

"Yeah." Connie looked at the photo of the body on the board. "So given that it's a public place, it's unlikely he's been there the whole time. Which means he was killed somewhere else and then dumped there. The question is when?"

Rhodri turned to Mo. "Is there anything to say he was moved?"

Mo nodded. "Good question. Hypostasis on his legs indicates that he was facing upwards immediately after death. That's not the way we found him."

"He looks like he's been arranged," Connie said. She bent her head to one side, taking in the tangle of limbs. "It's almost like he's doing yoga. Threading the needle."

Zoe smiled. They were thinking along the same lines she and Mo had. "So...?"

Rhodri stood up and joined Connie at the board. He wrote *Moved – when?* "We need to ask Pathology if they can identify when the body was moved."

"Or the forensics might help with that," Connie said. "I can talk to the FSIs in the morning." Her cheeks reddened.

"OK, so we've got the PM and the forensics," said Mo. "Connie, you've already volunteered for the PM."

"Ah. Yes." Connie looked at Rhod. "Can you go to the PM instead?"

"You need post-mortem experience, Connie," Zoe said. "You do that. Rhodri can talk to the FSIs."

"No problem, boss." Rhodri looked pleased with himself.

"You haven't seen this yet." Zoe got out her phone and pulled up the photo of the badge. She forwarded it to Connie and Rhodri's email accounts and their phones pinged.

Connie grabbed her phone. "That changes things."

"How?" Zoe asked.

"It's the same symbol the sarge found at the Boldmere scene." Connie pointed to the photo on the board. "Are the two crimes connected?"

"We don't know that yet," Mo said. "Could be a coincidence."

"Hell of a coincidence," Rhodri said. He looked at Mo. "Sorry, Sarge."

"We'll need to know who this victim was," Connie said. "That'll help us find a link."

"Good," said Zoe. The first step in any murder investigation was to identify the victim. That often led to the killer. "Rhod?"

"Er..." Rhodri dragged his gaze up from his phone. "DNA, boss. I'll ask the FSIs about it when I talk to them in the morning."

"Do you know for sure they've sent samples for DNA analysis?"

"Well, I suppose they always—"

"Can't assume anything," Mo said. "You might want to check. Or delegate that."

Rhodri looked alarmed. "Connie's got the PM to think about."

"Connie isn't the only person in the room."

"You want me to delegate to you, Sarge?"

"If you want to be a DS, you have to learn to make use of

all the resources at your disposal. Sometimes that's your senior officers. The DI and I haven't got anything to do yet."

"OK. Can you call Adi? Ask him if he's submitted samples for DNA?"

Zoe smiled. "Already spoken to Yala. She's Forensic Scene Manager on this one. Something you need to establish at the beginning of an investigation. And yes, she's submitted tissue samples to the lab."

"When will we get the results?"

Zoe shrugged. "She wasn't able to say."

"I'll follow up in the morning, when I talk to them about the scene."

"Good."

Connie was making notes on the board. Writing on the board was grunt work, and something Connie felt comfortable with. She needed to pull her focus away from recording, and spend more time thinking.

"Connie," Zoe said. Connie almost dropped her pen. "What else do we need to be looking at?"

Connie pointed at the board with the pen. "CCTV. We've already started on the footage from the Co-op. Nothing yet. Uniform have been visiting nearby premises, we can check for any other cameras. Sarge, can you take that one?"

Mo smiled. "I can."

"And then there's eye witnesses," said Connie.

"None as yet," said Zoe. "We've spoken to enough people, but none of them claim to have seen anything."

"That doesn't mean no one saw anything, just that they weren't there today," Connie replied. "Can we run an appeal?"

"We can use social media," said Dawson. Zoe had forgotten he was there. "For now. Wait till you know who the victim is before you think about anything else."

"OK." Connie looked at him, her posture stiff.

"Are we all done?" Dawson said. "I mean, this is all very lovely and that, but it's not the best use of a DI and DS, being bossed around by two constables."

"I want to give them some leadership experience," Zoe replied. "It won't hinder the investigation." She turned to the constables, smiling. "It might even help it."

Dawson snorted. "Just don't let it get in the way of you doing your job, Zoe. I'll be in my office if you need me. You lot planning to stay here chewing the fat for long?"

"Not long," said Zoe. She spotted the look of relief on Rhodri's face. If he had plans, that would have to come second. Especially if he wanted promotion.

"Right," she said as the door closed behind them. "What's the plan for the morning?"

"All back here, bright and early," said Connie. Rhodri flinched.

"Yes," said Zoe. "You'll need to prepare a schedule for the day, note who's doing what and what new evidence we're expecting."

"Are you making us the SIOs?" Rhodri asked.

"I'm not going that far. I'm still SIO. And if I need to, I'll lead. If things get ugly, or the investigation takes a turn we don't expect, it'll revert to normal. And I'll tell you when you can go home. Which is now."

Rhodri stepped towards the door, then thought better of it. He waited for Connie to gather up her things and the two of them walked out together.

"That was exhausting," Mo said after he and Zoe were alone.

"Interesting, though," Zoe said. "It'll do them good, and us too if it works."

CHAPTER THIRTY

Zoe was alone in the office. Normally when she found herself alone here at night, she would drop by Lesley's office on the way out. Connecting with her boss at the end of the day cleared her head and helped her see connections she might not have. And it was a relief not to be in charge.

She could go and see Dawson. She still wasn't ready to accept him as her line manager, even temporarily. But she had to admit he had authority. And it would be helpful for him to know why she was letting Connie and Rhodri lead this stage of the investigation.

No. He might stop her.

She picked up the phone and dialled Lesley. The DCI may be on ill health leave, but she'd made it clear she didn't want to be ignored.

"Zoe. Good to hear from you. How's it going with Frank?"

"It's improving. He might be less of a dick than I had him down as."

Lesley chuckled. "There, what did I tell you?"

CHAPTER THIRTY

"I'm changing the way a new investigation is run, giving the DCs some leadership responsibility. He didn't crap all over it."

"He trusts you, Zoe. He knows that throwing his weight around will be counterproductive and he'll let you do your job as you see fit. Just don't blank him out, yeah?"

"I'll try not to."

"So, you've got a new case?" Zoe could sense Lesley settling in for a chinwag.

"Two, sort of."

"Oh?"

"First there was a body found in an empty house in Sutton Coldfield. Turns out he was a copper, a DS from Erdington."

Lesley whistled. "And?"

"He was suspended two months ago. DCI Donnelly was his senior officer, he told me—"

"Hang on, Zoe. You're on speaking terms with Chris Donnelly?"

"Believe it or not. It's irrelevant now, Professional Standards have taken it off us."

"Not surprised, if he was suspended. Any idea who killed him?"

"None. But Mo found a symbol etched into the wall next to the body. We don't know who did it, the killer or the victim."

"What kind of symbol?"

"A bull, enclosed in a ring."

"The Bullring."

"Birmingham icon, I know," Zoe replied. "But we've also found the same symbol on a second body."

"Now you're getting me interested. I tell you, sitting around with Terry all evening is bloody dull."

Zoe shrugged. She didn't know how to respond to her boss's domestic concerns.

"So what now?" Lesley asked.

"I'm SIO on the second case. Unidentified man in Chelmsley Wood."

"Long way from Sutton Coldfield."

"Geographically, no."

"That's not what I mean."

"No." Zo thought of the two crime scenes. The house where they'd found Starling had been in need of some TLC, but it was a large detached property in an affluent suburb. The second body had been dumped in a patch of grass next to an industrial estate in an area struggling to improve itself.

"The symbol was etched next to your second guy too?" Lesley asked.

"It was on a badge. Embroidered."

"Like something a gang member might wear."

"Yes." Zoe had been thinking about gangs too. If DS Starling had been taking bribes, then they could be involved. But she wasn't aware of one with this symbol.

"You've spoken to Drugs?" Lesley asked.

"Not yet. I've got Connie and Rhodri leading on the planning. We're focused on identifying the victim for now."

"Makes sense. Find the victim, find the killer. Probably some guy who decided to leave the gang."

"He was too old for that. He was extremely bloated, but I could still tell he wasn't young."

"Family member?"

"Maybe." Zoe yawned.

"I'm keeping you," Lesley said.

"I'm not sleeping so well. Ian's trial."

"I can imagine it's stressing everyone out."

"It is. I'll be glad when it's done."

"Hmmm. I had an odd call today."

"OK." Zoe leaned back in her chair, stretching her leg muscles.

"I probably shouldn't tell you," Lesley said.

"But you're going to."

"It's been bugging me. And I'm not your senior officer anymore."

"Who from?"

"Hang on." Zoe heard muffled voices; Lesley had her hand over the receiver. Zoe yawned as she waited.

"Sorry about that. Terry tells me it's time to eat. It's like being a goddamn toddler here."

Zo grimaced. "At least he's cooking for you."

Lesley laughed. "Good job, too. With my cooking you'd have another murder investigation on your hands."

"I'll let you go."

"Ta. Call again, yes? It's good to hear from you."

"I will." Zoe hung up, realising she hadn't found out more about the odd call Lesley had received. She'd ask her, next time they spoke.

CHAPTER THIRTY-ONE

Zoe couldn't resist. Instead of turning right out of the station and driving home, she turned left and into the city. She passed under the tunnels, glad the rush hour was over, and made for Boldmere.

She pulled up in the street leading to the cul de sac. She didn't want her car spotted, and she had to admit that driving a British racing green Mini around made her easy to identify. She sat in the car for a few moments, staring out at the street and thinking.

That symbol. What was it? It could be a gang, could be something else. It was quintessentially Brummie, a bull in a ring. So much so, that it felt like a parody.

Whatever it was, both victims were somehow connected to it. And if the first victim was a bent copper, then the second might be too.

He was a middle-aged white man, like so many of her colleagues. She wouldn't be surprised to turn up to the crime scene tomorrow and find PSD there, sealing it off and taking over again. But in the meantime, she wanted to get her head around the connection.

She got out of her car and walked towards the cul de sac. A car stopped at the junction just as she reached it. She carried on walking, trying to look like she was a local resident making her way home.

"Zoe?"

She turned to see the car had its windows wound down. It was a green Polo: Adi.

She felt her shoulders slump as she approached the car. "You're working late."

"It was either that, or come back tomorrow. As it is, we're finished here."

Zoe looked towards the house. "Completely?"

"Don't get any ideas, Zoe. Those patio doors are a key piece of evidence. If you try breaking in there too, you'll contaminate the scene."

"You said you were finished."

He sighed. "You know what I mean."

"So are those patio doors still there?"

"Yes. We've taken paint samples from them, photographed the things till the cows come home."

"And?"

"Someone was in that house in recent days."

"The killer."

"Zoe, you know I can't..."

"I know. But I've got another case. A John Doe found in Chelmsley Wood. I think it's related."

Adi stared ahead, his grip tight on the steering wheel. "Yes or no answers, Zoe. I'm giving you no more than that."

Headlights swept across the car. Zoe turned to see a brown Vauxhall pulling up. A man got out: Mo.

"What are you doing here?" she asked him. She looked along the street. The residents would start to wonder what was going on.

"I knew you'd come here," he said. "I came to stop you doing anything stupid."

"You followed me."

He screwed up his lips. "You can't break into a crime scene."

"How stupid d'you think I am, Mo?"

Adi whistled. "I'm getting out of here. Don't want to be caught in a domestic."

"I'll buy you a drink," Zoe said.

"Zoe, I'm really sorry but—"

"Me too. I just want to compare notes. Answers of one syllable, Adi. That's all I ask of you."

"I could get fired for this."

"No one will know."

Adi turned to her, his face twisted. "You're dating Carl Whaley, and you don't think you'll mention it to him?"

"I keep my professional life and my personal life separate."

"I bet you do." Adi started the ignition. Zoe leaned through the window. "Please."

He thumped the steering wheel. "Alright. Nowhere round here, though. Find a pub in the city centre. I don't want anyone seeing me with you."

CHAPTER THIRTY-TWO

DAVID RANDLE PARKED his car by the Co-op supermarket, careful to stay out of sight of the police cordon. He reached into his pocket for his phone, then remembered he'd left it in his desk. Safer that way: no GPS.

His relationship with Frank Dawson wasn't established yet, and he couldn't have the informal chats with him he'd enjoyed with Lesley. And besides, the man wouldn't be in the job long. Soon there would be a permanent DCI in place. Hopefully Lesley would stay in Dorset.

So he had no idea how far Zoe and her team had got with this crime scene yet. He'd make a few calls in the morning, see what he could discover without drawing attention to himself. Meanwhile, he wanted to see it for himself.

He was wearing a black hoody and dark blue jeans with a pair of trainers he'd dug out from the back of a cupboard. Anita was normally meticulous about throwing out old clothes, but these had escaped. Birmingham's charity shops would be lost without her.

He slid out of the car and closed the door softly. He

pulled his hood up and walked towards the entrance to the supermarket, careful to look like just another shopper. It was coming up to 8:30 pm and the supermarket's lights shone out into the dusk.

As he approached the doors, he glanced off to the left, towards the crime scene. A cordon was still in place, roping off the patch of grass containing the forensic tent. There was a single uniformed constable standing next to it. Randle wondered if he had a colleague. Maybe he'd gone somewhere to get a coffee.

He'd done that himself, back in the day. Stood up all night, guarding a crime scene. Blowing on a cup of weak tea, stamping his feet against the cold. He knew how tedious it could get.

He dipped into the supermarket, walked up and down a couple of aisles – no sign of the other officer – and walked out again, putting a confident stride into his step. He lowered his hood partway, glad he'd changed out of his shirt and into a t-shirt.

As he passed the cordon, he slowed. "Evening."

The constable was already watching him. "Evening."

"Nasty business."

"Not my place to say, sir."

"I saw them taking him away earlier. Bit of a state. Can't be easy for you."

The constable grimaced. "He wasn't pretty, sir. I don't suppose you saw anything suspicious around here anytime? Last few days or nights?"

"Sorry. I'm normally at work at this time."

"Not necessarily this time, sir. Any time. We don't have much to go on."

Randle could get all this from his subordinates. What he

wanted was to get a feel for the scene. He'd turned up at crime scenes a few times since his promotion, sweeping in on the pretence of maintaining community relations. This one felt too close for comfort.

"Just you tonight, then?" he asked.

"My colleague's just gone to get a cuppa. She'll be back in a moment."

Randle looked backwards as if seeking out the other officer.

The constable pointed. "Costa over there. Never thought I'd see one of those round here." He coughed.

"Is the body still under there?" Randle knew the answer, but it didn't hurt to play dumb.

"Oh no, sir. Gone to the morgue. Evidence has been packaged up too. We'll do a final sweep of the area in the morning and then you'll have your neighbourhood back to yourselves."

"Great." So there was nothing inside that tent, nothing they'd spotted, at least. Randle wondered if it was worth trying to find a route around. To one side it was flanked by a steel fence topped with barbed wire. At the back was a hedge which looked like there might be another fence behind. But to the right were bushes, nothing he couldn't fight his way through.

The question was, could he do it without being detected? And even if he could, was it worth it?

He sniffed. "Anyway. Enjoy your evening."

The constable raised his eyebrows. "I'll try my best."

Randle turned back towards his car, his eyes alert for the female constable. He didn't want either of them seeing him get into his car. He'd brought Anita's Saab instead of his own

Audi TT, but it still didn't fit around here. And it didn't fit with his current outfit.

Satisfied she was nowhere around, he slid into the car, waited a few moments, then drove round to the other side of the supermarket.

He pulled up, checked his mirrors. Confident no one was watching, he reached round and grabbed the second, unregistered phone he kept tucked under maps and other junk in the pocket on the back of the driver's seat. There was someone he wanted to talk to.

CHAPTER THIRTY-THREE

Zoe parked in the 'cage', a multi-storey car park in Birmingham city centre encased in red wire mesh. She'd identified a suitable pub on Navigation Street, the Railway, one she'd never seen any other officers in.

The pub was large and dark, a cavernous space stretching around and behind the bar. She made for the far end, where she'd told Mo and Adi to meet her. They were both there already. Three glasses were on the table: ginger beer for Mo, a half of lager for Adi and a Diet Coke for her.

She sat down and picked up her drink. "Cheers." She raised the glass and gulped down almost half of it.

"No worries," said Mo. He sipped his ginger beer.

"I appreciate this," she said, turning to Adi. "I know you're sticking your neck out."

He nodded, his eyes grave. Words of one syllable, he'd said. Yes or no answers.

Here goes.

"You're still Crime Scene Manager at the house?"

"Yes." He blinked.

"Who's SIO?"

He gave her a *no you don't* look.

"Is Layla Kaur SIO?"

A shake of the head.

"Carl?"

The tips of Adi's ears reddened as he shook again.

"Detective Superintendent Rogers, in that case."

"Yes." Adi looked down as he took a swig of his drink.

"OK. Is Carl involved?"

"No." Adi licked his lips as his gaze rose to meet hers.

"Have you identified that inscription yet?" Mo asked.

Adi shook his head.

"Do you know about the other body we've found it on? In Chelmsley Wood?" Zoe asked him.

"Yala told me."

She leaned back and blew out between pursed lips. "Does anyone have any idea what it might be?"

"Yes."

Zoe perked up. "Yes?"

A nod.

"What is it, then?" asked Mo. "Sorry, mate."

Adi shrugged. "Yes and no answers, remember?"

Zoe clenched a fist. "OK. Did PSD identify it?"

"No."

"Drugs Unit?"

"Nope."

"Organised Crime?"

"Bingo."

She felt heat rush into her face. "Sheila?"

"No."

Damn. DS Sheila Griffin was a friend Zoe had worked

with plenty of times. She wasn't sure if anyone else in that unit would answer her questions.

"Is it anything to do with Trevor Hamm's organisation?"

"No."

"You sure?" Mo asked.

Adi turned to him. "Yes."

"Yes, it is, or yes, you're sure."

"Second one." Adi downed the last of his drink and went to stand up. Zoe put out a hand.

"Is it the callsign of another gang?"

Adi stooped over the table. "Yes."

"Which gang?"

"Uh-uh."

"Brum Boys?"

"No."

"Am I going to guess this?"

"No."

"Why not?"

Adi shook his head.

Shit. This was impossible. "Has Sheila been involved in the identification?"

A shrug.

"D'you think she might have been?"

"Yes."

"OK." Zoe looked at Mo. "We need to talk to Sheila."

"You think she'll help us?" Mo's voice was low. The pub was quiet but they couldn't be too careful. Zoe suddenly doubted the wisdom of holding this conversation in a pub they weren't familiar with.

She looked up at Adi. "Are there any new forensics? DNA, prints?"

"Yes."

"Which?"

He raised his eyebrows.

"Prints?"

A shake of the head.

"DNA?"

A nod.

"You've matched it?"

A shake.

She slumped back. "So you've got DNA for the killer—"

Adi raised a finger.

"Not necessarily the killer. Who?"

Adi stood straight. "I'm sorry, Zoe. This is getting too close to the knuckle. I suggest you talk to Sheila. Or Carl."

There was no way she was talking to Carl about this.

"OK. Thanks, Adi."

He gave her shoulder a squeeze and left the pub.

"Whose DNA d'you think it is?" she asked Mo.

"If it isn't the killer, or the victim…"

"We didn't ask Adi if it was the victim's."

"We had that already, Zo. You asked him if there were any *new* forensics."

"You're right. He didn't say it wasn't the killer, but he didn't say it was. Which means they think someone else was in the house."

"Maybe that patio door," Mo suggested.

"Yeah."

"The patio door was broken into not long before the body was found. Maybe the DNA they have is the person who did that."

"I don't get that. Starling was killed at least a week before we found him. He was dumped at some point in the intervening period. Adi might know when, but he's not telling us."

"Not unless you drag him back in here for another game of twenty questions."

"I know. It's not fair on him."

"Maybe we should leave well alone."

Zoe leaned forward. "But the badge. The bull in a ring. These two murders are connected. And I want to find out how before Carl comes in and takes the second case off us."

CHAPTER THIRTY-FOUR

Zoe shrugged off her jacket as she closed the front door behind her. She was knackered. Subjecting Adi to those questions had been draining, and she felt bad about it. If PSD got wind of it, his job could be on the line. He was a civilian, more vulnerable than she was.

She kicked off her shoes and slumped onto the sofa. She didn't have the energy to find the remote. Maybe she'd just grab a blanket and sleep here.

She was woken by the thud of paws on her legs. She sat up, smiling.

"Yoda."

The cat chirruped at her as it made its way up her legs and onto her stomach. Zoe ruffled between its ears. "Where's Nicholas?"

"Miaow."

"Yeah, you don't know either." Zoe leaned back and called her son's name. No answer.

The cat looked startled, its ears pricked up. Zoe gave it a stroke. "Just you and me tonight, huh?"

CHAPTER THIRTY-FOUR

"Miaow."

The doorbell rang. Zoe eyed the cat. "Can you get that?"

The cat cocked its head at her. She allowed herself a laugh and picked it up, placing it on the floor next to the sofa. "Guess it's up to me."

She opened the front door and her heart clenched.

"Carl." She stepped back to let him pass.

"Hey." He passed her, not pausing to kiss her, and walked into the living room. "Hey, puss."

"Yoda," Zoe said as she followed him in.

"Hey, Yoda." He picked the cat up and tickled it under the chin.

"You're here to take over my case," Zoe said, her voice flat.

Carl let the cat down to the arm of the sofa. "Don't be like that."

She shrugged. "So you are."

"Not quite." At least he had the decency to look chastened when he said it.

"I'm SIO."

"The cases are linked, Zoe."

"You don't have to tell me that."

"Look. The second case could be nothing. It could be a gang member who decided he wanted out. It could be someone from a rival gang. It might have nothing to do with DS Starling. But I need to know what leads you have."

"Which gang is it?"

He gave her a *stop it* look.

She thought back to what he'd said, a moment earlier: *Not quite*. "So, you're not taking over?"

He stepped towards her. "I'm not. But I need you to tell me what you've got."

"You could have done this officially. Spoken to Dawson. Come into the office."

"I wanted to ask you face to face. Just you and me."

She let him put his arms around her. "OK," she said. "But I need you to reciprocate."

"How so?"

"Tell me what you've got from the Starling investigation. Have you analysed the DNA yet?"

He stiffened, his hand heavy on her back. "It doesn't work like that, Zoe."

She stepped back and placed a hand in the centre of his chest to push him away. "It never bloody does."

"Zoe…"

She sat heavily on the sofa. Yoda jumped onto her lap and she swept the cat off. "I want us to work together. If this is a single investigation, then let's treat it as one."

"Look. I'll share with you what I can. But nothing sensitive. I wanted to do this amicably, Zoe. If you won't tell me what's happening with your case, I can always—"

"I know what you can do." She swallowed. "Alright, then."

She had little choice. Better to cooperate with Carl than to have Malcolm Rogers talk to David Randle and take yet another case off Force CID.

She looked up at him. "I'll work with you."

His face softened. "I appreciate it, sweetie."

"Yeah."

He sat next to her. "Thanks."

She nodded. "I'm tired. I just want to go to bed."

"I can stay?"

"Not tonight." She stood up and made for the front door.

CHAPTER THIRTY-FOUR

"I just need some time alone, Carl. Nothing personal. We'll talk tomorrow, yes?"

He kissed his fingertips and brushed them against her cheek. She put her hand to it.

"See you tomorrow. Zoe. I love you."

"Yeah."

I love you too, she thought as she closed the door behind him. But if she did, why did he piss her off so much?

CHAPTER THIRTY-FIVE

"This has got to be quick," Zoe said. "I have to be at the Crown Court in forty-five minutes.

She was wearing her court clothes again, the navy trousers and grey jacket that didn't quite work together, the feminine blouse and low heels instead of her usual boots and plain shirt. She felt trussed up like a turkey but she knew she had to create an impression.

Connie, Rhodri and Mo were lined up in front of her. Dawson sat at the back of the room. Next to him, a smile flickering on his lips, was Carl.

She watched him, feeling uneasy. She wondered who he'd spoken to before his visit last night. If Dawson had been in on it.

"DI Whaley is sitting in because he's linking our latest victim to the Raif Starling case. A Member of the Organised Crime team will be liaising too, but they couldn't send anyone this morning." She glanced back at the board, where they still had their notes on that case. She wondered if Carl would order her to remove them.

CHAPTER THIRTY-FIVE

"Right," she continued. "We've not got much time and we've got company, so we'll shift back to our usual format. Hope you don't mind, you two." She looked at the constables.

"No worries, boss." said Rhodri. Connie nodded and licked her lips. Zoe knew that Carl made her nervous. Another thing she had to get past if she was going to make sergeant.

"Good. So we've got four lines of inquiry on the Chelmsley Wood case." She pointed to the board. "We talked about these last night, and you guys allocated roles. Connie, you're heading over to the morgue this morning for the post-mortem, yes?"

"Ten am, boss."

"Good. I'll call you when I get a moment at the trial, see how you got on."

"I'll be fine."

"It's not a welfare call. I want to know what the report tells us. If we're any closer to identifying him."

"Oh. Sorry."

"It's OK." The body was in a gruesome state; she wasn't surprised Connie was looking a little grey around the gills.

"Rhodri, you're on forensics. Yala's the crime scene manager, find out if she's going to be there today."

"They finished packing the evidence away last night, boss. She told me she'll be going back for a final once-over later this morning then closing the scene."

"That was quick."

"Not a huge amount of evidence preserved."

"No. Anyway, I suggest you meet her there. Always better to get a feel for the scene instead of looking at the photos."

"That's what I was thinking."

"The priority is identification of the body. Ask her to sit on the lab, get that DNA analysis fast-tracked."

"No problemo."

Zoe rolled her eyes. "Good. Mo, you happy to take CCTV?"

"Of course. We've already got footage from the supermarket. I'll head over there with Rhodri, see if I can find any other locations that might have captured anything."

"What about you, boss?" asked Connie.

"Sorry?"

"We didn't allocate you a task."

Zoe smiled at her. "You were too reluctant to order me around, if I remember right."

At the back of the room, Dawson cleared his throat. Zoe wrinkled her nose.

"I'll coordinate," she said. "I've got the trial to contend with, and I'll be liaising with DI Whaley about links to the Starling case."

"Such as what?" asked Rhodri.

"All we have right now is the badge at our scene, which corresponds to a symbol that was scratched into the wall at the Starling scene." She looked at Carl. "Can you fill us in on that?"

Carl joined her in front of the board. "It's a sensitive case and I can't tell you anything that isn't directly linked to your own investigation. But we do think this symbol indicates a possible link between the two crimes."

"What is it?" asked Connie. "I've never seen it before."

Carl sighed. "It's the callsign of a gang."

"Hamm's lot?" asked Rhodri.

"I may as well tell you," Carl said. "It's a new gang. I'm sure Organised Crime can fill you in on the details. But what

CHAPTER THIRTY-FIVE

it does mean is that I need you to share anything with me from your case that relates to this symbol and potentially to the gang."

"And you'll share yours with us?" Mo asked.

Carl glanced at Zoe. She gazed back at him, not letting him see her reaction.

"Sorry," he said. "Too sensitive. But anything you can give me will be very helpful."

Rhodri muttered under his breath. Zoe flashed him a warning look and he stiffened.

"Sorry, folks, but that's the way it is," said Dawson. "Now, Zoe said she needed to get this over and done with. I suggest you all bugger off and do your jobs."

CHAPTER THIRTY-SIX

"What's this?" David turned towards Anita from the fridge, holding up a jar of chutney.

She felt a chill wash down her.

"It's new. From the deli in Great Western Arcade. I thought we'd try it."

"Says Fortnum and Mason."

She shrugged. "It looked nice."

"You spending all our money on posh food, now?"

"It's just a jar of chutney." She took it off him and placed it back in the fridge. She closed the door. "What do you need?"

"Just getting milk for a coffee."

"I can do that. You sit down." She could feel her heart pounding in her ears.

He gave her a suspicious look but did as he was told, sitting at the kitchen table and pulling his phone out while he waited.

She clattered around the kitchen, pouring the coffee

she'd already brewed and grabbing the milk jug. She spilled some on the floor and cursed herself.

He held out a hand for the mug and looked back down at his phone. "Thanks."

"That's OK." She stood at the fridge, watching him.

After a few moments, he looked up. "What?"

"Sorry?"

"You're freaking me out."

She blinked. "I'm just looking at my husband." She tried smiling.

"Well, don't." He slammed the mug down on the table. "I'm running late." He pecked her on the forehead as he passed. "Kiss the girls for me."

"It would be much nicer if you kissed them yourself." She turned to call up the stairs. "Carly! Maria!"

He frowned. "I haven't got time. You can do it."

Maria thundered down the stairs. "She said I can't have the leather jacket I wanted for my birthday."

"Who did?" asked Anita, snapping into this new conversation.

"Carly, of course. I hate her."

"Carly has no say in what you get for your birthday, darling," said Anita. She stroked her daughter's hair, resisting the urge to lean in and smell it. "Don't you worry."

"More expense," said David.

Anita turned to him. "You're doing well. You got that promotion. And you told me we could have the extension that we've been talking about for so long. Surely you don't begrudge—"

He waved a hand. "It's fine. I've got to go."

"Bye, Dad." Maria gave him a sheepish look. Anita tried to remember the last time he'd spent time with his daughters.

"Bye, sweetheart. Be a good girl for your mum." He turned to the front door.

"You're not dressed," Anita told Maria. "Quick, you've got to leave in ten minutes."

"That's an age."

"Just get a move on!"

Maria rolled her eyes and trudged up the stairs. Anita hurried outside to join David in the driveway. He had his car door open.

She put a hand on his back. "Is everything alright?"

He shrugged her off. "I worry about money. That's all."

"I don't mean that. You seem... distracted lately."

He turned to her, his face dark. She flinched.

"In case you haven't noticed, I've got this fucking trial to deal with. Then there's... nothing."

"What?"

"Nothing. Just leave it."

"You can talk to me, darling. I won't tell anyone."

When he'd been a DI he'd talked to her about all his cases. She'd even helped him see links in a couple of them that had led to an arrest. But now...

"I can't, Anita. Don't be so naive."

"Maybe not the details of your cases. But if there's anything that's troubling you... I can be a friendly ear."

He scowled at her, and grunted as he got into the car. He pulled the door shut.

As the car started to move, she backed away from it, her body feeling full and empty at the same time. She gave him a little wave. He responded with a nod.

At least it was something. He wasn't ignoring her.... yet. Not all of the time.

CHAPTER THIRTY-SIX

The car left the drive and Anita went inside. *Look at me*, she thought as she caught herself in the mirror. Letting him treat her like this. Like a mouse.

Was she turning into Margaret Jackson?

CHAPTER THIRTY-SEVEN

Zoe dashed out of the station and made for her car. She checked her watch: 8:45 am. She was running late.

As she dropped into the driver's seat, her phone rang. She plugged it into the car's system as she reversed out of her spot.

"DI Finch."

"That's very formal."

Zoe's heart sank. "Mum. I'm on my way to something important."

"So am I. Well, later."

"Oh?" It was rare for Annette to go out. Drinking at home was cheaper.

"I've got a hospital appointment. Six-month follow up from my mini-stroke."

Annette had suffered the stroke in October, when Zoe was working the Jackson murder case. "Sorry, Mum. I didn't know."

"I forgot myself. Doris next door reminds me, I show her all my letters so I won't forget things."

Zoe glanced in the rear-view mirror as she turned onto the Harborne Road heading into the city. She knew her mum was prone to forgetting things, but didn't realise she'd come up with a system to get round it.

"It's at quarter past three, love."

"Where?" Zoe reached the Hagley Road and turned right, heading into town.

"The QE," Annette replied.

"You know where you're going?"

"They've sent me a map. But you can show me, you go there all the time for work."

Zoe closed her eyes briefly. "I'm working, Mum."

"Surely you can tell them you're out on a case. It won't take long."

"I'm giving evidence at a trial today. There's no way I can duck out of that."

"Afterwards?"

"Surely you can get the bus?"

Annette's voice dropped an octave. "I hate the bus."

That was the first Zoe had heard of it. Her mum used the bus often enough to get from her house in Kings Norton to Zoe's in Selly Oak.

"You'll be fine." She was near the Crown Court now. She needed to concentrate on finding a space. "I've got to go."

"Zoe, please—"

"I'll call you later, Mum, yeah? Find out how you got on."

Zoe hung up and pulled into a space. She sat in the car for a moment, wishing she'd checked the caller ID before picking up. She felt a twinge of guilt, but pushed it aside. Talking to Annette had rattled her, as if she wasn't rattled enough already.

CHAPTER THIRTY-EIGHT

Zoe stared ahead as she was sworn in as a witness. *Here goes*, she thought. She was aware of Ian in the dock, his gaze on her. She didn't meet it with her own.

The prosecution barrister gave her an encouraging smile. Zoe had seen Fiona Hegarty in action before, in the Canary trial. The woman knew what she was doing, and she had thirty years' experience sending people down.

Zoe stood straight and shuffled her shoulders. She took a breath.

"DI Finch. Please can you tell the court how you know the defendant?"

"He was a member of my team in West Midlands Force CID. That's the unit that investigates major crimes."

"Was that how the two of you first encountered each other? In Force CID?"

"No. I was the Senior Investigating Officer when his children were kidnapped last October. At that time, he was working in local CID in Kings Norton. He joined Force CID after we returned the children to the family."

CHAPTER THIRTY-EIGHT

"You were sufficiently impressed with him during the course of the kidnapping investigation to request that he be transferred to your unit?"

"I received a request from the Professional Standards Department to have him move into my team. We had a vacancy." Mo had been temporarily moved into Dawson's team. It felt like a lifetime ago.

"Why did the Professional Standards Department want him in your team?"

Zoe scanned the courtroom. No sign of Randle. He was due to give evidence after her; he'd have to sit outside until then.

"It was in connection with another ongoing investigation. I'm afraid I can't say anything more about that."

She glanced at the jury, knowing that keeping information out of her testimony would dispose them against her. But there was no way she could divulge the fact that PSD were investigating Randle.

"So PSD, if you don't mind me calling them that, placed the defendant in your team so he could report back to them?"

"Yes."

"Why did they pick him in particular to do this?"

Zoe resisted a glance at Ian. "There was evidence that Ian – DS Osman – was involved with organised crime. He had connections to a particular group, he would be trusted by them."

"Tell me more about that."

"We'd been investigating a man called Trevor Hamm. Three of the men working for him are now serving prison sentences. Kyle Gatiss for illegally imprisoning a police officer, Simon Adams for the same, and Adam Fulmer for people smuggling. There was another man Hamm employed to do building work for officers who provided him with information. This man did some work on DS Osman's house."

"In return for giving Mr Hamm information about police operations?"

"I don't know the details, but that's what PSD officers told me, yes."

"So Sergeant Osman joined your team and was working cases with you as well as this undercover operation for PSD."

"Yes."

"How much did you know about his undercover activities?"

"Nothing other than that he was doing something. I wasn't given the details."

"Moving on, can you tell me how you and the defendant came to be together at Birmingham airport on the afternoon of the bomb on Pakistan Airways Flight 546?"

"I was in the office, working on paperwork. My DCI, Lesley Clarke, was called away to the New Street incident. Then Detective Superintendent Randle, who's the Head of Force CID, told me to go with him to the airport. It was Ian's day off, I didn't expect to see him. But when I arrived, he was already there."

"Had he had a call from the station?"

"He didn't tell me who'd contacted him. I was surprised, given that he had apparently been on a shopping trip with his family."

"And was off duty."

"Yes."

"In the event of a major incident like the bomb attacks that day, is it normal for officers to be called in from leave at short notice?"

"It happens, yes. But normally their line manager would be involved in notifying them."

"And you weren't?"

"No. I had no idea that DS Osman was aware of the incident until I saw him at the airport."

"Do you have any idea who might have called him?"

Zoe hesitated, thinking of Randle. "He didn't tell me. It was all very rushed, chaotic. He didn't tell me, and I was busy with incident response."

"So after you encountered him at the airport, did the two of you proceed to work together on incident response?"

"I was Bronze Command. Ian didn't have a formal role but he joined me."

"Doing what, specifically?"

"We went to the aeroplane with orders to preserve the scene. So that investigators would have the best possible forensics."

"Did you carry out those orders?"

"Firefighters were still on board, it was an active rescue operation. We were told to stand down until it was safe to go on board."

"Were you frustrated by that?"

Zoe heard a sob. She looked round to see an elderly male juror with his head in his hands.

The judge put up a hand, indicating for Zoe to stay quiet. Zoe watched the man, her muscles tense. After a few moments he sat up straight, taking a tissue from another juror and insisting he was OK to go on.

"Were you frustrated, DI Finch?" the barrister asked again.

"We wanted to ensure the evidence was preserved, so

there would be a better chance of identifying who had planted the bomb. But the rescue was more important."

She had been frustrated at the time. She'd been so focused on the police work that she'd lost sight of the rescue. She'd even argued with the firefighters. Looking back, she felt ashamed. She certainly wasn't about to tell a jury how she'd reacted.

"So you left the plane, and where did you go?"

"I went to where the pathology team was working."

"You and the defendant?"

"He was already there. He was bending over one of the deceased when I arrived there."

A raised eyebrow. "Were you able to identify the deceased?"

"None of the bodies had been identified at that time."

Zoe swallowed as she heard a sniff from the spectators. This was all so raw. Two bombs detonated in the city. She wondered if there were people in the gallery who'd lost loved ones. If that happened to her, she'd want to be at this trial.

"So you didn't know who it was that the defendant was bending over?"

"No."

"Can you remember anything about the person? Sex, ethnicity?"

Zoe took a breath. She'd run over this moment again and again in her mind. She'd even dreamed about it. But each time, the face was a blank.

"I'm afraid not. We were disturbed by the pathologist, who asked us to move away."

"Did you see the defendant place anything on the body he was bending over?"

"I didn't."

This was the crux of it. Ian was accused of planting explosives residue on the body of Nadeem Sharif, an innocent victim of the attack. They'd assumed the man had detonated the bomb, until Adi had worked out that the timings meant he couldn't have. The poor man had been killed and then his family had to go through the indignity of being questioned and having their house torn apart by police.

"Nothing at all?" the barrister asked.

"I didn't see anything leave the defendant's hand."

"But you did see him paying close attention to one of the bodies."

"Bending over one, yes."

"No further questions."

CHAPTER THIRTY-NINE

Connie swallowed as the pathologist arranged the unidentified body laid out before them. She had her fists clenched at her sides and her toes curled in the boots they'd made her wear.

Hold it together, she told herself. If Rhodri could do this, so could she.

It wasn't even as if this was her first post-mortem. She'd been to eight before. Three in Uniform and five in CID.

But she'd never seen a body quite like this.

It was impossible to tell whether the man had been overweight in life, or if it was just the bloating that made him look that way. His flesh was puffed up as if someone had blown into his mouth and inflated him. The skin on his stomach and chest was greenish-black but his legs were a purple-yellow colour, like a two-day-old bruise. His face had bite marks to the left cheek and the chin, and his teeth were visible through the tears in the skin and muscle.

Connie looked away, maintaining control over her stomach.

CHAPTER THIRTY-NINE

"Starting with external injuries," said Dr Adebayo.

"Yes," said Connie.

"This isn't for your benefit," the pathologist told her, pausing the movement of her hands on the victim's face. "I record it."

"Of course. Sorry." Connie clamped her lips shut.

"Subject has deep wounds to his left cheek and his lower jaw. Flesh has been torn away from the bone and mangled in places. Consistent with animal bites."

Connie kept her gaze on the pathologist's hands. She breathed through her mouth, not easy in the surgical mask.

Dr Adebayo turned to her. "Tell me you're not going to pass out."

"I'm not going to pass out," Connie mumbled.

"If you do, make sure you go that way." The doctor used her free hand to indicate away from the body. Connie nodded, hoping it wouldn't come to that.

"Right, where was I? Yes, animal bites."

The pathologist cut at the flesh surrounding one of the bites. She dropped a sample of the man's flesh into a metal tray and screwed up her face as she leaned in to get a better look.

"No sign of knife wounds to the head. Only trauma is teeth marks." She put her scalpel on the tray and picked up a swab, then wiped it across the bite wounds. She placed it in a bag, sealed that and picked up another which she ran around the man's teeth and gums before securing it. She stood back to let her assistant take photographs, then leaned in again.

"Moving down, subject has intensive greening to the abdomen. Indicative of post mortem interval of a week to ten days. Bloating of soft tissues confirms this."

"Would he have been overweight before death?" asked Connie.

"On balance, I would say yes. On a slimmer adult, bloating wouldn't be this severe."

Connie nodded. That might help with identification.

"Moving on to the legs. Hypostasis is present on the backs of the calves and thighs. Subject was found in a prone position lying face down, which would indicate the body was moved after death."

"Can you tell how long after death he was moved?"

The pathologist frowned. "Not with much certainty, but hypostasis normally kicks in around thirty minutes after death and becomes most prominent around twelve hours later. Temperature and environment will affect this, and as we don't know where he died..."

"But he was probably moved at least twelve hours after he was killed?"

"Given the post mortem interval and the fact he wasn't spotted until yesterday, I'd imagine he was moved later than that. But that's something for your forensics people to ascertain."

Connie nodded.

"OK. Time to open him up."

The pathologist picked up a scalpel and made the familiar Y incision into the man's torso. Connie gagged as the smell of rotting flesh rose from the bench. His flesh bulged under the knife, making squeaking noises. She could hear fluids seeping into the drain at the end of the table.

Connie turned away and cleared her throat.

"You OK?"

"Fine." Connie forced herself to turn back to the body.

"Right. Let's take a look." She clamped back the man's

skin to reveal his internal organs. The bright red of his insides contrasted with the green skin.

Dr Adebayo glanced at Connie. "This isn't the worst I've had this week."

"No?" Connie couldn't imagine anything much worse than this.

"Burn victim. Arson attack on his shop. Horrible."

Connie nodded. She didn't need to imagine a body more 'horrible' than this one.

The doctor moved around the table and bent down to get a closer look. She straightened abruptly.

"Can you smell that?"

"What?" Connie leaned forward, sniffing, then instantly regretted it.

"That smell."

Connie sniffed again. There was a strong and familiar smell, like cooking. She shook her head.

The doctor crouched down further, inserting her fingers into the man's chest and examining his organs. Connie couldn't see what she was looking at from this angle. The technician approached and the two pathologists muttered to each other.

Connie's eyes widened. "It's like... garlic?"

"A garlic-like smell. It indicates the presence of..."

The assistant, a tall black woman of whom Connie could see only her eyes, nodded.

"Of what?" Connie asked.

Dr Adebayo held up a hand to shush her. "It's the same as..." She put her hand to her mask. "I need to tell them about this."

"Who?" Connie said. "I can tell DI Finch."

The pathologist stood up. "Not your DI. Sorry."

"What is it? Was he poisoned?"

Dr Adebayo looked Connie in the eye. "I'm sorry about this, but I'm going to have to ask you to leave."

"I'm fine. If I was going to throw up, I'd have done it by now."

"It's not that. DC Williams, please can you leave?"

"The boss will want my report."

"And she'll get it, as soon as I've spoken to Superintendent Rogers."

Rogers? He was DI Whaley's boss. Connie looked back at the body.

"Can I at least tell her the cause of death?"

"Tell her it's arsenic poisoning. That's what killed him."

"Arsenic?"

"I'll talk to her after I've spoken to Superintendent Rogers."

"Doctor, please—"

"DC Williams. I've already asked you to leave once. Please, don't make my job any harder."

CHAPTER FORTY

Ian's barrister was a willowy Asian man in his forties. He looked down at his notes, pushed his glasses up his nose and turned to look at Zoe. She pushed her thumb into the palm of her hand, determined not to let him rattle her.

She knew the evidence she had against Ian was flimsy. There would be other evidence that Carl and his team had gathered, evidence that definitely showed Ian leaving explosives residue on the body of Nadeem Sharif. Not to mention the evidence connecting him to Trevor Hamm and Stuart Reynolds, the builder he'd employed.

How much of it was circumstantial, she didn't know. There was enough for the CPS to have charged Ian, but enough to convict him?

She glanced across at Ian. She didn't know for sure he was guilty, but her gut told her he was guilty of corruption at least, if not of planting evidence.

All she had to do was tell the truth. It would be for the jury to decide what that meant. She took a deep breath through her nose.

"Detective Inspector Finch," the barrister said.

She nodded.

"How would you describe your relationship with my client?"

"We had a good professional relationship."

"You weren't resentful of his presence on your team?"

"No."

"Who did he replace as your sergeant?"

"He replaced DS Mohammed Uddin."

'Who is now back in your team, is that correct?"

"It is."

"So DS Osman gets a brief spell in your team, you accuse him of planting evidence and then you get your old pal DS Uddin back."

"No."

"No? So what did happen?"

"DS Uddin was given a move to another team. It created a vacancy and I agreed to take DS Osman."

"Reluctantly, perhaps?"

"Ian Osman was a good detective. I was happy to have him on the team."

"When you were investigating the disappearance of his children, did you have reason to suspect Sergeant Osman?"

"Suspect him of what?"

The barrister raised his eyebrows. "I ask the questions here. Did you suspect him of being the person who took his own children?"

"There was a brief period during which we thought that he and his wife might have—"

"Based on what evidence?"

"The woman who took the children was masquerading as

Alison Osman, Ian's wife. We had no idea she existed so when we found evidence pointing to her, we naturally—"

"You assumed Mrs Osman was guilty, and you lumped my client in with her. Did your evidence point to him as well?"

Zoe licked her lips. "He'd been behaving strangely. We later learned that this was because he was connected to an organised crime gang."

"I know I'm sounding like a stuck record here, but on the basis of what evidence did you suspect him of involvement with this gang?"

"He had improvements carried out on his house by Stuart Reynolds, the man Trevor Hamm employed to do building work in lieu of payment. He disappeared on a number of occasions and we believed he was visiting members of the gang."

"You believed? Did you follow him to these meetings?"

"No." They had tried, but failed. Zoe thought of the evening Mo had borrowed Rhodri's ancient Saab, which had broken down before he was able to tail Ian.

"So you believed he was connected to organised crime, you took him in for questioning, and he was later released because there was no solid evidence backing up your theories."

"He was released by the Professional Standards Department. I can't answer as to why that happened."

"DI Finch, how did you feel about having a man you suspected of corruption and had recently accused of kidnapping his own children joining your team?"

"I knew the circumstances of his posting to Force CID. I gave him the responsibilities you'd normally give a DS in a major investigation team."

"Such as?"

"We were investigating the murder of a man in the gay village. DS Osman had responsibility for interviewing witnesses."

"Would you agree that during that investigation, you barely let my client out of your sight and you gave him no more responsibility than you gave to the two detective constables in your team?"

"I would not agree with that, no."

"DI Finch, did you like my client?"

Zoe gulped in air. "I was his line manager. Whether I liked him is irrelevant."

"You wanted DS Uddin back on your team. You didn't trust Ian Osman. And you wanted him off your team any way you could find. Is this why you're saying you saw him tampering with one of the bodies at the airport?"

"If you check the record of my evidence, you'll find I haven't actually said that. I observed him bending over a body."

"And that's all you saw."

She swallowed. "It is."

"His job on that afternoon was to preserve the scene, just like yourself. He was carrying out his normal duties as a police officer. He had every right to be near those bodies, as did you."

"He did."

"So why are you misleading the court into thinking he was undertaking a criminal act, when in fact he was just doing his job?"

"I'm just reporting what I saw."

"No further questions."

CHAPTER FORTY-ONE

Rhodri hated DS Uddin's car. It was a nondescript brown Vauxhall, cramped and dull. He'd rather have brought his own Saab, but the sarge had been worried it would break down.

He sat in the passenger seat, trying not to sulk. His Saab had passed its MOT only two weeks ago. It was fine. Just because it had let Mo down, back when they'd been following Ian Osman...

He sat up. "D'you reckon the boss has finished yet?"

The DS shrugged. "You know what Crown Court trials are like."

"I don't."

"You've never appeared at one?"

Rhodri shook his head. "Magistrates' Court, a few times. Back when I was in Uniform. But I don't even know where the Crown Court is."

"It's about a hundred yards from the Magistrates' Court. Maybe I'll show you on the way back."

Rhodri grunted. The longer he had to spend in this car, the more irritated he would get.

"How far now?"

They were on the M6 heading out of the city. The satnav had insisted it was the best route to Chelmsley Wood but Rhodri wasn't convinced. If it was up to him, he'd have taken the direct route via Stetchford.

"Fifteen minutes. What is this, a school trip? *Are we there yet?*" The sarge glanced at Rhodri, grinning.

"Sorry, Sarge. I'm not meself today."

"What's up? You miffed about not being put forward for promotion?"

"Nah. I knew that was a long shot. It's... it's nothing."

"You can tell me, Rhod. If something's getting to you, I want to know about it."

Rhodri gazed out of the window and yawned. "Woman troubles."

"Ah."

"Ah indeed."

Rhodri wondered if the sarge had ever had woman problems. He was married to that GP, Karine or Catrine or something. Two perfect little daughters and a tidy house in Northfield. Rhodri wanted all that one day. The job, the woman, the house.

"I'm sure it'll pass," said DS Uddin. "How long you been seeing her?"

"Two months. I think she's about to dump me."

"Ah."

Ah again. Rhodri wiped his nose on the back of his hand.

The DS pointed to the glove compartment in front of Rhodri. "Box of tissues in there."

"Huh? Oh, yeah. Sorry." Rhodri opened the glovebox

and pulled out a box of mansize tissues. He took one and blew his nose loudly.

"You got a bin?"

"Best if you pocket it," the sarge said. He indicated; they were filtering off the motorway. At last.

"Thank God for that," Rhodri said.

"You don't like my driving?"

"I'm just not a very good passenger, is all."

"Makes a change for me. The boss normally drives."

"In that Mini of hers. Must be a squeeze."

"I'm not a beanpole like you."

"Yeah. Sorry." Rhodri eyed the sarge, all five feet eight inches of him. Same height as the boss, which looked all wrong when you saw the two of them together.

"Don't be," DS Uddin said as he turned left past a supermarket.

"This it then?" asked Rhodri.

"It is. Let's hope we're not too late."

They pulled up opposite the police cordon. Forensics techs were dismantling the tent and Adi was trawling the grass beneath it for anything they might have left behind.

"Morning," the DS said as he approached the FSM, his arm outstretched.

Adi pumped DS Uddin's hand and then reached for Rhodri's. Rhodri flinched as he was subjected to the same powerful grip.

"Morning, lads," said Adi. "No Zoe?"

"She's in court," replied the sarge.

"Of course. Poor her."

"You almost finished here?" Rhodri asked.

"Yeah. Just doing final checks then we'll be lab-based."

DS Uddin gestured towards the industrial estate behind

them. "I'm going to go door-to-door. See if I can find any witnesses or CCTV."

"Uniform already knocked on doors," said Rhodri.

"I've got their list. There's a couple need following up." The DS walked away, his hands in his pockets.

"You in charge now?" Adi asked Rhodri.

"The boss is trying to give me and Connie some more responsibility."

"So you get forensics, and DS Uddin gets the grunt work."

"Not entirely grunt work."

Adi shrugged.

"I was expecting Yala," Rhodri told him.

"They released me from the Boldmere crime scene. Yala wanted to get a start on the lab work for this one."

"Fair enough. Anything new to tell us?"

"Come with me."

Rhodri followed Adi to the patch of grass, now standing empty.

"There's nothing here," he said.

"Not anymore. But I wanted to show you what there had been."

"OK."

Adi stepped onto the grass. He stood to one side, next to a hedge. "So this is where we found the body. You can see the stains on the grass."

"Blood?"

"Blood and other bodily fluids. He'd been dead a week, he was what you might call leaking."

Rhodri grimaced. "We still got no idea who he is?"

"That's what Yala's working on. We took DNA before he was moved to the morgue. Should get the results today."

CHAPTER FORTY-ONE

"And you found that badge on him."

"Hold your horses. Let me walk you through it first."

"Sorry." Rhodri put his hands in his jacket pockets, wishing he'd worn something more substantial than a suit.

"So. He was face down here. Tangled up. Like a yoga pose, Yala said. Thread the needle."

Rhodri nodded, feeling his flesh tingle. Izzy, his girlfriend, did yoga. If she still was his girlfriend.

"He was posed?"

"Well, you'd think so," Adi replied. "But he was put here at least a day after he died. Probably later, given that no one saw him. It's a busy area."

Rhodri looked across at the supermarket. Two kids stood outside it, legs astride their bikes, watching them. Rhodri wondered if they should be at school.

"So when d'you reckon he was dumped?"

"We've checked weather in this area for the last week. It rained on Monday night, and his clothes were damp, but not soaked. He'd been attacked by animals – foxes, judging by the bite marks – but not badly. I think he wasn't here more than twelve hours."

"So he was kept somewhere else in the meantime."

"We're examining his clothes for any fibres or debris from a location he might have been kept at."

"Or killed at."

"Or killed at, indeed. And then there's the badge you're so keen on."

"The same symbol found near the dead copper."

"I'm not s'posed to talk to you about that."

"The boss is working with DI Whaley. We're operating jointly."

Adi raised an eyebrow. "You are, are you?"

Rhodri nodded.

"I'll have to check that out. I've got strict instructions, and I've already... never mind."

Rhodri frowned but didn't push it. Adi's phone rang and the FSM raised a finger for quiet.

"Hi, Yala." Adi looked at Rhodri as he listened. Rhodri's heart picked up pace.

Adi's eyes widened. "You sure...? Yeah... I've got DC Hughes with me... yeah. OK, you do that."

Rhodri stared at him, shifting from foot to foot. Was it the DNA results?

Adi was still talking. "I'll tell him. They're not going to be happy... I know. See ya."

He hung up.

"Well?" Rhodri said.

"We've got a match for the DNA. It's probably not what you were expecting."

CHAPTER FORTY-TWO

Mo stood outside a scruffy looking building in the industrial estate opposite the spot where the body had been found. The two constables who'd been here yesterday had made a note of the CCTV camera above his head, and he wanted to follow it up. A sign above the door advertised the place as Chelmund's Cross Gym. From here it just looked like a neglected industrial unit.

He looked up at the camera, then turned to check the angle. The camera wouldn't be able to see the dump site, but it might have caught someone approaching it.

A voice came over the intercom. "We're not open yet. Come back after two."

"I'm with West Midlands Police. We're following up an incident in the local area."

"What kind of incident?"

"A murder. We're hoping your CCTV might have picked something up."

"It won't."

Mo looked up at the camera. The voice was female, Scottish.

"I'd like to check, if you don't mind." Mo pulled up his collar, it was starting to drizzle.

"Wait a minute."

Mo huddled into the doorway, trying to get away from the rain. Good job this hadn't started while they were taking the forensic tent down.

The door opened and Mo almost fell through. He grabbed his ID from his inside pocket and held it out.

A woman stood in front of him. She was skinny, with dyed purple hair and a cigarette hanging out of her mouth.

"That CCTV isn't working properly," she said.

"Not working at all, or not working properly?"

"Not working properly."

"What times is this gym open?" He looked at the sign on the wall. If it was a gym, it certainly wasn't Bannatyne's.

"Two pm till midnight. Six days a week."

"Do you have both floors of this building?"

"We do." She shoved a hand in her jeans pocket. Mo coughed as a blast of cigarette smoke hit him.

"Can I come inside please? I'd like to see what the view is from upstairs."

"Like I say, we're closed."

Mo bit down his irritation. He couldn't force his way in, but this woman wasn't doing herself any favours.

"Are you the manager?"

"I am."

"You own this business?" He got out his notepad.

She cocked her head. "Do I look like I own a fuckin' business to you?"

Mo stared at her. He could try and track down the business's owner. Or he could come back when they were open, hope there was someone more cooperative on site. If that didn't work, he could always go back to tracking down the owner.

"Who does own this business?"

"RJ Holdings."

"Do they have a director?"

She shrugged and took a drag on her cigarette.

He sighed. "Is there any chance I could take a look at your CCTV footage from the last few days?"

"We wipe it every morning."

She'd told him it wasn't working properly. Now she was saying it was wiped. "After you've checked it?"

"Look. If nothing's happened, we overwrite it. No law against that, is there?"

Mo looked up at the camera. It was the only thing on this building that looked cared for. He would bet it was digital.

He noted down the make of the camera. Connie could check how it operated.

"Thanks for your time," he said. "I'll be back later."

She grunted and closed the door in his face.

CHAPTER FORTY-THREE

Zoe sat in a café opposite Birmingham Crown Court, her mind racing. She didn't feel ready to drive yet, so she'd headed to a trendy corner cafe, and ordered a coffee and two slices of toast. They'd only had sourdough.

A young man with his hair pulled back in a man-bun put the plate of toast down in front of her. It was laden with butter, just the way she liked it.

She picked it up and tried to stop it dripping onto her shirt as she shovelled the thick toast into her mouth. She closed her eyes, trying to cast the image of that smug barrister from her mind. A solicitor had been sitting next to him, a large woman with blonde hair and ruddy cheeks. Zoe wondered when Edward Startshaw, Hamm's solicitor, had stopped representing Ian.

Her phone rang as she put the second half of the slice in her mouth. She gulped the toast down, almost choking, and grabbed it. It was Rhodri.

"Hey, Rhod." She licked her lips. "Sorry. Just eating some toast."

CHAPTER FORTY-THREE

"Sounds good, boss. Trial go OK?"

"Let's not talk about that. You in Chelmsley?"

"Yeah. Me and the sarge."

"OK." So Mo had given Rhodri the job of calling her. "What can I do for you?"

"They've got the DNA results, boss."

"Go on."

"It's a man."

"Well, that's no surprise." She slurped her coffee then cursed herself: it was hot.

"We know him, boss. Well, you do."

Zoe put her coffee down. "I do?"

"His name's Howard Petersen."

"Howard Petersen?" She cupped her hand around the phone, thinking back to the large, bloated body. The blond hair. "Howard Petersen from the Canary case?"

Howard Petersen had been one of three men they'd arrested for child abuse, just before she'd become a DI. He'd been given a suspended sentence for money laundering, and it still pissed her off.

"Same guy, boss. Checked against records from that case."

"Damn."

"What d'you want me to do, boss?"

"Is Mo with you?"

"He is."

"Someone needs to tell Mrs Petersen."

Zoe pictured the young, glamorous wife. She'd barged into the Petersen house last October, when they'd been searching for Ian's daughter. For a time, she'd worried the girl had been taken by the paedophile ring.

"You want me and the sarge to do that?"

"He lives in Four Oaks. Get the address from Connie. Talk to the wife, see if she's got any idea why someone might have done this."

"You don't see her being a suspect?"

"He was a big man. Unless she had help..."

And besides, domestic murders didn't generally involve keeping bodies for days then dumping them on waste ground.

"No," she said. "I don't. But watch her reaction anyway. You know what to look for, don't you?"

"Surprise, mainly."

"That and the authenticity of her reaction. Report back to me when you've spoken to her."

"Will do, boss. See you back in Harborne?"

"Yeah." Zoe hung up. She had someone she needed to talk to, and he was a five-minute walk away.

CHAPTER FORTY-FOUR

Colmore Circus was busy, office workers heading back to their desks after their lunch break. Zoe checked her watch: ten to two. She took the zebra crossing leading to Lloyd House, West Midlands Police HQ, and stopped outside.

She looked up at the thirteen-storey building, chewing over what Rhodri had told her.

If someone had killed both Petersen and Starling, then it had to be linked to the Canary case. To Trevor Hamm. And by extension, to Randle.

Carl might already know. But if she gave him the information, there was less chance of him pushing her out of the second case. She needed to know what would happen next.

But first, she needed a sounding board.

She strolled down a side street and huddled next to the wall. She dialled Lesley's number.

"Zoe, everything OK?"

"Yes, ma'am, why wouldn't it be?"

"You only call me when you're worried about something. Sometimes that something's me. But more often, it's a case."

"Am I that obvious?"

Lesley chuckled. "I don't mind. Bored off my tits anyway. Hit me with it."

"So you know about the Erdington CID detective we found dead in Boldmere?"

"DS Starling. I do."

"I don't suppose you know anything about the investigation into his death?"

"I thought you were SIO on that."

So Lesley hadn't been informed. No surprise there.

"PSD swooped in and took over," Zoe said. "Starling was bent."

"And you want an in on the evidence."

"We've found another body, this one dumped on some waste ground in Chelmsley Wood. There was a symbol found at both, the callsign of a gang."

"You think they're connected."

"Turns out the second body is Howard Petersen."

Lesley whistled. "Well, shag me sideways."

"Yeah."

"OK, Zoe. You know what you have to do on this. Tell Frank. It's his job to make the call to PSD."

"Petersen was one of the Canary paedophile ring. No reason to think he's linked to police corruption."

"Zoe, wake up. Who was SIO on Canary?"

"Randle."

"And you want him taking over this one?"

"No."

A grunt. "The only people who can take it off him are PSD. Malcolm Rogers needs to know."

"I'm at Lloyd House."

There was a pause. "Bloody hell, Zoe. You do like to stick your nose in, don't you?"

"DI Whaley is working with my team, liaising on the two investigations. I have a reason to bring him in on this."

"It's your funeral, Zoe. And your boyfriend. Just watch what you say, and who you say it to."

"Of course."

"I don't suppose there's any way I can talk you out of this, persuade you to go to Frank?"

Zoe said nothing.

"Thought so. OK, well good luck, Zoe."

"Ma'am."

"Don't call me that. I'm not your boss anymore."

"You're still my senior officer."

"On medical leave."

"Ma'am, before you go…?"

"What else?" Zoe heard Lesley mutter to someone in the background.

"You were talking about a call you had, when we spoke the other night."

"Oh, that. It was nothing."

"Not related to this case at all?"

"It was Anita Randle. She thinks David's having an affair with some young woman."

"I doubt he'd have the time."

"Exactly."

Zoe gripped her phone. "Hang on. Who is this young woman?"

"I didn't ask, Zoe. I've got no bloody idea."

Zoe thought back to the photo of Randle and the New Street bomber that the forensics team had found. She'd told

Sheila Griffin about it but had no idea if Organised Crime had pursued it.

"Did she get hold of that photo?" Zoe asked. "The one with Alina Popescu?"

"I damn well hope not, Zoe. But if she did, that's between her and David. I'm not sticking my big fat hooter in there."

"No. Thanks, boss."

"You've talked to Sheila about that, yes?"

"Yes."

"And?"

"I left it with her."

"That's not like you."

"I've been preoccupied."

"Sounds like it. OK, probably for the best. Leave well alone."

"Yes, boss."

"Lesley's my name."

"OK, Lesley." Zoe flinched at the use of the word; it felt odd on her tongue.

"Take it easy, Zoe. Don't do anything I wouldn't."

Zoe stifled a laugh and hung up. Her phone was blinking: Connie.

"Hey, Connie, PM all done?" She walked further down the street next to Lloyd House as she spoke. At this rate she was never going to get to see Carl.

"Sort of, boss."

"Sort of?"

"She kicked me out."

"You didn't throw up on her shiny white floor, did you?"

"I held it together. Just."

Zoe smiled. "So why did she kick you out?"

"She smelled something, on the body. Got all funny after that, then told me to leave."

"What did she smell?"

"She didn't say. But it was a bit like garlic. The doctor said—"

"Garlic," interrupted Zoe. "That can indicate the presence of arsenic."

"Yeah. But the state of him. I just assumed he was beaten up."

"He might have been that as well, Connie. But if arsenic was the cause of death, then it'll be in the report. I don't get why she kicked you out, though."

Two uniformed constables walked past Zoe. She turned towards the wall.

"She said she had to talk to Superintendent Rogers," Connie told her. "I think it was the same as Starling."

"She found arsenic on that body too?"

"She didn't say. But that's what I reckon."

Zoe looked up the hill towards the front of the building. "OK, Connie. You get back to the office. I've got someone to talk to, and I'll see you there."

"Yeah... that's the problem."

"What is?"

"I got a flat on my bike. Didn't replace the spare inner tube after the last time it happened."

"Where are you now?"

"On a bus from City Hospital into town."

"You should have called a cab."

"I'm used to the bus."

Zoe rolled her eyes. "I won't be long here. Meet me outside Lloyd House, twenty minutes. We'll drive back to the office together."

"Thanks."

"No problem." Connie whizzing around the city on her bike wasn't good enough. "See you shortly, Connie."

Zoe hung up and strode up the hill, hurrying to the building's entrance.

CHAPTER FORTY-FIVE

It was 2:00 pm now, and the manager of the gym had no excuse to send them away. Two men were hanging around outside, waiting to be let in. One was white with a shaved head, wearing a grey hoodie. The other was black with intricate designs shaved into his hair.

Mo stood beside them with Rhodri hanging behind, waiting for the door to open. The two men kept glancing at them, their faces hard. They might as well have been wearing uniform, they were so obviously police.

"Shouldn't we be heading over to Four Oaks, Sarge?" Rhodri muttered, leaning in towards Mo.

"I don't want to leave this one till tomorrow. It won't take long."

Rhodri shrugged.

After a minute or so, the woman appeared. She let the two customers in and stared at Mo.

"You again."

"It's two pm. You're open."

"Doesn't mean I have to let you in."

"I'm working on a murder inquiry. Your CCTV might help us identify the perpetrator. I can get a warrant and come back later, but it'd be much easier for you if I—"

"Oh, bloody come on then. You won't find anything." She stood back. Mo squeezed past her, followed by Rhodri. Rhodri had paled and was staring at the woman.

Mo frowned at him. "Where will I find the recordings?" he asked the woman.

"You won't." She closed the door behind them.

"Sorry?"

"I told you, we wipe them in the morning."

"Every day?"

Rhodri pointed towards the door. "That's a Bascom high-def system. Digital. Why would you delete recordings, when you can just keep them on your computer?"

"We like to be tidy." Her voice was harsh, the Scottish accent stronger than before.

"You gonna let us check?" Rhodri asked.

She put her hands on her hips. "You got that warrant?"

"OK," said Mo. "Can we come upstairs briefly? It would be helpful to see the view from your windows."

"We have blinds."

"Still..."

"Privacy. Our clients like to be secure. You won't see nothin'."

"Are you going to let us come up and look?"

She eyed Rhodri, who was staring at her, then looked back at Mo. "Go on, then. Won't do you any good."

"Thanks." Mo pushed down a sigh and hurried up the stairs. At the top he came out into a large space with a boxing ring at one end and mats at the other.

"You're a boxing gym," he said.

CHAPTER FORTY-FIVE

"Boxing, other stuff. Keeps 'em out of trouble." She nodded towards the two young men who were next to the ring, wrapping bandages around their hands.

"And you open from two pm to midnight every day."

"We do."

"I'd like to speak to your clients over the last three days, if that's possible."

"I don't fuckin' know who our clients were over the last three days."

"You're not a membership gym?"

"We are, we aren't. Flexible. No idea who's been here."

Mo doubted that. He glanced at Rhodri, who's eyes were alight. He looked like he might explode.

"What is it, Constable?"

Rhodri's eyes didn't leave the woman. "Nothing, Sarge."

Mo frowned at him. Rhodri pulled his gaze away from the woman and blinked at Mo. "Sorry, Sarge."

"Hmm." Mo turned to the woman. "I'll be back."

"With a warrant?"

"Maybe."

"Good luck getting one. We havnae done nothin' wrong."

"We'll see about that." Mo descended the stairs, Rhodri behind him. The woman slammed the door behind them.

"What was all that about?" he asked Rhodri. "You looked like you'd seen a ghost."

"It's that woman, Sarge. I know her."

"You do?"

Rhodri nodded violently. "Her name's Sheena McDonald. To be honest I thought she'd be in prison. She was the one that managed the brothel, where Trevor Hamm was keeping those Romanian women."

CHAPTER FORTY-SIX

"How's things?" Carl rounded his desk and approached Zoe, his arms outstretched. They exchanged a brief hug, Carl watching over her shoulder to be sure no one would see.

"I've given my evidence now, so we're safe to talk."

"I know."

"And I need to tell you something. Two things."

He rounded the desk and stood in front of his chair. "OK."

Zoe didn't like having the desk as a barrier between them. She shifted to its side, Carl at an angle to her.

"It's the body we found in Chelmsley Wood," she said.

"You've got further with the symbol."

"Not that. We've got pathology evidence, and DNA."

His eyebrows rose. "That was quick."

"Adi fast-tracked it."

"Tell me, then."

She chewed her bottom lip. "I need to know you're not going to boot me off this, Carl."

"Why don't you tell me what you've got, then I can decide what'll happen."

"Don't talk to me like I'm one of your sergeants. I'm SIO on this case."

"If it's corruption-related, you know we have to step in."

Her face felt tight. He was right.

"So are you going to tell me?"

"Adana, that's the pathologist," she told him. "Dr Adebayo. She'll be sending you a report. I don't have all the details but she seems to have found evidence of arsenic poising."

Carl put a hand on the desk. "Arsenic?"

"That's what you found on Starling, isn't it?"

His face darkened. "What about the DNA?"

"We've got a match."

"For your guy in Chelmsley Wood?"

"Yup."

He waited for her to elaborate.

"It's Howard Petersen," she said.

"The same Howard Petersen who—"

"Canary. Yes, that's the one."

He sat down. "OK."

"No reason to think it's corruption, Carl. It's organised crime. If anyone should be stepping in, it's Sheila Griffin."

He looked up at her. "If this is linked to Canary, then the SIO on that case will need to be informed."

"David Randle."

Carl nodded. "I'm going to have to talk to my super."

"We both know Randle's dodgy." Zoe lowered her voice. "The photo, with Alina Popescu."

"We can't discuss that, Zoe."

We can't discuss anything these days, she thought. "He's

due to appear in court today. He's a witness at Ian Osman's trial."

"How did your evidence go?"

"The barrister made me look like an idiot."

"I'm sure it wasn't that bad." He cocked his head. "Where's the original of the photo?"

"That photo is evidence in the Magpie case."

"It's not, Zoe. It's evidence in the Jackdaw investigation."

"The Jackdaw investigation?"

"Forget I said that. Where's the original?"

"Evidence store for Magpie."

"Right. This is out of your hands now, Zoe. All of it."

"No. Until we get more on Petersen—"

He leaned across the desk. "I've got no choice but to talk to my boss. You'll be formally questioned. Layla will do it. Or Superintendent Rogers."

Zoe nodded. "Fine."

CHAPTER FORTY-SEVEN

Connie was outside Lloyd House, looking uneasy, when Zoe emerged.

"Everything OK, boss?"

"Yes." Zoe didn't break stride. "I'm parked in the multi-storey on Dalton Street."

"No problem." Connie hurried to keep up. "Thanks for this."

'It's fine." Zoe strode ahead, her skin hot. Carl was going to move it up the line, and she'd be formally interviewed. As a witness in this Jackdaw case he referred to? She could only assume that was the investigation into Randle.

Who else? How far did this go? Was DS Starling a part of it? Was that why he'd died? And if so, what the hell was that bull symbol? She'd never seen any sign of it around Hamm.

She stopped at Steelhouse Lane, glancing down the hill towards the old central police station, where she'd worked for three years. She waited for the lights to change, jabbing her fingernails into her thigh. "Come on," she muttered.

The pedestrian light switched to green and Zoe sped across. "Come on."

"Sorry." Connie picked up pace. "You sure there's nothing wrong?"

Zoe said nothing. What was there to say? She was about to lose her second case in as many days, and Carl thought she was an idiot.

They reached the car park and she slowed. "I'm sorry, Connie. You don't deserve this. Tell me more about the post-mortem."

They walked as Connie filled her in. She talked about the state the body had been in, the size of him, even taking into account the bloating.

"Petersen was a big man," Zoe said. "Blonde hair."

"The body had blonde hair."

"Yes, well we've got a DNA match. It isn't as if there's any doubt."

Connie stopped walking just for a second, as if she was about to trip.

At the car, Zoe yanked open the driver's door. "We need to get back to the office. I'll talk to Dawson. Sheila, too."

"DS Griffin?"

"You know any more Sheilas?" Zoe turned the ignition and backed out of her space, almost hitting a car passing behind. "Shit."

"Boss, d'you want me to drive?"

Zoe turned to the constable, her heart pumping fast. "Can you even drive?"

"You can't join the force without a licence. Course I can drive."

"When was the last time you drove?"

"In Uniform I drove a panda car a few times. Did bike patrol mainly." Connie smiled.

"I want you to get a car."

Connie looked shocked. "How?"

"It's not good enough, you getting around on that bloody bike. Where is it anyway?"

"Locked up in the bike rack at City Hospital."

"What if you need to get from one end of the city to the other?"

"I can take a cab, like you said. I can get Rhodri to drive me."

"Rhodri isn't always going to be available."

They had left the car park behind and were heading through the city centre traffic.

"I can't buy a car," Connie said. Her voice was tight.

"Just something second hand, like Rhodri."

"My mum relies on me for money. There's Zaf's tuition fees to pay. She only does the odd bit of cleaning work. It's..."

Zoe pulled herself up short. She slumped into her seat. "Oh, hell. I'm sorry, Connie. I've had a row with – I've had a row with someone, and I'm taking it out on you. You don't deserve this."

"Is it anything I can help with?"

Zoe glanced at Connie. They were approaching the Bristol Road. How had she ended up on this route?

"Thanks, Connie. It's fine. I need to deal with it myself." She thought of Carl's face as she had left his office. He'd never looked at her like that.

The cars up ahead were stationary. Zoe slapped the wheel as she stopped behind them. "Damn."

"If we'd gone via Five Ways..."

"I know. I wasn't concentrating. It's, what, half past two?"

"Ten past three."

"Rush hour shouldn't have started yet. What's going on?"

"Roadworks, maybe. They had them near the uni last month."

"There was nothing this morning." Zoe turned to Connie. "OK, let's not worry about the traffic. We'll get there eventually. I want you to recap on where we are with the Petersen case. Where do you think the investigation should go next?"

"Surely it's out of our hands now."

"Assume it isn't. Tell me what you'd do."

"Well, we need to talk to Petersen's family. It might just be a domestic."

"I doubt it, but yes. Mo and Rhodri are there already."

"And then there's Jory Shand."

Zoe gripped the wheel. "Jory Shand. The other bastard who got off. You're right." She nodded. "What else?"

"Well..."

"Yes?"

"If both men had that callsign on them, and both of them were killed by arsenic poisoning, we can assume they were killed by the same person. Or people."

"Yes."

"A gang?" Connie suggested.

"I don't know of a gang with that callsign, but we have to assume Sheila's on it."

"In which case," said Connie. "Why would a new gang kill Howard Petersen, who was connected to Trevor Hamm, as well as a bent DS?"

"That's the million-dollar question," said Zoe.

CHAPTER FORTY-SEVEN

"Maybe Hamm's got in with a new gang."

Zoe shook her head. The car in front was moving again. She pressed the accelerator but couldn't go above ten miles per hour. "I don't see it. He wants to be in charge. He wouldn't join someone else's organisation."

"He's lost all his men. He'd be desperate."

Zoe looked ahead, her vision blurred. "Where is he? Where the hell has Hamm been hiding out all this time?"

"We need to find him, boss."

"You're right, Connie. Find Trevor Hamm, and we'll discover what's going on with all these cases."

CHAPTER FORTY-EIGHT

Ian watched as Detective Superintendent Randle walked from his seat to the stand. He was composed as ever, wearing a dark blue suit and white shirt with a pale blue tie. His hair was combed back and his face calm.

David Randle was like a goddamn duck. Legs belting away like mad under the surface but calm as a cloud on a spring morning where it could be seen.

Randle took his place and was sworn in. He kept his eyes up as he did so, his face still. He looked the epitome of professionalism.

Ian knew better.

The CPS barrister, Ms Hegarty, was going first. She approached the stand, her movements breezy. It was half past three and Ian knew from yesterday that the jury would be getting restless. They dipped after lunch; he'd even seen one of them nod off yesterday. It had been ten minutes before the foreman had noticed and roused him.

"Detective Superintendent Randle."

"That's me." Randle gave her a pleasant smile.

CHAPTER FORTY-EIGHT

"Mind if I just call you Superintendent? It's a bit of a mouthful."

"Not in the slightest." The smile didn't waver.

"Tell the court your connection to the defendant."

Randle's eyes travelled over Ian as he spoke. "DS Osman was a member of the Harborne Force CID team from late October last year to February this year. As the Head of Force CID, I was his indirect manager."

"Do you know how he came to be recruited to Force CID?"

"We had a vacancy. He was recommended to me by the Chief Inspector in charge of the South Birmingham Local Policing Unit."

"Was there a recruitment process?"

"A recruitment process isn't necessary for officers to undertake a transfer within the same force and at the same rank."

"So no, there wasn't?"

"No."

"Were there any other officers in line for the role?"

"We'd recently lost a few of our number. DI Finch had been promoted from Sergeant. DI Whaley had completed his stint in the team. It meant some shuffling around at DS level."

"You mention DI Whaley."

"He reported to my colleague DCI Clarke."

"And how long was he on the team?"

"Six months in total."

"What was DI Whaley's role in your team?"

"He was SIO on a couple of cases. He—"

"What was his *real* role?"

Randle pushed his shoulders back. Ian tensed as he

watched.

"He was an undercover officer from the Professional Standards Department."

"Were you aware of this at the time?"

"Not when I was a DCI, no. After my promotion to Superintendent, I was fully briefed."

"Fully?"

"Yes." Randle licked his lips. Was that sweat on his brow?

"So why was he placed undercover in Force CID?"

"We were working a major organised crime case, referred to as Canary. His remit, I believe, was to ensure that there were no opportunities for impropriety."

"So he was spying on you?"

"He was spying on all of us."

Ian remembered the briefing he'd had from Whaley when he'd been brought onto the team. His job had been to watch Randle, and report back.

Randle frowned at the barrister. "I fail to see what DI Whaley's role has to do with DS Osman planting evidence."

The hair on the back of Ian's neck was bristling, he could feel it. The man in the stand had told him to plant that evidence. *Find a body*, he'd said. Preferably male, preferably Asian. Leave this on him. No one will ever know.

Liar.

"Just setting the scene, Superintendent."

Randle took a sip of the glass of water that had been placed out for him. He nodded, stretching his neck.

"So, Superintendent. You were promoted to Head of Force CID, you discovered an undercover anti-corruption officer had been working alongside you. How did this make you feel?"

CHAPTER FORTY-EIGHT

"It didn't make me *feel* anything."

"Surprised? Betrayed?"

"No."

"Worried?"

"No."

"Were you concerned that PSD might have placed more undercover officers in your department?"

Randle's gaze flicked to Ian. Ian had never told him about his deal with Whaley. But that didn't mean he hadn't known.

"The officers in my department were long-standing members of West Midlands CID. DI Whaley had transferred in from another force. It was different."

"Yes, or no, Superintendent?"

"No. I was not concerned."

"It didn't occur to you that DS Osman might have been moved into your team as a spy?"

Randle looked at the barrister, avoiding Ian's eye. "If that had been the case, I would have been informed as the head of the unit."

"Unless it was you he was sent to spy on."

There was a gasp from behind Ian. He knew Alison was there, without her nasty bitch mother. He'd spotted her sneaking in at the back after lunch. What was she thinking, listening to all this?

"We all now know that Ian Osman was a corrupt officer," Randle said. "He was alleged to have taken bribes in local CID and he was observed by one of my team planting evidence on one of the bodies at the airport. He's not the kind of man you would use as a spy." He turned to the jury and gave them his most winning smile. Ian grimaced.

The barrister walked back to her paperwork and picked up a file. Ian noticed Randle's eyes narrow.

The barrister approached Randle. Ian hated the man, but was in awe of him at the same time. Most of all, he feared him. Not only did he have power over Ian's career, he had the power of life and death, too. The fate of DS Starling had made that clear.

"Superintendent, what do you say to the contention that the defendant was placed in Force CID to watch you and report back to DI Whaley?"

Ian felt ice run through his veins. He stared at Randle, his breathing shallow. He'd spotted Alison in the crowd, but what if Hamm's men were there too? He'd never be safe in prison, he'd never be safe on the outside.

Shut up, he thought, staring at the barrister. *Stop it*. He was taking the fall for this. It was better that way. Safer. For him and Alison. For the kids.

He wanted to throw up.

The barrister turned to look at him. Ian realised he'd made an involuntary noise.

The judge looked across at him. He was a middle-aged man wearing the largest glasses Ian had ever seen. "Are you alright, Mr Osman?"

He nodded. "Fine," he whispered.

Jane Summer, Ian's solicitor, leaned back in her chair and peered at him. "If you're not well, we can request a recess."

"I'm fine." He wanted to get this over with.

The judge pushed his specs up his nose. "Very well. Please don't disturb proceedings again, Mr Osman."

He clenched his fists. He longed to look round, to see who was watching. If they'd spotted Alison.

The barrister looked back at Randle. Ian forced himself to breathe.

"Superintendent. Where was I? Oh, the defendant being

planted to spy on you. Did you have any inclination this might be the case?"

"That's a preposterous idea." Randle looked across at Ian, his eyes hard. "At the time, I knew him as a good sergeant. A valued member of the team."

You valued me, alright, Ian thought. Randle had treated him like a puppy, his to order around at will. He'd sent him as a go-between with Hamm and his men. He'd summoned him to the airport.

"In fact, he was such a valued member of your team that you and he were in contact with each other outside your professional duties, is that correct?"

"I have no idea what you're talking about." Randle looked calm again. Boy, the man could lie convincingly.

"Very well, Superintendent," the barrister said. "Let's move on to the bomb detonated on Pakistan Airways Flight 546. You were involved in the operation at the airport, were you not?"

"I was Gold Command. My role was to ensure the police were working effectively with other emergency services."

"And you also oversaw the investigation into the bombing afterwards."

"Working alongside Superintendent Sanders from Anti-Terror, yes."

"The defendant's actions led you to initially suspect a Mr Nadeem Sharif, yes?"

"We found explosives residue on his clothes, he was one of the victims of the bomb. Our Forensics investigators later worked out that it could not have been him. We closed that line of investigation."

"And you moved on to looking into an international terrorist organisation."

"We eventually discovered, with a lot of international cooperation, that the organisation responsible was operating out of Pakistan. The man who planted the bomb managed to get away, we're still trying to track him down."

"We've already heard testimony from one of your colleagues that evidence was found that the defendant planted explosives residue when he was at the scene. Is this your understanding?"

"I wasn't present at the aeroplane."

"Do you know who gave the defendant the instruction to plant this false evidence?"

"I'm not sure if anyone did."

"You think he was acting alone?"

"I wouldn't know."

"Not with an organised crime group, maybe? Not with another member of Force CID?"

Randle blinked. "Like I say, that would be speculation."

"In your opinion, as someone who managed the defendant, would you believe him capable of working alone to do something like this?"

Randle looked at Ian. He shrugged. "He was a competent detective. I see no reason why not."

"Really? A lowly sergeant, taking it upon himself to plant explosives on a dead body?"

Randle shrugged. "It's not for me to say."

The barrister turned to the jury, made eye contact with a few of them, then returned to Randle. "On the same afternoon as the airport explosion, another bomb was detonated at New Street Station. Is that correct?"

"It is."

"Did you believe the two incidents to be connected?"

"Initially, yes. But our investigation led us to a local crime organisation in the case of the New Street bombing."

"Is this the same organisation which had advance warning of the planned incident at the airport? And which used that knowledge to smuggle a group of women and children off flight 375 from Bucharest?"

"They were running a people smuggling and prostitution operation. They weren't involved in the airport bomb, but they had prior information and took advantage of the diversion to take the women and children off the next plane on the runway."

"And now a number of them are in custody. Simon Adams, Kyle Gatiss, Adam Fulmer."

"Adams was already in custody following an earlier crime. The other two were involved in the people-trafficking."

"But you haven't tracked down the ringleader, is that correct?"

"He is still at large."

Ian noted that neither the barrister nor Randle mentioned Hamm by name.

"So this organisation was also responsible for the attack on New Street Station?"

"Yes. We believe the intelligence they received about the airport attack gave them the idea of launching a second attack in tandem, and hoping the terrorist organisation would be blamed for both."

"How did your officers work out that it was this organisation, and not the terrorists?"

A woman in the front row of the jury coughed. Ian jerked in his seat. He'd barely been breathing.

The barrister waited while the woman finished coughing. She held up her hand and apologised, then sat back.

"How did your officers work that out, Superintendent?"

"They found video and photographic evidence of the bomber which linked her to the prostitution operation."

The barrister checked her notes. "This woman's name was Alina Popescu."

"That's the name on her passport."

"She died in the attack."

"She did." Randle looked straight ahead.

The barrister tapped her file. "Superintendent, was this woman known to you or your officers before the attack?"

"No. She'd been smuggled into the country by the organised crime group and had barely left the house they were keeping her in."

"You'd never seen her before?"

"No."

"Met her?"

"No." Randle's gaze flicked to Ian, who had no idea what the barrister was getting at. He'd been taken off the case before they'd discovered Alina's identity.

"Did you know this woman, Superintendent?"

"No, as I've just told you."

"Did you know Trevor Hamm, the ringleader of the organised crime group?"

"Only by reputation."

"Did you work with this organisation, to give them information about police operations?"

Randle looked the barrister in the eye. "No."

"Was it you, Detective Superintendent Randle, who told the defendant to plant the explosives residue on Mr Sharif's body?"

CHAPTER FORTY-EIGHT

"I have no idea what you're talking about."

The barrister drew something out of her file. She placed it on the bench in front of Randle. He stared at it, his Adam's apple bobbing.

"Who is in this photograph?" the barrister asked. A murmur went through the jury.

"Myself," replied Randle. His voice had lost its smoothness.

The barrister pointed to the photograph. Ian couldn't see what she was indicating.

"This is you. And who is this woman, that you have your arm around here?"

"I'm not sure."

"Really?"

Randle said nothing. He stared at the photo. Ian held his breath.

What was in the photo? And why hadn't they told him about it?

The barrister drew another photo from her file. This was a mugshot of a woman. A passport photo.

"Would you say this is the same woman?"

Randle peered at the photo. His cheeks were pale. "I can't be sure."

The barrister turned to the judge and handed him the photos. "I'm submitting into evidence exhibits numbered 123 and 124."

The judge's eyebrows rose as he looked at the photos. He frowned at Randle. "You do know the penalty for perjury, Superintendent?"

"I do, your honour."

The judge nodded at the barrister.

"Just one more time," she said, "in case you've had an

opportunity to rethink. This passport photo..." She held up the photo for the jury to see. After a moment, she turned so the rest of the court could see it, including Ian. "This photo is of Alina Popescu, the woman who detonated a bomb in New Street Station on the orders of an organised crime group."

She held up the other photo. Ian drew in a sharp breath.

"And this photo is of Detective Superintendent Randle. Standing next to the same woman, Alina Popescu. With his arm around her."

CHAPTER FORTY-NINE

Selina Petersen was an attractive woman in her midthirties, which made her approximately fifteen years younger than her husband. She curled her lip at Mo and Rhodri as they stood on her doorstep, ID raised for her to check.

"Leave us alone," she told them in a thick Brummie accent. "We've got nothin' to say to you."

"This would be easier if we could come inside," Mo said. He hated doing this at the best of times, but with a relative who was already hostile to the police...

She folded her arms. "Whatever you've got to say, you can say it here. Howie's in bed. Hasn't left the house in... oh yes, five months. Since your lot slapped that tracker on him."

Rhodri cleared his throat behind Mo. *Yes, lad, I know*, Mo thought. He wondered where Mrs Petersen thought her husband really was.

He resisted the urge to test her, to suggest she wake Petersen. No, she was a new widow. Regardless of the lowlife she'd chosen to marry, she deserved to be treated with respect.

"Please, Mrs Peterson. I need to talk to you about your husband."

"He's done nothing wrong, like I say. Now fuck off."

Mo sighed. The woman started to push the door closed. He put out a hand to stop it.

"That's police harassment, that is. I'll be making a complaint."

"I understand you don't want to talk to us. But please. This is important."

"I'm not wakin' 'im."

Rhodri let out a high-pitched sound behind Mo. *Shut up*, he thought.

"No," said Mo. "I know you won't be waking him."

She scowled. "Why's that, then?"

"Mrs Petersen, where did your husband tell you he was going when he removed the tracker and left it here?"

She reddened. "What you talking about? You can't get those things off for love nor money."

He raised an eyebrow. "Did he tell you anything?"

She shook her head. "Howie's done nothing wrong."

"Mrs Petersen, I'm sorry to have to tell you this. But your husband is dead."

Her hand flew to the chain around her neck. Gold, thin. Tasteful, unlike the thick makeup she wore. "He's not. He's at a business meeting." She bit her lip, her eyes huge. Mo wondered how she could blink with all that mascara.

"Is that what he told you?" he asked.

She blinked back tears. "He's not dead. You just did that to get me to admit he'd broken his terms."

"I'm not concerned about him breaking his terms right now, Mrs Petersen. I'm more concerned about finding out about the circumstances of his death."

"Death?"

Mo nodded. "We found him yesterday. I'm afraid we weren't able to identify him until today. And naturally we came straight—"

He was interrupted by a howl. Selina Petersen stood on her doorstep and screeched like an animal. Rhodri shifted back. Mo stood his ground, his muscles clenched.

"Mrs Petersen, please. Let's go inside."

"He's not dead! My Howie is NOT dead!"

"Sarge." Rhodri's lips were near Mo's ear. "The neighbours are starting to come out."

The Petersens lived on a broad road in the affluent suburb of Four Oaks. The houses were separated by expansive front lawns and driveways that rivalled the Harborne police station car park. Even at those distances, the neighbours had heard the commotion. Mo looked round: of two houses opposite, one had a face peering from the front door and the other, a window in which the curtain had been parted a crack.

Mrs Petersen looked over the detectives' heads, easy with the steps leading up to her front door, and shouted. "Fuck off, all of you! You were bastards to him! Still are!"

Mo stepped up to put a hand on her arm. "Come on, Mrs Petersen. Let's get you inside." He turned to Rhodri as he steered her into the house. "Rhod, get a Family Liaison Officer sent out here asap."

CHAPTER FIFTY

The girls were upstairs doing homework. Anita could hear Carly's music blasting out. She'd have to go up and tell her to turn it off, it was one of the conditions of her curfew. The thought of it filled Anita with dread.

She scrolled through her phone, her mind far away. The conversation with Lesley Clarke had rattled her. She knew what the female officers thought of her and the other wives. Trophy wives, to be paraded at social events like dolls, hanging on their husbands' arms as if they were another medal. The force liked married men, even in these days of equal opportunities. Having a stable home life helped a man like David to rise up the ranks.

Stable home life, like hell.

Who was that woman? What was the event he'd attended with her? Something where wives weren't required. She wondered if his colleagues also had mistresses they took to these things. If there were specific events suitable for the illicit women, the ones without rings on their fingers and their names on the mortgage.

CHAPTER FIFTY

She stopped on the local news website. There had been articles about Ian Osman's trial for the last three days. David refused to talk about it, despite his agitation. She wished he'd confide in her.

There was a new piece. *Senior Police Officer in Liaison with New Street Bomber*. It was accompanied by two photos: a shot of David leaving the court, and a mugshot of a woman with long dark hair.

Anita held her breath. It was the same woman.

New Street bomber?

She jabbed on the photo to access the article, her chest tightening with every word.

When she'd reached the end, she threw her phone across the room. It hit the wall and clattered to the floor.

He'd not only been having an affair. He'd been having an affair with the woman who set off that bomb.

She stared out of the window, her mind numb. Did he have something to do with the bomb? Had he been working undercover?

She'd read about that undercover officer in the Met who'd cultivated a relationship with a suspect. He'd been sacked. Had he been prosecuted?

She ran to her phone and dusted it off. The screen had a small crack in the top corner but still worked, thank God. She dialled David.

Voicemail.

"David, it's Anita. Please call me as soon as you get this."

She hurried into the front room and stared out of the window. He wouldn't be home for hours. Knowing David, he'd creep in and go straight to his office. She had to intercept him.

She checked the clock on the mantelpiece: 5:15 pm. She could be in for a long wait.

She dialled for a takeaway pizza. The girls would be happy, and she wouldn't need to go to the kitchen to cook. A margarita and a ham & pineapple. Nothing for her, she felt sick already.

She put the phone in her lap – *call me back, David* – and watched the street outside, her nerves thrumming.

CHAPTER FIFTY-ONE

THE OFFICE WAS QUIET, Mo and Rhodri not yet back. Zoe dialled Mo and got voicemail. She tried Rhodri's number.

"Boss." His voice was low.

"Are you at the Petersen house?"

"Yeah. Hang on a minute." She heard him moving, walking to somewhere private.

"How did she react?" Zoe asked.

"She bloody howled, boss. She was a wreck. Still is."

"Genuine?"

"Looked it to me. She tried to make out like he was asleep, still in the house. She knows he's been going out, but we don't know where he told her he was going."

"Mo's interviewing her now?"

"The FLO has just arrived. There's a bit of an argy going on."

"About what?"

"The FLO thinks we're being too hard on her."

"What? Who is this FLO?"

"PS Lowe, boss."

"Never heard of her. Or him."

"Him. Bit of a jobsworth, if you ask me. From Erdington nick."

"That place keeps rearing its ugly head."

"Yeah. Anyway, there's talk of a lawyer being called. We're not going to get much out of her."

"She's not a suspect. She doesn't need a lawyer."

"S'pose not."

"But then," Zoe said, "she is the widow of Howard Petersen."

Connie was watching her, taking her coat off and sitting down at her desk. Connie gave a shrug which Zoe returned.

"OK, Rhod. See what you can get from her. We might have to bring her in for more formal questioning."

"A caution?"

"Let's hope it doesn't come to that. I'll see you back here when you're done."

"Er..."

"Rhodri. We're about to lose this case to PSD. We can't wait till tomorrow."

"OK, boss. See you in a bit."

Rhodri needed to understand that hours were fluid when they were working a murder investigation. Connie sat back in her chair and looked up at Zoe, showing no sign of going anywhere.

"OK," Zoe said. "Carl didn't say he was taking this off us yet, but we have to assume he will. In which case, we've got another fish to fry."

She walked to the board and scrawled *Trevor Hamm?*

"You think he's the key?" Connie asked.

"He was involved with Petersen. He might have got in

CHAPTER FIFTY-ONE

with this new gang. And there's still a warrant out for his arrest for what he did to those women. That case is open, we should be looking for him.

"But we already—"

"I don't care what we already did. He's the missing piece of the jigsaw. And I'm sure the CPS would be grateful to have access to him for Ian's trial."

"How was it today?"

"I'm not talking about it."

"That bad, huh?" Connie asked.

"It wasn't good. God knows which way it's going to go."

"But you saw Ian..."

"I saw him standing near a body, Connie. I can't be sure it was Sharif's body and I didn't see Ian plant anything. If they're relying on my evidence, he'll walk."

"They can't be. The CPS would never have prosecuted."

'That's what I'm assuming."

"DI Whaley hasn't filled you in on the details?"

"Something I've learned, Connie, is that when you're going out with a PSD officer you become the very last person he'll tell about his cases."

Connie nodded.

Zoe sighed. "Let's review what we have on Hamm. I think he's connected to Petersen breaking the terms of his suspended sentence. I want to have the right questions for Mrs Petersen, when she comes in. And there's Jory Shand to consider."

Jory Shand was a former newspaper editor, another of the three who'd been arrested in the Canary case. Just like Petersen, he'd got off with a conviction for money laundering and a suspended sentence.

"You want to go see him?" Connie asked.

"We'll probably need a warrant, I don't imagine he'll welcome us with open arms. But yes. He was one of that nasty little gang and we have to hope he can tell us something."

CHAPTER FIFTY-TWO

It was 8:00 pm when Carl was disturbed by a knock on his office door. He put a hand to the back of his neck, stretched and yawned.

"Come in."

The door opened and his visitor slipped inside, closing the door quietly behind him.

Carl caught his breath, his hand dropping to his lap. "Sir."

Randle nodded and took a seat. Carl glanced at the door. He walked to the window that separated his office from the one next door and closed the blinds. The neighbouring office was in darkness, but he couldn't be too careful.

"What brings you here?" he asked.

"You'll have heard about my evidence today."

"The photograph."

"Yes."

"I don't think you should be talking to me. We're already—"

Randle put up a hand. "I want to cut a deal."

Carl felt his mouth fall open. He closed it again.

"A deal."

"I provide evidence against Trevor Hamm's organisation, and you don't arrest me."

Carl stifled a laugh. He stared at the Detective Superintendent. Was he dreaming?

He put his hand up to the back of his neck again. He pinched the skin: fully awake.

"I think you should be talking to Superintendent Rogers."

"You're closer to this case. Jackdaw, you call it?"

Carl felt heat rise up his neck. How much did this bastard know about what he and his team were doing?

He stood up. "We can't have this conversation alone. Give me a moment, and I'll fetch a colleague."

Randle placed his perfectly manicured hands on his knees. He said nothing.

Carl opened the door to his office and scanned the corridors. Should he lock the door? The man wasn't under arrest. God knows, what had come out in court today had put a firework under PSD, but they didn't have a warrant yet. Randle was due to give the second part of his testimony tomorrow, and Superintendent Rogers wanted to wait for that. See if he incriminated himself.

The corridors were empty. Randle worked up on the tenth floor, five stops away in the lift. Carl had seen him moving around the building often enough. But he'd never appeared in Carl's office.

Superintendent Rogers's office was at the end of the corridor. Carl ran towards it, knowing it would be empty. He hammered on the door, but it was locked.

A door opened behind him. "Boss? Everything OK?"

CHAPTER FIFTY-TWO

"Layla. Thank God. David Randle's just appeared in my office wanting to cut a deal."

Her eyes were huge. "He's what?"

"You heard me. I can't do this alone. We need two of us."

"Yeah. Sure." She dived into her office and grabbed a pad and pen. "You got an audio recorder in your room?"

"I doubt he'll consent to us using it. He's not under arrest, remember."

"It's just a matter of time."

"Yeah." He pressed his fist into his temple. The door to his office hadn't budged since he'd been gone. "Come on."

Carl walked back into his office, trying to look like this was bread and butter to him. In truth, he'd never gone after such a high-ranking officer as Detective Superintendent Randle. And he'd certainly never done it without a senior colleague at his back.

"Sir. This is DS Kaur."

Randle turned and smiled at Layla. "I know."

She gave Randle an uneasy smile and grabbed the chair next to him. She pulled it away so it was at the side of Carl's desk, the three of them forming a triangle.

Carl rounded the desk, his heart racing, and sat down.

You can do this.

He leaned across the wood and placed his elbows on the table, his hands in a steeple grip. "Detective Superintendent Randle. Thanks for waiting."

A shrug.

"You say you want to cut a deal. What are you proposing?"

Randle leaned back in his chair, his legs crossed. "I tell you what I know about Hamm, and you put me and my family in witness protection. No arrest."

"Your family?"

"Two daughters. Carly and Maria." He nodded at Layla. "I suggest you write that down. And my wife Anita. She has no idea about all of this. Although after today…" He shook his head, just a little.

"I can't authorise witness protection just like that," Carl told him. "I'll have to speak to Superintendent Rogers, and things will need to be put in place."

Randle eyed him. "You work closely with Rogers, yes?"

"Yes."

"I bet you do. You're his eyes and ears. I'm sure the two of you are as one mind."

"Nothing I do here tonight can be inter—"

Randle waved a hand. "OK. Call him."

"And then you'll tell me what you know about Hamm?"

"Not until I have a guarantee that I'll be immune."

Carl pulled in a shaky breath. "My role isn't to catch Hamm. You know that PSD is here to—"

"I know what you people do." Randle leaned across the table. "But how would it feel to be the man responsible for bringing in the bastard behind the New Street bomb?"

Carl nodded. As far as he was concerned, Randle himself was the biggest fish. But for West Midlands Police as a whole…

Rogers would understand the politics of this better than him. But could Carl believe a word Randle said?

"Do you know where Hamm is right now?" he asked.

Randle smiled. "Uh-uh."

"If you don't even know where he is, why should I believe you'll have any valuable evidence?"

"You'll have to take my word for it." Randle scratched his chin. "Just ring your boss, like a good dog."

CHAPTER FIFTY-TWO

Carl bristled. He shared a glance with Layla then picked up his phone. It rang out six times, then Rogers picked up.

"I'm sorry to disturb you so late, sir, but I have Detective Superintendent Randle in my office."

"You have... what?"

"He wants to do a deal with us. He provides evidence on Hamm, we don't arrest him. And we put him in witness protection."

Rogers snorted. "Put him on the phone."

"I'll put it on speakerphone."

"Just hand him over."

Carl held his phone out to Randle, flinching as the man's fingers brushed his own. Randle put the phone to his ear, his face impassive.

"Malcolm." Randle sat back and jiggled his foot as he spoke. "Uh-huh... yes... of course... I will... that's for me to know... not yet... that's not good enough... I know you can... yes... I'll talk to her... very well."

Carl watched, wondering what Rogers was saying on the other end. Who was more important to his boss, Randle or Hamm?

Or did he hope to get both?

Randle cupped his hand over the phone, muttering. Carl felt irritation seep through his body. Layla shifted in her chair, her pen sweeping across her pad in terse strokes.

At last Randle lowered the phone. "Your boss will give you your instructions in the morning."

"Which are?"

"Like I say, he'll tell you in the morning." Randle stood up.

"Wait," said Layla. "You can't just leave."

"Why not?" said Randle.

"Because..."

"Are you arresting me?"

"No."

"Well, then." He tipped a finger to his forehead. "I'll see you around. Maybe."

The Superintendent moved smoothly to the door. Before Carl could think of the best thing to say, he was gone.

"What the fuck just happened?" Layla asked.

"No idea," replied Carl. He dashed to the door and opened it to see the lift doors closing, the corridor empty.

He ran back into his office and fumbled for his phone, which Randle had left on the desk. He dialled Rogers: voicemail.

"What the hell?"

"He's not picking up?" said Layla.

Carl shook his head. "I guess we have to wait."

CHAPTER FIFTY-THREE

"My client is prepared to talk to you, but only with me present," said the solicitor. He was a young man wearing a bright blue suit. Something about him made Mo want to wash his hands.

"Fine. She's not under arrest. Or caution."

"You can't be too careful."

Mo and Rhodri were in the kitchen of the Petersens' large house, with its ugly portico porch and white-rendered walls. The kitchen was vast and gleaming, the surfaces covered in grey granite. They'd been here almost two hours waiting for the FLO to arrive, and then the solicitor.

"Where is she?" Rhodri asked. He was perched on a stool at the gargantuan island and had been stroking the granite absentmindedly, humming to himself.

"She's in the snug. Follow me." The lawyer, whose name was Charles Greening, led them out of the room. They left the FLO behind, trying to figure out how the coffee machine worked.

The so-called snug was anything but. It was a room as big

as the downstairs of Mo's house, with a projector screen at one end and a vast wraparound sofa in cream leather at the other. Mrs Petersen sat on the sofa, her legs curled beneath her and a cat snuggled beside her. She'd removed her makeup, making her look like a child.

"I can't believe it," she said as she saw them enter. "Who killed him?"

Greening sat next to her and placed a hand on her knee. She flinched but didn't push it away. "It's alright, Selina. I'll tell you when to speak."

She nodded and rubbed the cat under the chin. It raised its head, eyes closed.

Mo took a seat in a deep armchair opposite Mrs Petersen. Rhodri took the other wing of the sofa. He perched on its edge, clearly worried about getting sucked into the thing.

"Mrs Petersen, we need to ask you some questions about your husband's movements over the last couple of weeks. I know it's hard, but it'll help us find the person who did this to him."

She looked up at him, her chin trembling. Greening's grip on her knee tightened. Mo wondered if they were more than lawyer and client. The solicitor was closer in age to her, certainly better looking than her husband, with his spiked blond hair and chin that looked like it'd been shaved to within an inch of its life.

"When was the last time you saw Mr Petersen?" Mo asked. He nodded at Rhodri, who pulled a pad and pen out of his inside pocket.

She sniffed. "I don't know."

"Can you maybe cast your mind back?"

She gripped the cat by the scruff of its neck. It mewed and she let go. "I think... last Monday. We watched Keeping

Up With The Kardashians together. Or was that on Tuesday?"

"That goes out on a Monday night," said Rhodri. Mo looked at him, surprised.

Selina stared at Rhodri like he'd sprouted another head. "We don't watch it live. It was Wednesday. Yes, because Mrs Brooking had been." She turned back to Mo. "She's our cleaner. Housekeeper, I suppose. She does everything for me."

"Is this Margaret Brooking?"

A frown. "Er, yes."

"How long has she been working for you?"

"I don't know. Howie found her after our old cleaner left. She was funny about his ankle thing. Four months. Three?"

Margaret Brooking had been Trevor Hamm's housekeeper, in his house outside Solihull. Another modern, soulless place. So he'd palmed her off on the Petersens when he'd gone to ground.

"So, last Wednesday. You saw your husband at what time?"

She stared at him. "Am I going to be in trouble for this?"

Greening removed his hand from her knee and leaned forward. "Mrs Petersen had nothing to do with her husband breaking the terms of his sentence. She knows nothing about it. If you try to insinuate that she did, then I will advise her not to answer any more questions."

"We're not implying anything," said Mo. "I just want to know when Mrs Petersen last saw her husband. Did he tell you he was leaving the house?"

She turned to her solicitor, who shook his head.

"No comment," she said.

Mo's least favourite words in the English language. "Your

husband is dead, Mrs Petersen. Even if I did believe you were an accessory to him breaking the terms of his sentence, I'm not going to arrest you for it. I just want to know what he told you."

"He didn't tell her anything," said the solicitor. "What is it you don't understand?"

Mo slid forwards on the armchair, staring into the woman's eyes, ignoring the man.

"That's not what you said, Mrs Petersen. I want to find the person who killed your husband. If we know where he was, it'll be much easier to do that."

She wiped under her eye. "He said he had a meeting."

"What kind of meeting?"

"I don't know. He didn't talk to me about that kind of thing."

"OK. Did he say where it was?"

She shook her head and sobbed.

"I think it's time you let my client have some peace," said Greening.

"Is there any possibility your husband could have been taken from the house?"

Her eyes widened. "You think someone came here?"

She'd said Petersen was going out. But that didn't mean he couldn't have been snatched here.

If so, it was a crime scene...

"They might have. Have you noticed anything out of place? Any sign of a break-in?"

She glanced at the solicitor, her eyes welling. "I did... there was a window open when I got up on Saturday. Patio doors." She gestured towards the back of the building.

Mo sat back, satisfied. "Could someone have broken in?"

CHAPTER FIFTY-THREE

"I don't know. Mrs Brooking had been the day before. They might have."

He stood up. "Do you have anyone you can go to, Mrs Petersen? Somewhere you can stay while we search your house?"

The solicitor stood up, standing toe to toe with him. "Oh no, you don't."

"This is a potential crime scene, Mr Greening. And as such, we have the right to search it. If you obstruct us, I'll have no choice but to arrest you."

CHAPTER FIFTY-FOUR

"OK," said Zoe. "What's the last known sighting of Hamm?"

Connie stared at her computer screen. "He was involved in the bomb attacks."

"We never actually saw him, though. He was arrested for supplying drugs to an inmate in Winson Green Prison... when was that?"

"October, boss. No charges pressed, his girlfriend was the one with possession."

Zoe shook her head. "A month after his wife died in suspicious circumstances and he's letting his new girlfriend take the rap for his crimes. We have to find this guy, Connie."

"Yeah." Connie stretched her arms out in front, her fingers entwined, and cracked her knuckles.

Zoe paced back and forth in front of the board. "If you were a nasty bastard trying to evade the law, where would you go?"

"Maybe he's got himself a false passport. Left the country."

"He's wanted in connection with a terror attack. Biometrics mean he'd never get out of the country."

"He might do if he went via Ireland."

"And once he's there..."

"Schengen Zone," said Connie. "He could be anywhere in Europe."

"You still have to show a passport to get from Ireland to the mainland EU, though. And in practice, getting to Northern Ireland, too. He'd be flagged if they checked his biometrics."

"You want me to check if he's crossed any borders?"

"Organised Crime will have had a watch out on him."

"Still..."

"If he'd been picked up at a border, we'd know. I reckon he's still in the country. More than that. I reckon he's still local."

"He'd have some neck to stay around Brum," Connie said.

"The slimy bastard is all neck. He'll want to know what's going on with Ian's trial. And he's got a gazillion business interests around here."

"Doesn't mean he can't export them."

Zoe tapped her teeth with her pen. She wrote Sheena McDonald's name on the board. "She's managing a gym in Chelmsley Wood. Opposite where Petersen was found. And she was managing the Hotel Belvista brothel for Hamm. We need to get her in."

"I've got a photo of her." Connie pinned it to the board. McDonald was skinny, with dyed red hair and a look that would melt diamond. "Can't believe she's not doing time."

"The punters never visited that house. We couldn't prove she knew they were being taken away and sold for sex."

Connie shook her head. "Those poor women."

"Kids, too."

"Yeah." Connie's shoulders slumped.

Zoe jabbed her thumb into the photo. "I say we watch her."

"You want me on that, boss?"

Zoe considered. Connie's strengths were desk-based. Taking apart tech, chasing down digital leads. But she was the only member of the team McDonald had never seen. And a young black woman would be less suspicious hanging around the gym than a forty-year-old redhead.

She turned to Connie. "I'll talk to Sheila. You and one of her guys can pose as a couple wanting to join the gym."

Connie's eyes widened. "OK."

Zoe put a hand on the constable's shoulder. "We'll give you a wire. You'll stick to the public places, we won't put you at risk."

"Yeah." Sweat had broken out on Connie's brow.

"You've gone undercover before, Connie. You did it on your own initiative. The cleaning company in the Osman kidnapping."

"That was a city centre office. This is..."

"You can refuse if you don't feel comfortable."

"I've been stuck behind a desk for too long, boss. I need to take some risks."

Zoe raised a finger. "Calculated risks. I don't want you doing anything silly."

"I'll have one of Sheila's guys with me. I'll be fine."

Zoe smiled. "Good on you."

CHAPTER FIFTY-FIVE

Anita was woken by the sound of a door slamming upstairs. She stretched her arms above her head and yawned. How long had she been asleep?

She pulled herself up from the sofa and dragged herself to the bottom of the stairs, listening. Carly normally shut herself in her room all night, but Maria wasn't normally this antisocial.

She trudged up and knocked on her younger daughter's door, then pushed it open.

"Hey, you."

"Mum. I'm on Discord." Maria pulled a face.

"Can I get you a snack?"

"Cornflakes."

"Please?"

"Please." Another face. Maria waved a hand to shoo Anita away.

Anita made her way to the kitchen, wondering when her daughters had gone from small mummy-worshippers to their current disdain. It was normal for teenagers, she reminded herself. Nothing personal. She just hoped it would pass soon.

As she opened the fridge, she heard another bang. She clenched her teeth, wishing the girls would learn to not slam the bathroom door.

She'd left her mug in the living room. She was thirsty.

She placed the milk carton next to the cornflakes on the worktop and padded into the living room. She needed to stop moving around, to watch for David. She grabbed her mug and took it back into the kitchen, flipping on the kettle.

She poured milk on the cornflakes and called Maria's name. No answer. Sighing, she took the bowl upstairs.

"Thanks, Mum."

At least she'd got an unprompted thank you. She returned to the kitchen and poured out a cup of tea which she took to the living room. The street outside was dark, the streetlamp across the road the only illumination. No sign of David's car yet. It was gone 9:00 pm. She needed to get Maria off her computer, school tomorrow.

She caught movement out of the corner of her eye and shivered, turning into the room.

"You can't be hungry again already."

There was no one there. She'd been imagining things.

You're losing your mind, she told herself. She sipped her tea and stood at the window, blinking to keep her eyes open. She could barely remember what it was she needed to talk to David about.

The photo. That woman, the New Street bomber.

Anita felt a chill fall over her as she remembered the image. David with his arm around the woman, smiling for the camera.

CHAPTER FIFTY-FIVE

Tears fizzed behind her eyes. She had no idea what she was going to say to him. But she couldn't let it slide.

There was the creak of a footstep behind her. She kept her gaze on the front driveway, her mind focused on her husband and not her children. She heard breathing.

"I know you're there."

Carly had liked to surprise her when she was younger. She could be playful even now, silly when she wanted to be. Anita smiled.

She felt air brush the back of her neck and turned to her daughter, gasping as she realised it wasn't Carly.

She looked up at the shadow in front of her, mute.

Something rushed in at her and she felt an object land over her mouth. She tried to scream but there was something across her mouth, inside it. It smelled of... what?

She threw her arms out, trying to fight. The girls! Where were they? *Oh, God. Don't hurt them.*

She tried to kick out but her legs were weakening. An ankle buckled beneath her and she felt heaviness wash over her. The gag was pushed further into her mouth, making her retch.

She felt herself being dragged towards the door. She struggled to gain control of her legs, but it was like they'd gone. She was numb from the waist down.

As they reached the hallway the numbness caught up with the rest of her and she flopped into her assailant's arms, unconscious.

CHAPTER FIFTY-SIX

CONNIE SAT in silence as they drove out to Chelmsley Wood. She was in the back of the car with DC Solsby, while the boss sat up front with DS Griffin. DS Griffin was on the phone.

"Yeah... OK... yes, of course... no, we won't... yes... thanks. I'll keep you updated."

Griffin turned to DI Finch. "I've got authorisation."

The boss nodded, her eyes on the road. Connie felt the butterflies in her stomach take flight.

DC Solsby grinned at her. She wondered how many times he'd done this kind of thing. Meat and drink to him, she imagined. How could she pretend to be this guy's girlfriend? He wasn't even good-looking.

Given the number of times Connie had to pretend to be something she wasn't, it would make more sense for CID to recruit people from drama school.

They pulled up at the back of the Co-op supermarket, out of sight of the gym and the spot in which Howard Petersen had been found. The boss turned in her seat.

CHAPTER FIFTY-SIX

"You ready?"

"Yup," Connie replied, giving the DI the most confident smile she could muster.

"All you're doing is checking the place out, OK? In and out in less than fifteen minutes if you can. See if you can have a nose around, pretend you want to see what equipment they've got."

"The sarge said it was a boxing gym," Connie replied. "I don't..."

"You don't have to worry about that," said DS Griffin. "You're not going to be using the facilities today. Just enquiring."

"Do people enquire in places like that?"

"It's OK, Connie," said DC Solsby. "I'll do the talking."

Connie swallowed the bile in her mouth. She could do this. She'd barged into Hatton and Banerjee and pretended to be a cleaner when they were looking for the Osman kids. She'd faced up to the bolshy supervisor, and she hadn't blown her cover. And this time, she wouldn't be alone and the boss would be just around the corner.

DS Griffin had her phone out. She tucked an earpiece into her ear. "Try saying something."

Connie resisted touching the wire under her shirt. "Can you hear me?"

DS Griffin nodded. "Loud and clear." She checked her watch. "Eight thirty pm. See you back here, no more than thirty minutes."

What happened if they weren't back in thirty minutes, Connie wondered. Would the two of them storm in after her, all guns blazing, DS Griffin and DI Finch to the rescue?

The thought made her smile despite herself.

DC Solsby opened his door and stood on the pavement,

stretching. He wore a pair of joggers, saggy around the bum, and Nike trainers that looked expensive. Connie was dressed in a pair of skinny jeans with a tight pink shirt and matching bomber jacket that looked like she'd bought it in the market. The cheap fabric made her neck itch.

She hauled herself out of the car, acknowledged Solsby's nod, and walked with him around the supermarket. As they rounded the corner he took her hand. She forced herself to relax. He was her boyfriend, they were out for a stroll.

"Don't grit your teeth," he muttered.

Connie stretched her jaw, unaware she'd been clenching.

"Come here." He stopped and pulled her to him. She felt ice travel across her skin, terrified he was going to kiss her. But instead he slid his arm around her neck and drew her in for a hug, his lips close to her ear.

"I'm going to pretend to be the kind of arsehole who treats a woman like he owns her. Hope you don't mind."

"OK." It was part of their cover. She'd be fine.

They'd only met an hour ago.

He draped his arm around her neck, hoisting her in, and bumped his hips against her waist. He was tall, well over six foot. She focused on dropping into the same rhythm as him, on walking like this was how she always did it. *Don't think*, she told herself. *Just feel*. She closed her eyes, aware of his movements beside her.

As they approached the gym she flicked her gaze around the scruffy tarmacked area in front, her eyes moving but her head still. She could sense Solsby doing the same.

"See anything?" she muttered, turning to bring her mouth to his shoulder.

"Just the CCTV we already knew about."

"Don't look at it."

"Don't worry."

They arrived at the door and he pressed the buzzer. He shoved her in front of him and leaned over her, draping his body over her shoulders. She stood as straight as she could, forcing herself to lean into him a little. He was calm, his body language fluid. How did he do this?

A voice came over the intercom. "Can I help you?"

"Hey," Solsby said. "You a gym, yeah?"

"That's what it says on the sign." The accent was Scottish: Sheena MacDonald. Connie had seen the woman in the video of her police interview, but they'd never met.

"Sick. We wanna check the place out."

"You want to join?"

"If we like it, like."

"Hmm." There was a buzz and the door gave under Connie's fingers. She pushed it, Solsby still draped over her from behind. He grabbed her arm and pushed her sideways so she was next to him. She wanted to tell him to fuck off, but then remembered his warning.

They sashayed up the stairs together, Connie considering how much easier this would be if they walked normally. At the top a skinny woman with purple hair was waiting for them.

"Well aren't you just the pair of love birds?"

Connie forced a smirk, her cheeks reddening. At least embarrassment came naturally.

Solsby looked down at her, a proprietorial look in his eye. "She's OK," he muttered. Connie flashed her eyes back up at him and caught a wink in return.

"So what d'you want?" the woman asked.

"Just moved into the area, yeah? Lookin' for the best gym."

"*Best* is a big word."

Solsby licked his lips and leaned towards the woman. "You know what I mean."

She met his gaze for a moment then raised an eyebrow. "Who told you about the place?"

He gestured down the stairs. "You got a fuckin' big sign, can't miss it."

"Not that big. Where else you been?"

"Place over behind Somerville. Checkin' out the new place, Fitness Fanatics, later."

"Those places are shitholes."

"Somerville was a dump. Not been inside the other one yet. So can we look around, or what?"

"This isn't David Lloyd, you know."

He shrugged. "Just wan' see what you got."

"Maybe I'd like to see what *you've* got." She looked him up and down. Solsby shrugged.

"Next time, no worries," he said. "But right now, me an' Rita here, we're on the clock."

MacDonald turned to Connie. "D'you talk?"

Connie shrugged and nestled closer into Solsby.

"She's shy, yeah? Don't talk for no one but me." He licked his finger and ran it down the nape of Connie's neck, making her shiver. "And boy does she scream!" He dissolved into laughter.

Connie fought to keep the shock off her face. The boss was listening to this. *Get on with it*, she thought.

"You want to join too?" McDonald asked her.

Connie shrugged. "Maybe."

McDonald sniffed and looked Connie up and down. "You need it." She blew out and returned her attention to Solsby. "Five minutes. Take a look. There's a couple of guys in the ring up the other end. Don't ask them any nosey questions."

Solsby gave a mock-salute. "Not too nosey, lady."

McDonald laughed. "I'll be watching you."

I bet you will, Connie thought. She scanned the space as Solsby led her further inside. It was a large room, spanning three units on the ground floor. Front and back were lined with grubby windows and there was a smell of stale sweat. At the other end two young men, no more than kids, squared up to each other in a boxing ring. A man stood to one side, watching with his hands on his hips.

Solsby snaked his arm around her waist and pulled her towards the ring.

"Hey," he said as they approached.

The man turned to him. "Who are you?" He was short and wiry, with light brown skin and neck muscles that bulged.

"Name's Zee." Solsby put out a hand which the man took reluctantly. "Just checkin' the place out. This is my woman, Rita."

Connie gave him a shy smile. The man's eyes travelled over her, making her squirm.

"So what d'you wanna know?"

"Does it get busy?" Solsby asked. "I don't like busy."

"Not if you know the right day to come."

"And what might that be?"

"Mondays is quiet. Tuesdays not so bad. Come just after they open and you'll have the place to yourself."

"It's open till midnight, yeah?"

"You don't want to be here then. Full of wankers."

"What kind of wankers?"

The man's eyes darted to McDonald, who was fiddling

with some mats and pretending not to listen. "Druggies, half of them. No way they'd beat anyone in a fight. They come to watch."

"And they can afford the membership?"

A shrug. "There are various ways of paying." He gave Solsby a conspiratorial look. "If you know what I mean."

"Shit!" One of the kids in the ring had fallen, his leg twisted beneath him. The man approached the ropes, wincing.

"Just a sprain, Elon. You'll be fine. Go on, get up again."

The kid who was still standing grabbed the other kid's hand and hauled him up.

"You run a youth boxing group?" Solsby asked.

"Nothing as formal as that, mate. This here's my sister's boy. Keeps him out of trouble."

"They got anything else here apart from the boxing?" Connie asked.

The man pointed along the space. "Some weights. There's some girls what do kick boxing Wednesday nights. You should try it."

"Maybe I will."

Solsby squeezed her closer to him. "Hush, woman."

She kept quiet, her eyes on the man. She hoped the boss could hear. Solsby squeezing her in like this would muffle the feed.

"Come on, sweetie, let's take the tour," she whispered to him. He nodded at the man.

"Good to meet you."

They bumped fists. "You too."

Connie started to pull her pretend boyfriend away. He stopped her, his arm around her neck. It made it hard to breathe, let alone to walk. After a few moments he muttered in her ear.

"Don't forget you move when I tell you to move."

She bristled but said nothing.

"There's nothing here," he said.

"Maybe."

"I can't see anything, can you?"

"Three doors leading off this space, all locked. Who knows what's behind them?"

"You want to see if we can get through them?"

"Not today. Maybe some other time."

He pinched her arm. "You're getting the hang of it."

"Shush."

McDonald was approaching. "You like what you see." She handed over a dog-eared leaflet with prices on.

Solsby took it. "So far," he said, the insouciance back in his voice. "Like I say, got a couple others to check out."

"Yeah, you'll be back."

"Whatever." He led Connie to the stairs and half-dragged her down. McDonald stood at the top, watching them.

They crashed out of the door together. Connie wanted to spring away from him, to stop and breathe.

"Keep it up," Solsby said. "She could be watching." He grabbed her by the hand and they strolled away from the gym, both scanning the area.

Connie could see the wasteground where Petersen had been dumped as they approached the street. And she'd seen it from the upstairs windows of the gym. She had no idea if that was significant.

If you were going to kill a man, would you dump him just across the road from your own business? And if MacDonald was working for Hamm, where was he? There was no fancy car out front, there'd been no sign of him inside.

Her gut told her this place would lead them to him. "We come back tomorrow," she said as they turned onto the street.

"Day after," Solsby replied. "Don't want to look too keen."

"OK." She held onto his hand as they made for the car, her heart racing.

CHAPTER FIFTY-SEVEN

David Randle bloody hated Carl Whaley. He hated all those bastards at PSD. Even Malcolm Rogers, who at least was being reasonable.

He was still itching with irritation when he hit the remote for the garage door, still muttering to himself as he heard it close behind him and opened the inner door leading from the garage directly into the house's kitchen.

"Arrogant fuckers," he said as he yanked open the fridge door. Anita had better have bloody left him something to eat.

He pulled a few things aside, looking for a plate. Finding nothing obvious, he searched for a Tupperware container.

"Anita!" he called.

Where was she?

The kitchen was quiet, a pizza box standing next to the sink. He flipped it open: empty.

Damn.

He was starving.

"Anita!"

No response. She'd been acting odd lately, looking at him as if she was trying to fathom him out. Anita never did that. One of the things he loved about her was her unquestioning nature, the way she lived her life and let him live his without any questions.

He went into the hall. "Anita!"

"What's up?" Carly stood at the top of the stairs. She wore an oversized Garfield t-shirt over bare legs.

"Put your dressing gown on," he snapped at her.

She came down the stairs. "You're pissed off with Mum. Don't take it out on me."

"I think with the way things have been for you lately, you'd better keep your mouth shut."

She flinched. "Sorry." He almost laughed at the unexpectedness of it. Carly never apologised.

She brushed past him into the kitchen. She smelled of shampoo.

"Where's your mum?" he asked.

"Watching TV, maybe. Gone to bed?"

Anita never went to bed before he got home. Even if he was out working till 1:00 am, she'd wait in the living room, dozing on the sofa. A few times, she brought a pillow and duvet down. But she always stayed downstairs.

He wandered into the living room. She'd be sprawled out on the sofa, fast asleep.

The room was empty.

"Anita!" he called.

"Still not found her?" Carly was behind him, holding a tub of ice cream.

"You can't eat that at this time of night."

"Why not?"

"Because..." He didn't know why not. "Where is she, Carly? Have you upset her?"

"Maybe she's finally decided to leave you."

His fist clenched at her words. "Don't talk like that."

She smirked and left the room, shovelling ice cream into her mouth. Chocolate. His stomach growled.

"Can you make me some dinner?" he asked his daughter.

She spat out a laugh. "No chance. Mum called out for pizza. You've got a phone, haven't you?"

Pressure filled his temples. "Tell me where she went."

"I already told you, I don't know. Perhaps she's gone to bed." Carly wafted up the stairs, apparently unconcerned that her mum was missing and her dad was going hungry.

Randle took the stairs two at a time and shoved open the bedroom door. He stopped himself as he entered the darkened room. If she'd been feeling unwell...

"Anita?" he whispered.

He reached a hand out to the bed, waiting for his eyes to adjust.

The bed was empty.

Maria's room was next door. He knocked softly and opened her door.

"Hey, sweetie."

"Huh?" Maria's voice was thick with sleep.

"Mum with you?"

"She bought pizza. She was waiting for you." Maria rolled over and went back to sleep.

He closed her door and turned back to the landing. Carly's door was closed and music came through it: Beyoncé.

Anita, where are you?

He pulled his phone from his inside pocket as he hurried

down the stairs. She knew. She'd seen the trial on the news and she'd left him.

No. Anita would never leave the girls behind.

As he reached the bottom of the stairs, her voicemail kicked in. He hung up.

"Anita!"

He stood in the centre of the generous hallway, his legs numb.

She couldn't have left him. Anita had stuck with him for the almost thirty years he'd been on the force. He'd confessed to his affair with Margaret Jackson many years ago, and she'd forgiven him. She'd tolerated the late hours, the sneaking into his study when he got home at night, the fact he'd been closer to Bryn Jackson than to his own wife.

She didn't know anything for sure. OK, so that damn barrister had brought out the photo of him with that girl. But nothing had been proven.

He could talk to her. He'd convince her, the way he always did.

He went back into the living room. *Anita, where are you?*

A glint of something caught his eye. He bent down to pick it up. It was her necklace, the one he'd bought before their wedding. A weekend in Rome, an escape from wedding preparations. It was the cheapest thing he'd ever bought her, picked up from a street vendor. But she'd worn it every day since.

The chain had snapped. It draped over his hand, accusing.

Had she torn it off, in her anger at him?

His phone buzzed. A photo message. The number was withheld.

He tapped to open the photo. It showed Anita, curled on

the floor of a grey room. Her mouth was gagged but her eyes were uncovered.

He sank into the sofa, staring at the screen.

His phone buzzed again. A text message this time.

Keep your mouth shut.

CHAPTER FIFTY-EIGHT

Connie lived in Gravelly Hill, on the other side of the city. Zoe drove her to University Station, having first checked there were still trains running.

"It's not late, boss. The last one's at half eleven."

"I'm not going to leave you stranded, am I? You sure you don't want a lift home?"

"Don't be daft. I get the train all the time."

Connie often took the train across town, bringing her bike with her, if the weather wasn't good. Tonight her bike was still parked in town, where she'd left it when she got a flat.

"What you going to do about your bike?" Zoe asked.

"My mum says she'll give me a lift to it in the morning. I've got a repair kit."

Zoe winced at the thought of Connie having to repair her bike before she could cycle to work. "Good luck."

"Don't worry about me."

A train approached the station. "Better go."

"You did good work tonight," Zoe said. "Well done."

CHAPTER FIFTY-EIGHT

"I actually quite enjoyed it, when I stopped being scared."

"DC Solsby said you were very convincing. You'll have him thinking you fancy him next."

Connie grimaced. "Don't." She slammed the car door and ran for the station.

Zoe waited a few minutes to be sure Connie had made the train, then started the car. She swung around the university and towards the Bristol Road, turning right for Selly Oak. But instead of turning into her road, she carried on driving.

Ten minutes later she was outside Mo's house. Catriona opened the door.

"Zoe, good to see you."

"I'm not interrupting anything, am I?"

"He told me you'd be popping in. Fancy a brew?"

"Please." Neither Mo nor Catriona drank coffee, but they did keep some very good Peruvian roast in for when Zoe came round.

She followed Catriona inside and closed the door. The house was quiet, the girls in bed. Zoe slipped off her shoes and left them at the bottom of the stairs with the rest of the pile.

In the kitchen, Mo already had a steaming mug of coffee in front of him, alongside a cup of herbal tea.

"You shouldn't have," Zoe said.

"I know you too well."

"Thanks, Mo." She raised her mug. "And you, Cat."

"My pleasure. I'll be in the dining room. Emails to check."

"You don't have to leave on my account."

"You'll be talking shop. Not my bag." Catriona patted Zoe's arm and left the room.

Mo sat on one of the stools at the large island. "So?"

"So." Zoe sipped her coffee. "Carl hasn't taken us off the Petersen murder..."

"But it's only a matter of time."

"Yeah."

"How much has he told you?"

"You know what it's like. Nothing."

"Hmm. You hear about what happened at the trial today?"

"If you mean me being made a complete prat of—"

"Not that. Randle."

"Oh?"

"That photo. The one of him with Alina Popescu."

Zoe felt her eyes widen, her mouth fall open.

"The CPS barrister had it."

"No." She grabbed the granite to keep herself from toppling off her stool. "How does that help their case against Ian?"

"They also asked Randle if it was him who told Ian to plant the evidence."

"Shit. I assume he denied everything."

"Oh, yes. Claims the photo is innocent too. Didn't know who she was. Certainly didn't know she was a prostitute."

"Has Ian's barrister cross-examined him yet?"

"That's to come tomorrow morning."

"Should be..." She hesitated.

"Explosive."

"Knowing Randle, he'll squirm his way out of it."

"I wouldn't bet on it."

"OK," she said. "So that makes it even more important we find Hamm."

"Hamm?"

"We're off the Starling case. We're about to get booted off Petersen. But the Magpie inquiry is still open. We have reason to be tracking Hamm down."

"We already tried that."

"I say we pick up where we left off. He'll be resting on his laurels."

"Or he could be on the other side of the world by now."

She shook her head. "He's wanted in connection with a terror investigation. There's no way he'll have risked flying."

"You think he's still in the country?"

"I think he's still in the city."

"No way." Mo slid down from his chair and filled the kettle; his mug was empty.

"I'll have another one, too," Zoe said. "If you don't mind."

Mo grabbed the tin of coffee. "The quicker you drink this stuff, the less likely it is to go stale."

"Seriously, there's no one else drinks this?"

"My mum drinks coffee. But she wouldn't know the difference between Nescafé and best Peruvian roast if it smacked her in the face. I keep this for you."

"You're too good to me."

"I know." The kettle boiled and he refilled his mug of tea. He took Zoe's mug and refilled it from the coffee maker.

"So how you gonna find him?" he asked.

"I reckon he'll want to know what's going on with Ian's trial."

"Makes sense. He won't turn up himself."

"But he might send one of his goons."

"They're all in prison, aren't they?"

"There'll be more. We keep an eye out for them. These thugs all look the same. And there's Sheena MacDonald."

"There is. That gym has to be a front for something."

"I sent Connie in there undercover tonight."

Mo put his mug down, spilling tea onto the table. "You did?"

"She was wearing a wire."

"Even riskier."

"I was two minutes away, listening in with Sheila. And she had DC Solsby with her."

"He knows his stuff."

"They put on quite a show." Zoe smiled. "Remind me never to go on a date with Solsby."

"He's fifteen years younger than you."

She shrugged. "You never know... Anyway, they spoke to some guy who was hinting at drugs use in the gym. And MacDonald wanted something from Solsby. She was checking him out."

"They're only letting people join if they're buying."

"Or selling."

"Connie will stick out like a sore thumb."

"As Solsby's girlfriend, she was pretty convincing. But they didn't see anything tangible."

"You can't send them back. MacDonald will have been warned."

"One more time. We wait a couple of days first."

"Even more time for her to twig who they are."

Zoe ran her finger around the rim of her mug. "You're right. OK, we send them back tomorrow. I'll talk to Sheila."

"Are you sure?"

"We have to find him, Mo. Tell me, how did you get on with the grieving widow?"

Mo shook his head. "Don't joke."

"She did stay married to a man who was arrested for child sex abuse."

CHAPTER FIFTY-EIGHT

"She was devastated."

"By him raping kids, or dying?"

Mo eyed her. "Dying. Her reaction wasn't faked. It isn't a domestic."

"In which case it might have something to do with our old friend Trevor Hamm."

"It might," Mo conceded.

"OK. I'll talk to Dawson in the morning. Our priority is finding him. Now we've got MacDonald and the gym, and the attraction of the trial, we're closer to finding him than we have been for weeks."

"You're going to talk to Dawson?"

"After the week I'm having, I need official backing for this."

"And he can take the fall when it all goes tits-up."

"I wasn't thinking like that. Dawson's surprised me with this case. He's supported me, let me do stuff I didn't think he would. I want to bring him in."

"And you'll get a bollocking if you don't."

She grinned at him over her coffee. "There is that."

CHAPTER FIFTY-NINE

THE HOUSE WAS QUIET, a looming hulk of darkness in the already gloomy sky. Randle waited for a moment, hidden by a prickly hedge.

He watched the house, trying to ignore the hedge that was scratching his face. No sign of movement.

This was the last known address of Trevor Hamm. The man himself hadn't been here since they'd rounded up his associates after the brothel in Hall Green had been exposed. But it didn't mean there weren't clues here to where he might be now.

Randle disentangled himself from the hedge and padded to the side of the house. He was dressed in trainers, black jeans and a black parka he hadn't worn for years. He pulled up the hood as he approached the house, wondering what Carl Whaley would say if he saw him now.

For all he knew, this was Carl Whaley's fault. How many people knew he'd started to cut a deal with PSD? Whaley, Rogers. And that DS he'd brought in with him as a witness. Randle hadn't even made a note of her name.

He'd need to rectify that.

He slid round the side of the building. There were no windows on this wall, and the hedge brushed up against the brickwork. He pushed through the thick foliage, cursing the barbs catching on his clothes.

At last he emerged onto a wide patio with views over the countryside. In the distance he could see the lights of the M42.

The back of the house boasted wide bifold doors. If there was anyone in there, they'd spot him as soon as he came near them.

He was confident there was no one inside, but it was best to play safe. He kept to the line of the hedge and continued down the garden, careful not to disturb the foliage too much.

When he was twenty metres away from the house, he reached into his pocket. He'd bought a night vision telescope online a few months ago. This was only its third outing.

He raised it to his eye and scanned the back windows. There were no curtains at the bifolds and the upstairs curtains were open. He squinted, trying to get a view into the rooms.

If someone was in there, they weren't at the window, watching him.

Randle slipped back along the edge of the lawn, raising the scope from time to time. Still no movement. Back at the house, he slid along the back wall until he came to the first set of doors.

These were modern aluminium doors. Expensive. There was no way he was getting them open. But there might be a side door on the opposite end of the building. He had skeleton keys with him.

He held his breath and stepped out past the edge of the

door, waiting for someone to shout out from inside. He wondered if there was an alarm, a hidden camera.

It was too late to worry about that kind of thing.

Silence.

He reached the opposite end of the doors – they had to be four metres long – and stopped to pull in breath. He was sweating. He shouldn't have worn the damn parka.

Past a second set of doors, he rounded a corner. Sure enough, there was a side door. Leading into a utility room, most likely, or a boot room. He'd looked into the kitchen as he passed it and the door leading out of that was internal, wooden.

He took out his set of keys and fiddled with the lock. It wasn't the easiest to break: Hamm had the money for a good locksmith. But after a couple of minutes he had it open.

He stepped inside and pulled the door closed behind him. He considered slipping off his trainers. No: they were soft-soled, and the floors in this house would be solidly made.

Now he was in a laundry room, pegs on the wall and a gleaming washer and dryer side by side beneath a white granite worktop. The hooks were bare. The shelf below them held no boots.

If Hamm had fled this place in a hurry, someone had come along afterwards to clean up. This was nothing new: Zoe had searched Hamm's flat near Cannon Hill Park when they were looking for Ian's kids, and it had been just as empty.

He gripped the handle of the door ahead and turned it slowly. He emerged into a vast kitchen. Dim light from the back doors reflected off the gleaming surfaces. He opened a drawer: empty.

CHAPTER FIFTY-NINE

This was hopeless.

Leaning against the counter, he stopped to think. He'd visited this place, just the once. Hamm had invited him for dinner. His Romanian girlfriend had been here, the one whose sister had died. Randle still felt bad about that. But he didn't even know the girl had a sister; what was he supposed to do about it?

There'd been a safe, in the study. He'd seen Hamm opening it after dinner, carelessly not closing the door behind him.

The study was at the front of the house.

He crept through the kitchen and into the hallway. Which side was the study on?

Beyond the door to his left, he found a bathroom. Not that one.

He opened another door: this was it. A single painting hung on the chimney breast, over the mantelpiece. It was two metres square, a modern landscape.

He stared at the painting, his breath short. This was the Diebenkorn that had been taken from Bryn Jackson's house on the night of his murder. The painting they'd suspected Hamm of staging a burglary to get rid of.

It was the only painting in the house. The hallway was devoid of decoration, and the living space adjoining the kitchen had been stripped bare, too.

Had it been left here for safekeeping, hidden in plain sight? Or was it just here to hide the safe?

Randle lifted the painting off the wall, careful not to mishandle it. He leaned it against the wall and turned back to the chimney breast.

He placed his ear against the safe. He'd seen this done in

movies, but had no idea how it worked. He turned the handle on the left and pulled. Nothing. He spun the dial in the centre a couple of times, then tried again.

Still nothing.

If Hamm had left the painting here, then chances were that the safe wasn't empty.

He stared at it as if he might open it by sheer force of will.

He knew people who could crack safes. Trouble was, they worked for Hamm.

A light shone outside. A car was pulling into the drive, headlights sweeping across the front of the house. Randle dropped to the floor. Had they seen him?

He crawled to the window. The door to the hallway was still open.

Did he have time to get out of the building?

Did he even want to?

He'd come here to speak to Hamm. It looked like that mission was about to be accomplished.

But being caught breaking into the man's house? Taking down a painting and trying to open a safe?

They'd kill him.

He scooted along the floor to the hallway, skidding as he rounded the corner. He had to hope the darkness inside meant they couldn't see him.

He darted into the kitchen and ran for the utility room.

As he reached it, he stopped.

His car. He'd left it along the road, parked partway into a ditch.

Had they seen it?

If they had, they would be waiting for him. Even if they hadn't, they might still be waiting for him. He had to get out.

CHAPTER FIFTY-NINE

He gritted his teeth as he turned the handle of the outer door. No one beyond it, thank God. He eased it closed behind him and leaned against the wall, panting. He'd wait until they were inside, and then he'd watch them.

CHAPTER SIXTY

"Hey." Zoe put a hand on Nicholas's shoulder and gave it a squeeze. "Anything good?"

He waved the remote at the TV. "Natural history. You'd hate it."

"I might surprise you." She flung her jacket on the arm of the sofa, ignoring his wince, and plonked herself down next to him.

"Tough day?" he asked.

"No more than usual. OK, maybe a bit more than usual. Kicked off one case, all but kicked off a second, and now we're back to..."

"Back to what?"

"I don't want to bring you into it."

"It's fine, Mum. It's not like you telling me will make some nutter more likely to go after me."

"We're not talking about the Digbeth Ripper here, Nicholas. These are serious people."

He shivered. "Sounds like *you* need to watch out. Did you manage to speak to Gran?"

Zoe sucked her teeth. "No." She checked her watch: past eleven. "Too late to ring her now."

"She keeps even later hours than you." Nicholas leaned forward to grab his mug of tea from the coffee table.

"I'll try. But it's your fault if she yells at me cos I woke her up."

He grinned and settled back into the sofa. Zoe took out her phone.

Annette's phone rang out. Zoe waited for ten rings then hung up.

"No answer."

"Maybe she's asleep," said Nicholas.

"Or..."

"She isn't always drunk, Mum. You're too hard on her."

Zoe rubbed her nose. Maybe she was, maybe she wasn't.

"If she had to go to the hospital, maybe she isn't well," suggested Nicholas.

"It was just a routine check-up. She's not ill."

"OK." He yawned. "Anyway, I'm off to bed. Got an assessment in the morning."

"You have them every bloody week."

"Tell me about it." He took his mug into the kitchen. Zoe listened, her eyes closed, as he ran the tap to rinse it out.

"Night." He passed through the living room and towards the stairs. Zoe stretched out on the sofa while the sounds of him going to bed rang through the building: footsteps on the stairs, the bathroom door opening, water running, then his bedroom door closing.

She glanced at her phone. Should she try her mum again?

No. If she's asleep, don't disturb her. She could try again tomorrow. Not too early though: Annette didn't do mornings.

She hauled herself up from the sofa and followed Nicholas up the stairs, wishing she hadn't stayed out so late.

CHAPTER SIXTY-ONE

Anita lay in the confined space, her legs and back repeatedly bumping up against a hard surface whenever she moved. Something was sticking into her shoulder, jabbing her again and again. She closed her eyes every time the car went over a bump, holding her breath and praying she'd be let out soon.

She knew that getting out of the car boot they'd put her in could lead to worse than this. But right now, this was torture.

The car rounded one bend, then another, taking both tightly. She tensed her muscles to brace herself against the jolts. The car slowed and stopped.

She could barely breathe: they'd taped up her mouth. Her hands were tied behind her back and her knees were drawn up to fit in the confined space. Every muscle in her body screamed at her.

But the pain was nothing. The fear for her own safety, her own life. All of it was nothing against her fear for the girls.

They'd both been upstairs in their rooms. Had her attacker known she wasn't alone? Had he been watching? Carly had come downstairs, getting that ice cream Anita had disapproved of. Maria had stayed in her room.

Please God, let him not have seen them. Let him have left them alone.

What was the last thing she'd said to each of them? Something about the inappropriateness of the ice cream to Carly. She'd offered Maria a snack, she couldn't remember if she'd fetched it before falling asleep.

Was that how they'd remember her?

The boot opened above her upturned face. She screwed up her face, trying to call out through the gag. Something hard and heavy hit her cheek.

"Shut the fuck up, bitch."

She whimpered. Blood ran down her cheek, warm and wet. It oozed into the creases of her neck.

She opened her eyes. She'd been blindfolded, but she could make out dim light behind the fabric. Street lights, maybe, or the lights from a house. She struggled against the ropes on her wrists.

"Stop it." Another blow to her cheek. Anita screamed in pain; she wondered if it was broken.

She gulped in what breath she could, worrying she might choke. A shadow fell over her and she felt a hand grab her under the arm. Two pairs of hands hauled her up and out of the boot. One at her shoulders, another at her knees. She kicked out and was rewarded with a slap.

Cool air brushed her skin. Within moments they'd have her indoors.

She wriggled in her captors' grip, doing her best to scream. Nothing but a muffled gasp came out.

CHAPTER SIXTY-ONE

Try again.

She closed her eyes, took the deepest breath she could, and yelled for all she was worth. Or attempted to.

"Shut the fuck up." She felt something being wrapped around her lower face; more tape. No, it was some kind of bandage. Either way, she could barely breathe. She decided to stop screaming.

Listen. Maybe she could work out where they'd taken her. Maybe she'd hear them getting the girls out of another vehicle. *Please, no.* She tried to push the sensation of movement away, to ignore her feet dragging against tarmac.

The tarmac. It was rough, with ridges and bumps. Not a road, then. A car park, or driveway?

Focus on the smells, she told herself. Anita had a good sense of smell; when the girls were young she'd been able to detect a dirty nappy as soon as she walked through the door. There was a smell of greenery. Trees, or bushes. Her guess was confirmed when she felt foliage hit her leg. She kicked out against it and her foot hit something hard. A tree trunk, maybe.

Was she in the countryside? She could hear the hum of traffic behind her but she couldn't hear birds. It was late, though; birds would be asleep.

Anita threw her focus outwards, her ears straining. She could hear rustling. Animals, or the men?

A door slammed and a light came on above her head, faint through the blindfold. If she didn't call out now, it would be too late.

She kicked and let out another muffled scream. This was useless. They could be miles from anywhere. No one could hear her, no one knew where she was.

She was propelled forward and dumped on the floor. She

heard a door shut behind her. A foot hit the back of her neck, making her writhe in pain.

"Now, bitch. Just do as you're told and we won't hurt you." The man's voice was local, a Brummie accent. There was a singsong quality to it. Anita didn't recognise it.

Don't hurt me. Don't hurt my girls, she thought. She consoled herself with the fact that they'd closed the door immediately after bringing her in. She hadn't heard other female voices, and no one else had been brought in after her.

She was lifted by the armpits again and dragged up a flight of stairs. Her back bounced off the steps.

She would be black and blue in the morning. If she was still alive.

CHAPTER SIXTY-TWO

Randle buried himself in the prickly hedge to the side of the house, watching the car. He was parallel with the side door. At least it was dark here.

The car sat for a while, the driver not emerging. Randle's chest rose and fell, his heart racing. He wasn't used to exertion. As a superintendent, he spent his working life behind a desk these days and the closest he got to exercise was when Anita forced him to take a canal walk.

He longed for one of those walks now. He'd never refuse her again.

The driver's door opened and someone got out. David pulled the night vision scope to his eye. It was a woman, dressed in a long coat, hair piled on top of her head. She had a prim expression, as if she disapproved of everything around her.

He flicked the scope's focus back to the car, wondering whether this woman was alone. The car was still.

She strode towards the house. Randle heard her tapping

a code into a pad. He edged towards the front of the house to see, careful not to disturb the foliage that shaded him.

He heard a long beep and then a door closing. A dim light shone out through the side door. He ran his mind over the route he'd taken through the house.

He'd moved the painting in the study, tampered with the safe. The room was in view of the front drive and he hadn't dared replace the painting.

Whoever she was, she would know someone had broken in within moments. She didn't seem to have Anita with her.

He had to get out of here.

He slid along the hedge and past the woman's car – a black BMW, nice. He bent to check inside; no one there.

Who was this woman? Was she an associate of Hamm's? His new girlfriend?

He would go back to his car. If it took all night, he would wait and watch.

Damn. He couldn't. He'd left Carly in charge, told both girls to go to sleep. He'd made an excuse about their mother, telling them she'd gone out to the shops. He'd seen the look in Carly's eyes; she'd known he was lying.

He had to go home.

As Randle reached the bottom of the driveway he turned to see the light come on in the study. The woman stepped towards the chimney breast. She bent down and held up the painting, her gaze moving between that and the safe. She put it down and went to the window.

She couldn't see him, all the way down here in the dark. But he had to go home. He could check the HOLMES database, find out who she was. If she was one of Hamm's people, chances were, she would have a record.

CHAPTER SIXTY-TWO

He took one last look back at the study – empty, light switched off – and ran for his car.

CHAPTER SIXTY-THREE

Zoe sat at the lights between the Bristol Road and Edgbaston Park Road, stifling a yawn. She'd slept badly, thoughts of her conversation with Carl running through her head. She'd had a dream in which she'd been kissing him and he'd morphed into her mum. The memory made her shudder.

She hit hands-free on her phone. It rang out: he wasn't picking up.

"Carl, it's me. I just wanted to talk. We're supposed to be working together, we can do better than this. Give me a call, yeah?"

The traffic started up again and she drove to the office in silence, thoughts whirling. She had no idea what she would be confronted with when she arrived.

Mo and Rhodri were already in. For once, Connie was the last to arrive.

"You heard from Connie?" Mo said.

"She needs to pick up her bike. She got a flat."

CHAPTER SIXTY-THREE

The door opened and Connie hurried in, out of breath. "Sorry!"

"It's fine," said Zoe. It was only 7:48 am. "Bike OK?"

Connie nodded. "I brought it on the bus. Too much hassle to replace the tyre on the street."

"I'd have given you a lift, if you'd—"

"Not with my bike. But thanks. I appreciate it." Connie thudded into her chair and pushed hair out of her eyes. Rhodri looked at her with a grimace and she stuck her tongue out at him.

"Right," said Zoe. "Mo and I have been thinking about the gym and we reckon it's best to go back today."

"So soon?" Connie said. "I thought you said it was safest to wait."

"I don't want to give them time to clear the place out. Sheila's on her way, and DC Solsby. Mo's going to be your backup this time."

"I am?" he asked.

"I want to go to the Crown Court. I'm sure Hamm will turn up, or he'll send one of his minions."

"*And* you want to see what happens when Randle is cross-examined by the defence barrister," Mo added.

"There is that. Do we have anything else pointing to Hamm's whereabouts?"

"He's still got the house outside Solihull," Rhodri said. "It was left empty after we raided the brothel."

"Check that out, just in case."

"He won't be there," Mo said. "He's got a dozen addresses."

"In that case, we check them too."

"The ones we know about," said Rhodri.

"It's a start," Zoe replied. "Talk to Uniform. See if a local patrol car can swing past each of them. Have a sniff around, let us know if there's signs of use."

"No problem." Rhodri scribbled in his pad.

"I want to talk to his goons, as well," she said. "Simon Adams and Adam Fulmer are both in Winson Green. Let's give them a visit."

"Who d'you want to do that?" Mo asked. "I'll be at the gym, with Connie. Rhod's—"

"The gym doesn't open until two pm."

"Fair enough. I'll call the prison."

"Don't call ahead. We turn up, don't give them the chance to tell anyone we're coming."

"Who would they tell?"

"Hamm'll have plenty of contacts inside that place. We'll get nothing if they're prepared."

"Right. Connie, you can come with me."

"Be right with you, Sarge."

"Good," said Zoe. "I'm going to talk to Dawson about the gym. I'd rather go there officially, save time with all this undercover stuff."

"What's the hurry?" asked Mo.

"We don't know how long the trial will go on. He'll disappear once that's out of the way."

The door to the team room opened: Sheila.

"Morning," said Zoe. "Any news?"

"This isn't about the gym."

"OK."

Sheila had DC Solsby with her. He gave Connie a wink as the two of them approached Zoe.

Sheila took a photo out of a folder and handed it to Zoe. "Another body."

Zoe turned the photo in her hands. It was of a man,

greying skin flaked off by water damage. She didn't recognise him, but that wasn't surprising given the fact that half of his facial skin was gone and his eye sockets were empty. "Who?"

"We can't be sure of his identity, but we do recognise his tattoo." Sheila handed over another photo. This one showed a close up of the back of a man's hand. The skin had fallen off in places but parts of a tattoo remained. It looked a lot like the bull symbol from the previous two murders.

Zoe peered at the photos. "Where did you find him?"

"Local CID in Edgbaston got a call. He was dragged out of Edgbaston Reservoir overnight. I think I recognise him, Zoe."

"Go on."

"Name's Jukes. Two of my team were watching him until three weeks ago. We'll have to check forensics, I could be wrong with the state he's in. But I'm pretty sure he's the ringleader of this gang." She pointed to the tattoo.

"Three weeks ago, you say?"

"We lost him. Assumed he'd rumbled us."

"But he could have been dead."

"He could," Sheila agreed.

"So if he's dead, who killed Starling and Petersen?"

"My question exactly."

CHAPTER SIXTY-FOUR

Anita could barely move her leg, it was so stiff. They'd dropped her with her knee bent beneath her and she was worried she'd injured it.

Tape still covered her mouth and a blindfold obscured her sight. They'd replaced the tape after dragging her up the stairs and dumping her in this room. She'd tried to cry out when they'd ripped off the original one, but one of the men had pressed down on her shoulders, pushing her into the floor. She'd stopped when she felt like he might push the breath out of her.

It was hours she'd been alone. It had been just gone ten when she'd woken up in the living room. And now she could see daylight through the blindfold. What time was dawn in April? 5:00 am, 5:30 am? Anita never paid attention to that sort of thing. If it was 5:30, she'd been gone for over seven hours.

She shuffled into the wall beside her, lifting her fingers to brush them against the surface. It was smooth. So she was in an inhabited building, not an outhouse or a shed. She knew that already from the smell: fresh paint. Beneath her was a wooden floor. She could be in a house.

She scooted along the wall, keeping her fingers against it. She didn't dare venture out into the middle of the room, with her blindfold on. There could be someone out there, watching her. She shuddered at the thought.

She came to a corner. She explored the wall with her fingers, contemplating standing up. But she knew she would collapse if she tried. She couldn't trust her knee to hold her.

Rounding the corner, she continued. After two feet or so she came to a window. She hauled herself up so she was kneeling, wincing at the pain. She turned away from the window so she could reach behind her and run her fingertips across the windowsill.

It was bare. Cold, and bare. So this house, if it was a house, was uninhabited. There were no objects on the windowsill, no sign of curtains.

Anita pressed her fingers against the glass: cold. How much effort would it take to break the glass? Was it even possible?

Anita thought of David, all his police training. He would know things like this. He would know what to do if he was captured. But here she was, silent and helpless.

David, where are you? He'd stayed out after giving his evidence. He'd been revealed as knowing the New Street bomber. Had they taken him, too?

And where were the girls?

Tears slid down her cheeks. She had to know if the girls were safe. She didn't care what these bastards did to her, so long as they didn't hurt her girls.

She faced into the room and pulled in her lips, trying to distance them from the gag.

"Hello?" she mumbled. "Is there someone here?"

No answer. Anita thumped her fist against the windowsill. She wanted to scream and shout and barge her way out of here. But at the same time, she wanted to collapse into a wrecked heap of bones and blubber on the floor. Did she have the strength to fight her way out of here? Would that even be an option?

She sank to the floor. Her legs shook. She had to conserve her strength. Someone would come eventually. To feed her, or to kill her. Either way, they would come.

CHAPTER SIXTY-FIVE

IAN STARED up at the judge's bench, wondering how long it would be before his old boss strolled in. The man had a way of carrying himself, an insouciance that was always there no matter how extreme the circumstances. He'd seen him in a room full of organised criminals, both of them knowing how likely it was they were armed, but Randle had behaved as if he was at a dinner party or a case meeting, utterly unruffled.

Yesterday afternoon, Ian had seen a chink in that platinum-plated armour. When the CPS barrister had asked if Randle had told Ian to plant the explosives, there'd been the barest of tics. Ian had only noticed because he was looking for it. But then when the photo had come out...

Randle had paled. The perma-tanned, immaculately moisturised skin had changed colour. The superintendent had looked, briefly, as if he might lose his temper. Then he'd composed himself, taking two visible breaths, and turned to the judge as the adjournment was announced.

Ian could only imagine what the press response would have been like outside those doors. Head of Force CID, photographed with the woman who'd detonated the New Street bomb.

Jane, his solicitor, was looking nervy. She kept looking up at the clock above the judge's high desk and frowning at his barrister. Proceedings were due to start in fifteen minutes. And they would be picking up where they'd left off yesterday.

Ian wasn't sure if he was relishing it, or not. Randle was his boss, in more senses than one. He'd protected Ian when PSD had brought him in after his kids went missing. He'd smoothed the waters with Hamm, meaning Ian's roof had been finished and he wasn't constantly in fear of Alison and the kids disappearing.

But Ian had had no idea about the woman. If Randle had known her, had he been told about the attack?

Ian hadn't known they were planning an attack on the station. He hadn't known about the airport until Randle called him and told him to get down there asap.

Randle, Ian was beginning to believe, deserved everything that was coming to him. The only problem was that if Randle went down, he would take Ian with him.

Alison was in the gallery, sitting halfway back as she had every day so far. She avoided his eye, but he was grateful she'd come. He wondered what she'd told her boss at the school. Although everyone in the city knew about this trial. Not much point in lying.

Jane approached him, her expression tight.

"What's up?" he asked.

"We've just had notice from the clerk. He's not coming."

"Randle?"

"Called to a major investigation, apparently."

"That's convenient." Trust David Randle to slip out of

this. But Ian knew the court had the power to override his police duties.

He glanced up at the judge, who was talking to one of the clerks. He didn't look pleased.

"He'll be here," Jane said. "They'll compel him."

Ian nodded. "So what happens in the meantime?"

"Forensic evidence," she said. "The jury isn't going to get the treat it was expecting this morning, after all."

CHAPTER SIXTY-SIX

"OK," said Zoe. "This changes things with the gym. Mo and Connie, stick with the plan to interview Adams and Fulmer. I'll talk to Dawson. But first I'm going to the reservoir."

"What about the trial, boss?" Rhodri asked.

She sighed. Was there really a chance Hamm would be there?

"I know someone else who'll be there. I'll call him."

Mo gave her a puzzled look which she chose to ignore.

"Go on, then," she urged. "Get moving."

Mo grabbed his jacket from the back of his chair and gestured for Connie to follow him. Rhodri buried his head in his computer.

"We'll go in separate cars," Zoe told Sheila. "I'll see you there."

Sheila nodded and left the room.

Zoe gave Rhodri a wary smile then looked into her office. She needed to make a call, and soon.

She shook herself out. She'd do it from the car.

CHAPTER SIXTY-SIX

"See you later, Rhod. Let me know if anything turns up."

"Right, boss."

The reservoir wasn't far from Harborne police station: a ten-minute drive. Zoe dialled as soon as she was out of the gates.

"Zoe."

"Morning, Carl."

He yawned. "Everything OK?"

"I've got a crime scene to go to. Will you be at the trial today?"

"Already there. Why?"

"I need someone to keep an eye out for Hamm."

"He's not going to be so stupid as to—"

"Maybe not Hamm himself. But his people. He'll want to know what's been said, if he's being implicated."

"Of course he'll be implicated."

"Have you heard his name being mentioned?"

"Zoe, I haven't been into the court room yet. Today's my first day."

"Because of what Randle did yesterday."

He ignored that. "Why are you back on Hamm, anyway?"

"Magpie is still an open investigation. I've got reason to believe he's in the city."

"On what grounds?"

The traffic ground to a halt as she approached the lights with the Hagley Road. Zoe gritted her teeth, her foot hovering over the accelerator.

"On what basis, Zoe?"

"He's going to want to know what's going on with Ian's

trial. And there's no sign of him having left the country. I think he's local. And now the ringleader of a rival gang has turned up dead."

The traffic started up again. Zoe shuffled forward, almost hitting the car in front. *Calm down.*

"You're just using this as an excuse to watch Randle," Carl said.

"I'm SIO on Magpie and Hamm is a person of interest."

"So is Randle, now that photo's come out."

"Did he finish giving his evidence?" she asked.

"The judge ordered an adjournment after he'd been questioned by the CPS. Today is cross examination by Ian's brief."

"Which should be interesting."

"Zoe. Don't get involved. If we need information from you, we'll get it formally. My boss is going to be in touch."

Don't I know it. Zoe had nothing to tell PSD that she hadn't already discussed with Carl. As long as they weren't questioning her about her own conduct...

She prodded the accelerator as the lights turned green.

"I understand," she said. "But please. Just keep an eye out for me."

"He won't be there."

"His people will be."

"How am I supposed to spot them?"

"You're a PSD officer. I imagine you've got a finely tuned nose for people who are out of place."

"I'll be busy doing my job, Zoe. But I'll tell you if I see anything that alerts my suspicion."

"Thanks."

"See you later." He hung up.

She was almost at the reservoir. She swung onto a pockmarked patch of tarmac masquerading as a car park, every nerve firing. Talking to Carl was becoming more and more stressful lately.

She forced herself to take three deep breaths then plastered on a neutral expression and left the car. A forensics tent had been erected near the water and white-suited techs walked back and forth between that and a van.

Zoe approached the tent. Sheila was inside, with Adi. He stood up and smiled at her.

"I was hoping we'd see you here."

"Hi, Adi. What we got?"

"White male, early thirties. Tattoos across his shoulders and on his forearms. Including that." Adi pointed at the partial tattoo on the back of the man's hand. It was faded from water damage and parts of it were missing where his skin had flaked away. But it was unmistakably the bull in a ring.

"The first victim, it was scratched on the wall," Zoe said. "The second, on a badge. With this one having a tattoo..."

"It means he's a member of the gang," said Sheila. "Marked for life."

Zoe nodded. "So he was killed by another gang? Or an internal feud?"

"We don't know enough about this gang to tell," Sheila said. "They only came to our attention before Christmas. They're nasty. Not as wide-reaching as Hamm, from what we can tell. But there's a vicious streak. Look at the lacerations on his chest."

Adi pushed the body slightly sideways and Zoe crouched to get a better view. Adi used a plastic stick to push the man's torn hoody aside so she could see his skin.

His chest had been given the same marking as his hand.

Only this time, it had been done not with a tattooist's needle, but with a knife.

"Is that the cause of death?" Zoe asked.

"Pathologist is on her way," Adi said. "We'll know then. But from what I can see, he didn't drown. Mouth is clean."

Zoe nodded. "I'm trying to work out the sequence of events. How long do we think he was in the water?"

"Again, you'd have to ask Adana," Adi told her. "More than a few days."

"If he was killed before the other two, then could those killings have been revenge? His gang members, leaving their calling cards?"

"Why would they avenge his death by killing a suspended police detective and a man who got away with child abuse?" Sheila asked.

"Petersen was associated with Hamm. Hamm provided the kids to him and his mates. If someone was pissed off with Hamm, they might kill Petersen to send him a message."

"But Petersen's been wearing an ankle bracelet for months now. He won't have been anywhere near Hamm."

"That might not matter."

"What about Starling?" asked Sheila.

Zoe stood. Her legs had seized up. She shook them out, cursing under her breath. "How much do you know about the Starling case, Sheila?"

"Not much. It's PSD's."

"Me neither. But my team were there at the beginning. Mo was with Adi when..." She turned to Adi. "Have they identified a suspect yet?"

He raised his hands. "I'm saying nothing."

"You've been processing the forensics. If evidence had been found, you'd know."

He shook his head. "Not again, Zoe. I can't."

"Someone has to join the dots. We've got Petersen, who I investigated as part of Canary. Starling, whose murder my team was originally assigned to. And now this guy. If I'm not going to put it together, who is?"

"We need to send this higher up the food chain," said Sheila.

Zoe grabbed her arm. "Your team was watching this guy. You want to give up the investigation into his murder, just like that?"

"Sometimes it's best to—"

Zoe let go. "If I send this up the chain, it'll go to Randle. You'll have heard about what happened in court yesterday."

Sheila paled. "He's still Head of Force CID."

"He's connected to Hamm. He knew Alina Popescu. We keep this away from him."

"I'm not getting involved in any of this," said Adi. "I'd prefer it if you left my tent."

"Sorry, Adi." Zoe knew how awkward this was for him. He wasn't a police officer, and he didn't belong to any one team. He had to work with everyone, with no bias. She pulled up the flap to the tent.

Adana was heading their way, kit bag in hand. Zoe bit her lip as she waited for the pathologist to reach them.

"Sorry I'm late," she said. "Domestic snafu. What have we got?"

Adi gestured for the pathologist to enter the tent. He gave Zoe a sharp look, which Adana caught. She frowned at Zoe who shook her head.

Clearing her throat, Adana crouched to get closer to the body.

"I'll see you ladies later," Adi said, throwing another stern look Zoe's way.

"We need to know what the pathologist determines," Sheila told him.

"Very well." He looked at Zoe. "But focus on *this* victim, alright? While you're in my tent."

Adana raised an eyebrow but didn't look up from the body. She leaned over to examine inside his mouth.

"He's been dead at least two weeks," she said. She looked through the gap in the opposite side of the tent, towards the reservoir. "Good place to dump someone. And he didn't drown."

"How do—" began Zoe.

Adana put up a hand. "See his airways? They're clean. Drowning victims tend to have froth in their respiratory tract. There's no sign of internal swelling, that you'd get with pleural fluid accumulation. There's water in his system, yes, but he didn't gasp it in. It could be this wound on his chest that killed him – there would have been a lot of bleeding. What is it, anyway?"

"It's a callsign," said Sheila. "A gang."

Adana's brow furrowed.

"How d'you know he's been dead that long?" Zoe asked.

"There's gloving on his feet and fingers. Where the skin has come away in one intact sheet. And this... Adi, does this look familiar to you?"

She reached into the victim's mouth with a plastic implement and brought out a mass of gloopy material.

"That's frogspawn," he said.

"Which forms in February and March. The reservoir is clear of it now. It means he's been in this water since at least the end of March. Possibly earlier."

Zoe exchanged a glance with Sheila. "He died first. Before Starling. Before Petersen."

Sheila nodded. "Question is, did the other deaths happen because of it?"

CHAPTER SIXTY-SEVEN

ZOE DROVE BACK to the office, struggling to get the image of Jukes's body out of her mind. Two weeks or more submerged in water took its toll on a corpse.

If he was the ringleader of a new gang and he'd been dead that long, then who had killed Starling and Petersen? Had someone else in the group risen up to take his place and give the orders? Or had they been subsumed into another group? If so, which? And how was Howard Petersen mixed up in it all?

They needed to talk to Mrs Petersen again, not that she was saying anything. And Mo's chat with Adams and Fulmer could be helpful.

She parked outside the office and hurried in, anxious to find Sheila and start tracing Jukes's movements in the days leading up to his death. As she passed the front desk, Sergeant Jenner stopped her.

"Ma'am, there's been a call from the hospital for you."

"The pathologist?"

CHAPTER SIXTY-SEVEN

His face darkened. "They didn't say. Said they could only speak to you. I gave the details to DC Hughes."

"Thanks." She walked towards the office, wondering why Adana was being so mysterious. She'd left the pathologist at the crime scene, in which case who was calling from the hospital?

Rhodri turned in his chair as Zoe entered the office. "Boss, there's an urgent call for you." He held out a post-it note.

"Adana's being bloody efficient today." Zoe opened the door to her private office, wondering what the initial post-mortem examination would reveal. She dialled the number.

"City Hospital, which department do you need?"

"I've been told to call this number. My name's Zoe Finch, Force CID."

"Hang on a minute... yes. Please hold."

Before Zoe had the chance to find out what she was holding for, on-hold music kicked in. Adana had her mobile number, she clearly hadn't given it to whichever of her team needed to get in touch.

"City Hospital morgue, can I help you?"

Zo breathed a sigh of relief. So it was Adana.

"It's DI Finch here, Force CID. I've got a message to give you a call."

"DI Finch?"

"Yes. Is the message from Doctor Adebayo?"

"She's out on a job right now... is that Zoe Finch?"

"Yes." Zoe tapped her foot. Rhodri looked in through the glass and Zoe gave him a smile which he returned with a brief wave, then dropped his hand, embarrassed.

"Are you the daughter of Annette Finch?"

Zoe's foot stopped tapping. "Yes."

"I'm very sorry to tell you this. I'm afraid your mother's passed away."

"Sorry?"

"Mrs Annette Finch." The man read out an address: it matched. "We identified her through her bus pass records."

"Hang on, when did this happen? When was she admitted?" Annette had had a routine checkup at the Queen Elizabeth hospital yesterday. Had she suffered another stroke?

"She was brought in to A&E yesterday afternoon after a collision with a car. I'm so sorry."

Zoe sank into her chair. Her head felt light.

"She... was she dead when they brought her in?"

"She was unconscious, it says on the report. I don't think she suffered, Ms Finch."

"DI Finch." Zoe swallowed. Her mum, dead? In a collision with a car?

"Had she been drinking?" she asked.

"I don't know the answer to that, I'm afraid. There was nothing untoward about her death, but we have to do a post-mortem on all vehicle deaths so..."

"Yes."

The door opened. "You OK, boss?" Rhodri asked.

Zoe stared up at him and nodded. "My mum."

Rhodri approached her, his movements awkward. "She OK?"

Zoe shook her head and spoke to the man from the morgue. "I want you to send the PM results to Force CID at Harborne Police station when you have them. Please."

"Is Mrs Finch part of a criminal investigation?"

"I'm a Detective Inspector. I work closely with Dr Adebayo. Just send the report, yes?"

"Right. Er, yes."

CHAPTER SIXTY-SEVEN

Zoe hung up. She threw her phone onto the desk like it was alight.

Rhodri stood over her. "You've gone white, boss."

"Oh my God." Zoe's hand went to her mouth. "The traffic me and Connie sat in in town yesterday afternoon. I read in the news, there was a crash. An elderly woman..." She shoved her fist into her mouth. "The stupid idiot."

"Is... was... the elderly woman..." Rhodri asked. "Was it your mum?"

Zoe nodded. "She's dead."

Annette Finch had lived through decades of abusing her body. She'd come closer to death than Zoe liked to think about. And now, hit by a car?

She'd been drunk, surely. She'd been nervous about the appointment, she'd stopped off in the pub, and she hadn't looked before stepping into the road.

Zoe ground her fist into the desk. "Stupid bitch."

"Are you sure that's how you want to...?"

Zoe's vision was cloudy. "It was always going to happen, eventually. But how am I going to tell Nicholas?"

CHAPTER SIXTY-EIGHT

"Report back to me if anything new emerges," said Detective Superintendent Rogers.

"Sir," replied Carl. He was standing outside the Crown Court, enjoying some rare sunshine. The trial had adjourned for lunch and he was waiting for the afternoon session. He'd sat through the morning's forensic evidence, not learning anything he didn't already know, and wondering where the hell David Randle was.

Rogers had no idea either. He'd called Randle's office in Lloyd House but his secretary had been cagey, insisting she could only take messages at this time.

Had he gone to ground? After that photo had been revealed yesterday, had David Randle decided to make a run for it?

He was a damn coward if he had. People were dead because of his actions and all he could do was flee.

"OK. I hope more comes to light this afternoon," said Rogers. "Otherwise I think we'll have to recall you to the office."

"I'd rather stay here and observe."

"I bet you would. Nice easy work."

"It's not like that."

Rogers chuckled. "Don't worry, DI Whaley. I'm not accusing you of laziness. Just tell me as soon as you have anything to report, yes?"

"Of course."

Carl hung up. He had twenty minutes before the trial resumed. Time for a sandwich. He ran to a Greggs and grabbed a meal deal. He perched on a wall and opened the sandwich.

As he ate, Carl scanned the crowds. Zoe was convinced Hamm would either be here, or would have sent someone. Carl hadn't been directly involved in the Canary case, so he wouldn't recognise Hamm's associates. Should he have asked Zoe to send him photos?

No. She was reaching. Hamm was miles away, if he knew what was good for him. Carl's job here was to focus on the trial. To listen for any evidence that might help them with Jackdaw.

He tossed the sandwich wrapper into a nearby bin and walked back to the court building. A tall dark-haired man in a blue suit was in front of him, making his way through the security checks.

Carl's heart skipped: Randle. He'd returned.

He needed to make sure the man didn't get away. Once Randle was through the barrier, Carl leaned towards one of the security guards and flashed his badge.

"That man you just let through," he said.

"Yes."

"Don't let him out again."

"I'm sorry, sir, I can't do that."

"He's an important witness in a trial. He didn't turn up when expected this morning, and I don't want him going anywhere. Who do I need to speak to, to make sure he's prevented from leaving?"

"The clerk of the court, sir."

"Good." Carl handed the man his card. "Meanwhile if he tries to leave, call me." He gave the guard a long look. "Please."

"I'll see what I can do. I'd be happier if it came through the proper channels, though."

"It will. Don't worry."

Carl hurried towards the court where Ian's trial was being heard. There was no sign of Randle. Carl scanned the corridor, wondering if he'd gone into the gents. Should he check?

Check the court room first. They had ten minutes until things started up again.

There was a lobby area leading to the courtroom, between two sets of doors. Carl almost stumbled over two people talking in hushed voices as he entered: Randle, and Ian's solicitor.

"Detective Superintendent Randle," he said. Trying to hide the surprise in his voice.

"Ah. DI Whaley." Randle gave him a patronising smile.

Carl frowned at the solicitor. Why was she talking to a crown witness? Was it even legal?

"Can we have a word?" he asked Randle.

"Certainly."

The solicitor looked between them. "Make it quick."

Carl gave her a smile and pulled Randle back out to the corridor. They stood against a wall, Carl glancing nervously at the passing crowds.

"What happened to you?" he hissed.

Randle squared his shoulders. "Unforeseen events. I'm here now."

"And you'll give the evidence you told us you would last night?"

"I believe it was your senior officer I discussed it with, not yourself."

"He isn't here. You'll have to deal with me."

"Indeed."

"Will you tell me the details of the agreement you made with Superintendent Rogers?"

Randle smiled. "That's confidential." He glanced towards the court room doors. The judge would know he was back; they would be waiting. "You'll find out."

"I hope we can rely on you," Carl said.

"I'm a serving police officer. I take deep offence at the suggestion of anything otherwise."

Carl pursed his lips. Randle gave him a wink and turned towards the court. Carl watched him enter, his body hot with frustration.

CHAPTER SIXTY-NINE

Zoe staggered up from her desk, grabbing her phone and shoving it into the inside pocket of her jacket. "I need to speak to Dawson."

"You need to go home, boss," replied Rhodri. "You're not in a state to—"

"Don't tell me what I'm not in a state to do. We need a warrant to search that gym. Hamm's been there, I know it."

"Is Hamm so important right now?"

Zoe glared at him. "I have to work. I need to be distracted."

She crashed out of the team room and almost ran to Dawson's office. He'd better be there.

She opened the door without knocking and was faced by a startled looking Dawson eating an apple. She stared at it; she'd never had him down as a fruit eater.

"Zoe? Are you OK? You look terrible."

"I need a warrant." She threw herself into the chair opposite him. "The gym in Chelmsley Wood."

"On what grounds?"

"Sheena MacDonald is managing the place. She works for Trevor Hamm. We need to track him down before he disappears for good."

"Sheena MacDonald was never charged. Maybe she's cleaned herself up, got a legitimate job."

"People like that never clean themselves up." Zoe reached for the glass of water on Dawson's desk. "Can I?"

He gave her a puzzled look then nodded and watched, scratching his cheek, as she downed it in one.

"I believe Hamm has either been in the area all along, or he's come back for the trial. He'll want to see first-hand what happens, what evidence is presented. He knows he can't rely on the news reports."

"There's no way he'd risk turning up at the Crown Court."

Zoe gritted her teeth and leaned back in her chair, fingers pressing into her neck.

"Zoe, are you sure you're OK?"

"This body we dragged out of Edgbaston reservoir. It's Dwayne Jukes. He's – he was the leader of a new gang. The same ones that killed Starling and Petersen. It's linked to Hamm, it has to be."

"Maybe Starling was working with the gang, and they killed him when he was suspended. Maybe Petersen has switched allegiances."

She shook her head. "Petersen was breaking the terms of his sentence. Removing his tracker and leaving his house. I believe he was meeting Hamm."

"And how would that get him killed, exactly?"

"I don't know. But that gym is the closest thing we have to a current location for Hamm. We need to search it."

"I'm sorry, Zoe. I don't know what's got into you, but I

can't authorise a search of a building on the basis of someone working there who we once arrested. Now if you can prove that Hamm owns the place..."

She stood up. "OK."

"You can prove it?"

"Not yet. But we will. I'm sure of it."

She stormed out of the office before Dawson had a chance to speak. People stared as she crashed along the corridor back to her office. *Let them*.

She threw open the office door, making Rhodri jump.

"Boss. You OK?"

"I'm fine. I've got a job for you."

CHAPTER SEVENTY

IAN FELT his fists clench as Randle walked into the court room. He was back. But just what was he going to say?

A murmur of surprise ran through the spectators as the superintendent walked towards the front and took a seat which had been saved for him.

Ian watched Jane acknowledge Randle in silence. Even with this new solicitor instead of Edward Startshaw, he knew he was a pawn in someone else's game. Whatever happened, he would be the last to know. And the first to be sacrificed.

The judge called for quiet and the room settled down. Randle looked up and gave Ian a tight smile. Ian felt his cheeks inflame.

Randle was called. He strode to the witness stand, looking quite different from last time he'd stood there. Ian wondered if he was feeling as calm as he looked, or if he was just a damn good actor.

The CPS barrister, Ms Hegarty, stood up. She turned to the jury.

"Welcome back, and I hope this warm weather won't

impact our ability to concentrate this afternoon. I know I was glad of a cool beer at lunchtime."

A ripple travelled through the jury. Ian wasn't sure if they were allowed to drink during a trial, or even if the barristers were (or indeed if Ms Hegarty really had). But it made her seem less removed from the jury, more of an everywoman. As if a woman who wore a flapping gown and a ridiculous wig to work could be described as an everywoman.

Randle watched all this, his face still. Ian's respect for the man was waning fast.

"Hello again, Detective Superintendent."

"Good afternoon."

"It's good to have you back with us."

Randle looked at the jury. "Please allow me to apologise for my absence this morning. Urgent police business."

I bet, thought Ian. He flicked his gaze around the court. Carl Whaley, at the front of the public benches, ran his finger inside his collar. Alison was three rows behind, her eyes on Ian. She looked away as she caught his eye. Two of the women in the jury fanned themselves with notebooks.

"We'll be continuing with your testimony from yesterday afternoon. As you were sworn in then, we don't need to do it again. You're still happy for me to call you Superintendent?"

Randle turned so his body was square to the barrister. "Of course."

"Good. So let's get straight to the point. The defendant is accused of planting evidence on a victim of the explosion on board flight 546. Is this correct?"

"I believe so."

"Were you present at the airport at this time?"

"I was. As I've already testified, I was Gold Command."

"Did you and the defendant work together during this operation?"

"Not directly. As far as I recall, we didn't even speak to each other."

Ian felt sweat drip down his back. So far, Randle was telling the truth. Ian had arrived at the airport and immediately gone with Zoe to the runway.

"You didn't give the defendant any orders with regard to what he was expected to do?"

Randle's gaze travelled over Ian. "The defendant is – was – a sergeant. There were a few officers between myself and him when it came to the chain of command."

"So who *did* give him his orders?"

"I assume it was DI Finch."

"Zoe Finch?"

"She was Bronze Command. She took Ian to the runway to secure the scene."

"So we've heard." Ms Hegarty glanced at the jury, then returned to Randle. "We've also heard that it was the defendant's day off. That he was disturbed while on a shopping trip with his family and told to report to the airport."

Randle shrugged. "Plenty of officers get called in from leave when there's a major incident."

"Who made that phone call?"

"I have no idea."

"DI Finch?"

Randle looked off to one side as if considering. "I didn't believe so, no."

"Why not?"

"Because I was with her. I drove her from the Force CID offices in Harborne to the airport."

"Why did you do this? Do officers not need their own transport?"

"Zoe's – DI Finch's – role was onsite. She didn't need to go anywhere."

"So you thought it made sense to give her a lift."

"Not a *lift*. I needed to be there, and so did she. I could brief her en route."

"Did you tell her that Sergeant Osman would be arriving?"

"I didn't know that Sergeant Osman would be arriving. So no, I didn't tell her."

"Are you sure about that?"

"Positive."

The barrister walked back to her bench. She picked up a sheet of paper and placed it in front of Randle. "Because we have records of you making a call to the defendant at three fifteen that afternoon. Which would be around half an hour before you arrived at the scene."

Randle leaned over and peered at the sheet of paper, unperturbed. "That's not my number." He drew his phone out of his pocket. "I can call you now, if you'd like to know what my actual number is."

"Superintendent Randle, would you agree that it's not unusual for people to have two phones?"

"Some people do. Not me."

"You wouldn't keep a service phone and another phone for private use?"

Randle shook his head. "Far too complicated."

"Interesting. Because we have text records from this number." She jabbed the sheet of paper with a finger.

"Can you hand that over please, Ms Hegarty?" the judge asked.

CHAPTER SEVENTY

"Certainly." She gestured back to her colleague who passed over a copy.

"And here's another printout, of a text message sent from you to my client an hour earlier." Hegarty picked up another sheet of paper. "This is a record of messages sent from this number to the defendant. There are only two, although there are plenty of calls. The second message says this."

She cleared her throat and turned towards the jury as she read.

"Instructions to come. Be ready."

Hegarty looked at Randle over the paper. "This was sent the day before the attacks."

Ian's stomach flipped. He remembered that text.

"There's no evidence this was me," said Randle.

"In this text, it seems that my client is being given orders."

"It does indeed. But not by me."

"Superintendent, the police have traced this phone's location on the day of the attacks. It was at the airport."

"I imagine plenty of phones would have been."

"On that same morning, it's been traced to the mast closest to your home."

"That mast must serve hundreds of addresses. I don't—"

"And we have one occasion, in February, when it was in the vicinity of Harborne Police Station."

Randle straightened in his chair. "Do you have the phone itself?"

"It's my job to ask the questions, Superintendent."

"Because if you don't have it, then—"

Hegarty raised a hand. The jury were getting antsy, two of the men in the front row leaning forward, their elbows on the barrier in front of them. Ian chewed his bottom lip and tried to control his breathing.

"Moving on," said the barrister. "Am I right in thinking that you were the Senior Investigating Officer in the Canary case?"

"I was."

"Please describe the Canary investigation for the court."

Randle took a moment to compose himself. A lock of hair had fallen over his eye. He swept it back and rubbed his nose. "Canary was a high profile investigation into a suspected child abuse network operating in the city. We arrested three men following covert surveillance and—"

"Who were these men?"

"Their names were Howard Petersen, Jory Shand and Robert Oulman."

"Were you investigating anyone else?"

Ian noticed Carl Whaley straightening. What was he expecting?

"No," said Randle.

"No?" replied the barrister. "Only three men. No one else involved in this significant criminal network?"

"We did not find any conclusive evidence pointing to other suspects."

"And two of the three men you mention received suspended sentences for money laundering, is that correct?"

"It is."

"Sounds like you failed to do your job."

"The men were tried in this very building. The process of justice was done."

"Hmm." Hegarty regarded Randle for a moment. "Superintendent, coming back to the photograph which was introduced into evidence yesterday."

Randle nodded, his eyes on the barrister.

"Can you remind us who this woman was?" Hegarty held up the photo.

"I didn't know her name. I met her at a social event."

"You didn't leave this event with her?"

Randle scratched his cheek. "I don't recall who I left the event with."

"Superintendent, we have already heard that this is Alina Popescu, the woman who detonated a nail bomb at New Street Station on the same day as the airport attack. So we're expected to believe your acquaintance with her was an unfortunate coincidence?"

"We weren't acquaintances. I didn't even know her name."

DI Whaley's foot was jiggling now, his leg crossed over the other. What was going on? Surely she wasn't expecting Randle to incriminate himself?

"Superintendent, do you recognise this man?" The barrister took another sheet from her assistant, who was leaning over the desks to pass it. She handed it to Randle.

"This is Trevor Hamm," Randle replied. "He was a witness in an investigation into his wife's death last October. The coroner ruled it death by misadventure."

"You didn't believe the death was suspicious?"

"The verdict was death by misadventure."

"Irina Hamm, the unfortunate lady who drowned, had been the victim of a violent robbery a few days earlier, is that correct?"

The judge leaned down from his chair. "Ms Hegarty, I do hope you can get to the point soon."

The barrister looked back at him. "Very soon, Your Honour."

"Because my patience is wearing thin."

"Apologies, Your Honour. I will get to the point."

The judge raised an eyebrow. *Go on, then.*

Hegarty stepped closer to Randle. "Superintendent, was Alina Popescu being held against her will by Trevor Hamm and forced to have sex with men for money?"

"We found evidence she'd been living at a brothel run by men we suspected of having links to Hamm. But we found no evidence she was involved in prostitution." Randle glared at the barrister as if daring her to go further.

Ian knew what the jury would be thinking. If Alina Popescu was a prostitute, and Randle had been photographed with her...

Ms Hegarty stared back for a moment as if weighing up her options. She sniffed and took a breath.

"Superintendent, did you believe Trevor Hamm's organisation to be behind the New Street bombing?"

"We found no concrete evidence implicating anyone except Alina Popescu."

Hegarty frowned. "Did you find evidence of an organised crime group having prior knowledge of the airport attack, and using that knowledge to take women from another plane? Did that group then force those women into prostitution?"

"We arrested a number of individuals relating to that incident."

"Were these individuals associates of Trevor Hamm?"

"As far as the evidence shows, the men we arrested acted alone."

Hegarty tugged at her sleeve. Ian could tell this wasn't going the way she expected.

The barrister returned to her notes and leafed through

them. "Superintendent, yesterday you told this court, 'We believe the intelligence they received about the airport attack gave them the idea of launching a second attack in tandem, and hoping the terrorist organisation would be blamed for both'." She looked up. "Are you now saying that isn't the case?"

"What we believed and what we found evidence for are different things. The beliefs I referred to yesterday were purely speculation."

A ripple went through the gallery.

Ms Hegarty scratched her neck. "Is a warrant out for Trevor Hamm's arrest?"

"I wouldn't be able to tell you the details of an operation I'm not directly involved with."

"Did you have direct contact with Trevor Hamm and his associates, in the run up to the attacks?"

"I did not. My colleagues interviewed him with regard to the death of his wife and the burglary at his flat, but that was some time before—"

"Did Mr Hamm introduce you to Alina Popescu?"

"I met her at a party. No one introduced me to her."

In the gallery, DI Whaley let out a strangled sound. Ian clenched his fists.

"Superintendent," said the barrister. "Did Trevor Hamm's organisation recruit you to provide information to them about police operations? And did they instruct you to tell the defendant to plant explosives residue on Mr Nadeem Sharif?"

Ian held his breath.

"Absolutely not," said Randle. He looked at Ian. "DS Osman acted alone. His only instructions as far as I'm aware were from DI Finch, to help her secure the crime scene."

CHAPTER SEVENTY-ONE

Zoe's phone rang as she was about to brief Rhodri. It was Mo.

"Boss. Rhodri called me. Your mum... I'm so sorry."

She pulled a face at Rhodri and retreated towards Mo's empty desk. "I'm fine. I need to work this case. It'll distract me."

"Zo, you need to go home. You need to talk to Nicholas."

"You know what she was like," she said through gritted teeth.

"More than anyone." Mo had known Zoe since before Nicholas was born. He'd seen the neglect and borderline abuse she'd suffered from Annette. The way she'd had no choice but to leave home after her dad died, and find a place to live with her baby son. "But she's your mum. Whatever happened between the two of you, it'll affect you."

"Yes, it affects me," she told him. "I'm bloody livid. She went out when she'd been drinking and she got herself run over. She was a liability."

"You know you don't mean that."

CHAPTER SEVENTY-ONE

She clutched the phone, her head pounding. "I don't know what I mean." She sank into Mo's chair.

"Go home, Zo. I'll come round as soon as I'm done at the prison."

"You don't need to do that."

"I want to. I've spoken to Fulmer, Connie is in with Adams. We wanted to make sure they had no chance to confer."

"Nothing to report?"

"I can tell you about it later. But no, nothing yet."

She felt herself deflate. "I'm sorry, Mo."

"Nothing to be sorry for."

"Nicholas. He loved her, despite everything. He'll be..."

"He'll get through it, because he's got you."

"How do I support him through his grief when I don't feel any myself?"

"I don't believe that's true."

She bent her head, her eyes screwed tight. "No."

"Go home, Zo." Mo's voice was gentle. "I'll make sure Dawson knows."

"Oh, *fuck*."

"What?"

"I just barged into his office demanding a warrant to search the gym."

"Did he—?"

"No. We need to prove Hamm owns the place."

"We can work on that."

Stop talking to me like I'm a child, she thought. She hadn't lived with her mum for seventeen years. She'd barely spoken to her until six months ago. This was nothing. She was needed on the case.

But Mo would never believe that.

"Can you work on that angle, Mo? I'll take some time, just today. Tell me if you find anything."

"Sure. What about the body in the reservoir?"

She'd almost forgotten about Jukes. "Sheila and I were going to run a briefing at two thirty." She looked at her watch: quarter to.

"Sheila can do it, and I'll help."

"Dawson will want to stick his oar in."

"Maybe he should. You need to let go. Let the rest of us take on the load."

"OK." Her voice was strangled. Her body felt light and heavy at the same time, like she might pass out or run a marathon.

"Go home."

"OK." She hung up and gave Rhodri a rueful smile. He nodded understanding and she grabbed her jacket.

CHAPTER SEVENTY-TWO

The morgue was the same as ever, only today it felt colder. Zoe drummed her foot against the hard floor as she waited for Adana.

The pathologist emerged from a set of swing doors, peeling off an apron. "Zoe. I'm so sorry."

"I want to see her."

"She's not ready. I—"

"Please."

"OK." Adana screwed up the apron and shoved it into a bin. "Give me ten minutes."

"Have you examined her yet?"

"I only got back from the reservoir twenty minutes ago. Jukes has to be a priority. You'll understand…"

"Yeah." Zoe pushed her hair out of her face. "Of course."

"But if it's any help, Vince, he's the person you spoke to, told me you were worried your mum had been drinking. He did a blood analysis. She was under the legal limit. Twenty milligrams per hundred millilitres of blood. That's the equivalent to half a unit of alcohol."

In a woman like Annette, half a unit would be the residue from the previous night's drinking. Annette had never been able to stop at one drink.

"She wasn't drunk?"

Adana shook her head, her brow furrowed. "No. Maybe if you talk to Traffic..."

"Yeah." Zoe sniffed. *Hold it together*. She wasn't grieving. Her mum had made her life hell, so why would she miss her?

She stood up. "I want to see her now."

"You know how it is, Zoe. We need to prepare her."

"I observe post-mortems all the time. You don't need to pretty her up for me."

Adana put a hand on her arm. "She's not some anonymous crime victim."

Zoe pulled in a shaky breath. "Fine." She thudded down onto the bench.

"I'll get someone to bring you a cup of tea."

"I don't drink tea."

"Coffee, then. Sugar?"

Zoe shook her head. Sugar for shock. She grimaced.

"No sugar. Give me five minutes." Adana hurried back through the doors.

Zoe leaned against the tiled wall, her head still throbbing. She felt like she might be sick. She still hadn't spoken to Nicholas. It was after two now, he'd be finishing school in an hour or so. She wondered what was happening at the trial.

After a minute or so, a man appeared with a plastic cup of coffee: Vince, she presumed. Zoe took it from him and blew on it. It smelled bitter. She sipped and screwed up her nose, then placed it on the floor next to her feet.

"We're ready for you." Adana reappeared wearing a clean apron.

"That was quick."

"She didn't need too much work."

Zoe forced down the lump in her throat and followed Adana. The pathologist led her past the familiar doors to the two examination rooms and through a set of wooden doors. Zoe found herself inside a small, dimly lit room. This room was less clinical than the areas of the morgue she was familiar with. The walls were papered and the floor was made of a material that wasn't scrubbable. Opposite her was another door, presumably leading to the outside. The way relatives normally entered.

In the centre of the room was a raised bench covered in a dark red cloth. Annette lay on it, covered by another, lighter, cloth up to her shoulders. Her skin was pale and grey, her eyes closed. There was bruising to her forehead, and what looked like road rash on her chin.

Zoe gulped in air.

She took a step forwards and held out her hand, leaving it hovering in mid-air. Annette looked smaller in death, like a different person. Her cheeks were sunken and her neck scrawny.

Zoe realised that she'd never properly looked at her mum, not in years.

She wiped a tear from her cheek. "Did she die at the scene?"

"She suffered internal bleeding, a ruptured spleen. I'm expecting to find brain trauma. One of her lungs collapsed. She would have lost consciousness immediately. She died in the ambulance."

Zoe's chest hardened. She let her hand float down to her mum's chest and rest on the sheet. It was chilly.

"She didn't suffer?"

"No."

Zoe looked up. "You're not bullshitting me, just to be nice?"

Adana's solemn face broke into a smile. "I never bullshit you, DI Finch."

"No." She let her fingers travel up to her mum's shoulder, where the skin was bare. It felt like wax. She pulled her hand away.

"Thanks." Zoe turned back to the doors.

"Stay as long as you need."

Zoe turned back. "Have you brought Jukes in? I should observe."

"No, Zoe. You don't need that right now."

Zoe's vision blurred. She'd call the office, send one of her team.

"I've already had a call from DS Uddin," said Adana. "He'll attend."

Zoe gasped. Mo, covering for her. Always there.

"I need to find my son." She pushed through the doors and hurried out of the building, her eyes filling with tears.

CHAPTER SEVENTY-THREE

THE TEAM WERE upstairs in one of the meeting rooms, DS Griffin and Mo together at the front. DS Griffin had a laptop open and was scrolling through photos from the reservoir.

"How did he die?" Connie asked.

"The post-mortem's later this afternoon," Sheila replied. "But Dr Adebayo says it isn't drowning."

"But he's been in the water at least two weeks," added Mo.

"Yes." Sheila met his eye. "He died before he went in. There were lacerations to his chest, who knows what else."

"So what's the timeline?" asked DC Solsby.

Sheila pointed her marker pen at him. "Good question." She turned to the whiteboard behind her and wrote *1. Dwayne Jukes* at the top. She then wrote the range of dates within which he most likely died.

"Starling next, or Petersen?" asked Connie.

"Starling was found on Monday," Mo said. "Pathology said he'd been there a week or so."

"But Petersen had also been dead at least a week," added Solsby.

"So we've got Starling and Petersen killed at roughly the same time," said Sheila. "Question is, why?"

"And are they the only ones?" added Connie.

"Let's hope we don't unearth more," replied Mo. Connie gave him a grim look.

"OK," said Sheila. "I don't know much about the Starling case. I'm not even supposed to be speculating on it. So let's focus on Jukes and Petersen."

Mo walked to the board. He held out his hand for the pen, which Sheila passed to him. He wrote 2. *Howard Petersen*.

"So was Petersen's death related to Jukes's?" he asked. "What motive would someone have?"

"Petersen was one of Hamm's lot," said Rhodri. "If Jukes was running this other mob, then maybe his guys killed Petersen for revenge."

"Petersen can't have killed Jukes. He's serving a suspended sentence, tagged," said Mo. "It doesn't make sense."

"Maybe it's a turf war," said Connie. "Two gangs, each trying to assert their authority. And besides, we know Petersen had worked his way around that tag."

"Hamm wouldn't have been best pleased if another bunch tried to muscle in on his turf," added Rhodri.

"They're different, though," said Sheila. She pointed at Jukes's name on the board. "This lot are small fry compared to Hamm. Drug dealing mainly, a bit of money laundering we reckon. Hamm's been involved in human trafficking, terrorism..."

"Yeah, but he lost his crew," said Rhodri. "The men he

relied on are all banged up, or stuck at home with tags on their ankles."

"You think he was trying to take over Jukes's gang?" Mo asked.

Rhodri shrugged. "I don't know what to think, Sarge. Just chuckin' ideas in."

"That's what we need."

Sheila shook her head. "We need solid evidence, is what we need." She turned to the whiteboard and wrote *Forensics, CCTV, Post-mortem, Witnesses.*

She turned to the room. "OK. Any volunteers?"

"I've already said I'll do the PM," said Mo.

"Cheers. And I've heard Connie's good with CCTV and digital evidence."

"Happy to take that," said Connie. "Anything after the morning I've had." She glanced at Mo. Her interview with Simon Adams had not gone well; he'd spat at her and refused to talk.

"We shouldn't have gone to the prison," Mo said. "They'll have got word to Hamm that we're looking for him."

"You really think he's in the city?" Sheila asked. "We'd have found him by now."

"He could have left, then come back. For the trial. I know it seems like a daft idea, but the DI's gut doesn't normally let her down."

Sheila's expression dropped. "How is she?"

Mo sighed. "She'll be OK." He wasn't about to tell everyone in the room what Rhodri had reported to him; that she'd been erratic and confused. He didn't blame her.

"Poor woman."

"Yeah." Mo had promised to go and see Zoe. She'd want

him to attend the PM first. He'd swing by her house afterwards.

"I'll talk to the forensics guys," said Rhodri. Mo saw Connie's lips twitch.

"You want to swap?" he asked her.

"No," she said, too quickly. "I'll take CCTV."

"That leaves me with witnesses," said Solsby. "I'll head back over there, see how door to door's coming on."

"Find out if anyone's got a camera on their house or business, will you?" asked Connie.

Solsby winked at her. "Why don't you come with me?"

She paled. "No, it's… OK."

"You know what you're looking for, Connie. It'll make your job easier."

"OK." She gave Solsby a look like he was a dog about to bite her.

Mo knew that Connie preferred to be behind a desk. But he also knew she had to drag herself out if she wanted to prove her readiness for sergeant.

"Good," he said. "Don't forget we're looking for Hamm, too."

"We need to prioritise Jukes," said Sheila.

"If Hamm is responsible for Jukes's death, you'll be grateful we were looking for him." Mo gave her a pointed look.

"Fair enough. Do we have any leads?"

"Uniform says there's signs of life at his house out past Solihull."

"Then we should get Uniform to knock on the door," she replied.

"And if he's there, he'll run. No, we need someone who's

working the case. And not alone. I'd come with you, if it wasn't for the PM."

"It's OK," said Sheila. "I can take DC Sarpong."

"Makes sense," said Solsby. "Femi terrifies me, she'll have Hamm eating out of her hand."

Sheila gave him a stern look. Connie curled her lip.

"Right," said Mo. "Let me know how you get on, yeah?"

"Yup."

CHAPTER SEVENTY-FOUR

Zoe was in the living room, staring at the blank TV, when the front door opened.

"Hey, Yoda." She listened as Nicholas stopped to fuss the cat in the hallway. The cat miaowed and led him inside. She'd be curling round his legs, guiding him into the kitchen and her bowl.

"Mum?"

She bit her lip and drew in a breath, then turned, attempting to pull her face into a neutral expression. "Hey, love."

"What's up? You sick?"

She stood up. "I've got something to tell you."

He tensed. "What?"

"Sit down."

"Is it my uni application? Damn, I knew I shouldn't have put Stirling first."

"It's not that. Sit down with me, yeah?"

His eyes didn't leave hers as he rounded the sofa and sat

next to her. The cat followed him, miaowing and jumping up to his lap. He pushed her off gently.

Zoe looked into his eyes. "It's bad news, I'm afraid."

"Just tell me."

She reached for his hand. He let her take it, his own hand limp.

"It's your gran," she said. "She was in a traffic accident."

His eyes widened. He pulled his hand away. "Is she OK?"

She shook her head. "She didn't make it. She's dead, love. It was quick, she wouldn't have been in pain."

He stood up, his foot brushing the cat to one side. Zoe stood to meet his eye.

"I'm so sorry, Nicholas. It happened yesterday afternoon. I only found out today."

"You should have called me at school."

"I've only been home quarter of an hour. I went to see her."

He shoved his hand through his hair, his eyes wild. "How... what was...?"

"She was peaceful. They said she didn't suffer."

"You've already said that. Of course she suffered!" He turned away and made a high-pitched noise.

Zoe sat down, the wind knocked out of her. Now she'd told him, the adrenaline had left her body.

He turned to her, his eyes wild. "She asked you for a lift."

"What? I—"

"If you'd helped her out for once instead of being so focused on your stupid job, she'd still be alive."

"Hang on, Nicholas. That's not fair."

"You're going to say she was drunk. You always blame everything on that."

She stood up. He bent to grab the cat. He bundled her up to his shoulder and buried his face in her fur.

"She wasn't drunk, Nicholas. She had the equivalent of half a unit of alcohol in her system. Nothing, for... Nothing."

"You were going to say nothing, for a drunk!"

"But she *was* a drunk. You didn't see her at her worst."

He flung the cat at her. She fumbled to catch it then let it drop to the floor.

"You're glad she's dead." He marched towards the door.

She stepped after him. "Of *course* I'm not glad she's dead."

"So how do you feel? You don't look like you've been crying to me."

"I wanted to be strong for you."

He slapped the side of his head. "Bollocks! You just don't care, is all."

She reached towards him, but he flung off her hand. He threw the front door open and ran into the street.

"Nicholas, come back. Be careful. I don't want you to..."

"I'll be fine," he shouted back at her. "Can't have two of us killed under the wheels of a car in twenty-four hours."

Zoe spotted movement from the corner of her eye. Ollie, one of the students living next door, was at his front door, key raised to the lock.

"Everything OK, Mrs Finch?'

"Fine." She caught herself. "Thanks."

Nicholas was halfway to the Bristol Road. There was no point running after him. He'd roam the streets for a while, and he'd come back. He was upset. He was angry. She didn't blame him.

She slipped inside, ignoring Ollie watching her, and

CHAPTER SEVENTY-FOUR

closed the door. She leaned against it and let herself slide to the floor. Why did she feel so numb?

CHAPTER SEVENTY-FIVE

Anita had now made a complete circuit of the room, and established that it had one door and two windows. She guessed that one window was at the front of the building, and one at the back. The door was to one side.

If she banged on one of those windows, would she be seen? The glass felt flimsy, like she could make herself heard. Or break it.

Right now, she was sitting behind the door. She'd worked out that the door opened into the room. In her current position, if someone came in, they wouldn't be able to see her. She wasn't sure what she'd do with this knowledge, but it was reassuring.

She heard footsteps beyond the wall. It sounded as if someone was walking up a flight of stairs. The ones she'd been bumped up last night. She held her breath and leaned into the wall, trying to ignore her damp trousers. She'd tried to pee in a corner when the need became too great but had only succeeded in soaking her clothes. It made her disgusted with herself.

"We can't keep her here."

Anita held her breath. That had been a woman's voice, with an accent. She pressed her ear closer to the wall.

"We can't take her anywhere else, not yet. You look after her for one more day, then we'll deal with her."

A man, Brummie.

"By then, we'll know if he's got the message." The woman again. She was Scottish.

"Who cares if he has? We're not sending her back to him."

Anita trembled. Were they talking about David? Who else would she be *sent back* to? And if so, what was this message he was supposed to have got?

She shuffled along the floor, away from the door. She wanted to be as far from these people as possible when they entered the room.

The smell thickened as she moved; she was heading for the corner she'd designated as a toilet. She backtracked.

"He's done as he's told so far," the man said.

"Lying his bent fucking mouth off." The woman laughed.

Anita heard the door open. She braced herself, waiting to be grabbed, or hit. She was hungry.

"I need food!" she cried.

"What's that, girlie?" the woman asked. "You're no making any sense." She laughed.

Anita faced in the direction of the voice. "Please. I need water." Her mouth was dry, her throat sore.

"Drink yer piss," the woman replied. "Looks like you've left plenty of it over there."

Heat rose to Anita's cheeks. "Where are my girls?"

"Girls, was that you said?"

Anita nodded.

"They're safe." The voice was closer now.

Anita didn't know if *they're safe* was good news, or bad. It meant that they knew about the girls. That they might have them.

"Don't hurt them."

"Wha' was that?" The woman was right in front of her. She was crouching, or bending down. Their faces were close. If Anita struck out...

She balled her fist and felt a hand clasp it.

"No, you don't. Your lasses are fine, don't ya worry. Just sit tight and everything'll be alright."

"Water."

"What does she think this is, the fucking Ritz?" The man laughed. He was over by the door. *Don't come any nearer*, Anita thought.

She felt a foot on her shin. She toppled backwards, unable to balance with the blindfold on. More laughter.

"I'll get ya yer water, Lady Muck. Just don't go expecting five-star treatment, eh?"

CHAPTER SEVENTY-SIX

It was 4:30 pm, and Nicholas still hadn't returned. Zoe had texted, phoned, and pinged him on WhatsApp and Instagram.

No response.

She dialled Connie.

"Boss. I'm so sorry about your mum."

"Thanks, Connie. That's not what I'm calling about."

"If it's the case, the sarge and DS Griffin are—"

"It's Nicholas."

"Oh."

"Can you find out if he's with Zaf? He buggered off after I told him about his gran and he won't return my calls and messages."

"No problem. Hold on for a moment."

Zoe stroked the cat as she waited for Connie to return. She'd moved from the hall floor to the sofa, but still felt numb. Worry about Nicholas cut through the blur.

"Boss, he's fine. He's at ours."

"He's at your mum's house?"

"Mum's fed him. He's pretty upset."

"Tell Zaf to pass on a message, will you?"

"Course."

"Tell Nicholas I love him and that I'm sorry."

"No problem," Connie replied. "You on your own?"

"I'll be fine."

"If you need company…"

"It's OK. I'm expecting Mo."

"He's at the post-mortem."

"As he should be. I can wait. See you in the morning, Connie."

"You're coming back in?"

"Of course I am. Thanks for your help."

Zoe stood up. Hanging around here would do her no good. And she didn't want to wait around for Mo.

She called his number and got voicemail.

"Mo, I'm heading to the Crown Court. Call me when you're free, yeah?"

She tossed some cat biscuits into a bowl and left the house. Twenty minutes later she was at the Crown Court.

She got through security in record time – more people were leaving at this time of day than arriving – and hurried to the courtroom.

This wasn't about work. She was looking for Carl. His voice on the end of the phone wasn't enough; she needed human contact.

The court room was empty except for a woman cleaning the desks at the front.

"You missed it, love."

"I can see that. When did it finish?"

"Only half an hour ago."

CHAPTER SEVENTY-SIX

Zoe considered asking the woman if anything interesting had happened. But she wouldn't know.

"Thanks."

She walked the corridors, searching for Carl. People were heading towards the exit, finishing formal business for the day. The lawyers would be going to their offices, to prepare for tomorrow. The accused – including Ian – would be in security vans on their way back to prison.

She walked out to her car and threw herself inside. She stared out of the windscreen. She could call Carl. If she told him what had happened, their argument would be forgotten.

But she wanted to do this face to face.

A shape appeared by the passenger door. It was a man in a dark suit, his hand on the door handle.

She flicked the central locking switch in the driver's door. This wasn't a rough part of town, but you couldn't be too careful.

The man tried the door handle, but it didn't budge. Zoe leaned across. It might be Carl.

He bent down just as she was putting her face up to the window. The two of them locked eyes. Zoe pulled in a tight breath.

"Let me in, will you? We need to talk."

She shrank back, mind racing. After a moment's thought, she disengaged the central locking. He jerked the door open and slid inside. His movements were fluid but his face was beaded with sweat.

"Sir?" she said.

Randle turned to her. "I need your help."

"What with?"

"It's unofficial."

"Sir, given the nature of what's—"

"Shut up, Zoe. I know what you're like. I've seen you pursue investigations you were told to leave alone. You're the only person I can trust."

David Randle, trust *her*?

She swallowed her pride, along with the lump in her throat. He was still her senior officer. Although the way he was talking...

She scanned the street.

"There's no one around," he said. "At least, no one you know."

She nodded.

Go along with it.

"What do you need, sir?"

CHAPTER SEVENTY-SEVEN

"I really feel for the boss," Connie told DC Solsby. They were hanging around in a street across the reservoir from where Jukes had been found, trailing two pairs of uniformed officers who were knocking on doors. The street was lined with modern houses that reminded her of those eco-living communities in Scandinavia. Most of them were uninhabited, many were still being built.

"She close to her mum?" Solsby asked.

"Not at all. But that doesn't make it any easier."

"Can be harder, sometimes. You grieve all the things you missed, the relationship you wish you'd had."

She eyed him. She didn't know this man well, but from the little she did, it wasn't like him to be deep. "What's your name?" she asked him.

"DC Solsby."

"Your first name."

"Gordon. Stick with Solsby, if you don't mind."

"Nice to meet you, Gordon."

He gave her a look of mock anger. "You too, Connie. Or should I call you Rita?"

She laughed: the name he'd used at the gym. "Don't get any ideas. I'm going out with a guy from the Forensics team."

"Good for you." Solsby – Gordon – gave her a nudge. "Lucky guy."

Connie blushed. She'd only been seeing Rav for a couple of weeks, but she had a good feeling about it. They'd met on a case, processing DNA samples after a student had been murdered at Birmingham University.

One of the PCs on door-to-door duty beckoned them over and they hurried to join her and her colleague. They were talking to a middle-aged woman who stood in her doorway dressed in her pyjamas.

"This lady says there's cameras on the industrial building over that way."

The woman pointed past the officers. "That building there, the one that looks like an old warehouse. They use it for events and stuff. I've seen cameras on it."

Connie followed the woman's hand. She doubted the building would have a view of the reservoir, but it didn't hurt to try. "Who do I need to speak to for access?"

"There's a sales office. Turn right onto Rotton Park Street. Can't miss it, flags outside."

"Thanks." Connie exchanged glances with Solsby.

"What're we waiting for?"

She grinned at him and they hurried in the direction of the sales office. A young woman with afro hair piled on top of her head sat behind a vast white desk.

Connie showed her ID. "We're investigating an incident in the area. One of your residents said there are CCTV cameras on the warehouse building over there."

"You mean Tubeworks. Yeah, there's cameras on all sides."

"Can we have a copy of the recordings?" Connie hoped this was the kind of outfit that didn't delete its CCTV every morning.

"You can. Do I need to be worried?"

"We pulled a body out of the reservoir," Solsby said.

The woman wrinkled her nose. "Edgbaston Reservoir?"

He nodded.

"Shit. Who?"

"Not one of your residents," Connie said.

"I didn't think it was. At least, I hoped not..." The woman leaned into her screen. "Here. What date d'you want the recordings from?"

"From three weeks ago to two weeks ago," Connie told her.

The woman nodded. "You want to watch it here?"

"Can you email it to me?"

"Course."

Connie handed the woman her card. "Can we take a quick look at where the cameras are?"

The woman shuffled out of her seat and rounded the desk. "I was about to finish up. I'll show you."

"Thanks."

Connie and Solsby followed the woman past more of the Scandinavian-style houses towards an area of open land. It had been recently landscaped, and was flanked on the far side by a large industrial building.

The woman pointed towards the far corner. "Up there."

Connie approached the building and looked up. There were cameras fixed on the corner of the building, just below the roofline. One pointed towards the estate, the other out over the canal that separated these houses from the reservoir.

"That could work," she said to Solsby.

"It could." He gave the woman a nod. "Cheers."

She gave them a thumbs-up and walked to her car.

"You want to go back to the office and check these?" Connie said.

"Why don't you head back? I'll stay here, follow Uniform around like a good dog."

"Er... I don't have a car."

"I've got my kit in my car," Solsby said. "We can watch the video there."

"Fine." Connie didn't fancy their chances of seeing much inside a car, but she didn't have much choice. Maybe the boss was right; she needed a car.

They sat inside his car and she forwarded the email to him. He opened up a bag he'd taken from the boot and pulled out a laptop. After a few moments the camera feed was onscreen.

"Those are expensive cameras," Connie said. The picture was clear, the view towards the reservoir excellent.

"It's a bit far away, though."

"Yeah."

"Still... when should I start?"

"We need to get this back to the office. Get a team on it."

"Let's take a look first, just in case."

"In that case, start two weeks ago today. Late evening."

He searched through the email attachments. The woman had sent them twenty-one files, three for each day covered.

"This is going to take forever," he said.

"We can speed it up." Connie reached over his shoulder, pointing towards a button on the screen.

CHAPTER SEVENTY-SEVEN

"I know." He slapped her hand away.

She gave him a mock hurt look. "Oi."

"You're fine."

"Play it, then."

He hit play. The view took in more of the site between the canal and the reservoir, which looked like it had been cleared for building work. It gave them an uninterrupted view.

"What's that?" Connie asked.

"I'll slow it down."

A car entered the shot. It crawled along the road leading to the reservoir then stopped.

"Ten thirty-five pm," said Connie. "Nothing to be here for at that time."

"Nope."

A figure got out of the car. Connie leaned over Solsby's shoulder to get a better view. He leaned back for her.

The figure was joined by another, emerging from the passenger door. The second person went to the boot and opened it.

Connie watched, her heart racing. Surely they hadn't found the right section of footage this easily?

The man leaned into the boot and seemed to rummage around in it. After a few moments, he closed the boot again. The driver, who'd been watching him, got into the car. The passenger closed the boot and got back in the car, which drove off.

"False alarm," said Solsby.

"It would have been too good to be true," said Connie.

"I'll drop you back at the station. You can make a start on these."

"Cheers." She was relieved to be able to get to work. What they had seen had raised her hopes.

"Come on, then," she said. "We haven't got all day."

He stuck his tongue out at her and started the car.

CHAPTER SEVENTY-EIGHT

"Just drive," Randle said.

"I'm off duty, sir. I'd rather you told me—"

He slapped the dashboard. "Drive. I'll explain when we're moving."

She started the car and headed towards Harborne. They drove in silence, Zoe occasionally muttering under her breath at other drivers. When they reached Five Ways, he shook his head.

"Not that way. Head out of the city."

She took the turnoff for the Hagley Road.

"Where are we going, sir?"

Did she need to worry?

"I'm just going to check in with my team," she said. "They'll be wondering where I am."

"You said you were off duty."

"My son will be expecting me."

"Your son is eighteen and living his own life, Zoe. You don't need to have someone follow your movements. Drive."

She tightened her grip on the wheel and drove out of the

city. At the motorway, he waved southwards. "Get on the M5."

She took the sliproad and joined the rush hour traffic. The speed restriction lights were illuminated on the gantry.

"I need you to tell me what's going on, sir."

He turned towards her, bringing his knee up to twist in the seat. "This is confidential, DI Finch."

"OK."

"When I tell you why, you'll understand."

Zoe thought of Carl. Had he been watching Randle today, at the trial? Had he seen the Superintendent get in her car?

"You can tell me, sir."

"I have to tell someone. Take the outside lane."

"The traffic here is—"

"Just take it."

She indicated to pull out. She knew what he was doing; making it as hard as possible for her to leave the motorway.

She only had to reach out to flick her phone on. She could have Mo tracking her.

But Randle was watching her. And despite her fear, she wanted to know what he was up to.

She forced herself not to prompt him. *Let him tell you in his own time.* He clearly had something he was aching to get off his chest.

"My wife's been taken."

She shot her head round to look at him. "What?"

"Look at the road. Last night. She was taken from the house. My daughters were there, but they're safe."

"How do you know she was taken? She could have—"

"She didn't leave me, if that's what you're thinking. I'm

sure she's thinking of it, after that photo came out in court. But Anita would never walk out on our girls."

"So who took her?"

He stared out of the windscreen, his jaw clenched. "Hamm."

Zoe felt a hard ball form in her chest. "Why?"

"Why d'you think? As leverage. He wanted to make sure I didn't incriminate him, or myself, at the trial today."

"Were you planning on doing that?"

"Ask your boyfriend. But I didn't. I made damn sure to shift blame away from Hamm in my testimony. Alina acting alone. Adams and Fulmer acting alone. No evidence of a conspiracy."

"Did the CPS buy it?"

"She kept asking about Hamm. She knew what was going on, alright, even if she didn't know why. But she didn't get me to admit to any of it."

"What about Ian?"

"What about him?"

"Did he plant that evidence?" she asked.

"You're the only person who knows that."

"I can't be sure what I saw."

"That's what you said in court. Were you protecting him?"

"No." She hit the brake as the car in front's lights came on. The two of them jerked forward.

"Easy, Zoe. Keep your mind on the road."

"It's not that straightforward, sir. I'd be much happier if we could pull over."

"I'm taking you somewhere."

"Where?"

"You've been trying to track Hamm down."

"We haven't been able to find him."

"There are two addresses you've been investigating. I believe my wife is at one of them."

"So why haven't you gone to get her?"

"It can't be me, Zoe. If I magically track the man down, it makes it look like I knew what he was up to all along."

She hesitated. "And did you?"

"I'm not answering that. What are the addresses you've been focusing on?"

"A house outside Solihull, and a gym in Chelmsley Wood."

They were approaching the junction with the M42, which led around the south of the city. Zoe changed lanes.

"What are you doing?" Randle asked.

"We'll need the M42 for both those locations," she told him.

"Fair enough. Stay in the outer lane, though."

She nodded and took the turnoff.

"When we get there," she asked him, "what are we expected to do? There's no way the two of us can overpower Hamm's men."

"I want you to call it in. Say you've seen him, and call for backup. Armed, if necessary."

"That'll take time."

"I'll make sure it's authorised."

I bet you will.

"I want to call DS Uddin," she said. "He's my best officer."

"Uddin is too clean."

She turned to him. "I'm clean."

"You're not bent, Zoe. But you walk a fine line. You don't always obey orders. There's no way I'm bringing Uddin in."

She blew out a frustrated breath. "I'll call it in to Harborne."

"You've worked with Force Response on this side of the city before. You know they're good."

She nodded. They were nearing Solihull, crossing over the M40 two junctions away.

"I'm not sure of the route to Hamm's house," she said.

"Take the next junction."

They took the turnoff for the A34 and he told her to turn right, away from the city. He guided her through a series of turns and bends, along increasingly remote lanes. She doubted she'd remember this route if she did it again.

"Pull over," he said.

She pulled onto the verge. They were in a quiet lane, no houses in sight.

"Where is it?" she asked, her voice low. She extinguished the headlights.

"A hundred yards up ahead. Call it in, now."

"Shouldn't we investigate first?"

"You want to go in there with a bunch of organised criminals inside?"

"You know they're in there?" she asked him.

"DI Finch, you need to trust me. Call it in. This and the gym."

She grabbed her phone.

"Show me the screen," he said.

She held out her phone as she dialled the number for Force Response.

"DI Finch, Force CID, here. Possible sighting of Trevor Hamm, wanted for terrorist activity."

She put her hand over the phone. "I have to tell them the location."

"What's your location, ma'am?" the woman at the other end asked.

"One moment. She opened the What 3 Words app. "Amps, masters, nuance."

"Received. We'll require authorisation."

"Operation pre-authorised by Detective Superintendent Randle." She eyed him.

He nodded, his face pale. "Tell them to be careful. Civilians."

"Possible civilians in the building," she said. "Care required."

"Received. We'll be with you in twelve minutes."

CHAPTER SEVENTY-NINE

"Rhodri, where are you right now?"

"Back in the office, boss. Spoke to Adi, didn't get much I'm afraid."

"Surely you got something?"

Mo was in his car, driving away from the hospital. The post-mortem had been ugly but not particularly helpful.

"Jukes had been in the reservoir for two weeks," Rhodri replied. "They've cordoned off a five-meter radius, but nothing so far."

Mo scratched his neck. He shouldn't be disappointed; the chances of finding forensics when a body had been left for that long would always be slim.

"Make sure he informs you if anything comes to light."

"Already asked him, Sarge. Any joy with the post-mortem?"

"Initial assessment was correct: he didn't die from drowning."

"How *did* he die?"

"Broken neck."

Rhodri winced down the phone. "Poor bastard. Not those cuts on his chest?"

"Nope. Looks like someone snapped his neck."

Another wince. "How?"

"Dr Adebayo's still working on that. Forensics would help."

"Like I say, Sarge, if anything comes to light... Connie's back, she's got CCTV on the go. I'm helping her."

"Where from?"

"There's houses being built just north of the reservoir. They've cleared a lot of the land, gives a good view."

"You'll need more people to go through it. We've got a hefty time window to work on."

Mo was approaching Selly Oak. He turned into Zoe's road and searched for a parking space.

"Most people have gone home," Rhodri said.

"What about Sheila's team?"

"Solsby is still doing door to door. DS Griffin and DC Sarpong are on their way to Hamm's house."

"Yeah." Mo parked his car and walked towards Zoe's house. "I'll be with you in a bit. Just need to check on the boss."

"Give her mine and Connie's best."

"Will do."

Mo hung up and knocked on Zoe's door. No answer. He leaned sideways to peer in through the bay window. A cat sat on the windowsill, miaowing at him. He put his hands against the glass to get a better view inside.

The next door along opened and a young man with messy blond hair emerged. "Mrs Finch has gone out."

"Mrs Finch?"

CHAPTER SEVENTY-NINE

The man shrugged. "That's what I call her. She says call me Zoe, but... well it's a bit odd, someone her age."

Mo resisted reminding the man that at forty, Zoe wasn't exactly a candidate for the retirement village.

"D'you know where she went?"

"She had an argument with Nicholas. He stormed off. I shouldn't be telling you this."

"It's OK." Mo showed his ID. "I'm her colleague. If she comes home, tell her Mo's looking for her, please."

"No problem." The man closed his door and reappeared in the front window of his house, trying not to look like he was watching Mo.

Mo turned away from him and dialled Zoe: voicemail.

"Zo, it's Mo. I'm at your house. Call me, I'm worried about you."

He hung up. Catriona was on call tonight, the girls were at their gran's. He could go home and keep his wife company while he waited for Zoe to get in touch and Cat waited to be summoned. Or he could help Connie and Rhodri out.

He got into his car and pointed it towards Harborne.

CHAPTER EIGHTY

Zoe's phone rang: Mo.

"Leave it," Randle said.

"He's worried about me. My mum died."

"Sorry for your loss."

"She was a drunk."

"You didn't get on?"

"No." She wasn't about to start telling her life story to David Randle. "What now?"

"We wait."

"We should investigate the house. What if there's no one there?"

"I saw someone yesterday. It's the perfect spot to hide a hostage."

"Hamm isn't exactly short of properties. And he knows we're aware of this one."

"I think he wants me to find her. He just doesn't want me making it official."

"So you dragged me in."

"You're a good detective, Zoe. You're the person I can trust."

She bit back the words she wanted to fling at him and put a hand on her door. "I'm taking a look." She slid out of the car before he could stop her.

The night was chilly, the air crisp. She could hear the distant hum of the M42 somewhere ahead of her. The road was lined with dense hedges and was wider than she would have expected for such a remote spot.

She peered in the direction Randle had told her the house was in. She wanted to confirm it was inhabited before she went barging in there with Force Response. But she knew this was risky.

She went to the Mini's boot and brought out her stab vest and baton. She clutched the baton, feeling its weight in her grip.

An owl hooted from somewhere above as she shuffled beside the hedge towards the house. She flinched and looked up, catching faint movement in a tree. She wasn't keen on wildlife, she preferred the city.

There was a gap in the hedge up ahead, a driveway leading off. She steeled herself and crept towards it.

Footsteps approached from behind. She flattened herself against the hedge and turned towards them: Randle.

"I told you to stay in the car," he hissed.

She shook her head, which felt tight. "I want to see for myself."

"Bloody idiot."

She glared at him. She'd given up caring about obeying orders from this man. Tonight's events had to mean he wouldn't be her boss for long.

"How d'you know it was Hamm that took your wife?" she hissed.

"I got a message. I'm not showing it to you. I deleted it."

"It's evidence."

"Zoe, don't be naive."

She turned away from him, aware that if she looked at him for a moment longer she would be tempted to hit him with the baton. She leaned around the hedge towards the house.

A light was on over the front door. Two cars sat in the drive, a black BMW and a red Jaguar.

"Whoever lives here isn't short of cash."

"It's Hamm's house," Randle whispered into her ear, making the hairs on her neck stand on end. "One of those cars might be his."

"He could be renting it out. Or he's sold it."

"I checked the ownership with the Land Registry. RJ Holdings."

"The house was registered under Hamm's name when we raided it." She turned to him. "Say that name again."

"RJ Holdings."

"That's the same company that owns the gym. He's transferred it."

Randle raised an eyebrow at her. "So now you know."

"I need to call Sheila Griffin."

"No, you don't. Force CID will be here in a few minutes."

"If we can prove Hamm is behind RJ Holdings, we've got grounds to raid the gym."

"I'm authorising all this, Zoe. You don't need to prove anything."

"I want to do this properly." She thought of Lesley: *above board, by the book.* Lesley knew the importance of following procedure if evidence was to stand up in court.

"I don't care about the fucking evidence, Finch," said Randle. "I want my wife back."

A light came on at the front of the house.

"That's the study," Randle said.

"How do you know?"

"I broke in. And... nothing."

"He invited you there, didn't he?" Zoe took a step away from Randle. What was she doing here?

When Force Response arrived, how could she find a way to tell them what he was up to? He was leading them all into a trap.

"Shush." He brought a finger up to his lips. She tightened her grip on the baton and turned back towards the house.

A woman entered the study. She went to the window and pulled a set of curtains closed.

"So much for that," said Zoe.

"*Think*, DI Finch. Did you recognise her?"

"She was fifteen metres away. It's dark."

"Blonde hair, pulled up in a bob. Prim expression. Solid, but not fat."

"Margaret Brooking."

His eyes flashed. "Hamm's housekeeper."

She shook her head. "Howard Petersen's housekeeper."

"So they share? I think you can guarantee that woman knows about more than how to clean Hamm's properties."

"OK, so say you're right and one of Hamm's employees is in there. We didn't have enough to charge her after the attacks. She's just a housekeeper. And she could be alone."

"Two cars."

She looked back at the cars.

"The BMW is hers," Randle said. "So whose is the Jag?"

They were interrupted by the sound of a car approaching from behind. Zoe leaned out to see better.

It wasn't the squad car she'd been expecting. Maybe Force Response had brought an unmarked vehicle.

She hung back, waiting to see if someone got out. The passenger door opened and a heavily-built black woman emerged. Zoe frowned.

Another woman got out of the driver's side. Zoe stepped forward.

"Sheila?"

"Zoe? What are you doing here? I thought your mum..."

"Long story." Zoe turned back towards Randle.

He'd gone.

"Fuck," she muttered. Had he gone towards the house, or was he hiding?

Coward.

"You OK?" asked Sheila.

"People keep asking me that."

"We've come to knock on the door, see if we can get a feel for whether Hamm might have been here."

"Force Response are on their way," Zoe replied.

"What? Why didn't you tell me?"

Zoe looked back at Sheila, who looked pissed off. "I can't..." She looked behind her again. If she revealed him now, he'd run. She'd never find his wife, and she'd never be able to take him to Carl.

She curled her fingers around her car keys. Her Mini automatically locked itself when she was away from it for more than thirty seconds. He had nowhere to go.

"Let's knock on the door," she said. "Might save Force Response a job."

CHAPTER EIGHTY-ONE

CONNIE ARCHED her back and yawned. "Sorry, Sarge. D'you want a cup of tea?"

"I'll get it," said Rhodri. He jumped up and grabbed the mugs from the four desks.

Connie, Rhodri, Mo and DC Solsby were all in the team room, trawling through the CCTV. Connie had set it to play at double speed and allocated a day to each of them, working backwards from two weeks ago. She'd rewatched the footage she and Solsby had found when they were in his car, but it hadn't helped. At least the picture was clear, even if there was nothing to see.

"You want to take a breather?" the sarge asked her. "We'll miss things, with tired eyes."

"I'm fine." She smiled. "Young eyes."

"Oi." He grinned. "I'm not that old."

"Sorry, I didn't mean—"

"Connie. You need to learn that it's OK to take the piss. Even out of your senior officers."

"So I can tease Dawson for those awful ties he wears?"

"There is a limit."

She laughed. Rhodri returned with a tray of mugs. "What's so funny?"

"Connie's about to have a go at DCI Dawson for his fashion sense," replied Solsby.

Connie gave him a look. "No, I'm not. But I'm allowed to take the piss out of the sarge."

Mo waved his pen at her. "To an extent."

"So how do I know?" she asked him. "How can I tell if I've crossed a line?"

Rhodri placed a mug in front of her. "You should know how to do that already."

"I do with *you*, Rhod." She blew on her peppermint tea, impressed that he'd remembered.

"You can say whatever you want to me." Rhodri placed mugs in front of Solsby and Mo. The sarge nodded his thanks.

"And you've got a pretty good feel for it with me," added Solsby. "At least, you're getting there."

"You're harder to read than Rhod."

"That's just because you haven't known him for so long," Rhodri said.

"We're becoming good friends, aren't we, Con?" Solsby gave her a wink. "Rita."

Rhodri looked between the two of them. "Ugh. Get a room, you two."

Connie felt her stomach dip. "Rhod! It's not like that."

"No? Course, you've got Rav, haven't you?" He turned to Solsby. "All loved up, they are." He poked his finger into his mouth, miming retching.

"Rhodri," Connie muttered.

CHAPTER EIGHTY-ONE

"OK," said Mo. "That's enough. I think we've all had a rest for our eyes. Let's get back to it."

"Thanks, Sarge." Connie was relieved to turn back to her desk. She could cope with this kind of banter with Rhodri, but throwing Solsby into the mix made her uneasy. She didn't want Rav thinking she didn't take their relationship seriously.

She leaned back and stretched her arms above her head. She rolled her head around, loosening her neck muscles.

OK. She had a fresh video to start on. From nineteen days ago. She clicked on the folder for the early morning recording.

She enlarged the video on her screen and shifted her chair forward. She sipped her tea, stifling a yawn.

After about twenty minutes of watching – forty minutes of screen time, putting her at 2:40 am – a car appeared onscreen. It drove along the same stretch of road she and Solsby had seen the car take in the earlier video. Maybe there was someone who made a habit of coming to the reservoir at night.

Connie reached her hand to the back of her neck and pulled, stretching out her muscles. There were God knew how many more videos to go through. *Stay awake.*

Once again, a person emerged from the driver's seat, then another from the passenger seat. Connie watched as the second person opened the boot.

"What have you got in there?" She tapped her pen against her chin. Opposite, Rhodri coughed and slammed his mug onto the desk, making her jump.

The man stayed next to the boot for longer than in the previous video. Connie became more alert as she watched. She leaned in.

"What you got, Con?" Rhodri was watching her across the desk.

"Probably nothing," she replied. "It's almost identical to something me and Gordon saw earlier."

Solsby flashed her a warning look from across the room: *don't use my first name*. She mouthed *sorry* and grinned as she returned to her screen.

"Hang on a minute." She paused it and zoomed in.

"What?" asked Solsby. He stood up from his chair.

Connie set the video to run forwards, but slowed down this time, not sped up. The sarge had also left his desk and stood behind her, his hand gripping her chair.

"Connie," he breathed.

She nodded, eyes glued to the screen. "I think we've got it, Sarge."

CHAPTER EIGHTY-TWO

"So DID Mo tell you we were coming out here?" Sheila asked as she and Zoe waited for the door to be answered.

"Something like that." Zoe stared at the door, not wanting Sheila to see the unease in her eyes. She should tell her colleague what was going on. But what would happen if she did?

The door opened and a woman with a blonde bun, wearing a blue striped apron, answered. She wiped her hands on a tea towel.

Sheila held up her warrant card. "Margaret Brooking?"

"That's me." The woman looked between the two detectives. "How can I help you?"

"Do you own this property?" Zoe asked.

"No."

"Can you tell me who does?"

"The company that employs me."

"Which is?"

"RJ Holdings."

"Do you also work for Howard Petersen?"

Her expression flicked. "I do. Mondays and Wednesdays. Can you tell me what you're here about, please?"

"We've had reports of suspicious activity in the area," Zoe said.

A frown. "I haven't noticed anything."

"Do you mind if we check inside, just to be sure? We want to make sure you're safe."

"I know you," the woman said to Zoe. "You're DI Finch."

Zoe held up her ID. "You have a good memory, Mrs Brooking."

"I'm not letting you in."

"Are you alone?" asked Sheila.

"Yes."

"Smells good," Zoe commented. A garlicky scent was coming from inside.

"It always smells good when I'm cooking. Now if you don't mind..." Mrs Brooking pushed the door.

"Whose is the other car?" asked Zoe. "Is it Mr Hamm's?"

Mrs Brooking laughed. "Don't be ridiculous. I haven't seen Mr Hamm for weeks."

"But here you are, cooking dinner in his house."

"It isn't his house now. He sold it."

"To RJ Holdings."

"Yes."

"Who you now work for," remarked Zoe.

"That sounds like quite a coincidence to me," said Sheila.

"I get my work via word of mouth. If my clients have other business transactions, then that's their concern." She pushed the door further.

Zoe put out a hand to stop it. "It will be much easier if you just let us in."

"Do you have a warrant?"

"Not yet," said Sheila. Zoe glanced back towards the road. She wondered if Randle was watching. Had he taken advantage of the diversion to break in again?

"Well, then. Good evening." The woman closed the door.

Sheila turned to Zoe. "That was a waste of time."

"Not entirely. We now know this place is owned by the same company that owns the gym. And that she's employed by them and by Petersen. I'd say that's enough of a connection to get a search warrant for the gym."

"You don't think we should search this place?"

Again, Zoe thought of Randle. "Maybe. But it's just a house."

She reminded herself that Sheila knew nothing about Anita Randle. Was Zoe doing the right thing, hiding her disappearance?

Had she even disappeared? Randle might have lied to get Zoe to go along with him.

"The gym is right next to the spot where we found Petersen," she pointed out.

"True." Sheila turned back towards the cars. "Come on, then."

"The gym?"

"I'll call for authorisation on the way."

"I'll do that," said Zoe, a little too fast.

Sheila eyed her. "Why are you here, anyway?"

"I had the same information as you. We came to the same conclusions."

"Shouldn't you be grieving for your mum? Sorry, that came out harsh."

"It's OK. We weren't close."

"Still..."

They were at the cars now.

"We need to move. She'll have phoned ahead," said Sheila. She jumped into her car. DC Sarpong already had her foot on the gas.

Zoe walked to her own car. Force CID would be here any minute. She had to hope Sheila wouldn't pass them.

Randle was in the driver's seat. Zoe yanked open the door.

"I locked it," she said.

He shrugged. "You were nearby, the key was in your pocket. Remote locking, see?"

"Let me drive."

"Get in the passenger seat, DI Finch."

"We have to wait for Force CID."

He shook his head. "Call them. She's not here."

"How do you know?"

"What do you think I was doing while you were chatting on the doorstep?"

So he *had* broken in. "The gym is definitely owned by Hamm," she said as she slid into the passenger seat.

"Course it is. You call Force Response, quickly. We need to hurry."

He floored the accelerator and she held onto the door handle as they sped off.

CHAPTER EIGHTY-THREE

"Play it again," said DS Uddin. "Can you get closer?"

Connie was glad the video was higher quality than the rubbish they usually got. With the dark night, and the distance to the reservoir, that was the only thing preventing this recording from being utterly useless.

"Good," said the sarge. "Start there."

Connie hit play and the car reappeared at the side of the screen. The team had gathered around her, leaning over her shoulders to get a better look. Her skin tingled.

Once again, the two men got out. One went to the boot while the other watched. The first man turned to speak to his companion, who approached him. The two of them manhandled something out of the boot.

"That's Jukes?" Connie asked.

"Has to be," replied Mo. She could feel his breath on her neck.

The bundle was misshapen, wrapped in something. It was the right size and shape to be a body, twisted over.

"What's he got round him?" Rhodri asked.

"Looks like a sheet," said Connie.

"Something we can trawl the reservoir for," added the sarge.

"Forensics are going to love that," commented Rhodri.

"Keeps the divers busy."

"Look," said Connie. She pointed to the other edge of the screen. Another car approached. It parked facing the camera.

"Thanks, mate," said Solsby. "Nice square view there. Good to know there are some considerate criminals about."

"Might just be a witness," said Connie.

"They've spotted him. If he's just a witness, he's about to become a second victim."

"There weren't any abandoned cars at the site," Connie said. "If they'd killed him…"

"They'd have moved it," said the sarge. "Hush. Let's watch."

The two men from the first car hauled the body up between them and walked towards the water. They looked confident, like they'd done this before. A shiver ran down Connie's back.

The man from the second car stayed by his vehicle. He leaned against its side and watched, arms folded across his chest.

"He's part of it," she said. "Has to be."

"Maybe he's the boss," Rhodri suggested. "Checking they're doin' their job properly."

"You want me to pause it?" asked Connie. "See if I can get a better look at him?"

"Please," said the sarge.

She clicked the mouse a few times. The image was of a balding man, heavily built, average height. Apart from that, she couldn't make out any distinguishing characteristics. His face was blurred.

"Zoom in on the plates," said Solsby.

Connie did as he suggested, her tongue moving across her teeth as she worked. "Whoah."

"Perfect," said the sarge. "Rhodri…"

"Got it, Sarge." Rhodri scooted round to his desk to bring up the vehicle database.

Connie's eyes flicked from the screen to Rhodri and back again. He stared at his screen, sniffing.

"Hurry up," she said.

"Going as fast as I can. This system is bloody slow."

She zoomed back out and restarted the video. Watching Rhodri wouldn't help him do his job. And the plates would be false, anyway.

"Got it," said Rhodri. He looked up, his eyes alight.

Connie stared back. "What?"

The sarge hurried round to Rhodri's side of the desk. He put both hands to his cheeks, his mouth wide. "We've got him."

"Who?" Connie's heart was thudding in her ears.

Mo grinned at her. "That car is a 2018 Jaguar XF. Registered to RJ Holdings."

CHAPTER EIGHTY-FOUR

"I'll get out here." Randle slapped the steering wheel. He stopped the car and slid out, disappearing into the shadows behind the Co-op supermarket.

Zoe shuffled across to the driver's seat and started the ignition. If she was going to alert Mo, or maybe Carl, now was the time.

Sheila was standing in the road as Zoe turned the corner past the waste ground where they'd found Petersen. Zoe stopped and opened her window.

"I've had a call from Gordon." Sheila was out of breath.

"Gordon?"

"DC Solsby. He's working the forensics and CCTV with your guys. They've got video of Jukes being dumped in the reservoir."

Zoe jumped out of her car. "When?"

"Eighteen days ago. It gets better."

"How?"

"Two cars. One had the body. Two guys got it out the

CHAPTER EIGHTY-FOUR

boot and chucked him in the water. The other car had a man. He stood and watched. He was part of it."

"And?"

"The second car is registered to RJ Holdings. It's a Jaguar."

"The one sitting in the drive back at..."

"I've put out an alert for that registration. And Uniform are on their way to the house. If he tries to run, we'll get him."

Zoe clenched her fists. She turned towards the gym. "We go in. Now."

"Shouldn't we go back? If his car is parked at the house..."

Zoe looked Sheila in the eye. She'd worked closely with Sheila on Canary, back when she'd been a DS. But she was the other woman's senior officer now.

She could give the order, and refuse to brook questions. Or she could give Sheila the respect she deserved.

"I think they're holding a woman in there."

"What? Who?"

Zoe scanned the area. It was too late to protect Randle; she had nothing to gain from it.

"Anita Randle."

"The Super's wife?"

Zone nodded, taking in Sheila's narrowed eyes.

"How long have you known about this, ma'am?"

"Not long."

"It's been reported?"

"Randle told me."

"How?"

"We just need to get in there. If they've seen us, they'll kill her."

Sheila turned towards the gym. "You got authorisation?"

"From the super."

"Really?"

"Check, if you need to."

"I will."

Zoe waited while Sheila called Command. She'd be in deep shit once this was over. Knowing a woman had been abducted and not calling it in. Working with Randle despite everything she knew about him.

And Carl would never forgive her.

"You're right," said Sheila. "Let's go." She started towards the fence that separated the gym from the road.

Zoe scanned the hedge opposite the gym and the railings closest to her as she ran to keep up with Sheila. Had Randle heard their conversation?

"We have to wait for Force Response," Zoe said. "They're on their way."

Cars pulled up behind them: two squad cars and a dark unmarked vehicle. PS Ford emerged from the unmarked car.

He put out a hand which Zoe shook, then Sheila.

"DI Finch. Good to work with you again."

"Likewise. This is DS Griffin from Organised Crime. Joint operation."

"What have we got?"

"The gym over there" – Zoe gestured towards it – "belongs to Trevor Hamm. Wanted on multiple counts of—"

"I know who Trevor Hamm is."

"That makes things simpler. We believe the premises are linked to the murder of Howard Petersen, found on that land over there, and of Dwayne Jukes, who was brought out of Edgbaston Reservoir earlier today."

"Organised crime, double murder and terror activities," he said. "It's your lucky night, DI Finch."

"Let's hope so."

CHAPTER EIGHTY-FOUR

"OK. I've got a team of six with me. Three of us will take the front, three are already finding position at the back. You've already got your stab vest on."

"Yes."

"We'll knock on the door, but you be with us. OK?"

Zoe had done this before. She nodded assent.

"There might be a civilian in there," said Sheila.

"Who?" asked Ford.

"IC1 female, mid to late forties," replied Zoe. "Not a purple-haired Scottish woman. If she's in there, arrest her."

He spoke into his radio.

"I'm waiting for your order, ma'am."

"Of course." Zoe took one last look at Sheila, who had adopted her pissed off look again. Right at that moment, Zoe hated herself.

"Go," she told Ford.

CHAPTER EIGHTY-FIVE

ANITA SAT HUNCHED in the opposite corner of the room from her toilet space. She was cold and dirty, her clothes felt slimy, and her stomach growled repeatedly.

They'd brought her a bottle of water, and a packet of Hobnobs. She'd devoured the biscuits greedily then thrown up. She'd brought up the water too, and it had been hours before they'd brought more.

If no one came for her soon, she was going to pass out. She didn't care who it was: at least if it was that Scottish woman, she might bring more water. Food, too. Not that Anita held out much hope of being given any. The woman had made her disgust clear when she'd brought the second bottle of water. "I'm not cleaning that up, yer posh bitch."

She'd heard people moving around nearby for the last few hours. It sounded like they were running, or lifting weights. Men's voices, sharp and easy. Her captors, or someone else? Were there people using this building who didn't know she was in here?

She'd tried using her tongue to push the gag off but had

CHAPTER EIGHTY-FIVE

only succeeded in making it tighter. When she'd drunk the water they'd yanked it down onto her chin. It had made it difficult to drink and she'd lost half of the water down herself. Her shirt was still damp.

Anita wrapped her arms around herself. David must have alerted his colleagues by now. Her captors knew who she was married to, they'd made that clear. Was this related to an investigation? Was it connected to that photo? And if so, did he know where she was?

He'd have been here by now if he did, half of Force CID in his wake. Even with the photo of that woman, Anita knew enough to understand that David would never abandon her.

A few cars had come and gone outside throughout the day but it seemed the people beyond the wall had come on foot. She wondered what this building was. Where it was. There were no clues from what she could hear. No trains, no buses, no factory sounds.

She scuttled along the wall and raised herself up to lean into the window, listening. If she heard someone, she would bang the glass as hard as she could. It didn't matter if she cut herself.

She heard voices, distant, from below. Was that...?

It was.

"Police!"

They were here for her. David had come.

She felt a gust of air as the door opened.

"Move!" came a voice. A man.

She shrank back against the wall. She put her hand against the glass and drew it back, but he grabbed her wrist and twisted it.

She cried out in pain.

"Shut up, bitch. Come with me."

He hauled her up and she struggled to get her footing. Her legs were numb and her right foot ached. He dragged her out of the door and along what felt like a corridor. She put out a hand as far as she could and swept it along a wall as they moved.

Another door was opened – kicked – and she was flung forward. She landed heavily on her front, her right shoulder catching the brunt of it. She felt pressure on her feet and pulled them in.

A door slammed. She turned, panicking: it had been behind her. She was in total darkness now, nothing visible around the edges of the blindfold.

She slammed her body into the door but it didn't budge.

"Quiet! You don't want me to come in there." The same man.

She pulled in a sour breath and fell back against something sharp, wincing. The ache in her foot had turned from a thrum to a stab. Her shoulder screamed at her. She wished she could reach it, to feel if it was damaged.

She tried to scream. She hurled herself against the door. The police were here. She had to tell them she was inside.

The door gave against her weight. She fell to the floor beyond it, every muscle on fire.

A kick landed in her stomach. She curled up, wishing her hands weren't tied behind her back. She wanted to fold in on herself, to protect her vital organs.

Another kick, this time to her back. She screamed, the sound muffled.

"Shut the fuck up." A mouth was close to her ear, breath hot on her skin. She trembled.

She felt something cold against her cheek. She jolted away from it, then felt an arm pull her back towards the man.

CHAPTER EIGHTY-FIVE

The knife was on her cheek again. He pressed the side of the blade into her skin.

"Shut the fuck up if you know what's good for you."

He stood up, withdrawing the knife. She struggled to pull away from him. He placed his foot against her back and shoved her back into the cupboard, then closed the door.

CHAPTER EIGHTY-SIX

Mo listened to PC Solsby as he spoke to DS Griffin on the phone. He kept glancing at Mo, nodding excitedly.

Zoe was off duty. She was grieving. She needed to find Nicholas.

But they'd just got their best lead to Trevor Hamm.

He grabbed his phone and dialled her number.

Voicemail. *Damn.*

"Boss, it's Mo. We've got video that links Hamm to Jukes's murder. Call me."

He ran his hand across the stubble on his chin as Solsby hung up. "Is DS Griffin at the house?"

"Not any more. She's gonna head to the gym. With DI Finch."

"Zoe's there?"

"She was already at the house. My boss isn't sure why."

Mo wasn't sure why, either. As far as he'd known, Zoe was dealing with personal matters this evening. If she was with Sheila, why wasn't she picking up?

"I need to speak to DCI Dawson," he said.

CHAPTER EIGHTY-SIX

"Yeah." Solsby licked his lips, his breathing shallow. "What d'you want us to do, Sarge?"

"Zoe and Sheila are already covering the gym. They'll need more evidence. We carry on with what we're doing."

"My DS told me they'd seen the Jag at the house, Sarge."

"Hamm's Jag?"

"The one registered to that company. Got to be his."

"OK." Mo turned to Rhodri. "First off, I want concrete proof that firm is his. Get on the Companies House website, trawl anything you can find."

"On it."

"Connie, carry on scanning the video. The twenty-four hours after we see them dumping Jukes. And find cameras from the vicinity. I want a timeline of them arriving at and leaving the reservoir."

"You're building a case," said Connie.

"That's what DCI Clarke would tell us to do, and that's what the DI needs from us now."

His phone rang: Zoe.

"Boss, where have you been?"

"Can't talk long. I'm at the gym, we're about to go in. I reckon Randle's wife is in there, Hamm's lot abducted her."

"They did *what*?"

"Long story. But Sheila's told me about the Jag you saw at the reservoir. We just walked right past it outside Hamm's house."

"You want me to get over there? I've got the team building a case."

"We'll have plenty of time for that," she said. "Grab one of them, and get over to that house. Uniform are on their way."

"What about Force Response?"

"I've got PS Ford with me here. He's called for another team to head over there."

"This is it."

"It is, Mo. We need to act fast."

"I'm there."

Mo shoved his phone into his pocket. Connie was on the phone, trying to identify more CCTV sources. Rhodri was leaning into his screen.

The proof that Hamm owned the car, and the business, was crucial. Without it, the bastard would slip through their fingers again.

"DC Solsby, you take over from Connie. Connie, with me."

CHAPTER EIGHTY-SEVEN

A SCRAWNY WOMAN with spiked purple hair ran down the stairs as Ford's team burst through the door. Zoe ran in behind them, Sheila after her.

Zoe snapped at the woman. "Sheena MacDonald?"

"Yeah. What the fuck's going on?"

"We have a warrant to search this property." Zoe shoved her mobile in the woman's face, the copy of the authorisation Randle had obtained.

Where was he?

"On what grounds?" the woman spat. "I'm calling my lawyer."

Zoe stood in front of her. "Edward Startshaw?"

"What's it to you?"

"Nothing."

The Force CID officers were already at the top of the stairs. Two more were downstairs, she could hear them moving through the building.

A door crashed open at the top of the stairs and two

young black men ran out. They stared at the uniformed officers, faces full of shock. One threw his hands in the air.

"We ain't done nothing."

The two PCs turned them to face the wall and patted them down.

"No weapons, ma'am."

"Drugs?"

"Nothing."

Zoe took the stairs two at a time. "Who are you? What are you doing here?"

The man closest to her wore a pair of grubby shorts and a vest that was torn at the shoulder. "Just doin' a bit of boxing, like."

"They're customers," MacDonald called up. "Leave them alone."

"Yeah." The young man nodded at Zoe, his sweaty hair bobbing.

"Get back in there. We'll need to talk to you." She pointed to the door the men had come through and followed them in. This was the space Connie had described. A large gym, boxing ring at the far end. A door beyond it, high windows on both sides.

Two of Ford's team were at the door, making ready to break through. They crashed through it then emerged after a few moments.

"Clear."

Damn. Zoe turned back towards the stairs.

"These two need to give statements."

"I'll keep an eye on them, ma'am."

"Cheers. Bring MacDonald up here, too."

Zoe went with the other PC, a woman, back to the stairs.

"Do I know you?"

"PC Janek, ma'am. I was there when we raided that kennels in Harmans Cross."

The day they'd found Zaf. "Right," Zoe said. "Thanks."

"Just doing my job, ma'am. What now?"

Zoe pointed to another door leading off the stairs. "Through there."

PC Janek opened the door and went ahead, another of her colleagues following her.

"It's clear."

Zoe followed them into a large room, not as big as the gym but still spacious. It stank of urine.

"What's that?" she pointed to an object against the far window.

PC Janek picked up a shoe with her weapon. "Woman's slipper, ma'am."

Zoe frowned. No one would wear slippers to a gym.

"She's here. Anita Randle. Find her!"

The room had no other doors. Janek and her colleague hurried out. Ford and two other men were rattling up the stairs.

"Nothing down there, ma'am," he said.

"Shit." Zoe slapped the stair rail.

"There's another door through here!" came a voice from the gym.

"Wait." Ford slid in ahead of Zoe and covered the room in a few strides. Zoe scuttled after him, her heart racing. She heard a crash behind her and turned to see Sheila entering.

"You OK?" she asked.

"I was downstairs. Storage rooms, no sign of Hamm. Or a hostage."

Zoe pursed her lips. "Through here," came a voice from the door they'd checked earlier. She followed it to find three officers in a small room, facing a locked door. Banging came from the other side.

"Wait," Zoe said. She approached the door and crouched down.

"Anita?"

A muffled cry came from inside.

"She's right behind that door," Ford said.

Zoe took a deep breath. "Anita, get away from the door. We're coming in."

More muffled sounds.

Zoe gave Ford a nod. "Be careful."

He gestured to his team. The male officer at the front tugged on the door. "Not budging."

"Get the hinges."

"They're on the other side, Sarge."

"We need to bust the lock then."

"You can't use the enforcer," said Zoe. "She's right behind the wood."

"Don't worry." Ford nodded to his colleague.

The man leaned into the door, pulling a chisel out of a bag PC Janek had placed on the floor behind him. He used it to jimmy the door. Zoe watched, her heart thumping against her ribs.

At last, the door crashed outwards and a woman fell out. She was blonde, wearing a stained shirt and trousers, along with a gag and blindfold.

Zoe rushed forward to remove the gag. "Anita?"

"Yes." The woman's voice was thin.

"Anita Randle." Zoe peeled off the blindfold and Anita blinked back at her.

"You're safe now," Zoe said.

"David?" Anita looked up and past Zoe.

CHAPTER EIGHTY-SEVEN

"He's nearby."

"I'm here."

Randle pushed past Zoe and gathered his wife in his arms. She melted into them, her limbs loose.

Ford and his team straightened. "Sir."

Randle waved an arm at them, not turning away from his wife. "Stand down, men. You did good."

CHAPTER EIGHTY-EIGHT

When Mo arrived at the house, Force Response were already parked along the lane, tucked into a lay-by.

"Wait here," he said to Connie, and got out of the car. She shivered.

"DS Uddin," he said as he approached the two cars. "Deputising for DI Finch."

"We know." One of the officers gave him a tight nod. "PS Gerry. We've taken a look. The house is quiet, one car in the drive."

"One?" Mo wanted to hit himself.

"Just a BMW."

"Shit." Mo thrust a fist into his mouth. "You didn't see a Jaguar?" He gave them the registration.

"Sorry."

"Wait a moment." He ran back to the car.

"Connie. Get onto command. If there's a sighting of that Jag, I want to know instantly."

"It's gone?"

"Of course it's gone. I can't believe we've let him get away again."

"I'll monitor, Sarge."

"Cheers." Mo ran back to the uniformed officers.

"We go in anyway. We've got authorisation for a search."

"We've been briefed," replied PS Gerry.

"You know what you're looking for?"

"I say we don't delay."

"You're right. Let's go."

Moments later they were at the front of the house. PS Gerry hammered on the door. Four of his team hung back in the shadows of the front drive. He gestured to two of them and they disappeared around the side of the building.

"Stand back, DS Uddin."

Mo hung back while they used the enforcer to break down the door.

"Police! Show yourselves!" he called as he followed them in.

Silence. He crossed through a generous hallway into a vast living space. Tall bifold doors filled the back wall and the biggest kitchen island he'd ever seen stood to one side.

He pointed at a door beyond the island and one of the PCs went through.

"Nothing here, Sarge."

Mo turned back to the hallway. He could hear boots upstairs, Gerry's officers searching the bedrooms.

"Clear!" came a voice. PS Gerry leaned over the banisters, looking down at Mo. "Sorry, mate."

Mo leaned against the wall. There was still one car, which meant Hamm had taken the housekeeper with him. If he'd been here at all.

Connie ran through the front door. "Sarge!"

"They've found the car?"

"Picked up on the M42, only three miles away."

"And?"

"There was a woman driving it. No passengers."

Mo's senses prickled. "So where's Hamm?"

"Dunno."

He stepped forward, suddenly alert. "Be careful, Connie. If he's here…"

"In here!" came a voice from the back of the house. Mo ran into the open plan kitchen.

It was empty.

"Hello?" he called. Connie ran in behind him.

"PC Nunn!" PS Gerry shouted as he entered behind them. "Where are you?"

A woman's head appeared behind the kitchen island. "There's a trapdoor."

Mo and Connie exchanged wide-eyed stares. Mo stepped forward but was stopped by PS Gerry's hand on his arm.

"He could be armed."

Mo nodded, his stomach clenching, and stepped back. He grabbed Connie's arm. She was breathing heavily, clutching her collar.

"Up!" barked PS Gerry. Mo heard movement behind the island. He ached to go round there.

Gerry looked round. "He's clean. No weapons."

Mo pushed past him, almost stumbling in his haste. Sitting at the bottom of a steep stairway, surrounded by row upon row of wine bottles, was Trevor Hamm.

Mo swallowed. "Trevor Hamm, you're under arrest."

CHAPTER EIGHTY-NINE

Zoe ran out of the building, Sheila following her.

"DI Finch!"

"One moment!" She threw a hand out behind to stop Sheila. On the road, Anita Randle was being wheeled into an ambulance. Her husband stepped up with her, his hand clasped around hers.

"Sir." Zoe stopped at the back doors to the ambulance. "We need to talk."

He squeezed his wife's hand. "Not now." Her face flickered.

"You can't expect me not to take action."

"I don't, Zoe. It's gone past that now."

"What's going on?" Anita croaked.

"Nothing, love." He lifted her hand and kissed the back of it. She smiled weakly.

How much did Anita Randle know?

"Sir, I have to make a statement about this to PSD."

"And so do I."

Her breath caught in her throat. "You're going to tell them?"

He looked up at the ceiling of the ambulance, then back at her. A paramedic brushed past Zoe.

"We need to get going."

"What are you going to do?" she called to Randle.

"Tell your boyfriend to expect a call."

The paramedic leaned out and pulled the doors shut.

CHAPTER NINETY

Zoe watched the ambulance drive away. Sheila stood next to her.

"You knew where Hamm would be," the DS said. "How?"

Zoe turned to her. "We got CCTV. That Jag."

Sheila shook her head. "You knew something else. What did the super tell you?" She looked after the ambulance. "Ma'am. I need you to inform me if anything untoward has happened here tonight."

Zoe was tired. Sheila hadn't called her *ma'am* for a very long time. Was this how things were going to be from now on?

"Detective Superintendent Randle has been working with Trevor Hamm for some time. PSD know about it, but haven't been able to gather conclusive evidence." *As far as I'm aware.*

"That photo..."

Zoe nodded. "Hamm must have set Randle up with Alina Popescu."

"You think he was connected to the bomb?"

"I don't know. I haven't seen evidence pointing in that direction. But he knew about it. I think..."

"What?"

Zoe had been about to voice her suspicions about the evidence that had been planted on Nadeem Sharif. Was Ian guilty? Had Randle ordered him to do it? And did Ian even know what he'd been doing?

Ian wasn't in Randle's league. But he was bent. He'd taken bribes when he'd been at Kings Norton, and he'd worked for Randle when he should have been spying on him for Carl.

"I need to talk to Professional Standards," she told Sheila. "I can't say any more right now."

Sheila pursed her lips. "I really hope you're not mixed up in this."

The accusation was like a jolt to Zoe's heart. Would Carl think the same way?

PS Ford approached them, pulling off his helmet. "Two men on their way to the station for questioning. What d'you want us to do with the woman?"

Sheena McDonald. Zoe couldn't be sure how closely she'd been caught up with Hamm's latest exploits. But she would know something.

"Caution her. We'll talk to her in the morning."

"Ma'am." He walked away.

"Zoe," Sheila said. "I really hope you're not getting yourself into trouble."

"I'll be fine," Zoe said. Her phone buzzed: a text from Mo.

We got Hamm.

CHAPTER NINETY

Her mouth fell open. She grabbed Sheila by the shoulders. "Hamm. Mo's arrested him!"

"Thank all that's holy for that. Where?"

"I don't know. But we *got* him, Sheila. We have CCTV of him when they dumped Dwayne Jukes's body, and I know my team is building a case now. By the time Connie's done, it'll be like a brick wall."

"Well done, Zoe," Sheila said. She looked hesitant. "You deserve credit for that, at least."

CHAPTER NINETY-ONE

ANITA LAY PROPPED against the pillows, occasionally placing a finger on her various injuries. Her ankle was sprained, her ribs were bruised and they'd put stitches in her forehead.

David knocked gently on the bedroom door. "How are you feeling?"

She grimaced. "Aching all over."

"You rest up for as long as you need. You've been through an ordeal."

She narrowed her eyes at him. "Who was that woman, David?"

He eased himself onto the bed, not meeting her eye. "It's not what you think."

"I *think* you've been having an affair. At least, that's what I thought until I read about your testimony in the trial of that sergeant."

He leaned towards her. She shook her head and he pulled back.

"Tell me, David. How did you know her? Did you have

anything to do with" – her voice was hoarse – "the bomb attacks?"

"I had no involvement in the attacks."

"Did you know about them?"

"I was Gold Command at the airport. I was one of the first to be told."

Pain gripped at her ribs. She wasn't ready for this. But it couldn't wait.

"That's not what I meant."

"No." He looked down at her feet beneath the duvet. The girls were both asleep, she'd made him call a neighbour from the ambulance so they would have someone watching them until she got home.

He'd left the girls alone in the middle of the night. Yes, he'd done it to find her. But he'd just walked out of the house and left them alone, knowing that someone had broken in just hours earlier.

What kind of man did that?

What kind of father?

"Tell me, David. Did that woman tell you what she was going to do?"

He looked up at her and shook his head. "She didn't know herself."

"Sorry?"

"She was forced to do it. Her family were threatened, in Romania. She didn't know it was going to happen until days before."

Anita put a hand to her throat. She couldn't imagine what it would be like to walk into a building with an explosive device strapped to your body. To have the – the what? It wasn't courage – to detonate it.

"She wasn't in control of the device, Anita. Alina was an innocent pawn."

"She killed people. That hostage negotiator..."

He nodded. "It wasn't her fault. It was the men who controlled her. Trevor Hamm."

"I keep hearing his name." She gasped in a shaky breath. She wanted to sleep. "Who is he?"

"He's a bad man."

"Don't talk to me like I'm five years old."

"He's a man I was stupid enough to get myself involved with. Bryn Jackson was mixed up with him when he was just into drug dealing and money laundering. They were different times. I found myself dragged into it."

"Don't make excuses. Bryn Jackson was the Assistant Chief Constable." She hesitated. "Is that why he died?"

David nodded. "Not entirely."

"But the verdict... it was his daughter, wasn't it?"

"She found out about what he was doing. She couldn't forgive him."

A lump formed in Anita's throat. "I understand how she felt."

Fear broke on his face. "Anita. Please. I'm going to talk to Professional Standards. I'm going to—"

"Did you sleep with that woman? Alina?"

"No. I swear it. She was just a pretty young thing to hang on my arm at a party."

"I could have done that."

"It wasn't that kind of party."

"No." She sank back into the pillows. Sleep pulled at her, despite the horror of what David was telling her. "Go. Don't wake me before you leave in the morning."

He reached for her hand under the duvet. She shrugged him off.

"Let me sleep, David."

CHAPTER NINETY-TWO

Zoe's phone rang as she drove home. The adrenaline had left her and her limbs felt heavy.

She checked the screen and felt a tug of relief.

"Nicholas."

"Sorry, Mum."

She wanted to melt. "It's OK. I can see why the relationship I had with your gran is difficult for you."

He sobbed. "It's different for me."

"I know." She'd worked hard not to infect him with her resentment of Annette. At least that had worked, to some extent.

"I'll miss her, Mum. I wanted the two of you to make it up. She wasn't all that bad."

"Maybe not." Was he right? Had she only seen Annette through the goggles of childhood neglect? Had her mum changed her ways?

"Where are you?"

"Zaf's. His mum said I should call you."

"Anabelle knows what she's talking about."

CHAPTER NINETY-TWO

"But I was going to anyway."

"Good. Are you coming home?"

"It's two am."

"And you've got school in the morning." He'd still been wearing his uniform when he'd stormed off. She wasn't sure how they'd react to him turning up in yesterday's clothes.

"Come home, love," she said.

"I'm tired, Mum. I just want Zaf to hold me."

Zoe's breath caught. She'd stopped being the person her son went to when he needed comfort.

She forced a smile, hoping he could hear it down the phone. "I understand. I'll see you tomorrow. I love you."

"I love you too."

CHAPTER NINETY-THREE

Zoe had another call to make. She dialled the number as she drove, heading towards the city centre now.

Carl yawned. "Zoe? What time is it?"

"Late. Sorry to call you like this, Carl, but we need to talk."

"Come to the flat. I'll put coffee on." Another yawn.

"No," she said. "I'll meet you at Lloyd House."

"It's the middle of the night. The place is closed."

"It's a police station, Carl. It doesn't just open nine to five."

"Why now? Can't it wait?"

"I've just been driving around the West Midlands with David Randle, looking for his wife. She was taken by Hamm's people."

"You've *what*?" His voice sharpened.

"We've arrested Hamm. Anita Randle is safe. And her husband has sworn to me that he'll contact your boss. But I don't trust him."

"Where is he now?"

CHAPTER NINETY-THREE

"He went with his wife, in an ambulance."

"Shit. Which hospital?"

"You're going to go after him?"

"I'm going to talk to you first. Be at Lloyd House front entrance in fifteen minutes."

"I'll be there in ten."

She blinked to keep her eyes open as she crossed the inner ring road and drove into the city centre. It was time to tell Carl everything she knew.

CHAPTER NINETY-FOUR

Anita listened as David's car left the driveway. The girls were moving around the house, arguing as they tried to get themselves ready for school.

She sat up in bed, wincing. Her ankle still hurt and her head felt thick. But she needed to be alert.

She went to the wardrobe and threw on the softest clothes she could find: a pair of faded joggers and a grey hoody. She pushed open the door to her room, forcing a mask of calm onto her face.

Maria was stood on the landing, her blazer on the floor beside her. Pens were scattered around it.

"Mum, she threw all my stuff on the floor."

"Just put it all back in the pockets. It's only some pens." Anita reached out for her daughter.

Maria gave her a puzzled look. "What happened to you?" She pointed at Anita's face. "Dad said you had to go to Aunty Julia's."

Anita nodded. "She wasn't very well. She needed someone to help out with the baby."

"You could have told us."

"Sorry, love." Anita pulled Maria to her and gave her a squeeze. It wouldn't be long before she couldn't fold her youngest daughter in her arms anymore.

"You're not going anywhere again, are you, Mum?" Maria's voice was muffled.

Anita squeezed harder. "No. Promise."

She bent to pick up her daughter's blazer, wincing. "Don't worry about this."

"Sorry, Mum. I'll pick it up. You look..."

Anita turned away, embarrassed by her injuries. She needed to be strong for her girls.

"You're getting a day off," she said. "Carly too."

Maria's face brightened. "Carly!" she cried. "No school today."

Carly emerged from her room. "How come?"

Maria turned to her. "Mum says."

Carly looked past her sister to her mum. "School's closed?"

"I just wanted to spend some time with you both. We're going on a trip."

"What kind of trip?"

"Not sure, yet. Both of you, go to your room and pack a bag. Clothes, phones. Any other stuff that's important to you."

"What's going on?" Carly asked.

Anita avoided her daughter's eye. She'd explain later, when they were safely away from here. She had money, David had put cash into a savings account over the years and she had access.

First stop would be the bank. Then... well, then she'd have to work something out.

"Go on, then!"

Anita turned back to her own room and opened the wardrobe doors. She didn't want much, it all made her think of David. Clothes she'd worn to fit with her life as the senior police officer's wife.

She thought of Margaret Jackson. The woman had moved into a house in Solihull, abandoning that massive place her husband had bought them. Now Anita knew how he'd paid for it.

Maybe Margaret would give her a place to stay, for a few days. She'd understand.

Carly ran into the room, holding a stuffed dog. "Should I take Hector?"

"Yes. Bring Hector."

"OK. Don't tell Maria."

Anita smiled as her daughter ran out. She sank onto the bed, pulling all her strength together. She could do this. It was the best thing, for her and her daughters.

CHAPTER NINETY-FIVE

"Zoe, a word." Dawson poked his head out of his office as she passed on her way to her own. She yawned and followed him in.

"Have you slept?" he asked.

"Not yet."

"You've come straight from Lloyd House."

She blanched.

"They called me, Zoe. You make a statement like that, and your line manager gets a call."

She sat down. "What did they say?"

"You're going to be recommended for a commendation. Yeah, I'm as surprised as you are."

"Yesterday I thought I might be arrested."

"You're a good copper, Zoe. You've made some mistakes, and you need to rein yourself in sometimes. But PSD knew you had nothing to do with what the super and Ian Osman were up to."

"Did you know anything?" Zoe asked him.

"I didn't even know that PSD had placed Osman in your team until the trial."

"Sorry."

"Don't be. The fewer people know about this stuff, the better."

"I want to be the one to interview Trevor Hamm," she told him.

"Of course you do. But it's not that simple."

"Why not?"

"PSD need to thoroughly investigate what happened with you and Randle yesterday. You went rogue, Zoe."

"But I thought—"

"You got Hamm. You seem to have uncovered the most senior corrupt officer in this force. But they still need to check you out. You're on paid leave for two weeks or until the investigation is concluded, whichever's sooner."

She jabbed her thumbnail into his desk. "That's not fair. It was my team that tracked Hamm down. I need to—"

Dawson raised a hand. "Did anyone see you come in here?"

She tried to remember if the corridor had been empty. It was only half past seven. Her team would be in, though.

"No one."

"In that case, we haven't spoken. You go and do what you need to do, then come and find me. No later than midday, though."

She stood up. "Right. Thanks."

He gave her a wink. Maybe he wasn't such an arsehole after all. She smiled at him.

"Thanks, sir. I appreciate it."

He laughed.

CHAPTER NINETY-SIX

"Boss." Connie looked over her screen and grinned as Zoe entered the team room. "Perfect timing."

Zoe grabbed a chair and pulled it to Connie's desk. "You should be at home. I told you to come in late, you need your rest."

Connie raised an eyebrow. "*You're* here."

"How long have you been in, Connie?"

"Not long." Connie looked away.

"Long enough to start trawling through the CCTV from the gym."

"They didn't wipe it at all, boss. I think they kept it deliberately. We found this recording in a separate file."

"We?"

Connie blushed. "I."

"Take credit where you deserve it, Connie."

"I'll try."

"Show me, then."

Connie brought up the file. It showed Anita Randle

being brought to the gym. Two men Zoe didn't recognise carried her. She flopped in their arms, drugged.

"Poor woman," Zoe whispered. "We got anything from inside?"

"Just the stairway." Connie showed her a video of Anita being carried up the stairs then taken through a door. Sheena MacDonald watched as the men carried her, her expression tight.

"So she was involved, then," Zoe said.

"Rhodri's gone with Uniform to pick her up."

"Blimey, you lot don't hang around, do you?"

Connie's eyes crinkled. "And there's this." She opened another file.

The shot was from a corner of the gym, at the front. It showed the road opposite, and the area of land where they'd found Petersen.

A van drove into shot. Two people got out and opened the back doors. They pulled what could only have been Petersen's body out and dragged it to the grass. Then they spent some time arranging him there.

"What was all that about?" Zoe asked. "The threading the needle thing."

"Could be relevant," Connie said. "Could be nothing. But I've traced the van. It was also involved in a drugs drop in Sparkhill two weeks ago. One that Organised Crime are investigating."

"Good work, Connie. Bring up the file for that investigation."

"Right here." Connie had the record open in another screen.

Zoe scanned it. "Dwayne Jukes."

"Seems they're from his gang," Connie said.

"And they'll have been mighty pissed off at Hamm killing their boss."

"Revenge?"

"Let's find out." Zoe stood up.

"Boss?"

"I'm going to find Sheila, interview Hamm with her. Then I've got to check in with Dawson. After that..."

"Everything OK, boss?"

"Fine. If you can't find me, just talk to Mo. He'll tell you what to do."

Connie frowned. "Course, boss."

CHAPTER NINETY-SEVEN

Hamm glared back at Zoe as she sat at the interview room table and placed her hands on the surface. Sheila took the seat next to her, slapping down a heavy file.

Zoe turned on the digital recorder.

"Present, Detective Inspector Finch."

"DS Griffin," added Sheila.

"Edward Startshaw, solicitor, and my client Trevor Hamm," added Startshaw. Zoe threw him a smug smile across the table. She wondered how he'd felt when he'd finally received the call to tell him Hamm had been arrested.

Zoe shuffled in her seat.

"Mr Hamm. Can I call you Trevor?"

"My client would rather you—"

"Trevor." Zoe flashed her eyes at him, then caught Sheila clearing her throat.

Calm down, she told herself. She wasn't going to nail him by getting over-excited.

"Let's start at the beginning shall we, Trevor?"

He stared back at her. His eyes were small in his red,

overweight face, and he breathed heavily. Not for the first time, Zoe wondered what it must have been like for Irina Hamm and Sofia Pichler to go home to him at night.

He folded his arms across his chest and grunted.

Zoe opened her file. "Let's start at the beginning, shall we?"

He cocked his head.

"Alina Popescu. The woman who detonated the New Street bomb. How did you know her?"

"No comment."

Zoe tensed. She'd been expecting this.

"I have here a copy of her passport." She pushed a photocopy across the table. "We found it in the brothel where you forced Alina to stay while you were selling her to men for sex and grooming her as a suicide bomber."

"No comment."

So he wasn't going to talk. No surprise there. Zoe knew she had the evidence. And if he failed to cooperate, it would be worse for him in court.

She scratched her nose, flipping to the next piece of evidence. *Bring it on.*

CHAPTER NINETY-EIGHT

Zoe was woken by her doorbell ringing.

"I'll get it!" called Nicholas.

She rolled over and checked her phone: she'd slept till gone nine. She never did that. Nicholas was downstairs, cooking pancakes by the smell of it.

She lay on her back and inhaled deeply. She and Nicholas had cried together last night, sharing memories of Annette. She'd even found an old photo album that she'd hidden away years ago. It had been cathartic, if challenging. And she'd managed to not mention Annette's alcoholism once.

"It's Mo!" Nicholas called up the stairs.

Zoe grabbed her dressing gown and hurried down to her friend. He stood inside the front door, his arms outstretched.

She stepped into them and gave him a tight hug. "Congratulations."

He pulled back to look into her face. "You too."

"You arrested Hamm. That must have been quite a moment."

"You got Randle," he replied.

"*Carl* got Randle."

"He couldn't have done it without your statement."

"Maybe not." She remembered she hadn't told Carl about her mum's death. And he'd been cool with her at Lloyd House. Ultra-professional. She had to hope that giving him everything she knew about Randle was enough to soften his attitude towards her.

"Give me five minutes to put some clothes on. We'll go for a coffee."

"You've got coffee here, haven't you? And your son needs you."

She glanced towards the kitchen, where Nicholas was playing loud rock music.

"Yeah. Come through. I'm getting changed, though."

Two minutes later she was wearing jeans and a t-shirt and cradling a mug of strong coffee. Mo sat next to her on the sofa with a mug of tea.

"You want pancakes, Mo?" Nicholas called.

"Please." He leaned back and crossed his legs, an ankle on a knee. "He makes a good cup of tea."

"He's a very talented young man."

"Like his mum."

"I've been suspended, you know."

"Not suspended. Paid leave until they clear everything up."

"That sounds a lot like suspended to me."

"It'll be fine. Dawson says you're up for a commendation."

"Don't count your chickens," she replied. She wasn't the commendation type. "Anyway, you're the one who took Hamm down."

"There's no way I'd have collared him if it hadn't been for you. And Connie and Rhod."

"How are they?"

"Itching for you to come back."

"Not itching to get themselves promoted?"

"Let's take things one step at a time."

She laughed. "They're both good, but in different ways."

"Maybe if you put the two of them together, you'd get the perfect sergeant."

"Or the sergeant from a nightmare."

Nicholas slapped two plates down. "Voila."

"Mmm." Zoe picked up a fork. "Thanks, love. You seeing Zaf today?"

"In an hour." Nicholas darted back into the kitchen. Zoe heard him shouting something about burning.

She grimaced at Mo. "Oops."

"Oops indeed. We're lucky we got these ones."

"So did you interview Sheena MacDonald?" she asked through a mouthful of pancake.

"She gave Hamm up. Didn't hold back. Seems she reckoned he was going to dump her in the shit and she wanted to get in there first."

"Specifics?"

"Murder of Dwayne Jukes. Raif Starling too. That wasn't Hamm himself, but he gave the order."

Zoe wiped up the last of her maple syrup with a pancake. "Why?"

"Starling was working with Jukes's lot. When Hamm killed Jukes, he took over that gang. But there were a couple of them that were having none of it, and Starling refused to switch allegiances, too."

CHAPTER NINETY-EIGHT

"Hamm was just that little bit too close to the knuckle for him, then?"

"We'll never know."

"Will she testify?"

"We've got CCTV, forensics and phone records to corroborate it. Hamm kept weapons, documents and phones in another room through that cellar I found him in."

"So he was using that house all along."

"With Margaret Brooking's help. She was more than just a housekeeper."

Zoe raised an eyebrow.

"She was his long-term partner. Business and bed. Irina and Sofia were just extras."

"Poor woman."

"According to Sheena, it was all Margaret Brooking's idea. The housekeeper thing suited her, gave her a cover."

"So she's in custody too?" Zoe asked.

"She is. DS Griffin and DC Solsby are interviewing her as we speak."

Zoe nodded. "It's going to be odd."

Mo's eyes crinkled. "Without your mum."

She hadn't thought of that. "I meant with Hamm in custody. Randle off the force."

Mo chuckled. "Odd. But better."

CHAPTER NINETY-NINE

The van door opened and the constable guided Ian out. His muscles felt tight from being immobile for so long. He was used to moving around, to going running after work and when he was at work, to being active. The six weeks in prison had piled on extra weight.

The officer watched as Ian unlocked his front door and shoved it open. A pile of junk mail was mounting up inside. So Alison was still at her mum's.

He scooped it up and dumped it on the counter in the kitchen. He ran water for the kettle.

The constable gave him a nod and walked back to the van. Ian knew most prisoners didn't get a lift home when they were released, but this guy had once worked for him in Kings Norton.

Ian stood in the doorway. He waved as the van drove away. The street went quiet, and Ian's body drooped.

This house should have been full of life. Maddy and Ollie, running up and down the stairs, fighting over some toy. Alison, singing to herself as she cooked their tea. The TV blaring. Even her mother's godawful voice was better than this silence.

A car crawled along the road: Alison's mum's Corsa. Ian gripped the doorframe. He looked terrible; he hadn't shaved and the trousers he'd been arrested in were too tight.

He rubbed his stubble and held his head as high as he could manage. He'd been married to Alison for five years, with her for two before that. She'd seen worse.

The door opened. Alison emerged, her back to him. She leaned over to talk to the person inside: her mum.

Ian felt his lip rise in a sneer. *Stop it.*

He forced a smile as Alison turned to him. The car drove off.

"Where are the kids?" he asked as she reached their front path.

"They're safe," was all she said.

"I want to see them."

She stopped walking. "Can I come in?"

"It's your house." He backed up and watched as she slid past him, careful not to make contact. She continued through into the lounge and he followed.

She sat on the sofa.

"So they let you off."

"There wasn't enough evidence to convict."

"Doesn't mean you didn't do it, though." She looked down the garden, not meeting his eye.

He knelt in front of her. Her cheek twitched.

"Alison, love. I was a bloody idiot. I gave them information, I let them do that work to the house. But I didn't know they were going to set off a bomb. If I had..."

"If you had, you'd have turned them in?"

"I'd like to think I would."

She turned to him. "I'm not sure you have the courage. And you haven't denied planting evidence on that poor dead man."

He pulled in a breath. "I don't want to lie to you, Alison. Randle told me to leave something on one of the victims. I didn't know what it was, and I didn't know..."

He *did* know why; of course he did. He was a detective.

"I was scared of him, love. The super. Of the men he was working for. They would have hurt me, you. The kids." He paused. "I was an idiot. I'm sorry."

She looked away, her eyes filling with tears. "I don't know what to think."

"I didn't hurt anyone."

"Mum says—"

"Your mum has always hated me. Don't listen to her."

"You put the kids at risk. Colluding with organised criminals like that."

His chest tightened. "Alison, I don't want to be hard on you. But the kids were taken because of your past. It was nothing to do with me."

Her head shot round. "Don't you dare accuse me of—"

He put a hand on her arm. She didn't push it off.

"I know," he said. "It was no one's fault. That insane woman who thought she could be their mum." He squeezed. "*You're* their mum. No one could have a better mum."

"Hmm."

"I love you, Al. I want us to give it another go. You can't be happy, all of you cooped up at your mum's?"

Her face hardened. "It isn't always easy." She stood up. "I don't know, Ian. I don't know what to do." She shook off his hand and walked past him to the door.

CHAPTER NINETY-NINE

"Please can we just give it a try?" he asked her. "You don't have to commit. Just try."

"It would confuse Maddy and Ollie. I can't do that to—"

"You don't have to move back in. Just see me. Let's spend some time together. It can be like when we first met."

"When we first met, I was with Benedict."

He smiled. "OK, so not *exactly* like when we first met."

She walked through to the hall. He followed.

"Please, Alison. Let's just try, please?"

She opened the front door.

"I'll think about it."

CHAPTER ONE HUNDRED

The house was in a quiet cul de sac in a town somewhere in Shropshire. Randle hadn't bothered to find out any more than that. He reckoned it was safer not to know.

He knew how these things worked. He would be moved a few times more. There was Hamm's trial to get through, he'd be moved around during that. And then, when the dust had settled, they'd put him somewhere permanent.

This place was modern, a nondescript red brick box with two bedrooms and the smallest kitchen he'd ever seen. Even so, he rattled around in it.

He hadn't seen Anita since the day after he'd got her back from that gym. He'd arrived home to find her gone, suitcases missing and the wardrobe half empty. The girls were gone too, Maria's blazer still on the floor outside her room and enough of their belongings vanished with them. Their posters, books and computer games were still in their rooms. He'd tidied up, hoping she might bring them back. That she might at least let him have time with them.

CHAPTER ONE HUNDRED

But the next day Sergeant Connell, his new handler, had arrived, and that was the last time he'd seen the house.

Two weeks, and he was starting to feel at home in this quiet corner of the Midlands. Maybe he needed the rest. The years of being first at Jackson's and then Hamm's beck and call had taken their toll. He was only fifty-one, but his hair was almost entirely grey and he had high blood pressure.

He would get fit. He'd asked Sergeant Connell to provide him with running gear so he could explore the woods behind the housing estate. She'd resisted, she resisted everything that involved him leaving the house. But he hadn't visited any places with people around, he had his groceries delivered and didn't go to the door to collect them. Those woods would be quiet.

He opened the back door. Birds were calling from the trees at the bottom of his tiny garden. He was lucky to have a house at the edge of the estate; the ones in the middle would drive him insane with claustrophobia. He imagined Connell liked this one better, it was more secluded. No one overlooking him.

He stepped outside, hands wrapped round a can of beer that had come in his last grocery delivery. At least they allowed him that.

He lowered himself to the back step and took a swig. Being here felt like a kind of nothingness, an empty part of his life that he would suffer until he was able to find Anita. But at least he wasn't in prison. A corrupt senior police officer in there, it didn't bear thinking about.

A blackbird landed on the lawn and dug its beak into the grass. He watched it, swigging his beer. Small pleasures. That was what he had to focus on now.

He could do it. Not for ever, but he could. He'd get by.

CHAPTER ONE HUNDRED ONE

It was inappropriately sunny on the morning of Annette Finch's funeral. Zoe had tried on almost all her clothes, attempting to figure out what was most appropriate. In the end she'd decided on the white shirt and black trousers she hadn't worn since ACC Jackson's retirement party.

Nicholas wore the dark blue suit she'd bought him for university interviews. Zaf was at his side throughout the service, also wearing an interview suit. Zoe stood next to them, proud of her son. Connie and her mum were in the row behind, along with Mo, Rhodri and Nicholas's dad Jim.

At last the service ended and they filtered outside. There was a row of wreaths to pass, handshakes and hugs to be shared. Zoe wished she could cry. She knew it was expected of her. And it wasn't because she didn't feel grief. She wasn't sure exactly what she was grieving for, but she knew it was something.

Nicholas, walking behind her, was convulsed with tears. He clung to Zaf, occasionally turning to grab her and cry all over her shirt. She pulled him in close, wanting to make it easier for him.

They reached the end of the wreaths. There was no burial site to walk to, Annette had wanted to be cremated. Zoe wondered if she would burn more easily with all that alcohol soaking her organs, then pushed the thought from her mind, ashamed of herself.

Carl stood at the end of the row of wreaths, his eyes sparkling in the way she'd noticed when they'd been investigating Bryn Jackson's death.

"Sorry I'm late."

She leaned into his embrace. "Sorry I didn't tell you."

"Mo called me."

"Good old Mo."

"She died the day before you…"

Zoe buried her face in his jacket. "Let's not talk about it, yeah?" She regretted not telling him about Annette when she'd gone to Lloyd House to make her statement. But she'd wanted to be dispassionate, professional. She didn't want anyone thinking emotions were clouding her judgement.

Carl nodded towards Nicholas, who was sharing a hug with Jim.

"Glad DI McManus made it."

"Yeah," she agreed. She noted that Jim was alone; he hadn't brought his wife Shula or their son Geordie.

"How does it make you feel, seeing Nicholas with him?"

Zoe considered. She was about to reply when she saw a woman getting out of a car up ahead.

"The DCI."

Carl followed her gaze. She stumbled across the car park. DCI Lesley Clarke took her hands.

"Ma'am. How are you?"

"How are you, more like? You look like shit."

Zoe laughed. Trust Lesley to be matter of fact at a funeral.

"Thanks, ma'am."

Lesley shook her head. "None of the ma'aming, yes? I'm not even based in the same force as you now."

"You're definitely going to Dorset?"

"Next month, God help me."

"It'll do you good."

"That's what they say." Lesley had been on sick leave for the last two months after suffering injuries in the New Street bomb.

Carl appeared by Zoe's side and shook Lesley's hand.

"Glad to see you two have decided to be friends again," the DCI said.

Carl put an arm around Zoe's waist. She grabbed his hand.

"More than friends," he said.

Lesley winked at Zoe. "He's a catch. I'll leave you two lovebirds to it." She walked off towards Mo.

Zoe turned to Carl. "Thanks."

"I'm just sorry I wasn't here earlier."

Nicholas tapped her on the shoulder. "D'you mind if I get a lift with Dad to the wake?"

She bit down the immediate urge to refuse. "Course not." She watched him walk to Jim's car.

"You find it tough, don't you?" Carl said. "Jim not being here when he grew up, but wanting to be the doting dad now."

She shook her head, thinking of her own dad. His funeral had been at this crematorium, nineteen years ago. She'd cried herself hoarse, worried she might hurt Nicholas, still growing inside her.

"No," she said. "I don't. Not anymore."

"Sure?"

She gazed at her son. Jim stood on one side of him, Zaf on the other. Zaf and Nicholas's hands kept brushing each other, even when the two of them were talking to other people. They might be going to different universities, but she felt confident those two would remain solid.

"He needs two parents," she said. "Not just me."

"That's very mature of you."

Zoe leaned back against Carl's chest. He was warm and solid. "I'm trying my best," she replied.

He planted a kiss on the back of her head. She closed her eyes, feeling the sun on her skin. She felt his hand run down her back and turned to him.

Carl put his hands on her shoulders and looked into her eyes. "You OK?" He wiped a tear from her cheek.

She put a finger to his wet one; so she had managed to cry, after all.

"I'll be fine," she said as she moved in to kiss him. "I've got you."

I hope you enjoyed *Deadly Fallout*. Do you want to read a short story starring Zaf? Read *Mystery at the National Gallery* for FREE at rachelmclean.com/zaf.

Thanks,
Rachel McLean

READ THE DI ZOE FINCH SERIES

Deadly Wishes

Deadly Choices

Deadly Desires

Deadly Terror

Deadly Reprisal

Deadly Fallout

Deadly Christmas

Deadly Origins, the FREE Zoe Finch prequel

Buy from book retailers or via the Rachel McLean website.

ALSO BY RACHEL MCLEAN

The Dorset Crime series – buy from book retailers or via the Rachel McLean website.

The Corfe Castle Murders

The Clifftop Murders

The Island Murders

The Monument Murders

The Millionaire Murders

The Fossil Beach Murders

The Blue Pool Murders

The Lighthouse Murders

The Ghost Village Murders

The Poole Harbour Murders

...and more to come

The McBride & Tanner series – buy from book retailers or via the Rachel McLean website.

Blood and Money

Death and Poetry

Power and Treachery

Secrets and History

The Cumbria Crime series by Rachel McLean and Joel Hames – buy from book retailers or via the Rachel McLean website.

The Harbour

The Mine

The Cairn

The Barn

The Lake

...and more to come

The London Cosy Mystery series by Rachel McLean and Millie Ravensworth – buy from book retailers or via the Rachel McLean website.

Death at Westminster

Death in the West End

Death at Tower Bridge

Death on the Thames

Death at St Paul's Cathedral

Death at Abbey Road

The Lyme Regis Women's Swimming Club series by Rachel McLean and Millie Ravensworth – buy from book retailers or via the Rachel McLean website.

The Lyme Regis Women's Swimming Club

...and more to come

The Detective Connie Williams series by Rachel McLean and Iain Grant – buy from book retailers or via the Rachel McLean website.

Last Breath

...and more to come